Part Three of the Okal Rel Saga

PRETENDERS

a novel by Lynda Williams

EDGE SCIENCE FICTION AND FANTASY PUBLISHING

AN IMPRINT OF HADES PUBLICATIONS, INC.

CALGARY

EDGE

Edge Science Fiction and Fantasy Publishing
An Imprint of Hades Publications Inc.
P.O. Box 1714, Calgary, Alberta, T2P 2L7, Canada

In house editing by Richard Janzen
Interior by Brian Hades
Cover Illustration by Lynn Perkins

EDGE Science Fiction and Fantasy Publishing and Hades Publications, Inc.
acknowledges the ongoing support of the Canada Council for the Arts and the
Alberta Foundation for the Arts for our publishing programme.

Alberta Foundation for the Arts

Canada Council   Conseil des Arts
for the Arts   du Canada

Library and Archives Canada Cataloguing in Publication

Williams, Lynda, 1958-
      Pretenders : a novel / by Lynda Williams.

(Okal Rel saga ; pt. 3)
ISBN-13: 978-1-894063-13-5

      I. Title. II. Series.

PS8595.I5622P74 2008   C813'.6   C2008-904669-2

FIRST EDITION
(h-20080726)
Printed in Canada
www.edgewebsite.com

Dedication

I dedicate Pretenders to the young people who
helped me realize the Okal Rel Saga was for
them, too, and kept me going with their interest
when I had doubts. In particular, I would
like to thank Krysia A., Mel F., Sarah T., Lisa O.
and my daughters Jennifer, Angela and Tegan.

Other Books In The Okal Rel Saga

1

Lost and Found

Into Exile – 175 Post Americ Treaty

The Green Hearth herald greeted Ev'rel with a look of pure shock. "You!" he cried in Gelack, registering his visitor's high rank in the pronoun.

Any other day Ev'rel might have laughed to see the poor man's dignity so overturned. Today she cared for nothing but getting past him.

Silver Hearth guards hovered uncertainly at her back, unsure of how to take charge of a prisoner so highly ranked. Not long ago, the Gelack Empire had been a toy her father dangled for her pleasure. Now she stood on Fountain Court under guard, seeking mercy at the door of the mentor she used to taunt with proof that she did not need to learn his harsh lessons.

Di Mon, the 103rd liege of Monitum, was her last hope.

Ev'rel shouldered past the disconcerted herald. Di Mon's errants sprang to attention and drew their swords.

Ev'rel had never feared a sword before. She had hated Di Mon's fencing lessons, down on Green Wedge below Fountain Court, but ever since Di Mon had told her about life on old Earth and Monatese theories about *Okal Rel*, she had felt nothing but contempt for the instruments of Sword Law. Now these weapons she thought of as stupid looked horribly lethal.

"Di Mon!" she cried, and humbled herself to beg. "Please! Let me see him!"

Silence fell hard, relieved only by her heaving breath, as the errants studied Ev'rel where she stood before them, trembling and barefoot, her black hair wild about her classic features and her face lit by a rising fever. Dark streaks soaked the front of her nightgown where her swollen breasts had begun to leak hours earlier, the warm milk gone cold enough to chill her.

She stood as still as she could, listening to the trickle of water sounds coming from the ivy-covered walls. The entrance hall was full of plants, some earthly green and the rest the dark turquoise of native life on Di Mon's homeworld of Monitum. The damp air, with its familiar smells, was a balm to Ev'rel's lungs.

Di Mon will save me, she thought.

"Take her to Liege Monitum," Di Mon's lead errant decided, putting up her weapon. "You can wait here," she informed the all-male Demish escort.

"Thank you!" Ev'rel gasped, elevating the errant to an equal with the pronoun to express her thanks.

The Monatese woman was not impressed. "This way, Immortality," she said, and led on.

Ev'rel followed her to the end of the ivy-lined hall and through a set of double doors that the herald held open. Inside was Azure Lounge, the first room of a series called the Throat. She looked about frantically for Di Mon, but the room was empty.

"He's in Ameron's old room, in Family Hall," the errant told her coolly.

Ev'rel nodded. The fever made the gesture feel out of control and exaggerated. She pressed her palm to her face and felt sweat there before hurrying to catch up with the errant. Glimpses of earth artifacts, old pictures and historical memorabilia flashed by her, reminding her that the

Monatese valued history over literature; philosophy over hope; and diplomacy over war — all things she had learned from her Monatese mentor.

He is a fair man, she told herself, for courage. *He won't hold past mockery and high spirits against me. He knows I'd never harm my own baby!* The very thought of the lost infant heaved a raw sob into her throat.

"Immortality?" The errant stopped to see what was the matter with her.

Ev'rel swayed against a leather chair in the last room of the Throat, called Family Lounge, often used for entertaining intimates. She and Di Mon had taken lessons here. And in his library.

The errant touched her bare arm. "You're hot," she said with concern.

Ev'rel shook her head. "Please, take me to him."

The errant took a knitted shawl from the leather chair and wrapped it about Ev'rel's shoulders. It must have belonged to some servant or a Sevolite too lowborn to be sensitive, because the patterns in it leaped at Ev'rel with unmitigated simplicity, setting her teeth on edge. Di Mon had always liked to play such tricks on her, to prove to her she had a highborn's navigational talent: an instinctive ability to discern complex patterns in star-scattered spacescapes while reality skimming through them. Ev'rel hated all such tricks — they made her dizzy. But she clung to the disturbing shawl today as if her life depended on it.

Family Hall intersected the Throat at a right angle. It was the deepest, safest part of Green Hearth, farthest from the spiral stairs that led up to Green Pavilion and the doors on Fountain Court that she had come through to get this far. Ev'rel wanted to feel safe here, but she had learned that all safety on Fountain Court was tentative. Property, here, could be guarded by nothing but swords, under Sword Law, and the social constraints of the Ava's Oath to which all hearths of Fountain Court must answer. That was the core prerequisite to holding power. Transgressors died, disgraced, for breaking Sword Law. But Ev'rel trusted none of it, not since her father's murder. Not when the half-brother who took her father from her ruled the empire.

She wanted Di Mon to be her new father, to forgive her everything and to shelter her. The need burned in her as physically as fever.

Seeing the door of the Ameron Room ajar ahead of her, Ev'rel could hold herself back no more. She broke into a run, leaving the errant behind in Family Hall.

Di Mon turned as she burst in. He had been standing in front of a portrait of Ev'rel's ancestor, Ameron Lor'Vrel of White Hearth. The historical Ava in the painting was a young man dressed in fencing gear who stood reading a book with his sword lying on the table in front of him. The portrait caught him in the act of glancing up, as if to greet a visitor. For some reason, perhaps because Ameron had always been the standard by which Di Mon judged her, Ev'rel's eyes fixed in mute appeal upon her ancestor.

The young Ameron had gray eyes and a lean, Vrellish build, just like Di Mon himself and all highborns who were racially Vrellish, but the resemblance between Di Mon and his idol ended there. Ameron's hair was a mop of chestnut brown — the Lorel color — and his sharp features were more pronounced, with a strong nose and a wide forehead.

Ev'rel felt no blessing in her ancestor's inquisitive stare. She fixed upon Di Mon, instead, who stared back at her, very much alive if unnaturally still. He had not expected to see her. He was not pleased about it, but he was not indifferent, either. She could see how it hurt him to see her like this.

Ev'rel would have given anything in that moment to force her way into his life. To seize a role, with him, in which she felt secure. On the heels of that longing, she suffered a pang of desire like a knife stabbing her.

"Ev'rel," Di Mon breathed, his tone encouraging her certainty of his concern.

She threw herself at his feet in a gush of tears and words. "Don't let them!" she begged, clutching at his legs. "Don't help them send me away into exile! You know I'm innocent! I loved Amel!"

Gently, he guided her up and sat down beside her on the bed. "You're feverish," he said, and touched her breast, sending lances of pain and passion through her. But his intent was clinical. "Milk fever," he concluded, and rose, "I'll fetch Sarilous."

"No!" she cried, rearing up to grasp him about the waist.

He tolerated the familiarity, touching her hair in an awkward attempt to be comforting.

"I loved Amel," she wept, indulging in her honest grief. "My beautiful, crystal-eyed baby."

"I know," he said curtly.

She clambered onto her knees, afraid to take her hands off him. His male smell was intoxicating. He had tried to explain that to her, as well. How she could never really be a Demish princess when her mother had been a Pureblood Vrellish warrior. She had to come to terms with her Vrellish nature, he'd always said. Learn to fight. Always he spoke about fighting, never the desire that was now consuming her.

"Then... you know," she floundered, trying to reconcile his tone and words. "You know I didn't do it!"

"Do what?" he said, his voice dry and bitter. "Order your *gorarelpul*, Arous, to hide Amel? And be careful — do not try to lie to me."

She clutched harder, tears cascading down her fever-spotted cheeks. "Yes! But to protect him from Delm!" she wailed.

"Maybe that was your reason," Di Mon said, still implacable, "maybe not. Delm says it was because you wanted to avoid a genotyping that would prove Amel was not his son, but Arous's. We will never know now. Amel is lost and could be dying as we speak, and Arous is conveniently dead."

Ev'rel gave a cry, stabbed to the heart by his cruel words. She pressed herself to him, hugging him and wanting him in every way. "No, no, no," she wept.

He pulled her from him with force and struggled to make her lie down, saying things about the fever and threatening to fetch his *gorarelpul* medic, Sarilous. But she did not want that kind of help. She wanted him. And fever had not sapped her Pureblood strength.

"Don't hate me!" she begged. "I didn't give Arous the overdose of Rush! It was Delm! I swear! I swear!"

His very resistance excited her. Their struggle became violent, but she — despite his efforts — was untrained. He struck her in the ribs. The pain snapped something emotional inside of her. She fought back with wild strength, as if she could solve everything by getting him down, beneath her, and having what she wanted.

She fastened her mouth on his, tasting blood, and for a heady instant she felt as if she'd tapped into a passion equally denied and violent. Then a sharp knee heaved her up, a hard hand slammed across her mouth, and her strength became useless against a genius for body physics that she had never mastered.

She came to herself on the floor, at his feet, staring up at him breathless and humbled.

"You are not guilty of all Delm accuses you of, perhaps," Di Mon ground out at her. "But Amel was Arous's child. You hated Delm. So you used a *sla* sex drug on a conscience-bonded commoner — on Arous — a man your stupid father let you take from the *Gorarelpul* College for no better reason than his good looks. Did your father know that you were disappointed when Arous proved to be impotent due to pain training? Did you even care that Arous was a brilliant student, slated to become a college father? Did anything matter to you except his body, Ev'rel?"

"I didn't—" she started, and gulped as he yanked her to her feet.

"Kill him?" he finished. "No, but you gave Delm the idea. You made it possible for him to implicate you with your *slaka's* corpse. He knew that using Rush would implicate you when I investigated."

His grip bit into her upper arms, making her gasp.

"You are Vrellish inside, oh yes!" he said. "But in the wrong way! Did I never teach you man-rape is a crime even in Red Reach, Ev'rel! When I taught you Green Hearth's history, of the commoner-Sevolite alliance that defined its origins, did I fail to make it clear that the humans we call commoners are not toys to be used for a Sevolite's dishonorable pleasures! Should I have made that an explicit part of the curriculum!"

He shoved her away from him.

She staggered back, bumping into the bed behind her. Ameron's portrait looked down at her over Di Mon's shoulder, the two of them united in a supernatural blow of condemnation.

"You disgust me," Di Mon told her. "If you were not the empire's last female Pureblood, I would see you slain, not exiled."

"You!" she groped for anger to sustain herself, panting with injured pride and indignation. "You would condemn me, when you voted with the rest of them to bind me to a ten-child contract with Delm — the brother I hate — the brother who had our father slain!"

He wavered then. "I am not proud of my part in that, Ev'rel. I could not blame you, as a person, if you chose to thwart the empire's need for heirs and bared the door to Delm. But what you did with Arous — it was *sla*, Ev'rel. Wrong and obscene. Think about that in your exile and learn to be a Vrellish woman in a more wholesome way!"

"If I do," she begged, stinging from the lash of his anger, "would you forgive me? C-could we start over?"

"I will fetch you a medic," he said coolly. Then he turned and walked away from her.

Hopeless desperation tried to swallow her and failed. Outraged pride and a pilot's will vomited her back to face the exile awaiting her.

"I enjoyed Arous!" She shrieked at Di Mon's retreating back. "I enjoyed the fact he hated pleasing me!"

He didn't give her the satisfaction of a flinch, but he slammed the door behind him hard enough to jar the portrait of her venerated ancestor.

Amel Found — 16 years later

"Amel?"

The name failed to claim Von's attention. He was too busy peering out the window at the wonders of a living planet, visible at last through the fluffy clouds of Barmi II's rich atmosphere. He had never seen anything like this on the barren surface of Gelion. There were streams and fields and ribbon-thin roads with a few tiny vehicles moving on them. In some of the fields there were animals and most of the vehicles looked as if they were being drawn by horses, although their shuttle was still too high up for Von to be sure. He had never seen a real horse before except in pictures. He was less interested in the long trucks that must have been powered by *rel*-batteries or some locally generated fuel with eco-safe waste products.

It was all so amazingly beautiful he forgot to breathe regularly.

"Are you doing all right, Amel?"

He smiled at the big blonde woman sitting opposite him with clouds streaming past the window at her back.

"Air—ee—yum," he said aloud, and laughed.

"Yes?" she asked, puzzled by the way he emphasized each separate syllable.

"It's in your name," he told her, pointing towards the window. "Air." *And yumminess,* he added to himself.

They were speaking the old Earth language, English, for the sake of his nervousness concerning Gelack pronouns. In Gelack, he was still prone to talk like a commoner, although he understood he wasn't supposed to anymore. Ayrium indulged him with English. She had been wonderful to him about everything.

Von looked out the window again the moment they were out of the clouds. They were closer now. The patchwork of fields below him looked like a scene from one of the Demish storybooks he loved.

"Oh, Ayrium," he gushed, "no wonder it's *okal'a'ni* to even dream of hurting green worlds for absolutely any reason at all! No wonder there is Sword Law, instead, and *Okal Rel*."

Ayrium's mouth spread in a generous smile, warm golden highlights in her short hair. "Mom," she said, "is going to love you."

'Mom' was the infamous mutineer, Perry D'Aur, who had taken the world below from the last liege of Barmi, a reputedly dreadful ruler who also happened to be one of Amel's relatives.

One of my relatives, Von reminded himself, and felt his anxieties regroup to mass in his chest.

Ayrium squeezed his arm again before she sat back. She was large and strong, but shapely in the womanly, Demish way, with sky-bright eyes and a sunny disposition. There was just no denying her sexiness, but Von felt bad about noticing. He preferred to think of her as a big sister. There had been too many lovers in his short life and only one dearly loved sister, even though he now knew the girl he'd grown up with was nothing like him. He was Amel, a Sevolite Pureblood and heir to the empire, as well as a potential Soul of Light sacred to the gentle sect of *Okal Rel* known as *Okal Lumens*.

It was all pretty daunting for a boy raised in seclusion on Gelion, who had been earning his living in the sex trade for the last three years.

Ayrium leaned over to point. "There's the palace!"

Von peered down at a U-shaped building coming up fast, below. A junkyard of agricultural vehicles filled what might once have been a garden at its back. Beyond that lay the runway they were headed for.

"We still call it the palace," said Ayrium, "although we don't keep it up like one. Mom runs the Purple Alliance from there."

He looked at his big, sunny savior. "I thought you were Liege Barmi, Ayrium."

"I am!" she said, grinning. "I have to be, to keep up appearances for Fountain Court. They don't recognize the Purple Alliance, just my title. Mom can't be Liege Barmi because she's just a Midlord and Liege Barmi has to be highborn." She paused, studying him with a worried expression. "You do know, I hope, that you have a better claim to Barmi than either Mom or I. I've been thinking about that ever since Dad insisted I bring you here, and how Mom says she would never have taken Barmi II away from a deserving liege to start! Not that we're going to give it back or anything!" she added quickly. "Well, if things go the way Dad hopes, at court, maybe one day I can swear to you as Ava, which will fix it all up." She grinned. "Mom wants to be respectable again, so I think she'd like that."

It took Von five seconds to grasp that this person who was not him... not really... not yet, this Pureblood Prince Amel, was a threat to his new friend and the other people who had taken over Barmi II. The realization coalesced his free-floating anxiety, bringing on one of the fits he could not control.

His memory locked on a trauma in his past and his senses took him there. For an instant he was back inside the chamber called a visitor probe with his brain interfaced to a half-living computer called an arbiter.

"Amel? Amel!" Ayrium was out of her seat belt and kneeling on the floor beside him.

"It's what the Reetions did to me," he told her, not knowing who else to confide in but afraid to admit too much. "It makes me clear dream — except I don't remember past lives like a real clear dreamer does. I relive bad memories."

Ayrium was looking at him with such open pity that he felt ashamed. "It's no big deal," he tried to convince them both.

"Sure," she said gamely, but he could tell she knew it was a lie.

She got back into her seat to prepare for landing while Von tried not to think about anything at all. Instead, he let himself enjoy the feel of touching down on the ground.

As soon as they came to a complete stop, Ayrium was up. "Let's not keep Dad waiting!" she said, taking his hand.

He went ahead of her down the aisle to where their pilot was busy deploying a ramp. But the moment he caught sight of the people outside his hands locked on the frame of the shuttle door.

People of all kinds, from workers in overalls to Sevolites wearing swords, were watching from windows or standing in one of the many doorways lining the machine-choked courtyard. Some stood on balconies peering down. The net effect was as if a giant hand had squeezed the palace to make people pop out of it through every window and door. Even more alarming were the two people waiting to greet him formally: one a large man who had to be Ayrium's father, D'Ander, and the other a small woman who would be the liege-killer, Perry D'Aur.

Ayrium put a hand on Von's shoulder and leaned forward to whisper encouragement. "Inhale! Breath the air! Go on. You'll find it very different from what you're used to underground on Gelion."

Von closed his eyes and felt the air on his face. It felt cool, moist and wonderful in his lungs, full of smells that spoke of plants, people and the machines parked in the ruined garden of the courtyard.

He opened his eyes again and tilted his head up in amazement at the way the sky went up and up, blocking out the
blackness of space beyond: no ceiling, no walls and no bonds.

"It's beautiful," he said, awestruck.

"You're beautiful!" said Ayrium with a laugh. "It's a joy
the way it just pours off you."

Fortified, Von found the courage to look down.

Prince D'Ander was gloriously Golden from head to toe,
with gently curling locks of hair the same color as Ayrium's,
a handsome face with a pronounced dimple in the chin, a
chest encrusted in designs that proclaimed an illustrious heritage, and a jewel-hilted sword. He was busy scanning the
people-laden balconies and doors with a look of ferocious
displeasure that gave Von qualms.

"Don't be frightened of Dad," Ayrium coaxed. "You are
his miracle. He couldn't be more protective if you were
Ameron himself, back from his last jump — and that's saying
a lot! Dad is nuts about Ameron. It's a toss up, in fact, whether
he's more devoted to Ameron or the Golden Emperor back
on the Golden home world of Demora. Of course," she added,
leaning so close her clean breath tickled Von's ear lobe, "there
is something those two worthies have in common. Neither
one is likely to contradict Dad's opinion of how best to serve
them; that might be what makes them so attractive to him."

She freed a hand to point at the short, dark-haired woman
beside Prince D'Ander.

"That's Mom," said Ayrium. "They're not married. Dad
gifted me to her in the Vrellish fashion twenty-five years ago.
I'll run you through the niceties some other time. For now,
the gist is: my parents are still allies but not lovers. You don't
want to screw up on that front because Dad's got a wife on
Demora and plays by Demish rules of romance. Fortunately,
Mom's not the kind to be broken up about such stuff. She's
got a husband of her own, named Vrenn, or rather a Vrellish-
style *mekan'st*. She's been known to look elsewhere, and Vrenn

certainly does. End of briefing," she concluded, giving him a gentle nudge.

Von's gaze slid from the formidable Golden prince to Perry D'Aur. She was dressed in work pants and a close-fitting tank top with a well-worn flight jacket worn loosely over it. She looked neither old nor young, but weathered enough that she couldn't be highborn. Von remembered hearing she was a Midlord, the lower of the two classes of nobleborn, which made her tougher and longer-lived than any commoner, but not regenerative like D'Ander and Ayrium.

And Amel, he reminded himself. He tried to think *me* instead of Amel, but still couldn't.

A breeze ruffled Von's hair, blowing it across his eyes. He clapped a hand to his head, surprised, and tucked the stray hair away behind his ear. Then he took a deep breath and went down the ramp.

"—didn't tell a soul you were bringing Amel here, I swear!" Perry was explaining to D'Ander. "Rumor spreads faster than highborns can fly, that's all. Besides, you had better get used to him being exposed to the crass curiosity of my irregulars if you want to stash him here while you figure out—"

"Look, Mom!" Ayrium interrupted, pulling Amel around in front of her. "See what I found! Everyone's missing heir."

Von managed a watery smile.

D'Ander's handsome face erupted in a much more extravagant one.

"Immortality," the Golden prince addressed Von with lofty formality. "I give you Perry D'Aur, a nobleborn of the Blue Demish. And this," he introduced Von to Perry, "is the Pureblood Prince Amel, Soul of Light, and future Ava of the Gelack Empire!"

Von's ears buzzed. He heard voices speaking in Reetion — the language he had acquired by force inside the visitor probe; then he came to himself braced in Ayrium's strong hands.

"S-sorry," he stuttered, a cold lump of fear in his stomach. He dared not use a pronoun because, if he did, he would have to decide how to cope with being up-spoken by the liege of Golden Hearth and Sword Champion of all Demora.

"He's fragile as glass!" exclaimed D'Ander. "The least stress and he has one of his episodes!" He seemed oddly pleased about it.

Perry, on the other hand, fixed Von with a dark blue stare that opened him lengthwise, like a knife, as if she could see perfectly well he was only a commoner courtesan playacting fine sentiments.

"Why don't you take him to Demora?" she asked D'Ander, applying the form of 'him' fit for a Pureblood, but with something closer to resentment than reverence about it.

"I will, of course," D'Ander floundered, "when the time is right. At the moment there are still, uh, concerns there about his... mmm... career, while a commoner."

"Tough sell back home, is it?" asked Perry. "A Soul of Light surviving as a prostitute for three years?"

"Once he's Ava—" D'Ander began to argue.

But Von could take no more. He bolted past Perry, shied from D'Ander, and took off across the machine yard, vaulting the first obstruction he encountered. Rough, uneven engine parts stung his soft palm as he cleared a broken-down car. He landed cleanly only by good luck.

This is no way to behave! he thought. Not that there was a Demish handbook of etiquette to cover this situation, but he knew what he was doing was futile and possibly dangerous.

A dirt mover with a high cab for the operator loomed up. Von sprang inside with a bound. The seat was wide and padded at the back. He threw his head against it, panting without being tired.

Soon he became aware of a lone figure walking towards him.

It was Perry D'Aur. Watching her approach, he noticed how the nipples of her small breasts asserted themselves against her tank top and frowned at himself with annoyance. This was not the way he wanted to react!

Perry trudged over and set one calloused hand on his dirt mover. "May I come up?" she asked, addressing him in *pol-peerage*, as if they were both commoners.

The low-stress, grammatical fiction calmed him down. "Of course!" he said, blushing, then formally accepted her offer by working in a pronoun to match her grammar. "I would like that."

Perry heaved herself up and settled into the seat beside him. "Must have been fun being a courtesan on Gelion," she said, straightfaced, adding an appreciative grin, "for your clients." She paused while he registered the compliment, then asked, "Vrellish women, weren't they?"

"Mostly," Von said, to be agreeable, then decided to tell the truth. "Actually, half of them were Demish ladies."

Perry raised an eyebrow. "Sexual workout one night, flattering chit-chat over tea the next?"

"Something like that," he said, "but you'd be surprised about some Demish women... particularly the widows. And Vrellish women talk sometimes." He considered. "Usually afterwards."

Perry chuckled. "I know what you mean. I have a Vrellish *mekan'st*."

He nodded. "Vrenn," he remembered.

"Not exactly a lady, am I?" she said with a good-natured smile. "I served in the Blue Demish fleet, led a coup against my liege over two decades ago, have a Vrellish lover... and there's Ayrium, the bastard."

"I like Ayrium," Von enthused.

"Me too." Perry shifted herself to get comfortable. She didn't mind bumping him to do it. Her casualness felt companionable.

"D'Ander helped me out in a tough spot," she gave him her own version of the briefing Ayrium had offered earlier. "So yes, we were lovers. And Ayrium did the trick, for the Vrellish at least, at court." She paused to rub an itch along one side of her nose. "In any case, D'Ander and I were *mekan'stan* for a while — regular lovers in the Vrellish fashion — and we get along all right still, as allies, even now he's married. But he's D'Ander, Sword Champion of the Golden Emperor and liege of Golden Hearth on Fountain Court, while I'm not even sure I have a title. It's Ayrium who is Liege Barmi."

"I know," said Von, trying to be helpful, although he wasn't sure where this was going at all.

"My own people call me Cap," said Perry, "whether or not they ever served under my command." She stirred in discomfort. He was patient.

"Look," she told him, bluntly, "the point is I'm not up to messing with who gets to be the next Ava." She looked at him seriously. "That's something you need to understand."

He had no idea what she meant by saying all this to him. He was busy resisting his curiosity about her breasts, instead, and wishing he could turn his sexual awareness of women on and off. He wasn't a courtesan anymore. He could afford to be discriminating, maybe even fall in love. There had been one woman in particular, a Reetion he'd met named Ann....

But I'll never see Ann again, he remembered, *not if Prince D'Ander wants to make me Ava.*

"I think," he said, "I'm going to find it hard to adjust."

"I'd say that's a safe bet," said Perry D'Aur. Then she added deliberately, "Pureblood Amel."

"Can't you call me Von?" he asked.

"No."

She climbed down out of the cabin and put up a hand to help him down. He accepted it, although he didn't need help. He enjoyed the firm feel of her hand.

"You are Amel," she said, switching her grammar to match. "You have to start thinking like a highborn."

Something in the way she said it made the warning clear. He nodded dumbly, half afraid and half determined to survive.

Amel, he told himself as Perry led him by the hand back to where D'Ander waited with Ayrium. *I have to learn to be Amel.*

"Ayrium will show you to your room," Perry said as she transferred him back to her daughter. D'Ander looked inclined to argue before Perry headed him off.

"You have to give the boy a chance to relax," Amel heard her telling D'Ander as Ayrium led him into the palace.

Inside, they were met by a large-boned, lanky woman with gray eyes and short black hair.

"All clear, Ayrium," she said, with a casual salute.

"Thanks, Maverick!" Ayrium called back as she hustled Amel up a sweeping flight of stairs off the main entrance.

The room he'd been assigned was on the second floor.

"Big, four-poster bed with the original burgundy velvet curtains," Ayrium said with a gesture towards that stately piece of furniture. "Clean sheets... clothes in the dresser." She moved around the room, demonstrating as she talked. "The bathroom articulates with Mom's room, in case you need anything. Dad will be sleeping on the other side while he's here." She smiled. "I'll leave you now, to settle."

She gave him a hug and was gone.

For a moment, Amel felt terribly alone. Then he started to explore his new environment, finding it reassuringly familiar after his first exposure to the great outdoors.

His room's ornate wooden dresser would have been a treasure back home on subterranean Gelion, where all green-world products were imports. He found a pair of stretch pants ideal for exercise and put them on. He also selected a dressing gown and slippers for later, and left them on his bed. Then he closed the drawers and cabinets of the dresser again, one by one, leaving their contents messier than he had found them.

Amel had to move only a few things in the bedroom to clear enough space for a workout. When satisfied, he stood at the center of the room, struck a starting pose, and summoned up a routine suitable for the space available. Then he let all his tensions unfold in his chosen art.

He danced.

The door cracked open a slit, and Von caught a glimpse of the woman Ayrium had called Maverick watching him, but he didn't mind. Other people gathered in the doorway as the minutes ticked by. He accepted them as an audience, unconcerned so long as the logic of his movements kept him occupied.

When D'Ander shouldered past the spectators, Amel was too busy pouring himself backwards onto his hands to notice.

"Immortality?" D'Ander tried politely. But Amel only righted himself and let his body flow into the next move, snapping out an arm and then spinning his body to join it while keeping the arm still until it was time to switch, suddenly, into another pose.

"Dear One!" D'Ander boomed.

The endearment, in a man's voice, jarred Amel out of blissful absorption in the dance. He came to a standing position and centered his body. His heart hammered. Sweat trickled down his sides. Reason caught up with the chill on his skin as he schooled himself to get past the knot in his guts.

"That's an *Okal Lumens* thing, right?" Amel asked, in an edgy manner. "Calling me 'Dear One'?"

"Of course!" D'Ander folded his powerful arms across his chest. "Dear One, Divine Goodness, Sweet Soul. You dance beautifully," he added, using an elevated pronoun for 'he' with religious significance among Luminaries.

Amel swiped at his feathery black hair with splayed fingers, embarrassed by his adverse reaction.

"Thanks," he said, "but, really, I am so out of shape! All that flying and—"

D'Ander's look of pained sympathy shattered Amel's fantasy that his dancing skills still mattered. "Never mind," he muttered, feeling wrong-footed and bereft. It had only just occurred to him that being Amel meant he probably shouldn't practice courtesan arts.

"Show's over! Let's go!" Maverick interjected loudly as she came to life and began to herd the rest of the audience out.

Amel picked up a towel to dab at his face before draping it around his neck the way he might have after a workout back at Den Eva's, the establishment where he had worked on Gelion. The exercise left him with a warm, capable feeling of competence. Even his sometimes annoying vanilla scent — which he had learned was a symptom of being a descendant of the Golden Emperor — was light, not sweet and cloying the way it could be when he was stressed. But D'Ander still made him feel small and inadequate.

"You ought to get some rest," D'Ander told him reasonably.

Amel knew that, but he hadn't slept well since his run in with the Reetions and their visitor probe. When he slept, the clear dreams took control.

Ayrium stuck her head in the door. "Any luck putting our teenage miracle to bed, Dad?" she asked.

"Amel is a Soul of Light," D'Ander told his daughter with strained patience. "Doesn't that mean anything to you?"

"Sorry," said Ayrium. "Figured you were treating him with enough respect for both of us."

"Do I *have* to be a Soul of Light?" Amel asked in a small voice.

The thunderous look D'Ander cast at him made him babble. "I mean," he said, "I'm only thirty-four percent Golden Demish, which is just one percent more Golden Demish than you are, Your Highness. So why am I a Soul of Light if you're not?"

D'Ander's impatience evaporated in a smile. "Of course," he said, indulgently. "You have a sweet nature and a modest one. Any true Soul of Light would be reluctant to acknowledge himself one! But believe it, Amel! For I have no doubts."

Amel looked at Ayrium. "Ayrium is Golden, too, through you. If anyone I know is a Soul of Light, Your Highness," he insisted, in dead earnest, "it's Ayrium."

Ayrium gave an astonished laugh. "Please! Don't get Dad started on all the things I'm not!" She smiled to show it didn't matter. But Von saw through her in a flash of insight so clear that he lost track of his argument. He had always been aware he had a gift — or curse — of intuition about people, although there was nothing metaphysical about it as far as he was concerned. He was simply alive to the subtleties of the emotions between father and daughter. D'Ander was uncomfortable with Ayrium because she excelled at those things a Demish father wanted in a son, and his bastard daughter's mere existence mocked him somehow. It was equally clear that Ayrium knew.

"What is it?" D'Ander asked excitedly.

Amel gave a start. "What?"

"Just now," said D'Ander. "You saw beyond our words. You felt something. I have seen that look in Fahild, the Golden Emperor. Something changes, and it is as if he sees your naked soul. Fahild I cannot press to explain himself. He's too fragile. But you—" D'Ander gripped Amel's shoulders in his big hands. "Tell me, Amel, what were you thinking just now?"

Amel stared back at the larger man, wide-eyed, his mouth too dry to answer even if he'd wanted to.

Ayrium came to his rescue. "Dad," she said, and tugged gently on D'Ander from behind, "give the kid a break and back off."

"Can't you see how important this is?" D'Ander flared at her. "It proves his heart! Ava Delm never glimpsed souls!"

"Maybe he did," Amel said as the idea occurred to him, "and used his insights to control his courtiers."

D'Ander blinked, his face blank with shock. "That would be evil!" He paused to swallow. "The foul corruption of a gentle gift."

"I... I'm sorry," Amel stammered, wishing he had kept the idea to himself. "I'm sure I must be wrong."

The chill left D'Ander's features in a hot gush. He seized Amel and crushed him in a hug. To Amel's surprise, it didn't feel the least threatening or sexual. In fact, it made D'Ander seem less fearsome. He hugged the Golden prince back willingly enough, returning strength for strength to prove he wasn't as fragile as D'Ander said his great grandfather Fahild was.

D'Ander released him with tears standing in his eyes, which captured Amel's attention. He had always felt foolish about how easily he cried, but if D'Ander did it maybe it was just a trait of Golden Demish men, the same way being unable to cry was typical of very Vrellish people. No one could accuse a great sword champion like D'Ander of being anything less than a manly Demish man, whether he cried or not.

"Forgive me," D'Ander said, with anguish in his tone. "There are moments when I cannot bear to know what you have suffered without having a throat to slit for it or a face to smash."

Amel blinked. "Oh," he said, a bit stunned. He had not been thinking along those lines at all.

D'Ander touched him again lightly, with reverence, and hurried out of the room.

"I've never believed in the Soul of Light thing the way Dad does," said Ayrium, "but since I've met you, I am put out for the first time about his never letting me meet Fahild for fear I'd make him faint on sight or something."

Amel was sure she meant it. But the next minute Ayrium denied any disappointment with a laugh. "Oh, stop emoting in all directions!" she ordered, and gave him a playful shove.

"Time to sleep," she followed up, pointing at the bed like a stern matron of novices at Den Eva's.

Amel swallowed. "I'm afraid to try. Ayrium, you know how the Reetions tried to fix two memories of things I'd done wrong in the past, to make me braver? Well, ever since, whenever I go to sleep, it is as if the truth of what I really did is trying to reassert itself, to put things back the way they really were. I have to relive those mistakes over and over, as vividly as if I were really there. I can't do it, Ayrium!" He warmed to his confession. "I'm afraid!"

She took him briefly in her arms. Then she held him away from her to fix him with a serious stare. "It's your Demish memory correcting itself," she said, "just as if you'd taken damage *rel*-skimming. But it can't last forever and you have to sleep." She winked to reassure him. "We'll be close by." She squeezed his hand, once, and left.

Amel remained standing where she'd left him, staring at the bed. At last he shed his clothes and got in. He liked to sleep naked because bedclothes made him feel encumbered, but no sooner had he closed his eyes than he worried about what would happen if he woke up in the grip of a clear dream. He got up, took a bath, put on pajama bottoms, got back into bed, and thrashed around, getting comfortable, for what seemed like a very long time before he fell asleep.

The first thing he dreamed about was pleasant. He was in bed with Ann, the brown-skinned Reetion woman, trying to get her to explain to him what she meant by declaring a relationship with him. He never could figure it out because she kept distracting him with sexual invitations he found impossible to turn down.

Things went wrong suddenly. One moment he was with Ann and the next he was sealed in the visitor probe with a Reetion medic flipping through his memories like a stack of cards.

"What should you have done?" the medic asked as she selected one.

"No!" he protested. "I don't want to remember!"

But it was too late. His sister was there before him, once again, telling Princess H'Us of Silver Hearth how H'Reth was abusing him, putting her livelihood on the line for him, and he couldn't back her up. He couldn't look the princess in the eyes and say, "Yes, it is all true." He wanted to, but he was afraid to die. He couldn't form the words.

"Amel!" a man's voice penetrated the dream.

A man. Like H'Reth.

"No!" Amel cried. Lashing out in anguish, he groped to get back into the moment when his silence condemned his sister to an unknown fate.

Something went thump.

Amel hurled himself into the drapes around his bed, trying to run after his sister as she was led away. He expected no physical obstruction. Reality contradicted him in the form of velvet drapes. He blundered through those, his actions incompatible with his surroundings, and struck his face hard on the floor.

Stunned, Amel lay where he'd fallen, not trusting his senses. Pain radiated from his nose, followed by a hot gush of blood.

There were other people in the room. Ayrium knelt to help him. On the far side of the bed, Perry was helping D'Ander up.

"I'm sorry, I'm sorry," Amel choked out, not sure if he was thirteen or sixteen, commoner or Pureblood.

Ayrium pulled over a heavy wooden chair upholstered in embroidered flowers. "Your nose is bleeding," she said as she made him sit down.

"I'm all right," D'Ander was saying in a rough voice to Perry D'Aur. "It's my fault. I should—" His words were cut off by a rasping cough.

"D'Ander, don't be stupid," Perry said with force. "He almost crushed your windpipe with that blow! You are coming with me to get it looked at, and tomorrow night, if necessary, we strap Amel down!"

"You can't—" D'Ander started and broke off in a spasm of coughs. "He's a Soul of—" D'Ander croaked, and was forced to stop.

"He—" Perry said with a special emphasis echoing D'Ander's choice of pronoun, "is a one hundred percent Sevolite highborn, and obviously stronger than he looks! Now you're coming to sick bay — Your Highness," she added as an afterthought, as if to mitigate her disrespectful manner.

Amel could not hang onto all the details. Perry meant to strap him down. In the wake of this idea, terror bloomed. He burst into tears, his face throbbing, and clung to Ayrium, staining her loose pajamas with blood from his bleeding nose.

2

Old Friends

Out of Exile

Ev'rel raised her eyes to track the shuttle descending over the highlands as she lowered the communicator in her right hand. Cattle lowed behind her. The wind whipped a strand of black hair about her lips like a lash.

"Who is it?" asked the smaller woman at her side.

"My old mentor," Ev'rel answered with unnatural calm, then spoke the man's name like a prayer. "Di Mon."

"After sixteen years?" exclaimed her companion, prepared to be angry on her friend's behalf.

Ev'rel looked down at the very young woman by her side whose expression was as intense and abstract as ever, her slight frame crisscrossed with the straps of an equipment pouch and a collection bag half full of plant samples. She was lucky to have found Mira when she sent her scouts out looking for bioengineering expertise three years ago. The girl was brilliant, and unfettered by superstitious dread of biosciences. Out here, in the isolated reaches called the Knotted Strings, so far from the society of court, Mira had become a teacher and a confidante, someone Ev'rel needed as much for mental stimulation as she did for the work they pursued together. But Mira was still just a commoner with no Sevolite blood, and apart from her scientific training, quite ignorant.

How can or should I weight that, Ev'rel thought, *against the man whose disapproval defined the shape of my rebellion as a child?*

But it was too late now to try to instill respect in Mira for Di Mon. Not after all the long walks they'd shared together and the late-night talks where Mira had listened to Ev'rel complain about her early life at court.

"What do you suppose he wants?" Mira asked, refusing to dignify the pronoun with a differencing suffix, although she did Di Mon the minimal honor of up-speaking him with a *rel*-case pronoun.

"Something important, I would imagine," Ev'rel said, managing to sound more indifferent than she was.

Mira returned her attention to the scruffy-looking plants, strewn across the windy hillside, which she'd modified with DNA of Earth origin in contravention of prevailing laws against meddling with genetics of any kind. The improvements meant FarHome cattle could graze outside environmentally controlled enclosures, which was more important to Ev'rel than the risk of discovery so far from densely populated areas; she wondered, briefly, if Di Mon had come to admonish her about the plants. Certainly, if anyone could deduce what she was up to from as far away as Fountain Court, it was Di Mon. But the altered plants did not feel important enough.

Ev'rel felt sure something much bigger was up.

"He still matters to you, doesn't he?" said Mira.

Ev'rel turned her head to smile down at the smaller woman. "Oh yes," she said, "he does. But don't feel threatened."

Mira shrugged, never one for focusing on feelings. Instead, she turned away to contemplate the unfinished sampling job ahead of her.

"You will have to see what he wants then," Mira acknowledged. "I can finish here."

Ev'rel resented the suggestion she was being dismissed, not the other way around. "No," she commanded, "come with me."

Mira looked up, her narrow face redeemed from plainness by the bloom of youth and her intense air of intelligence.

"All right," she said, in the carefully neutral tone she used when she sensed the ground between them shifting, and put the scissors back in her bag.

They trudged down the side of the hill in companionable silence towards the old battlewheel serving as Ev'rel's base of operations for the plant experiment.

Battlewheels were huge rings able to simulate gravitation while under rotation in space. This one looked uncomfortable on the ground, as if it might rise at any moment and fly off, even though battlewheels in service never did that. They were designed for deep-space operations. This one had crash-landed near the end of the clan wars in the Knotted Strings, wars in which Ev'rel had taken sides in order to unite the people she now called her own. The clan wars had been hard to extinguish and stupidly wasteful. In all the Knotted Strings no highborns remained, save Ev'rel and the two sons she had been obliged to gift to each of the dominant houses in the war. The grounded battlewheel was also a reminder of stupidity of an even more dramatic sort: if it had flown into the planet while still under skim, there would be no life on FarHome anymore.

Di Mon's envoy class *rel*-ship had landed by the time Ev'rel and Mira trudged up to the awning erected over one of the battlewheel's shuttle bays that served as a door. Ev'rel took every breath in the expectation of seeing him, but she was greeted, instead, by an excited retainer who rushed up to tell her that the liege of Monitum was waiting in her study for her.

"Thank you," she told the retainer, making a point of keeping her excitement in check. When the rough, Knotted Strings natives in her service talked about Di Mon's arrival, she wanted it said that she took her time getting back down the hill and showed no sign of eagerness.

She and Mira shed their outdoor clothes together, servants taking charge of their muddy boots, warm coats, and Mira's collection gear. The first section of the corridor they passed through after that was stark and serviceable. Evidence of Ev'rel's taste for finer things appeared as they went deeper. Corded rugs hung on the walls, made from local fibers, alternating with nervecloth displays of young men laboring in fields, herding cattle, or servicing shuttles. She had a preference for seeing them bare-chested and glistening with sweat, which was easy to indulge since she was the artist.

Not until they reached her study door did Ev'rel become self-conscious of her desire to keep Mira with her. "Wait here," she told the medic, not bothering to catch Mira's reaction to this sudden reversal of plans before she went inside and shut the door behind her.

Di Mon stood with his back to her, inspecting the contents of her desk, his long fingers drifting from one object to another. With a growing sense of irritation, she watched him touched her plans for solar collectors displayed on a flat screen, then one of Mira's reports on the plant project printed on poor-quality paper, and finally a request from a vassal to rule on a matter considered childishly simple by court standards. With rising anger, Ev'rel set her teeth. The last time she'd seen Di Mon he had damned her. Now he was back, reviewing the contents of her desk as if he had the right to check up on her. Or was he, perhaps, afraid to turn and face her?

Armed with that happy thought, she schooled herself to demonstrate patience.

In due course, Di Mon turned to look at her.

It was no good — she was still unprepared. But if he sensed the unwilling confession in her eyes of his importance to her, he gave no sign.

"Your brother, Ava Delm, is dead," he told her bluntly.

"Dead?" Ev'rel swallowed her surprise. "An accident?"

He shook his head, once. "By the sword."

"Oh," Ev'rel said, her left hand drifting nervously to her throat. She had not expected that! The shortage of Purebloods had defined Ev'rel's life. It had brought her grief and even horror, forcing her into the ten-child contract so painfully aborted by her exile, but it had also made her life — and her brother Delm's — sacred to Sevildom. Or so she had thought.

"By the sword?" she heard herself repeat, in an aloof tone. "My goodness. Delm must have distinguished himself to have inspired that."

Di Mon's thin mouth hardened.

"Who killed him?" Ev'rel asked.

"I did," said Di Mon.

Ev'rel's mouth went dry, eyes drawn to the dueling sword Di Mon wore on his right hip. Swords were polite attire among Sevolites: a statement declaring the wearer was prepared to abide by Sword Law instead of threatening mass destruction over quarrels that were ultimately personal. *Okal Rel* was the name given to this pact. Sevolites were expected to observe it, religiously, or be toppled by the wrath of those they dared to put at risk through their ambitions. This curious social contract empowering a weapon as archaic as the dueling sword was one Ev'rel had never hated more than at this moment.

"I presume," she said, struggling not to feel vulnerable, "that my dear, departed brother must have given you some cause for offense?"

Di Mon had not moved since he first spoke. Such stillness in him was a weapon: an unnatural exercise of discipline.

She won the war of wills.

He blasted air through his thin nostrils and swept the back of one hand across the sweat in his hairline. The Vrellish could never keep still, not even the infamous Di Mon, 103rd liege of Monitum.

But she could be Vrellish or Demish by turns as it suited her. Therefore, she would never wind up sword-slain like Delm. The insight made her feel safer.

"There is no right way to say this," Di Mon told her although his eyes darted around the room as if to seek escape before he made himself look straight at her. "It was Delm we should have exiled, not you. It was Delm who conspired against the life of his own child and heir." He barely paused. "We have genetic evidence that Amel was indeed Delm's, as you said, not the result of your... other activities."

Ev'rel's throat locked around an aborted breath. There was so much she could have felt. Instead, she remembered her lost baby's clean smell, his feather-soft hair and the wordless love staring back up at her out of his crystal-clear eyes — her beautiful, beautiful Amel, snatched from her by the ravenous thirst for power that had made Delm fear his own son. She had given birth twice since, for political reasons, but had never dared to love a child again.

"What do you mean?" she blurted. "What genetic evidence? Is Amel alive?!"

"Yes." Di Mon gave her a moment to collect herself. Damn him. She did not want to owe him anything.

"But first," he continued, "I must beg you to accept Fountain Court's apology for sending you into exile."

Fountain Court's apology, she thought, *not yours*. Politics had brought him to her. His personal distaste over the 'other activities' alluded to would never be forgiven. An answering bitterness welled up in her.

"Second," he sighed, and his shoulders lost their razor straightness. "Amel is more than merely alive. He is a sixteen-year-old Pureblood, mild natured by all accounts and raised as a commoner — the perfect pawn — and we don't have him. Prince D'Ander of the Golden Demish does. Ev'rel, he's your rival now." He inhaled deeply. "D'Ander even has the audacity to claim he acts as Ameron's disciple, which is the crowning arrogance."

"For you," she said curtly. "I am rather more put out by D'Ander's claim to ownership of my firstborn."

Di Mon nodded. "I can win Amel for you against D'Ander's daughter, Ayrium. She is why D'Ander has Amel now. The two of us agreed on a duel to first blood during a crisis in Killing Reach where, in order for us to take over a hostile battlewheel together, I had to let her take custody of Amel."

"What makes you think D'Ander's bastard will keep her word about a thing like that?" Ev'rel demanded. "Especially when Amel is her rival for Barmi II? She'd be better off marrying him." She paused to consider. "Or killing him."

Di Mon was shaking his head. "There would be war in Killing Reach if Ayrium or her mother acted dishonorably," he insisted.

"Mm," Ev'rel said, tight lipped, as she contemplated the alternatives. Amel persisted in her memory as a sweet infant, but he could not be so now. "Better if she slays him, all in all," she concluded, on political grounds alone.

Di Mon said nothing. She wondered what he thought, and found it pleased her to imagine that he found her hard. She was a liege now in her own right, by her own cunning, and no longer the shocked and desperate child who had thrown herself upon his mercy sixteen years before.

"What I mean," Ev'rel elaborated, "is that revenge would be easier to pursue, in claiming Barmi II, than a rival who was also a daughter-in-law." The prospect, once spoken, dismayed her and she asked abruptly, "Is Ayrium smart enough to realize it?"

"D'Ander has his own ideas for Amel," Di Mon assured her. "And he'll have a hard enough time making those plans palatable to the Golden Demish, given the boy's past, without the liability of marrying him off to his bastard daughter. He is putting Amel forward as a Soul of Light and heir to Fahild, the Golden Emperor."

"His past?" Ev'rel asked. "What is wrong with Amel's past?"

Di Mon tried to sound matter-of-fact. "He was working as a courtesan when he was found. A sword dancer."

Ev'rel arched a single, exquisite eyebrow. "My," she said, and felt a tickle of amusement threaten. *Talented*, she thought ironically. *A mother should be proud.* It made sense at the same time. *What other trade would a lost child with Delm's good looks wind up in, on Gelion?*

She was silent for long, breathless seconds, in which she weighed her ambitions against D'Ander's, and decided she understood him well enough. She, too, wanted everything within her grasp: the Avaship, Demora, and even the renegade Purple Alliance that had hung onto Barmi II for a quarter of a century for reasons fast becoming obsolete.

"I will, of course, have you as my First Sworn," Ev'rel told Di Mon. She toyed with the desire to tease him and her better judgment lost out. "Do you think you can take Ayrium D'Ander D'Aur? I've heard she's better than most Demish women on the challenge floor."

"Anything can happen in a duel," Di Mon trotted out a truism of Sword Law.

"Of course," Ev'rel snapped, annoyed with herself for forgetting he was too Vrellish to be insulted by the suggestion that he couldn't beat a woman. The Vrellish made no distinction between women and men as fighters. But she knew Ayrium had very little Vrellish blood — just a splash on her mother's side. Surely she'd be no competition for a swordsman of Di Mon's caliber. "I would like you to kill her," Ev'rel ordered. "Alive, she might obstruct my claiming Barmi II on Amel's behalf."

"Our agreement was to first blood," said Di Mon.

"We'll talk of it later," Ev'rel said, and was pleased to watch him frown. *Did you expect me to come to heel without a nip or two, after all these years?* she thought. Much to her annoyance, at the same time, she was worried by the blood vessel pulsing at his temple and the white-hard tension in his jaw.

"But you are tired," she said suddenly, letting her concern show. "It is a long flight here from Gelion and I suspect you flew hard. You will, of course, take the usual three-day respite before returning to court." An impish mischief crossed her mind. "And while we've nothing like Den Eva's to offer here on FarHome in the way of professional courtesans, I know a woman or two who is Vrellish enough in her manners to be honored by the opportunity to help you relax, if you will accept such hospitality at my hands."

"Thank you," he replied curtly, "no."

"Still the only Vrellish prude in living memory, my dear Di Mon?"

"Hardly," he said in a brittle tone. "I have a *lyka* now on Monitum, and a *mekan'st* at court."

"Ses Nersal," Ev'rel blurted, and immediately regretted seeming interested. She covered it up with a shrug. "I send envoys to court from time to time, and I am always glad to hear news of old acquaintances." She did not need to force a smile. She was suddenly glad just to see him standing there before her, unchanged and unassailably alive.

"I thank you for your hospitality," Di Mon told her with a distant courtesy, "but I must return to court at once. If necessary, I will rest at way stations along my route on my way home. So if there is anything we must discuss before I leave, let it be now."

She regretted the offer of women then, for she suspected it was why he would not take respite. He had always been more reserved about sex than any Vrellish highborn — male or female — she had ever known.

And one day, she promised herself, *I will know why.*

Ghosts

Space was not large enough to make Di Mon's problems feel small on the way home from his meeting with Ev'rel.

He kept thinking about his late *gorarelpul*, Sarilous. She had urged him to kill his new friend, Ranar of Rire, but he could not do it. Sarilous had died of bond conflict, trying to do it herself against Di Mon's explicit orders.

But was she right? Di Mon thought as he stared into the shifting stars ahead. *By protecting Ranar, have I doomed everything she and I worked to preserve?*

All because he was boy-*sla*.

For three decades since the death of his first forbidden lover, Darren, he had tried to imagine their affair had been an aberration. He had needed to believe that as he watched Monitum's stability teeter in the aftermath of Darren's disgrace. But he knew, beneath the longing for a wholesome normalcy, that he had been passionately in love with the 102nd liege of Monitum. And never, if he forced himself to brutal honesty, had he been truly able to refocus his desire. He took female lovers chosen for the men that he associated them with, and he hated himself for it: his commoner *lyka*, Eva, for her dance partner Von; and his nobleborn *mekan'st*, Ses Nersal, to sustain a connection with the self-exiled Hangst Nersal of Black Hearth.

Now there was Ranar, and for the first time since Darren he had dared to love a man. But what a strange man! The brown-skinned alien from Rire, infuriatingly decent and unshakably rational, had guessed what Di Mon felt and calmly said he felt likewise, as if it shouldn't matter to anyone except the two of them.

What, then, of Monitum?

After a millennium of influence, Di Mon's ancestral house now survived more on reputation than real power and could not sustain a second scandal. Darren's disgrace had happened on the brink of a great war when the Monatese fleet could still boast a hundred highborns — a tenth the number of its Nersallian and Red Vrellish allies, but still enough to be a power. Thirty years later, Di Mon could field nothing but nobleborns, either in space or on the challenge floor; his ruin could close Green Hearth forever and leave Monitum vulnerable to takeover. Ev'rel herself might do it. She was looking for a more hospitable world to give her Dem'Vrellish vassals than FarHome. She had asked, before he left, whether it was time to admit the Lor'Vrellish line was extinct and yield up White Hearth to her son D'Therd. She had barely conceded that Brown Hearth must remain open to the Lorels of *TouchGate Hospital* and hinted that nothing but slavish Demish respect for tradition left Monitum in command of three votes on Fountain Court, despite two of the hearths concerned standing empty. Ev'rel would never have dared such opinions while Black Hearth and Red Hearth looked to Monitum as their wily Vrellish advisor on how to contend with Demish powers, but within the past year, Vretla Vrel of Red Hearth had spurned Di Mon for sending her to *TouchGate Hospital* against her wishes, and his comrade in arms against the Nesaks, Black Hearth's Hangst Nersal, was showing signs of teaming up with their old enemy. It was a very bad time, as Sarilous had realized, to be courting disaster in the shape of Ranar of Rire.

Easily fixed, the voice of Sarilous seemed to whisper to Di Mon. *Finish my work and kill the Reetion.*

Di Mon gritted his teeth against gap-induced fantasies, meaning to endure in silence, then decided to fight back out loud. "You're not one of the Watching Dead, Sarilous," he said gruffly. "You're a commoner."

What of it? came her acid answer. *Only Nesaks believe we lack souls, Master.*

I am debating a ghost, he thought, and shook his head to clear it, but could not resist getting in the last word. "More to the point, Sarilous, neither of us believe in souls or the reincarnation cycle."

The way she laughed convinced him she was nothing but his own guilt tormenting him. *Tell me, then*, she taunted him, *why you keep looking for Ameron in Ev'rel. Or do you consider your expectations of her to be scientific because you think in terms of genes not spirits? Sevolites breed true — isn't that what you told Ranar? What happened to Ev'rel, then?*

Di Mon cut out of skim farther from the Gelack system than he normally did, more willing to put up with zero gravity than self-inflicted mockery. Blood rushed to his head. Nettled, he nudged his envoy vessel into a technique known as cat-clawing, which drew energy from the skin of the universe by engaging the reality skimming phase-splicer without skipping much space between engagements. A cat-clawing ship resembled a shimmering centipede on the nervecloth of another *rel*-skimming vessel and moved about as quickly. The technique provided a comfortable level of acceleration for a highborn at a low level of threat to defenders.

He was promptly surrounded by three ward ships. The lead vessel danced a pattern at him that registered on his ship's nervecloth, requesting he identify himself.

Di Mon stopped cat-clawing long enough to dance back: *Liege Monitum*.

A pause was followed by a short flurry of patterns translating into a request to communicate by radio, which struck Di Mon as curious.

Dropping out of skim in a space lane as heavily traveled as any of the approaches to Gelion was not a recommended practice, but curiosity got the better of him. He cut out of skim. The other ship followed.

Di Mon and the other ship would barely register as mass until a reality skimming ship was about to manifest on top of them. They would have to trust the two ships still under skim to ward off other travelers while they conversed. But the risk was necessary because reality skimming ships could not communicate with each other using electromagnetic signals and shimmer dances had a limited vocabulary — not to mention being indistinguishable from an attack if the conversation got too vigorous.

"Liege Monitum," the other ship greeted him by radio, "I am *rel-sha* Taff of Rocky Coast in Lion Reach."

Silver Demish, Di Mon realized with a sigh, as the *rel-sha* launched into a recitation of his birth rank, territorial affiliation, and the titles of both his military commander and the liege of his family of origin.

"You have a message for me?" Di Mon interrupted before the list was quite finished. Zero gravity was getting to him.

"Yes!" exclaimed the Demish fighter pilot. "But I wanted to tell you, first, that I... well, damn it — Vrellish or not — you did the right thing. I mean about exposing Ava Delm for the dishonorable monster he was, once you turned up the evidence of his lying about Amel being a *gorarelpul*'s bastard. And some people thought Delm was a Soul of Light! A man who could condemn his own innocent infant to—"

"Yes," Di Mon said, losing his grip on diplomacy, "thank you. The message?"

"Right!" There was a short, disconcerted silence. "Our admiral, Prince H'Us, was informed of a Reetion incursion into Killing Reach and has dispatched the battlewheel *QuickSilver* to monitor the situation. Since you were away, your *pol*-heir was consulted about providing a Monatese embassy on board, to round out the sense of this being a Fountain Court initiative and not strictly unilateral. Oh, and she said to tell you she took along the Reetion, Ranar, to act as interpreter if necessary."

Di Mon's heart lurched. "What?" he got out, unable to believe Ranar could have escaped his custody in Green Hearth so easily. His niece Tessitatt had no idea why it was so important to keep Ranar in Green Heath, of course. How could she? He dared not trust even Tessitatt with the knowledge that he shared Darren's flaw. But Ranar knew his dangerous secret, and was now at risk of passing beyond his control, maybe even returning to his own people.

"Did you want me to repeat—" began Taff of Rocky Coast in Lion Reach.

"No!" Di Mon snapped. "Just tell me where to find the *QuickSilver*."

Ninety seconds later, Di Mon was under skim again and headed back towards the jump, away from Gelion. He flew hard. After twenty minutes at five *skim'facs* his nose began to bleed and gap hallucinations gathered, still shapeless but threatening, at the edges of his conscious awareness. He cut back to three skim'facs with a cry of frustration. It was mad to be flying so hard after the long trip to FarHom*e* and back with no rest except a few nerve-wracking stopovers on semi-hostile way stations. He knew better, but his anxiety drove him to fly harder.

It was an hour before he calmed down enough to think out the implications of being met so fortuitously with the message that the annoying Demish *rel-sha* had delivered. To be sure of catching him along his route in the vastness of space, Prince H'Us must have charged every Silver Demish ship warding Gelion with its delivery. It was a safe bet, there-fore, that *rel-sha* Taff of Rocky Coast had been parroting Silver Hearth policy concerning Di Mon's exposure of Ava Delm. Di Mon knew he ought to be relieved about that, and by his niece, Tessitatt, being asked to set up a Monatese presence on *QuickSilver*. But all he could think about was the liabil-ity posed by Ranar.

The fastest route to Killing was through Golden Reach, and Di Mon feared interminable delays if he stopped to chat, so he picked up the pace again hoping to look like an over-flown Vrellish renegade from Red Reach, on a joy ride. The Golden Demish usually warded such ships through to the Killing Jump without a word of protocol, pleased to let the lawless of Killing Reach contend with the lawless of Red Reach without risking their pilots.

Instead, Di Mon's telltale highborn streak across space at-tracted two whole hands of D'Ander's highborn ward ships.

One came at him from the front and one from behind. He was impressed enough to cut speed and shimmer dance, which probably saved his life. The two hand leaders did not believe him, even so, and buzzed him half a dozen times trying to get a whiff of soul touch to confirm he was telling the truth about who he was.

Di Mon gritted his teeth against the invasive feeling of being brushed by the wings of martial angels so absolutely sure of what was right and wrong that it invoked the snarling Vrellish warrior in him, not the contemplative scholar. Both Goldens were male highborns, which was no surprise, although his sudden awareness of their maleness caused Di Mon to panic for fear he might reveal his *sla* perversion. To get away he threw open *gap* wide enough to skip outside the sphere of ships surrounding him in one stitch of shimmer, but the Goldens had set up an outlying guard. He was caught between two of these at once, which gave the others time to close. There was no escaping such odds. He could drop out of skim and hope not to get trampled, but that strategy depended on patience, good luck, and more tolerance for zero gravity than Di Mon felt he possessed at the moment. Ashamed of his terror at the thought of tolerating further soul touch, he signaled his willingness to dock.

The slow process of approaching the designated battlewheel, flanked by wary Golden highborns who clearly considered him as mad as any Vrellish fool possessed by a life-starved ghost, was interminable. Di Mon's teeth were on edge by the time he climbed out of his cockpit. His flight leathers felt gritty with sweat. Blood from his nose, which had stopped bleeding after just a few minutes, soiled the front of his jacket. He had the strange sensation, as he snatched his sword out of its place behind his seat, of watching someone else perform the action.

Opening his hatch required no special powers of concentration. He felt primed and ready to contend with anything from flying at six *skim'facs* to taking on both Golden hand leaders hand-to-hand. The part of his brain that knew how to fight felt like an optimized nervecloth pattern with all of its channels clear for input.

Di Mon felt surreal enough that it hardly phased him to find Hangst Nersal, liege of Black Hearth, waiting for him in the outer airlock. It felt like meeting someone in a dream. Dream logic dressed Hangst in the emotions of their long friendship, from Di Mon's apprenticeship under his tutelage in the last Nesak War through the long decades in which they'd worked together for the Vrellish cause, as lieges of Fountain Court.

Hangst Nersal was a hybrid, like Ev'rel: part Vrellish, part Demish. He was big and broad-shouldered with a narrow waist — solid, timeless and indomitable — outfitted in red and black decorated in Nersallian braid. His sword had a dragon guard and a crimson dragon spanned the black cape that declared him admiral of the most respected fleet in Sevildom, even though both metallic Demish houses could command more highborn pilots. Di Mon recognized the admiralty cloak, the dragon on it reaching its arms about Hangst's neck as if in an attack. From the front, one could see nothing but the dragon's claws on either side of the winged collar. The cloak symbolized the *kinf'stan*: crack swords and pilots who stood within challenge right for the title of Liege Nersal. There were over a thousand such Highlords in clan Nersal: men and women who would defend their liege against enemies to the last drop of Nersallian blood, only to threaten that same liege, themselves, on the challenge floor. Di Mon had always feared the *kinf'stan* on his friend's behalf. It seemed impossible to him that anyone but Hangst could ever be the liege of Nersal.

For a moment, Di Mon almost believed time had rolled back and things were as they had been before Hangst rejected the Demish court in favor of their erstwhile enemies, the Nesaks.

Hangst narrowed his large, blue-gray eyes. "Are you *rel-fatigued*?" he asked.

It was a politer term than space drunk, lacking the connotation of irresponsible behavior.

"No," Di Mon said, knowing it was a lie. "Not much," he amended, feeling like the younger highborn again, despite his sixty-five years. Hangst was the older of the two of them: more than one hundred, an Old Sword who had survived so many challenges most people had lost count.

The kinf'stan *will never take him down*, Di Mon assured himself, and realized that was not what he ought to be worried about anymore. Hangst was on the brink of becoming an enemy and, at the very least, had ceased to be an ally the day he had abandoned Black Hearth to a skeleton staff.

Hangst's wide, full lips turned down in a frown. "Where are you going?" he asked.

The question sobered Di Mon up. "To Killing Reach. The Reetions have begun building a station there. Silver Hearth sent a battlewheel to observe."

"I have just returned from *QuickSilver* myself," said Hangst. "I met with a Reetion representative there, named Ranar."

That name on those lips sent a shriek of alarm through Di Mon, making blood beat in his ears. "What for?" he heard himself demand.

Hangst's laugh was sudden and generous. "Same old Di Mon," he said, "assuming all the business of the empire must also be yours. Do you still do it in the name of the lost Lor'Vrellish Ava, Ameron?" He shook his head. "Forgive me, we were friends once. It is small of me to mock you for your belief in an empty hearth."

There is nothing small about you, thought Di Mon with an involuntary pang of admiration.

"The Silver Demish don't want Reetions in Killing Reach," Di Mon said quickly. "I hope, therefore, you told this man, Ranar, to make them stop building and withdraw, as I will when I get there."

Hangst's expression hardened. "I had dared to hope, when I heard you killed their pompous Ava, that you might be developing a mind of your own instead of waiting to be told what to think by Silver Hearth."

As he processed the insult, Di Mon experienced an abstract sympathy for Hangst's hearth-child, Horth, who suffered from a particularly extreme and disabling version of the linguistic limitations typical among the Vrellish. As Sarilous had explained it to him, Horth had to make a conscious effort to put words together, like a puzzle, and draw meaning from them after they were assembled. This was exactly how Di Mon felt now. He took in the words one by one and fitted them together. It took an effort to make himself accept what Hangst had said. But the moment he was sure, beyond all hope of doubt, he cleared his sword and charged.

Hangst drew as he stepped back to block. Di Mon was furious. Hangst was cool. The big Nersallian's free hand struck Di Mon's head like a battering ram. It did not knock Di Mon out; instead, it made him stagger aside and buckle onto one knee on the airlock floor. Hangst moved to hold him at sword point. Di Mon got his sword up in time. Their blades crossed, both men paused, looking into each other's eyes.

"Reetions are commoners," Di Mon gasped, seeing Hangst through a fading haze of anger with the side of his head pounding from the blow. "What can you want with them?"

"The Nesak high priest says your Reetions are *okal'a'ni* for what they did to Pureblood Amel," Hangst told him in a chilling voice. "Best we get to know them better, to be sure."

"You don't care what they did to Amel!" Di Mon seethed as hot as Hangst was cold. "Amel is just another foppish Demish prince to you!"

Hangst stepped back far enough to put a sword's length between them and watched to see what Di Mon would do.

Di Mon's mouth had gone dry and his sword arm was aching from holding off Hangst's sword. He forced himself onto both feet, sword ready, but did not renew his attack.

"Commoners cannot be trusted to honor *Okal Rel*, you who were once my *brerelo*," Hangst said in his rich, deep voice, using the Gelack naming word for comrade that touched Di Mon's aching heart. "You should know that."

"But Nesak priests can?" Di Mon answered in a broken voice.

"While you would put more faith in Lorel ideas," Hangst said in a lighter tone, glancing towards the door, "I cannot." He sheathed his sword.

Di Mon turned to see three Golden Demish men coming towards them, resplendent in braid aglitter with embedded jewels.

"Yes," Hangst told their hosts briskly, "he is Liege Monitum. But he is badly over-flown." He looked back at Di Mon with a maddeningly friendly smile. "I know the signs well. I recommend a three-day travel respite."

"Thank you, Liege Nersal," the leader said, and executed one of the many gestures in the Golden Demish repertoire. Hangst responded with an all-purpose Nersallian salute.

"Come to court," Di Mon appealed in desperation as Hangst prepared to leave him to their hosts. "Swear to Ev'rel. Heal the empire."

Hangst leaned towards him, hand on the hilt of his own sword and fearlessly indifferent to the naked one in Di Mon's left hand. "You have less respect for Ev'rel than you had for Delm, or have you forgotten?"

Di Mon could not refute it. He stood, watching Hangst's broad, retreating back, unable to force false words from his stubborn throat.

"If you will come this way, Liege Monitum," the Golden leader said with another elegant gesture in his direction, "we will find servants to show you to your quarters."

"Don't be ridiculous!" Di Mon snapped.

All three Goldens drew their swords.

Di Mon actually thought about it for two seconds, which proved — even to himself — that he really was space drunk.

"All right!" he snarled instead. "But just one day, not three!"

In the end, it was two days before Di Mon was ruled sober enough to cross Golden Reach under a heavy escort. He was met by two sets of escort ships in Killing Reach on the far side of the next jump: three of D'Ander's *rel-sha* from the contingent left to guard Amel, and two Nersallians from the Bryllit clan who constituted the only stable power in Killing Reach apart from the Purple Alliance, although their holdings lay far outreach, well away from the controversial Reetion jump.

It was a long, slow trip to reach the *QuickSilver*. Di Mon had never experienced such a buildup of battlewheels clumped together in too little space as he found in the area surrounding the jump that led to Reetion territories. The nervecloth of his envoy craft's nose cone showed what pilots called bright weather — the glimmering tracks of tiny *rel*-fighters painting their webs in careful patterns around and between the blurry glow of battlewheels that throbbed in place at lazy intervals in order to remain visible to ships under skim.

Now and then a *rel*-fighter would pull clear to dance a pattern, and Di Mon flagged them with labels. Demish pilots rarely bothered with such things, but, in a field of moving pinpoints this busy, Di Mon trusted his nervecloth better than his memory. What emerged was a frightening array of Golden Demish, Nersallian and Silver Demish highborn power, with fainter scatterings of Purple Alliance nobleborns, all concentrated in a sphere of space no more than an hour's radius from the jump at a single *skim'fac*. It was enough to make any reality skimming pilot feel the urge to tiptoe towards dock.

QuickSilver was not under skim itself but Di Mon was able to identify it from its attendant swarm of ward ships, and was glad to drop out of skim well clear of the invisible challenge sphere enforced by its defenders. His envoy ship carried conventional fuel, but he put up with zero-G rather than pollute the hard vacuum required for *rel*-skimming. The last leg of the journey seemed to take forever, which was always frustrating, but at least he was able to raise Tessitatt on the radio.

"Yes," she answered his question about Ranar, "I brought the Reetion. He pointed out, sensibly, that he could translate for us. The Reetions have their own translation devices, of course, but I prefer to trust a person over whatever they extracted from Amel's brain when they were mistreating him. Besides, Ranar can also act as an advisor."

"Ranar pointed that out, too, I suppose," Di Mon replied sulkily.

"You don't approve?" Tessitatt asked. "I thought you trusted him."

"You did nothing wrong in bringing him," Di Mon assured her quickly, fearing his anxiety about Ranar might seem out of proportion to the situation. "I am not at my best with my head pounding for lack of G force, that's all. We'll talk later."

"I'll be waiting," she said.

And she was waiting as promised, with Ranar.

The Reetion was decked out in some of Di Mon's own clothes, minus any house braid or insignia of office. Di Mon frowned, wondering how Ranar had talked Tessitatt into that. No doubt he had made it seem sensible, since it was true he was no Monatese commoner, even if he wasn't a Sevolite either.

Tessitatt embraced Di Mon once. "Did it go well with Ev'rel?" she asked, as she drew back.

"Well enough," he said, glancing at the Silver Demish honor guard that had turned out to receive him.

Tessitatt got the hint. "This way to the Monatese embassy," she said, and led on.

Di Mon avoided looking at Ranar. He was afraid to find the Reetion staring at him in a conspicuous way. But when he did risk a glance in Ranar's direction, he was disappointed not to make eye contact.

Their Silver Demish escort left them at the edge of a beautiful challenge floor ringed about by comfortably upholstered seats. On the far side of this was a suite of rooms designated as the Monatese embassy, where Di Mon found two of his own errants standing guard in a pleasant, albeit Demish-looking antechamber.

A herald in his livery opened the door for him. Inside, he recognized the inferior Sevolite who jumped up from behind a big wood desk to bow to him, and the two *gorarelpul* who conferred together in another corner. The *gorarelpul* reminded him that he must pick a permanent successor for Sarilous. *When I do, will I tell him what Sarilous knew?* he wondered. *And will he advise me to kill Ranar, just like she did, if I do?*

Ranar moved up beside Di Mon, making him tense for fear they might touch. But the Reetion was attending to Tessitatt who was talking about setting up the embassy, proud of managing it herself in his absence.

"—with sixteen staff, not including two hands of nobleborn *rel-sha*, housed elsewhere. The *rel-sha* can also be called upon to help diplomatically, if required. I picked at least some of them for that potential."

"A good idea," Di Mon complimented her, catching Ranar's eye just long enough to note approval there. "We may need to rely on a surrogate here from time to time, although I want to plan for either you or me being in residence as much as possible."

Tessitatt answered him with a sober nod. *She is growing up*, he thought. *She would be the only heir I need, if only she were highborn.*

"The core rooms are the most private," said Ranar.

Tessitatt picked up on his prompt and beckoned to the captain of the embassy errants and a *gorarelpul* named Ekous. "Please tell my liege-uncle about security measures," she instructed them.

Di Mon listened with a growing awareness of Ranar. At last he interrupted.

"Good, Tessitatt! Ranar, I want to see you in the briefing room. Ekous: protocol on all meetings in that room will be the same as in my library at Green Hearth. No one is to enter without warning. Understood?"

The *gorarelpul* bowed with more deference than Sarilous had ever shown, which inspired mixed feelings in Di Mon. No replacement could ever be as much a partner as his first mentor had been, and he would miss her, but he liked being able to subtract the subtext of his shameful flaw from every interaction with a *gorarelpul*. Better, then, not to tell her replacement. Better for him, that was. Sarilous would have added, *Not better for Monitum*.

Tessitatt began talking as soon as she, Ranar and Di Mon were alone in the briefing room. "The Silver Demish have been very gracious about inviting us to take part, but—" she gave Ranar an apologetic look, "—they do not want the Reetions building a station here, and they are offended by the deal you made with Ayrium concerning custody of Amel."

Di Mon nodded impatiently, already aware of both facts. "Liege Nersal was here," he said. "Why?"

"I was about to tell you," Tessitatt said, "D'Ander invited Hangst to act as Judge of Honor for the custody duel over Amel, and the Silvers agreed to it."

"Liege Nersal spoke to me, as well," Ranar said. "He made it a condition of the deal with the Silvers and Goldens that my people be allowed to build an outpost in Killing Reach."

Di Mon could stand such foolishness no more. He rounded on Ranar so swiftly that the Reetion took an involuntary step back. "Haven't you wondered why he wants Reetions in Killing Reach?" Di Mon demanded.

"I know what you're thinking," Ranar defended himself. "I've heard the rumors of Liege Nersal's intention to invade Reetion territory with his Nesak allies. But how will we convince him not to if we're not here to talk?"

"Talk!" Di Mon suffered a sharp pain between his eyes as his blood pressure spiked. He paused to pinch the bridge of his nose. "Leave us for a little, will you, Tessitatt?"

He was grateful that she gave him no argument. Ranar was another matter.

"You, yourself, believe your friend Hangst Nersal is an honorable man," Ranar was saying even before Tessitatt closed the door. "He treated me respectfully enough. I cannot believe he views all natural humans as vermin to be slaughtered, as Tessitatt has told me the Nesaks do. His connections with the Nesaks might even provide a conduit through which to influence—"

Di Mon seized Ranar by either shoulder, squaring him to face him. "You are a fool," he told him, angry with himself for the passion the connection aroused, "a young, idealistic fool!"

"Tessitatt has told me about Hangst Nersal," Ranar protested. "And you are hurting me," he added crossly.

Di Mon let go with a snort and turned away. He closed his eyes, concentrating on his headache instead of the young, boy-*sla* Reetion who had become his lover — so willingly — on Gelion. His thoughts swam. To keep ahead of them, he prowled about the room.

"Hangst Nersal wants to learn the jump into the Reach of Paradise," Di Mon said, heart broken by the conclusion. He wished to believe better of the man he had once called *brerelo* and whose honor he had trusted more than his own. "For a long time, we agreed the Ava's Oath must hold together to prevent the Nesaks conquering the empire in a future war. Now Hangst considers the Nesaks to be better than the Demish court. Conquering your Reetion territories would be the warm-up for their joint assault upon the empire to restore Nesak orthodoxy and the rule of priests on Gelion, which cannot, must not, happen."

Ranar intercepted Di Mon with a touch as he walked past on his next circuit of the room, making Di Mon start.

"It is safe in here," Ranar assured him. "We can talk."

"We *are* talking!" Di Mon spat back, although he knew perfectly well what the Reetion meant.

"I expect you're angry to find me here," Ranar said reasonably. "I know you wished to keep me under your control, but I warned you I could never accept that. I am a free man with my own work to do." He paused. "We have to trust each other, Di Mon."

"How?" Di Mon blurted, desperate for some relief. "How can I trust an alien I barely know with the safety of my very house! Ah, gods! I wish I could burn this vile affliction from my flesh, or die in the knowledge I might be reborn clean of its taint!"

It was impossible to miss the impact of his outburst on Ranar's face. "Is that how you think about... me?" he asked.

Di Mon reviewed, with lightning speed, the precautions in place and the rules about interruptions in this room, which matched those of his library back on Gelion. "Not you," he said, hating the dawning awareness of wrongness in Ranar's expression. "Your acceptance of what you are amazes me. Never do I want you to feel as I feel about this... thing."

"Thing?" Ranar repeated with a frown. "Just exactly how do you think of us? What is the naming word you use, in your language, for what we are?"

Di Mon was loath to use it. The sounds formed and bunched in his throat. They forced themselves out. "*Slaka'stan.*"

"Mmm," Ranar said. His hurt expression becoming introspective. "That's wrong."

Di Mon reacted as if he had been slapped across the nose by a Demish lady's gloves. "What do you mean wrong?" he demanded. "It's not wrong."

"The defining thing about a *slaka'stan* relationship, as I understand the word thus far," Ranar lectured, "is the pairing of an abuser and a victim: the *slaka'st* and the *slaka*." He paused. "I am not your victim." He toyed with the beginnings of a smile. "Or do you think you are mine?"

Di Mon scowled. "That is not the point."

Ranar tipped his head slightly. "Why?"

Di Mon shook his head with much the same feeling he got when he had water in his ears, but his head refused to clear. "We have no time for this," he grumbled.

"Later then," said Ranar, still maddeningly calm and self assured.

3

Courtships

New Deal

Ev'rel hated flying but she was reassured by the confidence of her son, D'Therd, who was piloting their shuttle. At fifteen, D'Therd was already one of those splendid young men who did everything right the first time. He had proved himself in space as a *rel*-pilot against his father's rival clan, the Lekkers, when they last attempted to rebel against the new order, but combat in space was not his first love. In a space war it was too easy to die unnoticed and unsung. Where D'Therd excelled most was on the challenge floor. She knew he was aching to take on the empire's best to establish her fledgling house of Dem'Vrel as a court power. She had not decided yet exactly how she felt about that. He was an important asset, naturally, but with too much popularity he could become a rival.

From the air, Gelion was dry and barren, with an atmosphere too thin to block the harmful radiation of its old yellow sun. She spotted a single vehicle at work clearing dust, but no one out walking around. People stayed inside when they could.

The landing field lay between broken cliffs. D'Therd soared into the rocky chasm, disdaining the chutes that led to the highborn docks.

The landing platform for the Ava's Way was tiny compared to the chutes and the docks they articulated with below, but it was the most exclusive landing site on Gelion.

I am coming home, Papa, Ev'rel thought.

D'Therd set down on the lip of the Ava's Way as if he had done it a dozen times before. Its doors were open for them. Inside, the deck overlooked a square, ringed with rising banks of gardens in which Demish ladies strolled about in layered dresses, attended by flocks of servants and a few gallant princes. Ev'rel had read, in one of Di Mon's books, where a ship overshot the landing deck and tumbled down the terraced banks below.

"Why didn't the next Ava build a barrier!" Ev'rel had asked Di Mon, horrified.

"Because UnderGelion's design has a purpose," Di Mon had told her. "It reminds us how our lives depend on trusting each other, and it encourages us to respect the harm reality skimming ships or Lorel biosciences can do to the environments all life depends on. The apartments below the deck are filled with young adults of powerful families visiting court for a swearing or other special occasions like the pan-Demish tournament. By sending their children to live under the arrival deck, the families express their trust in the Ava, and the Ava hosts them grandly as hostages to honor."

So, Ev'rel thought coldly, *the trick is not to care about the hostages.* It pleased her to know this was not the conclusion Di Mon had wanted her to extract from the lesson. Nonetheless, it was the one that she was bringing home with her.

"Mother?" D'Therd touched her arm. "It is time to get out."

She frowned at her prosaic son. He was so unimaginative, just like his father, the previous D'Therd, a title meaning "Liege Therd" in the dialect of the Knotted Strings. The senior D'Therd had demanded a Demish-style marriage rather than a Vrellish-style child contract, but Ev'rel had only had to put up with him until the first war with the rival clan of Lekker.

She'd had a second son by the liege of Lekker, afterwards, as part of her stratagem for hammering together a nation. The younger son, D'Lekker, was a brooding, emotional piece of work. D'Therd was the better raw material, although she often wished he was less attached to his title and would go by the name she had given him at birth, which was Chad. But from the moment his father died fighting Clan Lekker in space, her Chad had become D'Therd and would not respond to what he called his "baby name" anymore. She counted it as a rejection, as well as due notice that they had more in common than she would have preferred.

D'Therd helped Ev'rel out of their shuttle and followed her down the ramp to the floor. The first thing he did there was buckle on his sword as an expression of his willingness to live by Sword Law.

Di Mon came to greet them dressed in the full regalia of his position. He had chosen to wear house braid and a selection of Monatese heirlooms but not his admiralty cape, which may have been a tacit admission of his weakness in that quarter.

Silver Demish pages rolled out a carpet patterned in the designs of Ev'rel's mixed heritage. Ev'rel spotted Vretla, liege of Vrel, in the receiving line and was glad she had insisted that the Demish not play down the red threads in the carpet too much.

Vretla was a vigorous woman with a lean build and a feline cast to her features suggested by her eyes and cheekbones. The nobleborn Vrellish attending her favored bright dyes, beaded bands, leather vests and exposed skin. They injected a riot of colors into the blue-and-silver mass of Demish in attendance.

Among the Demish, Ev'rel noted that men's fashions had changed less than women's in the sixteen years of her exile. Even the changes in women's attire were not startling, just a new froth upon the surface of century-long traditions.

There were no Golden Demish in attendance, and no black-clad Nersallians, either. D'Ander of Golden Hearth had set himself against her by laying claim to Amel. Hangst Nersal of Black Hearth had subtracted himself from the equation when he left court.

"Welcome home," said Di Mon.

Ev'rel inhaled deeply of the recycled air of UnderGelion and smiled. *Yes*, she thought, *home at last*.

"Thank you, My Lord of Monitum," she addressed him in the gendered, Demish fashion, and watched him frown.

Politics, she thought at him. *It is the Silver Demish who dominate the empire. You should be proud of your pupil, Di Mon.*

Three princesses came forward to receive her and curtseyed in unison. She acknowledged them with a nod and gave each her naked hand. Their hands were gloveless as well, enacting a ritual of trust left over from evil times in which bioscience was equated with Lorel crimes.

The princesses withdrew to make way for the real head of their house, the Silver Demish admiral, S'Reese H'Us. There were thousands of princes in the house of H'Us, but this big, blocky man was the one meant when people said: *Prince H'Us*. All the same, his flowery words of welcome did not catch Ev'rel's interest. Instead, she remembered the last time she had seen him, his sand-colored eyebrows massed above the condemnation in his eyes as he told her she was to be exiled for conceiving Amel by a commoner. "Like a Vrellish slut!" were the words he had used on that occasion.

Isn't it a charming world? Ev'rel thought, as she smiled at him.

"...tragic proportions, for yourself and your lost son, Prince Amel," H'Us was saying, "a boy of sixteen, in the hands of my wild, ambitious nephew D'Ander, who has so badly misled his mother's people that they trust him above their Silver cousins, who wish them nothing but good. I pray D'Ander does Amel no further harm, and humble myself on behalf of all Silver Demish in extending our apology to you for the mistake made in blaming you, so wrongly, sixteen years ago for the child's loss. If there is anything I can do—"

"Yes," Ev'rel said crisply, cutting off the stream of empty words.

Beside her, Di Mon tensed.

"Yes?" asked Prince H'Us, blinking blue eyes overshadowed by those thick, bushy eyebrows.

"There is something you can do to redress my injuries," said Ev'rel with a womanly smile.

She liked the suspicious way Di Mon was looking at her. D'Therd just looked puzzled and a bit embarrassed. Ev'rel noted Vretla Vrel's appreciative grin at the discomfort she was causing H'Us. *That's right, my very Vrellish cousin,* she thought. *I might wear a dress, but I'm not harmless.*

"I want," Ev'rel told H'Us, "a hearing to review the disposition of my late brother's Blue Demish assets. There is Delm's flagship, for example, the *Vanilla Rose.* I understand Di Mon very carelessly left it in Killing Reach while, at the same time, he took it upon himself to make bargains concerning my firstborn."

H'Us looked to Di Mon for help.

Not used to women asserting themselves, are you, my lord admiral? Ev'rel thought at the big H'Usian leader.

Di Mon spoke in a clipped tone. "I conceded possession of *Vanilla Rose* to Liege Barmi under *rel*-combat circumstances, where we were obliged to trust each other in order to cooperate against a common enemy who was, potentially, *okal'a'ni.*"

"But was it yours to give away?" Ev'rel declined to take direction. "Oh, I know," she waved away his next objection, "you conceded your own right to fight over it, then and there. But it didn't belong to you to start with. It was the property of the liege of Blue Dem, and as such should fall to his successor." She smiled at H'Us. "A flagship isn't such a large thing to ask, I hope, for sixteen years of exile I did not deserve."

"Perhaps not," Di Mon said tersely, "if it weren't that your claim rests on usurping a title that has larger implications."

H'Us looked flustered. "Certainly a hearing is in order concerning the *Vanilla Rose*. Perhaps when your son, Prince Amel, has been secured? Because Di Mon has a point, you know. Prince Amel is the most convincing claimant to the title of Liege Blue Dem, now that your brother, Delm, is..." H'Us cast a quick glance in Di Mon's direction.

"Dead," supplied Di Mon.

"Indeed," H'Us agreed and rushed to get past the awkward moment. "You would be the natural heir, Immortality," he told Ev'rel, "if not for Amel. Amel is the grandson of your father on both sides, since he is Delm's son as well as yours. And then there is the Golden Demish factor, as well, through Delm's mother, rather than, in your case..." He glanced in Vretla Vrel's direction and ran out of words.

"My very Vrellish mother?" Ev'rel said, making eye contact with Vretla.

"Er, yes," H'Us admitted, and struggled to be gracious in an irksome male-Demish way. "But I must say I am ever so pleased to see you looking so entirely feminine yourself, Immortality. You will grace the palace with your presence. May we show you to the royal apartments? I am sure you will want to rest after the trip here."

"No," Ev'rel said crisply, swishing the long skirt H'Us had alluded to in his remarks as she used her other hand to adjust her hair, "I am not going to be living in the royal apartments. I will set up residence in Blue Hearth."

She arched one thin eyebrow at Di Mon. "It *is* empty?" she inquired.

Di Mon was too angry to answer. He had advised her not to claim Blue Hearth, but to stay in guest rooms at the Palace Sector until the question of Amel was settled on the challenge floor. Then she could rename Blue Hearth something appropriate for her Knotted Strings vassals, solving the problem of finding a Fountain Court hearth for the Dem'Vrel without challenging his proxy management of White Hearth for the absent and possibly extinct house of Lor'Vrel. She could almost see him thinking his way through her motives for ignoring him, to arrive at the goal of unseating D'Ander's bastard daughter on Barmi II.

Exactly, Ev'rel thought, as she watched Di Mon glare at her. *I need a green world.*

Di Mon turned away to leave, no doubt angry about her riding roughshod over his deal with Ayrium because it tweaked his precious honor.

Politics, dear heart, she thought as she watched him depart. *You'll swear to me whatever I do, so long as I seem to agree with you about the Nesaks. And that gives me room to maneuver on other fronts.*

She worried briefly about her rivals taking alarm at her maneuvers and doing something drastic, like attempting to marry Amel to Ayrium to consolidate their claim to Barmi II. But Di Mon did not think D'Ander would permit that, and if Perry was rash enough to try it on her own, Ev'rel would have a Silver Demish force occupying Barmi within a month, which was fast by Demish standards. Perry was a liege killer after all. Only Vrellish support for Ayrium, as a gift child, and the support of a princess known as a Golden Soul, important to the *Okal Lumens* religion, had delayed a much-needed purge long enough for Ayrium to grow up. Things were changing. The Vrellish alliance was fractured and Luminaries everywhere were squabbling over whether to accept D'Ander's claims concerning Amel.

As Di Mon departed, Vretla Vrel made a decision and walked towards Ev'rel through ranks of Silver Demish men, who drew aside to make way for her.

Ev'rel stood her ground with trepidation. She and Vretla shared an ancestor in Ev'rel's Vrellish mother, who was Vretla's grandmother, but Vretla was unquestionably the more Vrellish of the two.

"When you are settled in Blue Hearth," Vretla said, tacitly accepting Ev'rel's claim to the title, "I would like a word with you in private."

Excitement thrilled through Ev'rel. "Certainly, cousin," she answered, using the Vrellish term for a near, but not intimate, relative. "In fact, I would be grateful if you saw fit to escort me to Blue Hearth yourself. We can talk there."

Vretla's grin told Ev'rel that she knew her sword had just been engaged in Ev'rel's defense should Blue Hearth try to deny them entry. "Immortality," she answered, "I would be honored."

D'Therd looked thoroughly displeased.

"I think we will find we have much in common," Ev'rel said to Vretla, as a clump of Vrellish nobleborns fell in around them as an escort.

H'Us watched with a rather stupid look on his face, which amused Ev'rel. She was less pleased to notice that D'Therd chose to stay with the Demish to see their rather laborious welcoming ceremony through to the end. He did so want to be respectable, did her boy, D'Therd, the son of the Knotted Strings clan leader who chewed *ignis* leaves and spat out the wads at the dinner table. Maybe she shouldn't have rubbed his nose in his father's uncouth behavior quite so often. *Ah well*, she decided, leaving D'Therd to his own ambitions, *perhaps it might prove useful if he manages to make friends as well, without, of course, getting above himself... or... rather, me.*

Ev'rel wound her way down off the landing deck and crossed the decorous, flowery world below at a brisk clip, surrounded by half-naked Vrellish. The males in Vretla's entourage amused themselves by making eyes at women who shrank back from their suggestive grins. The females frowned at their male companions, but only because they disapproved of Demish females in general. They were just as apt to tease the men they encountered, and with even lewder invitations. In fact, the more the Demish flinched and stared, the worse it made both sexes.

Ev'rel was beginning to wonder if she was sacrificing too much reputation on this ploy when Vretla took charge. "Behave!" she snapped at her people. And they did.

"They are only doing it because the Demish half expect it of us," Vretla said, by way of apology.

"Thank you for controlling them in any case," said Ev'rel. "One cannot antagonize the Demish too much, however much fun it is."

Vretla gave her an appreciative look of camaraderie. "You understand, I think. You are Vrellish — here." She clapped her hand over the generous genital mound between her legs just long enough to be clear what she meant. Female Vrellish genitalia were noticeably larger than other women's.

Ev'rel floundered despite herself. "Ah, well, not entirely. Not, perhaps, in the way you might think."

Vretla was walking along with her eyes front again, scanning sidewalks and gardens in a casual, predatory manner. "I don't hold the business with your *gorarelpul* against you," she told Ev'rel. "Arous was his name, yes?"

"Yes." Ev'rel cleared her throat, feeling uncomfortable to be in this territory, with this person. "He was bonded to me when I was just a girl."

Vretla nodded without looking at her, and continued in her matter-of-fact manner. "A girl, yes, but not just any girl. You were a Vrellish girl living with Demish restrictions. Do not mistake me, Ev'rel — I understand Di Mon's abhorrence for what Arous suffered, but Di Mon has cold blood for one of our kind. You had no one but Arous, and before Arous your father— neither good choices, but you had no better guidance, only impossible Demish demands for self-denial. You found your own way, under bad circumstances, and once you lost your father you had access to no male but Arous and Arous was impotent. It happens to some *gorarelpul* due to pain training procedures. Of course you used Rush." She gave Ev'rel a frank look. "And it was Delm who gave Arous the overdose to make you look bad. You used Rush, but only because Arous could not be your lover without it." She paused a couple of seconds. "Yes?"

"Yes," Ev'rel said, feeling hot. She had not meant to be having this conversation. She was used to relying on Demish reticence about unpleasant things, or Di Mon's meaningful silences. It was rather dreadful to discuss the whole business surrounding Arous openly and bluntly without any warning it was going to come up!

Vretla seemed satisfied. "That's what I thought," she said, "and listen, if you ever need a man..." She smirked. "I can find you more than one who would be honored, and smart enough to keep his mouth shut." She winked at her. "I know you can't afford the Demish knowing fright is not what makes you giddy at the thought of males."

Ev'rel was flushed by now, and feeling acutely uncomfortable. "I'll remember," she said, "but I am able to manage, thanks." She hoped none of the Demish people making way for them could hear what was being said.

"There's one more thing," said Vretla as they reached Demlara's Walk, the promenade connecting the Palace Sector to the Plaza. "Your son."

"D'Therd?" Ev'rel asked, startled.

Vretla shook her head. "Amel. He was my favorite den boy when he was a courtesan, and it's giving me trouble with Spiral Hall. They like to tease me about being taken with a Demish prince who writes poetry. That's my problem, of course, but I want you to know it wasn't like that. There was nothing of what the Demish would call romance between us." She stopped them by stepping in front of Ev'rel and squeezing her arm. It was a gentle squeeze, but Vretla's hand had such unconscious power in it that it made Ev'rel catch her breath and pay attention. Vretla delivered her next speech like a friend complimenting a proud mother, which was a sentiment — given the topic — that Ev'rel had no idea what to do with.

"The truth is," explained Liege Vrel, "your Amel could put some Vrellish highborn males I know to shame for sheer sexual stamina. He was smart, too — there with you all the way. Damn worth it. That's why he was my favorite, not for the poetry," she insisted. "I never knew he wrote it or had Demish blood of any sort before all this *sla* muck came out of Rire about him!"

"Well," Ev'rel said, in strained tone, "I'm so glad we cleared that up."

Vretla let her go, but they stayed stopped where they were on Demlara's Walk. Blessedly, no one was anywhere close.

"The problem Di Mon caused me is much worse," said Vretla, looking grave now. "My own kind, back on Cold Rock — other highborn Red Vrellish, not the nobleborns here at court — don't trust me anymore, Immortality. Not since Di Mon sent me to *TouchGate Hospital*. They think I may have been changed by the Lorels there. And the worst is, I don't know if they are right or not. I don't know how to be sure."

"Vretla," Ev'rel said as gently as she could, oddly moved by this bold woman's sudden descent into helplessness, "I do not believe there are any Lorels left on *TouchGate Hospital*, just people who inherited their knowledge of medicine."

"So Di Mon says," agreed Vretla, "and I am grateful for my life. But I am still concerned there might be something they did to me without my knowledge. Something that might harm my people. I was not prepared to take the risk, but Di Mon overruled me when I could not stop him."

Ev'rel nodded. "Trust is a hard thing to fix once it is broken," she said.

Vretla grinned. "I like you, Immortality."

"I think," Ev'rel assured her, "the feeling is mutual. But please don't talk to me quite so openly about sex. I have no quarrel with the way the Vrellish live among themselves, but I am only part Vrellish. It isn't something I am used to."

Vretla shrugged a shoulder. "If you like," she said.

They walked on across the Plaza, with its open-air businesses lighted by glowing poles, and enlivened by colorful tents in which people gave fencing lessons, told stories, served drinks, watched skits, placed bets, traded money, or made plans for economic transactions for anything from marriage to flying goods around the empire.

A handful of Silver Demish errants were guarding Blue Pavilion.

Here we go, thought Ev'rel, trying not to hold her breath.

She couldn't help fixating on the swords. From Di Mon's failed attempts to teach her swordsmanship, she knew that it was easiest to kill using the point, although deaths occurred in other ways. A Gelack dueling sword was sharp for the final third of its length to accommodate engagements to first blood, the most common sort among the Demish. Demish gossip assumed the Vrellish always fought to kill, which was not necessarily true, but watching the faces of the Demish men guarding Blue Hearth as she approached with Vretla Vrel, Ev'rel decided it might be a useful superstition.

"I am Ev'rel, liege of Blue Dem," Ev'rel told the guards. "Let me pass."

The captain of the guard was Highlord according to the braid on his jacket, and therefore eligible under Sword Law to contest Ev'rel's claim as a fellow member of the highborn challenge class, which included Purebloods, Royalbloods and Highlords.

He eyed Vretla as if wishing someone would make it clear whether the Vrellish woman was Ev'rel's champion or merely walking with her. The Vrellish nobleborns with her did not count. They could not engage him unless he granted them the right to fight on Ev'rel's behalf.

"Of course, Immortality," the captain of the guard decided at last, "just as soon as word comes from Prince H'Us telling us to yield Blue Hearth to you."

Vretla cleared her sword with a casual gesture and stepped clear. "Let her in," she said, "or let me see what color you bleed. I've heard it's supposed to be silver."

There was a stir among the errants on duty and silent appeals to each other for guidance. Ev'rel guessed that none of them had come on duty today expecting to be called on to make critical, and possibly fatal, decisions without greater guidance from their superiors.

Naturally, this being Gelion, the standoff was also attracting an audience. Witnessing duels under *Okal Rel*, it was also a popular subject of conversation for days, and sometimes years, afterwards. The longer the captain hesitated, the more embarrassing his situation grew.

"I suppose you could wait inside, Immortality," the captain floundered, turning red as he backed down from drawing against Vretla.

As Ev'rel passed, she heard one of the Silver Demish nobleborns remark, "He could have taken her, she's just a woman."

"She's the liege of Vrel!" another man hissed back. "You don't get to be Liege Vrel from being good at embroidery, whether you're a man or a woman!"

Vretla let the chatter roll off her.

Ev'rel went ahead down the spiral stairs inside Blue Pavilion to Blue Hearth's reception room, where she stopped, ambushed by unexpected feelings of nostalgia.

This was the room where she had enjoyed her birthday parties, spoiled and flattered by her Papa. It was the hearth where she had learned to hate and fear her half-brother, Delm, who had engineered their father's death by sending stupid, prudish, Demish princes to come upon the two of them in bed. They had blamed Papa of course, not her. She had been young. And female.

Vretla brought her back to the present.

"Can you prove to me that I am still myself?" Vretla spoke up boldly from behind her. "Prove I have not been turned into a weapon subject to a will not my own or given a disease I will spread to my people if I go home to Cold Rock to confirm my title."

"Why?" Ev'rel asked, and immediately raised her hand. "I see, of course, why you would want to know. But why should I do this for you?"

"I have heard you have a medic trained on *TouchGate Hospital* who understands Lorel sciences," said Vretla, "a medic who is not a *gorarelpul* but a free woman, one who serves you. If you trust her, and she tells you I am not compromised, I can live and act as a free woman once more. For her service, I would offer my oath to you... although it will have to be my oath alone, and not the support of my Red Reach kin, until I can convince them to swear to me once more."

Vretla stood with her feet apart, asking to be justified in feeling she was truly herself, but neither the big empty room nor her own doubts had managed to dwarf her. She was prepared to make whatever bargain was necessary to be whole again.

"Fair enough," Ev'rel agreed. "It will be adequate, for the Demish, that you occupy Red Hearth, whether or not you are acknowledged on Cold Rock as Liege Vrel. But you must swear to me first. The medic is already on her way to court, but she is a commoner and will not be able to get here before the Swearing is over. Will you trust me?"

"I will, Cousin," said Vretla. She clapped Ev'rel on the shoulder. "Think about my other offer as well."

"Offer?" Ev'rel asked, mildly puzzled.

"Men," said Vretla. "It isn't good or safe for a Vrellish woman to do without for too long." Then she took to the stairs in quick bounds, before Ev'rel could remind her she had promised not to talk about sex again.

Courtesan Memories

Amel caught sight of himself in a mirror as Maverick led him down the stairs and marveled at the creature he saw reflected there. He watched himself blink with a slow, gliding motion as if the act consumed his last strength, and thought, *Liar*. The pallor of his skin against the darkness of his lashes, a general emotional exhaust, and the oddly luminous way his eyes reflected light all connived at the impression of glimmering beauty on the brink of collapse while, in truth, health stubbornly persisted beneath the surface.

His nose had healed perfectly. So had D'Ander's throat.

D'Ander had left soon after the incident to tend to his court on Demora. Amel missed the man, if not his lessons on how to be a Soul of Light and future Ava. He worried about his Reetion friend Ann, as well. Perry had told him about the Sevolite forces gathering to invade Rire, and he couldn't help believing Ann would be on the front lines. He wanted to do something to help. Instead, the face in the mirror mocked him with its helpless beauty masking useless strength.

"There is someone here from court to see you," Maverick said, at his side. She spoke in hushed tones, as if talking to a high-strung child.

Amel turned his head from the mirror to blink at her. "I thought it was hard getting here from court," he said perfectly lucidly, "because of all the ships gathering."

"Yeah," Maverick replied with a rueful smile, "what more can a reach do to discourage visitors? Guess there's just no stopping some pilots."

"Who is it?" Amel asked.

"Vretla Vrel," Maverick said.

Amel nodded and stepped clear of Maverick to walk unassisted down the stairs.

"I know a few Nersallians," Vretla was telling Perry, in the deep, female voice that resonated for Amel with profoundly physical memories of good, aggressive sex. "They helped. I am here to satisfy myself you've got Von, then I'll go back to tell Ev'rel."

"He's not Von," said Perry, "he is Pureblood Prince Amel."

Amel missed his footing on a stair. Maverick caught him by the elbow and helped him the rest of the way down.

"What have you done to him?" Vretla demanded. "He looks like someone left on ward duty for ten hours straight."

"He's been having trouble sleeping," Perry explained.

Vretla looked sleek and robust, standing on a Blue Demish story carpet at the base of Perry's stairs and wearing bright red flight leathers. She wore her sword with courage, given the PA's reputation for disrespecting Sword Law. Perhaps she trusted the vengeful power of Fountain Court if something were to happen to her.

Vretla crossed to the base of the stairs, took Amel's chin in one large, strong hand and turned his head from side to side.

"Huh," she said, "did D'Ander wear him out with all his Demish nonsense about Souls of Light?"

"No," Perry answered with an air of forced civility. "It was the Reetions. The medical device they used on him makes him keep reliving things better forgotten."

"Hard flying will cure bad memories," said Vretla.

"For you," said Perry, getting caustic, "not a Demish Pureblood."

"Be easier to tell with his clothes off," said Vretla, tipping her head as she felt Amel's upper arm.

"Not on the menu," said Perry.

Vretla answered with a snort. She rubbed Amel's face with her thumb above his eyebrow, as if to check that he was not someone else wearing make up. Then she said, "Applesauce"... and watched him blush.

"It's him," she concluded with a grunt. "Only courtesan I ever knew who did things he couldn't talk about afterwards." She turned on her heels and strode out the way she had come, heading for the runway behind the palace.

"Applesauce?" Maverick asked.

Amel willed his cheeks to cool down. "Culinary experiment," he said evasively, "at Den Eva's."

Maverick held his eyes a moment before saying, "Liege Vrel's into cooking, huh? Who'd have thought."

"And I suppose it will be my fault if she gets herself killed getting home," Perry grumbled. "I offered her travel respite. She refused — but who will believe me if it comes to a trial of honor?"

"I wouldn't worry about it, Cap," Maverick remarked. "Anything that Vrellish *rel*-skims like fish swim. Besides, I'm betting the Nersallians will let her rest up on one of their battlewheels, seeing as she's got a friend or two in the Dragon House." Maverick grinned. "Or a couple of *sha'stan* more likely, seeing as they're all Vrellish."

"I hope so," said Perry. "Getting blamed for dishonorable conduct towards the liege of Vrel is the last thing we need right now, and the best way to bring the Red Vrellish swarming out of their bolt holes to help Ev'rel go after us."

Maverick cocked an eyebrow at Amel. "Applesauce?" she remarked again, in a suggestive way, as she slowly rubbed the side of her nose. "So tell me, Cap, because I'm ignorant about these Golden Demish matters — are culinary experiments an acceptable part of the Soul of Light repertoire? I mean, with Vretla Vrel no less!" She wolf-whistled. "Our Golden boy's got to be some chef."

"He's no more Golden than he's Blue," Perry snapped back, "and I expect he's had enough backhanded comments from the entire staff to last a lifetime, so please lay off."

"He's no more Golden than he's Vrellish might be more to the point, Cap," Maverick begged to differ, unperturbed, and stuck her hands in her belt. "Thirty-four percent each, Golden and Vrellish. Another twenty-six percent Blue Demish means our side comes up a bit short, and the last little bit is Lorel. Quite the mongrel, our Pureblood, when you look at it like that."

The percentages made kaleidoscope pictures in Amel's imagination, trying to be poems, then people, and finally shattering into shards of colored glass — twenty-six, thirty-four, thirty-four, six.

Who am I? he asked himself. *Von the courtesan or Amel the Pureblood?* An answer slapped back at him out of his childhood.

Shatenous, his harsh foster father, stood behind his desk agreeing to make him the slave of a *slaka'st* — a man so afraid of anyone finding out he was boy-*sla*, that he wanted his *slaka* conscience bonded to him like a *gorarelpul*.

"Why?" cried the terrified child who was — and was not — Amel. "Why do you hate me? What have I done?"

"It is not what you've done," Shatenous told him bitterly, "but what you are."

The betrayed child had felt only confused grief and terror. The current Amel understood at last, because Shatenous had despised all Sevolites and must have known, even then, who Amel really was. But he had no time to appreciate his overlapping perceptions of the situation because he was being dragged away. He came to himself in the act of striking out, inexpertly, just as he had then. Maverick cursed. Perry seized him from the other side, but he had already gone still, staring in dismay at Maverick who stood hissing in pain with one hand clamped over one eye.

"Go get your eye seen to, or it will swell," Perry told her.

"Right, Cap," said Maverick, taking down the hand. Her eye was shut but didn't look too bad. She spat blood and wiped her mouth on the sleeve of her jacket. "But watch yourself. Believe me, he only looks like he's made of glass!"

Perry led him upstairs and nudged him gently through the door of his room. She came after him and closed the door.

"Into bed," she ordered.

Amel looked at the offending piece of furniture with loathing. They had ruined the big four-poster bed in his room to make it suitable for strapping him down every night, and whenever his fits took him during waking hours. Holes were punched straight through the mattress. Thick leather straps rose through them, secured to heavy weights below.

He tried to stay calm as Perry helped him loosen his clothes and get settled on his back, but as soon as she reached for the nearest strap he caught her wrist. Their eyes locked. He wasn't sure what his eyes said, but he saw pity reflected back at him from hers.

"Stay with me?" he preempted the speech he had already heard about why this was necessary. "Just lie beside me and the clear dreams won't start, I'm sure. I don't want to be tied up — and I don't want to be alone. Please, Perry?"

Her stern expression wavered. "All right," she decided all at once and slapped him on the flank. "Move over."

Desperate for the comfort of contact, he threw an arm about her and closed his eyes. He liked her earthy female smell with its lingering trace of grease and leather, as if she could never get her work out from under her fingernails. He had noticed how she liked to putter with farm equipment whether or not it was necessary for her to do it personally. He suspected it relieved stress. She also flew more than Maverick said she should, and the smell of flight leathers seemed to have seeped into her skin and hair. But that was how Perry was supposed to smell.

She shifted to get comfortable, muttering to herself about being a mad fool. He snuggled up against her. They remained that way for long moments, both afraid of something going wrong. Then, slowly, they began to relax together. He promised himself he could not possibly clear dream with Perry beside him. As soon as he started believing it, sleep pounced.

The next thing he was aware of was drifting in a fantasy, half dream and half memory, in which he was making love to someone friendly, like Eva, his den mother. His hand shifted along his lover's side and took an interest in the contours it discovered. He indulged himself lazily, tracing his nose along the inner ridges of her ear. She was fully dressed, which seemed odd. His hand explored a small, firm breast that did not match Eva's figure and, undeterred, began to drift gently downward.

"Amel!" Perry said sharply.

The command startled him awake and pitched him straight into a clear dream. He was bound to the floor in a back room of the Bear Pit, the *sla*-den that supplied children to clients with unhealthy appetites. A Vrellish woman leaned over him, watching his face as her knife cut a wound ever so carefully in his side.

He jerked, shocked to find no resistance. Double signals about his body's size, deployment, and condition confused him. He got a noseful of Perry smell and, like a blow, his dual perception was gone.

Perry was sitting on top of him. In his confusion, she had managed to get the upper hand, although she looked spooked by the sudden change in his behavior.

It dawned on him that he must have been taking liberties earlier, and he wondered if he ought to apologize. On the other hand, he knew the Eva dream hadn't been about Eva's body for a little while, and he knew how to diagnose the flush on Perry's face and throat.

Wanting to prove something to himself, he flipped them over so that he was the one looking down at her. Either it was no contest or she let him — he suspected it was a bit of both. She looked confused about what was happening between them.

He, on the other hand, was quite sure. He wanted the kind of sensory feast that would keep him anchored in the moment and safe from the terrors of his childhood.

He leaned down into a kiss she did not refuse, his conscience doing battle only weakly with her being a Demish woman, while any objections D'Ander might have voiced on his own behalf lacked traction in his current state of mind. He had seldom wanted a woman more, and he needed to be close to someone he dared to trust. It was a decision his body made, at odds with his emotional desire to do better than he had, to date, with the task of uniting sex with romantic love. But despite the intensity of his desire, it would have taken no more than a push or a "no" to have dragged him out of the intoxicating mire of sensation he was intent on plunging them both into. Instead, Perry slowly began kissing back, which was more than enough to encourage him to lose himself, blissfully, in the work he loved.

Half an hour later, minus stress and clothes, he drifted off in Perry's arms to the feel of her stroking his hair near his temple.

"You poor, messed-up kid," he heard her mutter, "if D'Ander kills me for this it will be no more than I deserve." Too drowsy to find words to reassure her, he simply snuggled closer, not quite sure he believed it when she gave a throaty chuckle and whispered to him, "But that was art."

4

Serviceable Lies

Forsworn

"So," said Ses Nersal, lounging in bed as she watched Di Mon finish dressing, "are you going to swear to her? To Ev'rel?"

"Your liege leaves me no choice," Di Mon answered, busy lacing his vest closed in the correct patterns for his rank and house. He paused to admire his handiwork in the mirror, judging it as good as any valet's efforts. He was once again fit to attend Ev'rel's Swearing, despite the stopover to check in with his court *mekan'st*, Ses Nersal, who was sworn to Hangst Nersal of Black Hearth.

Di Mon had hoped for a message from Hangst, or a last-minute appearance. But Ses had confirmed that Black Hearth would send nothing but the tacit message that Hangst Nersal had lost faith in the Ava's court regardless of whether Delm or his sister, Ev'rel, ruled over it as figurehead.

Ses heaved herself out of bed and hunted about for her own clothes, unself-conscious about her middle-aged, nobleborn body with its impressive collection of dueling scars. She drew her pants on slowly with a grunt for the sake of an old wound and came to join Di Mon. She did not take liberties, despite the passionate turn his visit had taken, rather unexpectedly on his side, just half an hour earlier. Instead, she maintained a respectful distance and spoke in *pol*-to-*rel* address without explicit differencing, which was friendly without being presumptuous.

"I am sorry there's a rift between you and Liege Nersal," she told Di Mon.

He nodded. "He is your liege. I do not expect you to tell me any more than Hangst wants you to convey."

"I never know more than he wants me to convey," Ses assured him, and then added with a bit of a growl, "I could wish he made less of those Nesaks of his, myself, I don't mind telling you. But it's going the other way. Young Branst Nersal tells me that his eldest brother, Zrenyl, is as good as a Nesak by now, and even Horth, the youngest hearth-child, has accepted a commission in the joint fleet."

"Horth as well?" Di Mon said, feeling all the tension he had managed to relieve, with Ses, creeping back into his bones again. "Isn't Horth sworn to Liege Bryllit, not his father?"

Ses was nodding. "And you are thinking, as many of us are, that Bryllit may be Black Hearth's last chance for a break with the Nesaks, if she sees fit to challenge. If so, you are right to take Horth joining his sire as a bad sign, because he wouldn't have done it if Bryllit wasn't willing to follow Hangst." She scowled. "There are those among the *kinf'stan* who don't like what's happening. But Hangst is an Old Sword. He's killed too many younger challengers who thought they were better than him. A lot of them are expecting Bryllit to decide. She's been his *mekan'st* and his heir at different times, and no one doubts her honor, even though she is half Nesak herself on her father's side. Bad business there, but no one blames the child, and it was two wars ago. If Hangst is really planning something *okal'a'ni* against the Reetions, Bryllit will challenge him."

"*Okal'a'ni*," Di Mon muttered wearily. Environmental stability was the only thing sacred to *Okal Rel*, not the lives of Reetion commoners. Even if the Nesaks planned attacking habitats in space, he doubted if religious scruples would be enough to stop the avarice fueling Nersallian outrage over Amel's mistreatment by the Reetions, especially now that forces were amassing to invade. The whole stupid, repetitive predictability of greedy wars made Di Mon's teeth grind. Ameron had wanted to do something more than repeat history forever. He had struggled to find ways that mankind could move on, inspired by books of history, literature and social science written at least a thousand years ago on Earth. But even Ameron had been stymied at every turn by class and racial conflicts, the determination of minorities to amass power, mindless superstitions about biosciences, and the equally foolhardy arrogance of those who believed in nothing but their own desire to triumph through superior technology, which Di Mon feared he sometimes glimpsed in Ev'rel.

More importantly, even Ameron had failed.

Why did I ever believe I could do better? Di Mon thought bitterly. *I, the last highborn of a weakening house possessed of no special weapon beyond an uncommon knowledge of history. How arrogant, to imagine myself as Ameron's heir and executor in the quest for a better world. A world a bit more like Ranar's Rire.*

The thought of Ranar made Di Mon hopeful and miserable at the same time, because if Rire was a better world, it was a world in which he could not live. He would resist to the death, in particular, the ubiquitous surveillance all Reetions inflicted on each other. Honor was a better way to keep the world safe from atrocities.

The honor my own pupil Ev'rel despises, he reminded himself. *And even Hangst, the man who taught me honor, seems prepared to set it aside to gain power.*

He had stopped to see Ses on his way to Ev'rel's Swearing, hoping to hear last-minute news of a miracle, and had wound up in bed with Ses instead, which might have pleased him if he hadn't been thinking so much about Hangst at the time. How could he be angry with Hangst for being seduced by his Nesak wife's ideas, when he was unable to master his need to think about men when he lay with women? Now he was going to be late for Ev'rel's Swearing and he hardly cared.

Ses Nersal touched Di Mon's arm, making him start.

"Are you well?" she asked.

"What?" he shook his head as if to dispel the ghosts of demanding ancestors. *The least Ameron could do is keep the rest of the Watching Dead at bay,* he thought, and frowned at himself for thinking in religious metaphors when he did not believe in the spiritual side of *Okal Rel,* apart from its utility in restraining those less wise and self-disciplined than himself.

"I'm fine," he told Ses, "and I should already be at the Swearing, to attend the preliminary receptions."

"Putting it off as long as possible are you?" she guessed, folding her arms. "So tell me, did she really use Rush on her *gorarelpul,* Arous? Is Ev'rel a man-raper?"

Di Mon drew breath to repeat the obfuscating babble that was current in Demish circles, excusing Ev'rel of anything to do with *sla* sexual practices.

She's paid for her mistakes, Di Mon told himself. *I must defend her.*

His hesitation betrayed him.

"I'll take your silence for an answer," Ses said. "It's enough to make a decent woman hope Prince D'Ander wins the duel for young Amel — if only it wasn't you who will be going up against him!"

Di Mon listened without grasping what she meant. Comprehension collapsed about him with a stinging shock, leaving him too angry to be coherent. "Don't be absurd!" he chastised her.

"You are probably right," Ses decided, frowning, "she's too smart to be that stupid, politically."

Di Mon's throat went dry. "Gods, woman!" he barked angrily. "How can you think such a thing?"

"How can anyone help thinking about sex, first, when Amel's name is mentioned? It's all people talk about: his past, rumors leaked about him from his ex-clients, and those Reetion pictures. If you ask me, he's the last dish anybody should be serving a woman with a bad habit. You know what they say: 'first a *slaka*, next a *slaka'st.*'"

The old maxim set Di Mon's teeth on edge. He should have recognized the signs of a caged and powerful sexuality budding in a half-Vrellish girl being raised as a spoiled Demish princess, but he'd been afraid of her attraction to him coupled with her razor wit and willful nature. He could never have hidden what he was from her. She had turned, instead, to her besotted father — an old fool obsessed by her half-Vrellish nature.

I failed her, Di Mon refused to spare himself.

"Forgive me," Ses misinterpreted his glum mood, "I know such sordid things offend you."

He shook his head. "No, you do well to warn me to be wary." But with a dismal flash of insight he thought, *My life has been defined by sordid things.* First Darren, the lover who had taught him he was different; then Ev'rel's father, who simultaneously spoiled and abused her; now, Ev'rel, twisted by her uneven upbringing, and Ranar, who could destroy him utterly.

He took his leave of Ses without further comment.

"The Citadel," he told the driver who had been waiting for him outside Ses's garage complex on the Palace Plain.

Six of his nobleborn vassals were milling about the base of the Citadel when he arrived. They aligned themselves like iron filings on a magnet as soon as he stepped out of his car.

"Everything all right?" asked the liege of one of Monitum's oldest demesnes, which had been highborn-led until the last Nesak war.

"Yes, fine, Liege Eversol," Di Mon assured her. He gave no explanation for his lateness, just led them up the long flight of stairs ahead. They did not pause to rest at the top of the first flight but went straight on to the highborn promenade, where foot traffic gained access to the docks through eight gates controlled by the houses of Fountain Court. Di Mon remembered clashing with Vretla Vrel's clan mother here, over the business of sending Vretla for treatment on *TouchGate Hospital Station*. He entertained the idea of Ev'rel inviting Vretla to be her First Sworn as a punishment for his lateness and, for one lovely moment, he didn't care. Then he nearly panicked. Neither he, nor Monitum, could afford to lose Ev'rel's favor on the very day that she was sworn in as Ava!

Ameron's Wound! he thought. *I have time slipped and I am not even* rel-*skimming!*

He broke into a run, his right hand at his side to control his sword. His entourage matched pace; the guards of honor filling the mouth of the Palace Shell passed them through without a word. So did the Demish errants holding back the people on the Plaza, who lined the route from the highborn docks to the Palace Sector where the Swearing would take place. The commanding officers looked relieved to see him.

Di Mon kept jogging down Demlara's Walk, ignoring the Demish attendants who bowed as he swept past. He had missed all the preliminaries. All he could hope to make now was the Swearing ceremony itself.

Striding in late, parting guests, and silencing conversations, Di Mon felt as if he'd stepped onto a stage. The decor of the Greek Room where Ev'rel had decided to hold the event looked ludicrously fake with its pseudo-Ionic pillars; artificial olive trees; servants dressed in togas offering expensive slices of raw fruit flown in on high gap to prevent bruising; sea-scented breezes generated by a hidden fan; and a nerve-cloth wall projecting a stretch of Mediterranean waterfront mocked up to suggest a vaguely Athenian setting, all based on knowledge previously reconstructed by Earthly historians two thousand years after the fall of the Greek empire.

Ev'rel was flanked on the right side by Prince H'Us and a group of Demish princesses wearing long, tasseled gowns. Vretla Vrel stood on her left, attended by a dozen Spiral Hall nobleborns dressed in bright red leather with wide swatches of skin exposed. Ev'rel herself had opted for a style that acknowledged her mixed heritage. Her dress was simply cut and worn beneath a Vrellish-style vest displaying her house braid. Her hair was long, like that of Demish women, but worn loose in the way the Vrellish favored. Although her house braid was accurate enough to please a court herald, her dress and vest were dyed the rich sapphire of Blue Hearth, reminding every attendee that she meant to reclaim Barmi II from its usurpers.

Demish guests held their breaths to see how Ev'rel would respond to Di Mon's entrance. Vretla gave a low growl. Di Mon imagined Ev'rel inclining her elegant head just a fraction in Vretla's direction and saying, with all the sweetness of a Demish princess asking how much sugar one took in one's tea, "Liege Monitum is late. Do please go and kill him for me?" He really wasn't sure if he could take Vretla, and the sense of being in touch with his mortality caused him an uncanny moment of dissociation in which he regretted nothing but his loneliness. He missed Ranar.

Ev'rel brought him crashing back down to reality by putting out her hands and coming forward.

"My First Sworn is here," she declared, clasping his hands with a warm smile. "We can begin."

He could not have asked for a stronger endorsement of his value to her, and he thanked her as graciously as he knew how, after he had bowed over her hand and then embraced her in a more informal, Vrellish manner. But the feeling that dominated the rest of the affair, for him, was jealousy of Hangst Nersal, who was not obliged to swear to an Ava that he profoundly doubted and increasingly feared.

Honor and Contraband

"And then?" Mira asked, lying ensconced on a couch in Blue Hearth's family lounge. She had missed Ev'rel's Swearing six days earlier.

"Then they all swore to me," Ev'rel continued, "first Di Mon, then H'Us, and then Vretla, making me Ava Ev'rel!"

"For now," Mira cautioned, "until D'Ander makes his play using Amel."

"Yes, yes, that wretched duel Di Mon promised Ayrium," Ev'rel said. She pulled her shawl about her shoulders. Beneath it she wore a long dress of dark blue with no decoration about her except for the flowers embroidered on her light beige shawl. "Let me enjoy my Swearing for a few days before fretting me about duels. You should have seen Di Mon! Oh, he drew his sword as required, and handed it to me, hilt first, declaring himself my First Sworn. He just didn't mean a word of it, damn his simple-minded Vrellish honor! Oh, yes," she insisted, as if Mira was about to object, "it's all about honor. He killed Delm because honor demanded it! No matter how much he tries to make it sound rational and calculating, *his honor* was the real reason." She whacked a cushion off the end of Mira's couch, making it plop to the floor, and frowned at it where it lay. "And he pretends to be a statesman!"

"Does rationality have to preclude honor?" Mira asked.

"Yes!" Ev'rel rounded on her. "Or are you going to insist there is something rational about running one's enemies through with a sword, when there are so many better ways to kill people?"

"Or avoid killing altogether," said Mira.

"Don't be a child!" Ev'rel scoffed and gave her shawl a tug. "So long as there is something one man wants that another man has, people will kill each other any way they can."

"Making the only improvements possible through science more efficient methods of slaughter?" Mira challenged her with equal cynicism.

"Are you about to make a case for *Okal Rel*, Mira?" Ev'rel mocked her.

"You know what I think about the way that *Okal Rel* throttles development," said Mira. "But abuses of bioscience by people who argued much as you do are the very reason that the medical sciences are feared now. I find myself uncomfortable with the idea that such superstitious dread should be overcome in the service of exactly the sort of reasoning that made *science* synonymous with *atrocity*. If it can form the basis of trust, then maybe honor has its uses."

"Trust?" Ev'rel said, with a sneer. "Sword Law is nothing but a game played by men like my own dear D'Therd, who wants nothing more than to be admired as a great swordsman and a man of honor. And I suppose it is true that among men like Di Mon and Prince H'Us, that is exactly what would make D'Therd powerful. But it is no use to me or you or any other woman who is not so Vrellish that she might as well be male for most intents and purposes. The only power a woman can trust is her own, not anything contingent on a man's good graces! You know that. Or has making the trip here from FarHome softened more than your bones?"

"My bones are fine," Mira said, sounding nettled. "My wits, too, and the rest of me will be fine again in a week or so."

"Are you tired?" Ev'rel asked, her irritation wiped out by a sudden concern. "Am I pushing you too hard, too soon after a hard trip?"

"I am tired," Mira answered with a thin smile, "but I am lying on a couch with a cup of tea beside me and a throw over my legs to keep me warm, which is not terribly stressful." She hesitated. "I have missed your company, in fact. So, tell me what you think the problem is between you and Di Mon. Does he lack confidence in you as Ava?"

Ev'rel smoothed her dress as she thought about an answer. She knew she looked good in the blue dress. Mira, of course, was indifferent to female rivalry as far as Ev'rel had been able to deduce. It was one of the things that fascinated her about her commoner confidante. Mira was no competition as a woman. She did not seem to care about anything except her work, and Ev'rel.

"I think," Ev'rel said, "it's the old trouble."

"Arous?" asked Mira.

Ev'rel flicked a hand at her. "An old mistake."

"There have been a few times—"

"Nothing serious," Ev'rel rejected the suggestion. "Besides, I did not kill Arous! Even Di Mon knows that, now."

"You did not kill him," Mira said quietly, "but Di Mon knows what you did do."

Ev'rel pulled off her shawl, folded it, and put it down on the couch. She felt inclined to be annoyed with Mira for harping on the business about Arous. Papa would have understood. At times like this she knew why people liked to believe in the Watching Dead, because it would have been nice to imagine the late Ava Relm watching her from a supernatural dimension and cheering her on.

Di Mon, of course, had spoiled such comforts for her. She had absorbed his cynicism about all things supernatural. It was necessary to pretend belief, of course, but that was not hard. She pretended about everything all the time, except with Mira. With Mira, she indulged in the sanity-saving luxury of saying what she really thought, even though that meant accepting insolence from an inferior. There was no harm in that so long as Mira depended on her. Utterly.

"You are missing the point about Di Mon," Ev'rel insisted. "He has no right to make heavy weather about honor when it was he who taught me to apply my mind, and not my heart, to problem solving. But never mind all that, now!" Ev'rel beamed a wide, eager smile at her companion. "I have a present for you!"

Presents from Ev'rel were usually things Mira needed for her work. "What is it?" the medically trained commoner asked, irrepressibly curious.

"I must show you," Ev'rel said, helping Mira up with a hand under her elbow to hurry her.

Ev'rel led Mira to a big room at one end of Family Hall and urged the medic to press her palm over a nervecloth panel in the wall. This revealed a lock Ev'rel opened with a physical key she handed to Mira afterwards.

"I have a duplicate," Ev'rel told her friend, "but no one else has access, not even Di Mon. He installed the nervecloth, which is why I insisted on the second lock, as well. I couldn't help suspecting any nervecloth locks of Monatese manufacture might have back doors known to the Monatese, and I want you to feel safe doing anything you want in there."

Mira stepped into the room and began to look around while Ev'rel held back, holding her breath, as she waited for her friend to react to the splendid thing she had done for her.

The room had once been the Blue Hearth library. Now it was a complete medical lab, containing a one-bed ward screened off in a corner; a portable toilet unit in the tiny, but functional, bathroom; a workbench with internally regulated plumbing; a set of the best Luverthanian diagnostic machines Monitum could legally import under the terms of its treaty with *TouchGate Hospital*; a freezer and an autoclave; a well-stocked drug cabinet; and a very sophisticated examination and operating table at its center, with adjustable fittings overhead and instrument trays that folded away against its side when they were not needed. There was even a nervecloth console in one corner connected to a medical database, and a set of books bound in green leather, bearing Monatese crests.

"What do you think?" Ev'rel asked eagerly.

Mira walked the length of the workbench, eyes devouring everything in sight. When she turned back to look at Ev'rel her eyes were bright with pleasure. "This is for me?" she asked incredulously.

Ev'rel was delighted by her friend's amazement. "I will expect you to continue teaching me about medicine when I can spare the time," she told her excitedly. "But apart from that, yes. It is yours."

Mira looked back at the miracle surrounding her. "It must be the best equipped infirmary in all UnderGelion," she marveled.

"I told Di Mon it had better be," said Ev'rel, "but knowing him, he will have a better one tucked away on the highborn docks. I do believe, though, it is the best he could muster on short notice."

Mira roamed the room in silence, opening drawers and checking the equipment.

Ev'rel watched with a growing sense of suspense. It had been foolish, really, to demand this lab of Di Mon. He had warned her, as he always did, about the hazards of appearing too Lorel. But she wanted Mira to be happy, and the feeling that the room bordered on transgression against *Okal Rel* gave her a secret thrill that nourished her through all the pretenses she had to maintain for people like Prince H'Us and Vretla Vrel.

"You really like it?" Ev'rel asked, needing more praise.

The commoner medic addressed her as a friend, speaking English. "Ev'rel, it's amazing! I know it represents some risk for you politically, and I swear I will do nothing to abuse the trust you are placing in me."

"Good!" Ev'rel said happily. "It would hardly do me any good to be caught red-handed in my own hearth, helping you turn Vrellish highborns into programmable zombies or making killer viruses."

Mira was looking through the medicine cabinet. She turned around holding a vial of brown oil and a case of needles. "*Klinoman*," she guessed, "and..."

"*Sish-han*," Ev'rel said quickly, "a general sedative and a general stimulant, two of Luverthan's most common exports, used by Sevolites everywhere."

"You know I don't like to use either," Mira pointed out.

"The addictive complications of both drugs offend you, as well as the inexplicable impurities and lack of specificity in targeting what's treated," Ev'rel recited Mira's objections to avoid a lecture. "But the fact is they are both ubiquitous across the empire. Any well-stocked medic ought to have some."

Mira put the vial back but retained the smooth black case of needles. "This looks familiar," she said, in a guarded tone.

"It is only *sish-han*, not Rush!" Ev'rel insisted. She took the case out of Mira's hands. "But if you are so contemptuous of my presents, I will take it back and keep it elsewhere."

"No," Mira said, "you were right. It belongs here." She took the case of needles and placed them on their shelf beside the vial of brown, resinous fluid.

Ev'rel ran a hand along the surface of the examination table, focusing on the superior features of its design in an attempt to quell the anger Mira had stirred up in her. The top of the table was padded but the padding, while firmly affixed, could be removed to turn it into an operating table. The way everything folded away tidily and locked in place when extended made Ev'rel suspect the design was Nersallian. That would be interesting, given Di Mon's falling out with Black Hearth. Or had Di Mon lied to her about that? Would he side with Hangst Nersal against her as soon as he could?

"Ev'rel," Mira began hesitantly, retrieving Ev'rel's thoughts. "Are you sure I should be here?"

Ev'rel was taken aback by so ungrateful a remark. "A moment ago you seemed happy enough I'd done all this for you."

Mira dropped her eyes. "It's not that. It's just being here, at all, on Fountain Court. Three years ago I came here to work as a Silver Star medic, newly qualified and proud of being personal physician to the princess-liege of H'Us. Then I ran into my brother, the boy I grew up with at the *Gorarelpul* College, and I threw it all away like an idiot because I was too innocent to imagine he might have changed in the three years we'd been out of contact." She pursed her lips. "If your agent hadn't recruited me for work on FarHome, I would probably have died in the UnderDocks."

"That is behind you," Ev'rel reassured her.

"Yes," Mira said in a dead tone, and stirred herself, "certainly I won't go looking for my brother again now that I'm back. He's made his choice. Yet, I wonder if I wouldn't be better off tucked away back on FarHome."

Ev'rel answered instantly, "No."

"I didn't grow up the way most commoners do here on Gelion," Mira continued to express her doubts. "My father had contempt for Sevolites. He lived to prove the Lorel heresy about their origins. My little brother and I spent a lot of our time pretending to be Sevolites who would change the world for the better, and rummaging through old archives predating current orthodoxy. It didn't prepare me for knowing my place as a commoner. I have already learned the hard way, once, how dangerous that can be on Fountain Court."

Ev'rel put her hands on Mira's narrow shoulders and looked into the thin face of her brilliant young friend. She had to look down, being taller, but she spoke to her in English to avoid Gelack pronouns. "You are here," she reminded her, "under my protection. And I am Ava."

"The last two Avas were murdered," Mira said in her surgical manner.

Ev'rel did not appreciate the reminder. She withdrew her hands with a scowl. "You have never talked much about the incident with your brother. Tell me about it."

Mira looked away.

"It isn't idle curiosity," said Ev'rel. "I need to know if it is going to prove a liability with the Demish, since you were working for princess H'Us at the time. I won't let them lay a hand on you," Ev'rel dismissed the ghost of fear she saw cross her friend's face. "I simply need to know details. Your brother's name was Miff, wasn't it?"

Mira cleared her throat with difficulty. "Yes, Miff. It was short for his *gorarelpul* name, Imifilious. He used to worship me."

Ev'rel nodded. "Yes, yes. But you did something to try to help him — denounced a Sevolite you believed to be abusing him. Wasn't that it?"

"Does it really matter?" Mira asked, a little sharply, and mended her tone if not her underlying resistance to the topic. "It's princess H'Us I offended, and she's dead now. The story won't have gone far. She was disgusted by my accusations and would not have spread them." She broke off unexpectedly, more tension in her face than Ev'rel was accustomed to seeing there. "I don't want to talk about my brother, Ev'rel."

"The liege of Monitum, Ava," announced the herald. He'd been one of Delm's people who had come with Blue Hearth like the furniture.

Ev'rel rose, feeling suddenly flustered.

Di Mon wore his sword, of course, but apart from that was dressed in oddly casual attire: just a plain shirt and stretch slacks.

"This is the medic you told me about?" he asked, with a quick glance in Mira's direction.

"A Silver Star medic," said Ev'rel, "the best on Fountain Court, since you have lost your *gorarelpul*, Sarilous. Feel free to make use of her services."

Di Mon looked at Mira again, but made no comment.

"She was just telling me," Ev'rel said, with a wry smile in Mira's direction, "how much she appreciates the trouble you went to in outfitting this lab to my specifications."

"I am glad it meets with her approval," Di Mon answered with acid precision in measuring pronouns that pegged Mira as five ranks his inferior. "See to it she does nothing to make me regret the indulgence."

"Indulgence, Liege Monitum?" Ev'rel asked, arching manicured eyebrows. "Is that what people call it these days, at court, when a vassal honors the request of his liege and Ava?"

"Save your word games for the Demish," Di Mon told her, in peerage, which implied a tacit putdown, since she outranked him by two birth ranks. His next words both mended his pronouns and made Ev'rel forget the insult. "The Nersallians are gathering at court to endorse Hangst Nersal's decision to join the Nesak crusade against Rire. Hangst may be challenged, but it isn't likely any challenger will win. I must assume the worst. So I am going to Killing Reach to face it there. We need to talk." He looked at Mira pointedly. "Alone."

Mira got off the stool she was perched on and left the room in silence.

Ev'rel plucked a test tube from a rack, turned it in her fingers, and put it back into its slot again. "You cannot go to Killing Reach, Di Mon, it's absurd. You just need to have something to be grim about, I think. Fortunately, I find it endearing."

"I wish you found it persuasive instead," he said.

"Because, of course, you advise me in my own self-interest?" she asked archly.

"I am your First Sworn."

"Yes," she said, "and you were also sworn to my late brother Delm when you ran him through with a sword."

He frowned. "I wish you no harm, Ev'rel."

"You wish me no more power than necessary, either," she challenged.

Muscles clenched and relaxed in Di Mon's jaw. "The Blue Demish are nothing but a few thousand families of nobleborns scattered across the empire," he lectured her. "There is little to be gained by presuming to lead them."

"Really?" Ev'rel disagreed. "How about Barmi II? Wasn't it you who taught me it was hard to overemphasize the importance of green planets? Like Demora. Like Monitum." She leaned towards him. "I don't have one."

"You have FarHome."

She made a face at him. "Hardly a green world," she quibbled, "little better than Gelion — a brown world, perhaps." She smiled at her witticism.

He held her stare for long seconds, making her pulse quicken to imagine she might have succeeded in making him angry. But he overcame his temper and relaxed.

"Since Barmi II is in Killing Reach, and Killing Reach is full of ships poised to invade the Reetions, it is a moot point at the moment to whom it rightfully belongs," he pointed out.

"You and your precious Reetions," she muttered back.

Di Mon frowned. "They are not *my* Reetions."

"Then why so adamantly opposed to invading them?"

"Because the rest of us will be next," said Di Mon, "and I don't plan to live through another Nesak War."

"Nesaks, Nesaks, Nesaks!" Ev'rel dismissed her ex-mentor's favorite hobbyhorse. "Don't you think it's time you worried less about the empire and more about your own house? You need a highborn heir. You can't run off to stand alone against your old friend Hangst when you haven't taken care of that!"

Di Mon stiffened.

"Your personal infertility must be a source of great frustration to your people," Ev'rel goaded him. "Maybe an infusion of new blood via one of your sister's children? Ack! But I forgot, you tried that and it didn't work out. Vretla explained it to me. She also explained how unhappy she is with you for sending her to *TouchGate Hospital* against her wishes."

"If I had not sent her to *TouchGate Hospital*," Di Mon said stoically, "Vretla would have died."

"Apparently death is preferable to risking one's soul in the hands of Lorel doctors," said Ev'rel.

Di Mon remained impassive. "If you have a point, make it."

She leaned forward, aware of him as an attractive male and irritated by his lack of vulnerability to her as a woman. Everyone said he exerted more self-discipline than was healthy for someone of a Vrellish disposition. There had to be a way past it.

"The point is, my dear Di Mon," she said, their faces so close her breath touched his lips as she formed the words, "you need an ally."

She drew back. "Why not me? After all, you are my First Sworn. Isn't that supposed to mean something to an honorable man?"

He remained stiff for a moment, then he pulled a stool over and sat down, adjusting his sword to keep it out of his way.

"Trust and respect must flow both ways, Ev'rel," he said. "Why confound my arrangement with Ayrium, over Amel, by declaring yourself liege of Blue Dem?"

"I have the best claim after Amel," she snapped back at him, "and he is only sixteen, so he should be living here, with me."

He fixed her with a frank stare. "Do you still have a mother's feelings for him?"

She surprised herself with honesty. "How can I, when I haven't seen him in sixteen years? Frankly, it is hard to equate a young man whom Liege Vrel assures me is quite sexually mature with the infant I fawned over when I was myself a mere girl."

Di Mon pursed his lips. "All the same, I wonder if it is wise for you to view the data extracted from Amel by the Reetions. None of it is pretty. It is like seeing and hearing a series of Amel's worst experiences from his own perspective. I haven't watched more than a few minutes of it myself and am glad the Silver Demish have declared it contraband. You said you wanted a copy from me in order to deduce how hard a time D'Ander will have of it making Amel acceptable to

Demora. I can give you my opinion, instead: Amel is going to have a long, hard struggle living down material in which he is portrayed, repeatedly, as a *slaka*."

Ev'rel boiled inside at his refusal. How dare he presume to act as censor?

"Let me try again," she said, when he had finished lecturing her. "You hold three hearths on Fountain Court, but only nominally. Brown Hearth and White Hearth are vacant. Your real source of power is your *de facto* leadership of the Vrellish houses, but Vretla isn't talking to you and Hangst Nersal of Black Hearth is about to invade Rire, a point of policy I know you differ with him over. Eight hearths, and you command only one, in reality. Work with me, Di Mon, and be on the right side when the ships dock and the swords are sheathed."

She knew she was getting to him. Logic and strategy were the tools he had given her. For a moment, she was certain he wavered. Then Di Mon drew a deep, shuddering breath and mastered his emotions again. "Have you no real idea what's going on in Killing Reach, right now?" he asked her dully. "Or do you simply not care?"

Ev'rel folded her arms. "Nesaks again, is it? Very well, will the victory be as quick as Hangst Nersal and his Nesak allies expect? Given what you know about Reetions, that is."

"No," Di Mon said coldly, then added, "but before it is over, the invaded reaches may be damaged beyond repair. At the very least all hope for reasonable relations with Rire will be shattered." He continued grimly, "The invaders will triumph in the end. Nersallians and Nesaks are both hybrids. They learn quickly. The Nersallians, in particular, are Sevildom's best engineers. But what they learn about war from the Reetions won't be healthy for the rest of us, Ev'rel."

"What better reason for the Demish to secure a buffer zone in Killing Reach between us and whatever mess arises in the conquered Reetion territories?" Ev'rel said. "I can do that, for them, by upholding my claim as liege of Blue Dem. Or do you seriously mean to convince me Perry D'Aur's Purple Alliance could stem the tide of undesired change by itself?"

"D'Ander—" Di Mon began to protest.

"Is a problem, yes," Ev'rel agreed. "Everything will have to wait until the question of Amel is settled, naturally. Presuming it is. The way things are going we may not be able to get him off Barmi II until the war with Rire is over, which, now that I think of it, must be a violation of your agreement with Ayrium! Perhaps I should convince Prince H'Us to fetch him back by force immediately!"

Di Mon reacted as if she'd knocked the breath from his chest. "You mean that?" he asked her bleakly. "You would provoke more havoc with rel-ships than is already brewing in Killing Reach, just to snatch Barmi II for yourself?"

"It is an uncertain universe," said Ev'rel. "I must entertain all possibilities." She smiled at him. "My teacher would expect no less of me."

"True," Di Mon admitted with a defeated air, and no matter how much she wished to bring him to heel, the unexpected twist in her stomach at the idea that she may have succeeded was hard to bear. It was all the more galling because she did not wish to feel anything. He did not put her first. He had exiled her. Why should she care? And yet she seemed to need him to remain strong, if only to endure her attacks on him.

"I am going to do what I can for the Reetions," he told her. "That is what I came to tell you."

"How?" she demanded. "You have no highborn fleet, just nobleborn flyers. Surely you don't intend to try holding off the combined forces of the Nesak and Nersallians fleets single-handed? With a sword, maybe?"

"I don't know what I intend," he said, "I just know I have to be out there, whatever happens. Beyond that — ack rel. But yes, if I challenge him, Hangst would indeed pause to fight with me."

A tingle of alarm swept over Ev'rel. "Di Mon!" she exclaimed. "You can't. I order you not to. You aren't thinking clearly."

His steady gray stare laid hold of her just as it had when she was a child, forcing her to share something vital with him as a fellow being.

"Be better than you need to be," he told her. "It pays off in the end."

Then he left her.

"Di Mon!" she cried, and took a halting step after him before her captain of errants dashed into the lab looking excited.

"I've got it!" he told her, and held out a slim silver box. "It cost enough. H'Us has been raiding the UnderDocks to confiscate them!"

Ev'rel refocused on Captain Kandral, a nobleborn who had demonstrated ruthless loyalty to her during her war of unification in the Knotted Strings. He was a rough-looking man, weathered by too much *rel*-skimming exposure and glad to serve her now in other ways.

"What?" Ev'rel croaked, her stomach still churning at the thought she might never see Di Mon again.

"The smut on Amel," Kandral told her with a wide grin. He stroked his hand over the little Reetion device called an info blit. Holographic images appeared above it in miniature.

Kandral put the info blit down on the padded examination table as Ev'rel was drawn to join him, intrigued by the prospect of getting to know her long lost son in this unique fashion.

Di Mon will be all right, Ev'rel told herself. She really knew so little of what ships did in space during shake-ups — a quaint and harmless-sounding term for combat between *rel*-skimming vessels. Many of the terms pilots used for *rel*-skimming experiences seemed ordinary, like referring to *rel*-skimming conditions as *weather*. She couldn't picture how Di Mon, with all his years of flight experience, could get himself into any real trouble. As to challenging Hangst Nersal, surely his concern for the future of Monitum would prevail.

"Gods!" Kandral exclaimed, as the images stolen from Amel's memory resolved themselves into a scene. "What's this? It's not sex or violence. It's nothing but the inside of a station somewhere!"

"*TouchGate Hospital*," said Ev'rel, recognizing it from pictures she'd seen in the Green Hearth library as a girl. "The reception area."

"Hey!" said Kandral, pointing, "The girl there looks like—"

Ev'rel felt a fist clench in her chest. "Mira."

Kandral had clearly been expecting pornography and was disappointed. But he rallied. "Should I get her, Immortality?"

"No," Ev'rel said, watching the sensory avatar of Amel's remembered self looking long, and searchingly, into Mira's face. She could not give up this secret — not until she knew what it was worth to her. "Turn up the volume," she said instead.

5

Swords!

On the Sidelines

Amel was jealous of Vrenn. He thought of the tough ex-Nersallian as Perry's husband. They called themselves *mekan'stan*, of course, but he suspected Perry would have married him if he hadn't been too Vrellish for it. He was also afraid of Vrenn, which didn't make for a good combination of emotions whenever the grim highborn set down on the runway behind the palace and stalked back into Perry's life, looking lean and space-gnawed without any sign of being weaker for it. Vrenn was the sort of Sevolite the commoner in Amel shied from.

Those mixed emotions were the main reason Amel hovered outside Perry's parlor off the lower lobby of the palace, listening to Perry and Ayrium talk to Vrenn. He did it to prove he wasn't jealous, and was not afraid, either. But he didn't go in, and he wasn't sorry to have Maverick beside him as he hovered just outside the door.

It was not a secret conference. The door of the parlor was ajar. He knew Perry wouldn't mind him listening or Maverick would have taken him away. But he couldn't quite get up the courage to go in, either.

"All right, all right!" Perry's voice rose above the hard rumble of Vrenn's.

Maverick touched Amel's arm. "Shall we wait somewhere else till they're done, Your Sweetness?" she asked, using the pet name she'd come up with for him.

He overcame a peevish impulse to jerk away from her. "No. Please," he said instead, "I want to hear."

Ayrium had taken over the argument from Vrenn. "There is no immediate threat to us, anyway, Mom," she said. "Dad has Barmi II covered by the Golden Fleet."

"Don't give me that," grumbled Perry. "If Vrenn wasn't worried about all those Nesaks and Nersallians getting ready to tromp through the jump to get to Rire, he wouldn't be standing there in a flight suit. And neither would you, Ayrium."

Amel moved closer to the door to catch Vrenn's deep-voiced answer. "Someone has to stay here, on the ground, for stability."

"Don't patronize me," Perry countered sharply.

"Mom—" cautioned Ayrium.

"If I must be blunt," said Vrenn, suddenly applying suffixes to pronouns, "*I* do not want *you* to fly because you will be no use to us in space. You're just a Midlord."

Amel heard Perry inhale before Ayrium interrupted the incipient row with forced enthusiasm. "Right, then! Let's go!"

Something leaped in Amel's chest and drove him through the door. "Wait!" he cried, holding out a palm.

At his elbow, Maverick gave Perry an apologetic shrug. Vrenn was looking at Amel as if he was something one scraped off a boot before entering the palace. Ayrium's beautiful face glowed with excitement, but it wasn't on his behalf. She spared him a quizzical look.

"If highborns are needed in space—" Amel blurted, determined to be useful, "let me come!"

Vrenn gave a snort of disdain that made Amel's face flush.

Perry hid her expression behind half-curled fingers.

"Amel, you're not a *rel*-fighter," Ayrium said kindly, "even if you are a highborn."

Amel swallowed, eying the hard ex-Nersallian beside her. He had no doubt Vrenn could take him apart before he got a chance to find out whether being Pureblood mattered. *Would Vrenn be my superior in space, as well*, he wondered? It was true he had never flown combat.

"But I'm a highborn," Amel insisted. "What good am I if I can't help when there's trouble?"

Vrenn cast Perry a sidelong look as a grin stole across his face. "You can help all right, Courtesan," he told Amel. "Make sure this damn woman stays on the ground where she's the most use, even if you have to stay on top of her the whole time to do it!"

"Time to go!" Ayrium cried, a bit shrilly, stepping in front of Amel to prevent him catching more than a glimpse of the exchange of looks between Vrenn and Perry. Amel heard Vrenn laugh at something Perry said. Ayrium distracted Amel with a hug. As soon as she released him, Ayrium followed Vrenn out the door.

Perry let out the breath she had been storing up for some retort. "Don't let him bother you," she told Amel, speaking in the casual *pol*-to-*rel* address they had settled on using in the bedroom.

Amel identified the thing in his chest as stirrings of something like manly pride, freshly crushed. His eyes stung and he blinked to stop himself from tearing up. "No," he said, "he's right. I'm not a proper Sevolite. I can't protect you."

Perry put an arm around him. Thwarted bravado tried to take offense, but he enjoyed the contact too much. "What's happening in space, Perry?" he asked.

"A lot of looming, mostly," she quipped back, giving him a sideways hug. "The Nersallians are waiting for Liege Nersal to arrive from court. Then they'll zip past us down the jump to Reetion territory — presuming they've got someone to teach them the jump."

"You're worried about Ayrium, aren't you?" Amel asked sympathetically. *And Vrenn, too*, he thought, trying to be charitable.

"I worry a lot," Perry said, and kissed him lightly. "Come on, we'll get the news by radio when it comes, so we may as well set up for a vigil."

§ § §

Ev'rel woke to find Mira leaning over her. "The staff sent me in to wake you up," she said, and smiled. "Seems you intimidate them."

Ev'rel sat up. She'd fallen asleep watching the info blit. Her mind was still filled with disturbing images from Amel's childhood memories. Seeing Mira, a shiver of guilt went through her.

I ought to tell her my Amel is her Miff, she admitted to herself. *Her foster brother, who didn't betray her, exactly. He was conscience bonded. Backing her up would have killed him.*

"Come on, get up," said Mira. "The *kinf'stan* will be gathering on Black Wedge within the hour. Everyone expects you to be there."

"I don't want to go," complained Ev'rel. It would be a sweaty, bloody business with swords if Hangst Nersal was challenged, and a boring bit of ceremony if he was not.

"Suit yourself," said Mira, straightening.

Ev'rel scowled. She knew she needed to make a good impression on House Nersal. She just had no inkling how, or if Hangst Nersal would even notice if she did not make an appearance. Besides, watching Amel's visitor probe record had helped her keep her mind off Nersallians, Nesaks, and Di Mon's gloomy pronouncements about them.

"Is Di Mon back?" Ev'rel asked.

"No," said Mira. "There is no word about him at all." She left the room then, and was immediately replaced by servants.

Ev'rel put up with them hurrying her through her toilet and into some suitably stately clothes.

D'Therd was waiting for her by the spiral stairs with a hand of errants led by Kandral.

"There you are!" he greeted Ev'rel with impatience.

"Afraid you might miss a duel?" Ev'rel remarked, smoothing her bright blue gown before she looked up. "You could have gone ahead alone."

"Don't be absurd," he snapped. "You are the Ava."

"Yes," she said, surprised by the quiver of anxiety in her gut, "I am."

It is nothing, she told herself, *just the prospect of a duel. I hate duels.*

"Do you anticipate Hangst will be opposed?" she asked D'Therd conversationally as they started down the spiral stairs together.

"I hope so," he said, the hilt of his sword clasped in one large hand. "I would like to see Hangst Nersal defend his title."

"You must be careful not to blink, then," teased Ev'rel. "He makes short work of challengers, as I remember."

§ § §

Perry and Amel began their vigil in her parlor, but it wasn't long before the room had filled up with too many bodies for comfort, forcing Perry to move the radio reception equipment to the more spacious entrance lobby of the palace.

There was a holiday feeling about the whole affair, with people passing around snacks and warm drinks. But Amel could tell Perry was worried. He took up a post behind her and began to work with his strong, clever fingers at the knots of tension in her shoulders. Perry put her head back. "Don't stop," she told him.

Maverick edged over, grinning, "Not, at least, until it's my turn!"

It wasn't until he was working on his fifth customer, with a line forming in front of him, that it dawned on Amel that Pureblood Demish princes didn't normally give massages to their social inferiors. He was acting like a courtesan again! He glanced at Perry to check for disapproval, but she was much too introspective to be paying much attention to him.

Oh well, he thought, and got back to work on the person waiting in a chair for his attentions.

§ § §

"She isn't going to challenge!" D'Therd hissed in disappointment.

Ev'rel was relieved. Liege Bryllit, everyone's best bet for challenger, had just finished declaring she was going to let her liege decide whether the Nesaks were worse or better than the Reetions.

"Pity," Ev'rel said, dripping sarcasm.

She'd been impressed by Liege Nersal's speech to his followers. There was enough of the politician about him to work with, once he and his Nesak allies were done with Di Mon's precious Reetions. He wanted this alliance, and was prepared to waive *Okal Rel's* prohibition against destroying inhabited space stations in order to get what he desired. That felt promising.

Then, just when it seemed certain no one among the gathered *kinf'stan* would challenge where Bryllit had declined, one of Hangst's own entourage stepped forward.

"Yes!" D'Therd hissed excitedly beside her.

Ev'rel did not recognize the challenger, but suspected he was balking over the business of station-killing, which meant he must be an idealist: dangerous and unpredictable.

He won't win, of course, she thought, *not against Hangst Nersal.*

§ § §

Ayrium's voice on the radio electrified the room. Everyone shut up, put down what they were doing, or swallowed whatever was in their mouths.

Perry locked both hands on the neck of the massive old microphone set up on the floor amongst the array of speakers broadcasting Ayrium.

"Good to hear you!" Perry greeted her daughter heartily.

Ayrium's voice arrived after the short delay caused by the limitations of light-speed transmissions. "The strangest thing has happened on the *Quicksilver*," she said.

"Strange?" Perry was taken aback. "Can you explain?"

Ayrium was in the solar system but beyond the orbit of Barmi II. Amel could tell without thinking about it, but only once he'd picked up on the length of the round trip delay between exchanges. Ayrium compensated by giving a full report all at once instead of waiting to be asked questions.

"Di Mon is on the *Quicksilver*. He caught a Nesak priest stealing the jump from some Reetions. Zrenyl Nersal, Liege Nersal's oldest son by his Nesak treaty-wife, showed up with Di Mon's niece, Tessitatt, in his custody. Di Mon challenged him to a duel for custody of both hostages."

Excited gasps went around the room.

"Come on, Ayrium," Perry muttered under her breath, "this is no time to be demonstrating your storytelling talents by keeping us in suspense."

But Ayrium had only been pausing to catch her breath.

"Di Mon won the duel," she continued. "He recovered his niece and executed the Nesak jump-stealer. But I heard he was wounded."

"Wounded?" Perry gave Amel a tense look. "How badly?" she asked Ayrium.

Moments later, Ayrium's voiced replied, "My informant was not sure. But if it was trivial, I doubt it would have been reported at all."

Maverick said what half the room was thinking. "If Di Mon cannot speak for himself at court, it will fall to his liege to do it. And that means Ava Ev'rel."

"I've told you all I know so far, Mom," continued Ayrium, out of synch with the conversation, "so I'd better go back up Vrenn. Hangst Nersal has not arrived from court, yet, and I can't imagine he is going to be too happy when he finds out Di Mon has killed his son, Zrenyl. Bye for now, then."

Perry looked as if she wanted to say something quite different, like "no, come back, you've done enough," but she simply acknowledged Ayrium's sign-off.

Immediately, the room began to buzz.

Important things are happening, Amel thought, *things that threaten Perry and Ayrium and all my new friends. And all I can do right is massages.*

§ § §

The duel was over so fast Ev'rel's sense of reality had a hard time keeping up. D'Therd was riveted, of course. He really didn't seem to blink as he watched.

The challenger was a lean man in Nersallian black who looked like half the other *kinf'stan* present. But he quickly proved to be something quite different.

It was over in a single lunge. Ev'rel couldn't follow it precisely enough to know why the challenger had won, but she heard D'Therd suck in his breath beside her, which was testimony enough to the challenger's genius.

"I am going to fight that man one day," D'Therd said, as Hangst Nersal staggered and began to fall, "and then I will be the best sword in all of Sevildom."

Ev'rel was angry. Once again everything had changed — in an instant! — over the slightest wiggle of a man's wrist at the end of a fatal length of metal!

This is no way to run an empire! she brooded, darkly.

"Who is he?" D'Therd asked excitedly.

"I do not know," said Ev'rel's captain of errants, and left at once to find out.

I suppose I had better go congratulate the new liege of Nersal and commander of the empire's best disciplined fleet — all won by virtue of swords on a challenge floor! Ev'rel thought, overtly calm but inwardly furious.

Before she had even decided how to tackle the unsavory task, however, the mysterious winner was pelting up the stairs into Black Hearth, followed by Liege Bryllit and a few other *kinf'stan*.

"Horth," Kandral reported, on his return, "the late Hangst Nersal's third son by the Nesak Princess, Beryl."

"Wait a minute," said D'Therd, "isn't Horth the one who hardly speaks?"

"Gods ignore us!" Ev'rel despaired, pressing three fingers to her forehead.

Long Jump

Di Mon revived from a dead faint to discover he was moving swiftly beneath panels of glow plastic. He had not expected an afterlife, and this one failed to match any he could remember reading about in the extensive historical archives of Sanctuary. Therefore, he concluded, he was not dead. Then he remembered the rest of it.

He had fought a duel, taken a wound in the liver, and been treated with a Reetion nanotech plaster that had held him together long enough to preside over greeting the new Liege Nersal. Miracle of miracles, the new liege had called off the pending invasion.

Sometimes the universe goes out of its way to surprise cynics, Di Mon thought, with a smug, giddy feeling.

Then he remembered. *Hangst is dead.* A sick feeling of personal loss filled him. He stared up at the panels overhead, bearing the grief of it silently.

Then he heard the voice of the Reetion medic jabbering away nearby and remembered he wanted nothing more to do with Reetion medicine. Di Mon launched himself off the automated Reetion stretcher, eliciting a yelp from the brown-skinned woman attending him.

He landed pretty well for a dying man. Then he buckled to his knees, with an arm to his chest as if he needed to hold the pain in.

"I told you we shouldn't have rehydrated him!" a Reetion voice said, shrill with frayed nerves.

Di Mon half smiled. Ranar's people weren't used to physical violence. It was oddly endearing.

Ranar knelt in front of him. "Let us help you," the Reetion begged him.

"I have to get... into my ship," Di Mon ground out between his teeth, in English.

Ranar looked like a man who'd had the air knocked out of him. He was worried, Di Mon realized, but did not know what to do with the warm feeling it generated in him.

"You have to get back on the stretcher," Ranar insisted, gently but firmly.

I'm feverish, Di Mon thought. It was the nanotech plaster they'd used on him. His Sevolite immune system objected to the helpful invaders. Between his body's response and the severity of the wound, he could go *rel-osh* within the hour, and then he would be better able to make decisions and carry them out. But the cost of the uniquely Vrellish overdrive would be that he would use up his energy reserves until he dropped dead. The Reetions would not know how to treat a Vrellish highborn who had gone *rel-osh*.

"*TouchGate!*" Di Mon growled at his friend, willing Ranar to do the rest of the thinking for both of them.

Ranar's distressed look dissolved into a calm, stubborn expression. "All right," he said, "*TouchGate Hospital* it is, then. But we go together."

Di Mon shook his head and laughed out loud, thinking about how their situation paralleled Ameron's two hundred years before. Ameron had been wounded in Killing Reach and rushed to *TouchGate Hospital* for treatment by the contemporary liege of Monitum. Except she had been a Royalblood to Di Mon's Highlord. She had also been Ameron's *mekan'st*, not half of a cross-cultural pair of *slaka'stan*.

Di Mon laughed again, a bit hysterically.

Ranar shook him. "Pay attention!"

Di Mon knocked the Reetion's hands away, afraid the Reetions and Silver Demish watching them would guess what they were to each other.

"You *will* take me with you," Ranar demanded.

The look on the Reetion's face made Di Mon afraid to refuse for fear the Reetion would do something demonstrative.

"All right," he gasped, wanting them both out of sight and in a *rel*-ship, together, the sooner the better.

One of the Silver Demish stepped forward, displacing all the Reetions except Ranar. "Would you like me to ask the captain if we could loan you a pilot to take you to *TouchGate*, Liege Monitum?" he offered.

"No," Di Mon said, harshly. If he was going to die, it was better he took the Reetion with him. And if he and Ranar were going to share a cockpit, it was better there not be anyone else in it, just in case they experienced soul touch en route.

Fortunately, their Silver Demish hosts did not argue. They contented themselves, instead, with getting him and Ranar prepared for launch as efficiently as possible.

Di Mon drank all the fluid he was offered. He even let the Reetion medic repack his wound to stabilize it, after making sure Ranar told the woman she must not use nanomeds on him. He accepted, with trepidation, a Reetion drug meant to keep his fever down, but declined the pain killers.

The medic frowned. "You should be feeling more pain than you say you are," she warned, "which means either you are lying or the metabolic state Ranar warned us about, called *rel-osh,* is at fault."

"It will get us there," Di Mon said, feeling optimistic, which was also a bad sign, but he figured he might as well work with it. "The Lorels of *TouchGate Hospital* can do the rest."

He stumbled as they stepped into the airlock and shied from Ranar's touch when the Reetion tried to steady him. Ranar looked impatient over the rejection, but he held his peace.

They launched from the station and accelerated away from it, cat-clawing. It was minutes before Di Mon dared to think of anything else. Then he turned to look at Ranar's profile in the eerie lighting of the cabin, and asked, "If I die, would you be able to pilot for yourself?"

"No," Ranar said, bluntly but without fear.

Di Mon reminded himself it would be unwise for his *sla-*lover to survive him. But he heard himself saying, "If you end up stranded, set a beacon. There is a chance of being found."

"Right," said Ranar, although they both knew the odds of a rescue to be astronomical. Space was just too big. Of course the more likely scenario, should Di Mon die in the cockpit, would be for them to time slip, but Di Mon found the idea of becoming Lost together oddly comforting.

There were arguments against reality skimming on the ground that each successful trip meant someone else had to suffer time slip. It balanced the books of the space science principle of conservation with regard to cheating the time dilation effects. Theoretically, of course, even one ship boosted into an infinite future, to become Lost, would be able to absorb all finite time debts. In practice, Di Mon suspected time slip was never truly infinite. Monatese scholars believed there had to be some cosmic equation awaiting completion of a workable subset of inputs, within proximate bounds of time and space, before it solved itself and dished out penalties.

Di Mon had worried about such things in his teenage years, intrigued by the exponential function of the time slip curve. The fact that time slip varied exponentially as a function of its duration meant the longer you slipped for, the lower the chance you would return within living memory. Slipping forward by as much as a day was fairly common. Making it back a week ahead of yourself was exceptional, and missing pilots were written off as Lost after a year, although there were recorded cases of pilots who survived time slip of over a decade and legends about even longer slips. All probabilistic data plot had its outliers.

Di Mon glanced at Ranar in the seat beside him and tried to reassure himself that his Reetion friend was young and healthy, even if he wasn't a Sevolite. He knew Ranar had *rel*-skimmed before, as well, but that was less comforting because the shimmer-damage component of *rel*-skimming stress on a non-regenerative body was cumulative. But the choice had been made.

"Going to skim," Di Mon warned, before he did.

The transition coaxed a grunt from Ranar in the seat beside him as the Reetion shifted to get comfortable, but couldn't.

"Have I mentioned I hate reality skimming?" Ranar muttered between clenched teeth.

"Talk," Di Mon advised him. "Talk about anything. Tell me about Rire."

At first Ranar did, describing everything, from his travails getting Gelackology recognized as a valuable discipline before contact was re-established, to the details of expansion voting. But by the time they made it across Killing Reach to the first jump of their journey, he had fallen quiet.

Unwholesomely alert himself, Di Mon extended his right hand, keeping his eyes forward on the nervecloth display of stars ahead of him, and gave Ranar a firm nudge.

"Wha — oh," said Ranar, and straightened up in his flight harness.

"Jump ahead," Di Mon said. "Ready?"

Ranar failed to answer. A quick glance in his direction revealed him staring, waxen-faced, into oblivion.

"Nervecloth circuits," Di Mon said, gruffly.

Ranar turned to look at him. "What?"

"Nervecloth circuits," Di Mon repeated. "That is my jump mantra for this one... how I visualize it — my jump hallucination, as you Reetions put it."

"Isn't it bad luck to share a jump mantra with someone else?" Ranar asked, blinking owlishly in the light of the cockpit beside him.

Di Mon shrugged. He wanted to protect Ranar somehow, to share something intimate with him. He didn't know how else to attempt it.

"Do you think," Ranar said in a still voice, "this might be a good time to discuss which naming word, in Gelack, applies to us?"

Slaka'stan, Di Mon thought involuntarily.

"Apart from *slaka'stan*," Ranar said, as if he had heard.

Fine, Di Mon thought, annoyed, *let's play word games. Anything to keep you from lapsing into a coma on me.*

"Then I suppose you would be my *lyka*," Di Mon suggested, "since I am Sevolite and you are commoner."

"I am not," Ranar insisted, "anybody's *lyka*."

Di Mon laughed despite himself. "What then?" he asked. "Do you think we may be *cher'stan*?" He meant it as a ludicrous suggestion, since *cher'stan* were as far from *slaka'stan* as possible. They were the sacred soul-lovers of legend, fated to seek each other out in each life, and mutually exclusive to each other. Even the Demish liked the idea of *cher'stan*, and had adopted it, although Di Mon was fairly sure the term had originated with the Vrellish. The Vrellish themselves claimed it only sparingly, at the risk of being laughed out of Red Reach. It was the sort of thing young lovers sometimes proclaimed in a fit of enthusiasm, and then later regretted having made fools of themselves.

"Maybe we will find out," Ranar answered quite seriously, "if we soul touch."

They fell through the jump before Di Mon could be sure how he felt about Ranar's remark. But when they emerged on the other side all he remembered was the usual mantra of nervecloth patterns that he associated with this jump.

"Next time, perhaps," Ranar said wistfully, looking nauseous.

Nausea won't kill him, Di Mon thought. The key thing was to keep his mind engaged.

Ward ships gathered to escort them safely past properties in Golden Reach and this time they passed him through without a fuss, since he was heading away from Amel in Killing Reach, and not towards him.

"Why not *mekan'stan*?" Ranar spoke up again suddenly, after long minutes of silence.

Di Mon had forgotten the topic of conversation. "What?"

"Why can't you think of us as *mekan'stan*?" asked Ranar.

Di Mon frowned. "*Mekan'stan* are a man and a woman."

"Not necessarily," Ranar countered. "There isn't a male and female case involved, grammatically, just the *pol* and *rel* forms: *mekan* and *mekan'st*."

"The Vrellish do not use *mekan* much," said Di Mon, trying to change the subject, "not like *lyka* and *lyka'st*."

"Which also lack gender-specific cases," Ranar pointed out.

"It's understood," Di Mon insisted.

Ranar paused a moment, then said, "I do not like the term *slaka'stan*. It isn't right. I suppose we could use the English word for lover to skirt the issue. But Gelack is your native language. I suspect its entrenchment in your makeup will always make you mock my efforts to dismiss the problem as unimportant. You need a naming word for us, in Gelack, that you aren't ashamed of."

"That is ridiculous," said Di Mon.

Ranar responded with a long argument about grammar and noun cases, gendered and otherwise, in which Di Mon was happy to encourage him without paying much attention.

After the jump into the Reach of Gelion, which also failed to induce soul touch between them, Ranar took out a med kit he'd brought and injected himself with a stimulant, but he still looked drawn and sat limply in his flight harness.

Di Mon gave him a longer look than was wise, given how quickly the universe could become unpredictable at *rel*-skimming displacements.

"Don't think too hard," Di Mon warned, "feel instead. Feel anything. It's safer."

There was no response.

"Talk to me!" Di Mon ordered, getting anxious about his passenger.

"I am curious," Ranar said, "about soul touch. It does not always happen, correct?" He spoke like someone who had enjoyed one too many drinks on a den crawl.

"No," Di Mon acknowledged. "It is hit and miss, capricious."

Ranar bobbed his head in a nod. "There's one more jump between us and *TouchGate Hospital*, one more chance to experience it." He paused. "There is so much anecdotal evidence for soul touch in your culture, it could be a real psychological phenomenon, based on some sort of physical overlap of mental processes. The subjective aspects of jump physics are not well understood."

"The scholars of Sanctuary believe it is folklore," Di Mon said, and added, moments later, "but they don't fly much."

They continued in silence.

"So it does happen?" Ranar asked, long minutes later, showing signs now of losing his coordination as he flipped up a hand in a gesture. He frowned at his own increasing impairment, and put the hand back in his lap with a purposeful effort.

"What?" Di Mon asked, through the haze of his returning fever.

The jump to *TouchGate Hospital* was just ahead. On the
nervecloth display, it looked as if space had been peppered
with flecks of light — an effect of enhanced telemetry. A jump
was invisible to the naked eye. It was nothing but a thin patch
in the stuff of the universe.

"Soul touch," Ranar answered Di Mon's forgotten question
as they tipped into gap between reaches.

The soul touch that followed smashed Di Mon's usual jump
mantra. He was fleetingly aware of Ranar as something he
had to protect, but the next instant both of them were caught
up in a third perspective. Someone was dying — a woman.
With fierce glee, she latched onto Di Mon through their shared
identity as liege of Monitum, as if it gave her the right to
command him. At the same time, Di Mon was battered by
a roaring, hurting, hell-bent demand to reach the space
beyond, where things undone awaited the hand that would
complete them. The roar had no name; it was raw and pri-
meval. It stripped them all of anything but the drive to succeed despite death, despite reason, ravaging identity with
purpose, while the ghosts of the void gathered in the dark
corners of Di Mon's vain attempt to wrap images around what
he was experiencing.

Two ships burst into the reach containing *TouchGate Hospital*. Di Mon's shot past the first one and into the lead. The
other ship flickered on his nervecloth display and then followed them steadily.

Di Mon stared at the stars ahead like a man who had nearly
drowned rediscovering the glories of ground beneath his feet.
He was soaked in cold sweat. His wound sent shooting pains
into one shoulder. The clarity of *rel-osh* was gone; a metabolic crash was imminent.

"Ranar!" he shouted raggedly.

The Reetion did not respond.

Di Mon reached across and shook him. "Ranar!"

The Reetion coughed, moved his head, and came around. "Was that... soul touch?" Ranar asked, stunned.

Di Mon reacted with a wordless curse, afraid he was going to die before he knew exactly what had happened to them.

"I'll take that as a... maybe?" Ranar said, and coughed again, bringing up blood. He whispered hoarsely, "Oh damn."

"I don't know what it was," Di Mon admitted, "but look at me! Pay attention. I must show you how to signal the station via radio in case—"

"No!" Ranar demanded. "You must live."

Di Mon gave up on rational arguments against the absurdity of trying to obey such an order. He could already feel his strength crashing. Anger refreshed him briefly, but by the time they made dock with *TouchGate Station*, Ranar was the one in better shape. Di Mon barely made it out of his flight harness, gasping in pain and stumbling. He did not even attempt to get his sword. Ranar had to help him walk with an arm around his waist.

A man and a woman in flight leathers had made it to the sterile-looking reception area ahead of them. The woman was laid out on the floor with a blue-clad medic kneeling over her. A second medic stood ready with a stretcher for the man who must have carried her this far. He was dressed in white clothes spattered across the chest in dried blood. His right leg was crudely bandaged and oozing sluggishly from a deep wound in the thigh. His face was unwholesomely white from blood loss.

The wounded man in white looked maddeningly familiar, but Di Mon could barely keep him in focus. He had to hitch himself up against Ranar, and blink to clear the gray spots from his vision.

"I am sorry," the medic said in Gelack, up-speaking the bloody man in white without appending suffixes, which amounted to a guess.

The stranger spoke in an out-of-date dialect, using *rel*-peer-age. "She is dead," he said, "dead the moment we made the jump together, or dying in it — be that possible — dying and refusing, still, to fail me."

He broke off as he spotted Di Mon and Ranar. His eyes fixed on Di Mon's flight jacket.

"Monitum?!" the white-clad man exclaimed, his voice like a cracking whip. "*Thou* art Liege Monitum?"

Di Mon struggled with his failing body as the medics closed in. He glimpsed the Monatese heraldry on the dead woman's body and saw it matched his own. She had to be some kind of relative.

"How long?" cried the white-clad stranger. "How long?"

But Di Mon was spent. He felt Ranar's arms go around him with a sudden, desperate grab as he lost consciousness.

6

Bracing for Change

Promises

Ayrium watched from the second storey balcony as Amel danced in the lobby below. Palace staff had formed a circle around him, with more spectators leaning over the railing of the balcony to either side of Ayrium. Amel had inspired an impromptu orchestra to play for him, and was dancing with a novice partner he was making look good.

But then, Ayrium thought, smiling at him with affection, *I suspect a stuffed doll would look good in Amel's arms.*

"Hell of a security risk," Maverick grumbled beside her. "I don't even know who all is in the palace right now!"

Ayrium tried to worry, but she just couldn't believe anyone enjoying Amel's artistry could wish him harm. In the short time he'd been with them, Amel had transformed from an exotic invalid to a social superstar. If he wasn't dancing, he was listening to people's troubles, organizing play recitals, telling stories, or writing playful, satirical poetry that was already becoming part of Barmian folklore, including a ditty about Perry herself which was also, unfortunately, getting around.

Serves Mom right, thought Ayrium with a grin, as she remembered the rather catchy tune. The song was flattering to Perry, on the whole, although it gently poked fun at her

"I'm-just-the-janitor" attitude, when she was clearly the one in charge.

"It's impossible to keep people away from him," Ayrium sympathized with Maverick, making a point to scan the crowd, at least, rather than watching the performance below. "He attracts them like—" She laughed. "A Soul of Light, I suppose."

"Yeah, he's happy," said Maverick, more prosaically, and gave Ayrium a mournful look. "Your dad is back. He just called down from orbit."

Below them, Amel set his dance partner down before springing away into a series of elated twirls to the cheers of his small but appreciative audience.

"Soooo," said Maverick, "how have you and Cap been making out with the not-a-courtesan-anymore lessons for His Sweetness down there? Let's see," she proceeded to answer her own question, "what sort of stuff do courtesans get up to? Dancing, writing poetry, entertaining the folks, and then there's Perry's cure for clear dreaming...."

"Dad's not going to be very happy with us," Ayrium acknowledged with a sigh. "But we don't have to be forthcoming with that last item, all right? There's no reason D'Ander needs to know about the sleeping arrangements."

Maverick gave her a who-are-you-kidding look. The whole palace staff knew. The whole planet probably did, too, by now.

Ayrium sighed. "Right." She conceded to the skepticism in Maverick's expression. "Good point."

Below them, Amel continued to twirl and leap, inspiring oohs and ahhs.

"He's going to wipe out," Maverick predicted, just before he appeared to lose his balance and career into the arms of his waiting admirers. She leaned her head closer to Ayrium's. "Uncanny how it always seems to happen right in a spot where there are a handful of sturdy people plain delighted to catch him and make a fuss."

Ayrium tried, and failed, to raise a smile. "I'd better go tell him to get cleaned up to receive Dad," she said, and headed down the stairs.

§   §   §

Hours later, D'Ander stormed into Perry's small but well-appointed parlor, making Ayrium shoot up out of her chair, alarmed at the prospect of quarrel.

"These rumors I've heard!" he demanded of Perry, who remained seated with a civilized Demish tea set before her. "Are they true?"

"I am not trying to get pregnant," Perry defended herself in Vrellish terms, as she poured tea with Demish aplomb.

"It was my fault!" Amel cried, using the potent pronouns D'Ander had foisted on him often enough. "You can't be angry with her!"

For a moment, Ayrium was afraid a clash of wills was going to result, but D'Ander melted with a wide grin at the sight of Amel dressed up in Demoran garb.

"You look wonderful!" he exclaimed with pride.

"Because of Perry," Amel said, "and how everyone has made me feel welcome. But I'm not perfect, Prince D'Ander, especially not where women are concerned. It was my fault and you won't be angry with her!"

"It's all right, Amel," Perry said, coming over to put a hand on his arm. "Much as I appreciate the two of you squaring off like good Demish men to make all the decisions, allocate the blame, and so forth."

She turned to D'Ander with Amel at her back. "It's not important and it's done him good."

"Not important!" D'Ander erupted, taken aback.

"It might have been unwise," Perry admitted, "but it's worked wonders." She shrugged. "And, as I said, I am not trying to get pregnant."

"The rumor alone—!" D'Ander began.

"Yes!" she said sharply. "Not good for your efforts to rehabilitate him on Demora. I'm sorry. It just happened. That's all."

"Sorry!" D'Ander exclaimed, and gestured in exasperation as if he would rather be faced by six angry Vrellish highborns than a single ex-*mekan'st*. "Perry, one is sorry about taking someone else's glass of water at the dinner table, not about bedding a Soul of Light without permission!"

"She had my permission!" Amel exclaimed, his sleek voice pitched higher and rougher than usual. He seemed to have surprised himself, as well, because he caught his breath and swallowed. But he didn't give up. "Prince D'Ander, I know you are trying to do what is right for me and maybe for the empire, or maybe it is all about nothing more than what this or that group makes of who I am, but I know this: you will not shout at Perry for comforting me!"

Dressed in flowing Demoran robes that trembled with the strength of his emotion, his crystal clear eyes snapping with indignation on Perry's behalf, Amel was too much for D'Ander. The big Golden prince began to blink, tears rising in his eyes.

"Very well, Dear Amel," he said, softly, and smiled at him. "But would you leave us for a short while?" He raised a palm. "If I promise to treat Perry with the proper respect owed a woman, of course."

Ayrium glanced at her mother, expecting her to roll her eyes, but she was looking down, askance, more awkward over Amel's defense of her than she would have been going up one side of D'Ander and down the other.

"All right," Amel said, and drew a deep breath, making the soft cloth of his long, white Demoran robe quiver.

"Come on," said Ayrium, putting an arm around him to lead him out of the room.

No sooner had the door closed behind them than Perry lit into D'Ander, making him break his word and bellow back at her.

Amel balked and looked into Ayrium's face with alarm.

"Listen, you beautiful idiot," she told him, unable to resist the urge to ruffle his hair with her free hand. "I know Mom. She's a treasure. But you don't need to feel chivalrous about whatever happened between you and her in bed just because D'Ander is doing a bit of stomping and foaming at the mouth. Got that?" She gave him a nudge to get him moving again, her arm still around his shoulder, and his face still turned to hers as if he could drink purest wisdom there.

Ayrium made a fist and knuckled him in the ribs to elicit a laugh. "I think you like the idea of being the bad, lusty man here," she teased him, "instead of the seduced innocent."

Amel stilled the hand she was tickling him with. "Ayrium," he said gravely, "I am not innocent."

"Sorry," she said, capturing his hand in hers. "I don't mean to make light of what you've been through."

"It isn't just that! I've killed people!" he confessed to her. Then he burst into tears, which undid any impact he might have made with the fact.

Ayrium led him to his room under the shelter of her arm, and pulled him down to sit beside her on the bed.

"I killed Jarl," he said, sniffling, "with my bare hands!"

She stroked his hair. "No one regrets the loss."

"I killed a man on Gelion once, too, with a throwing knife. He was... he was..."

"Going to hurt someone you cared about?" Ayrium guessed.

"And me!" Amel flared up. He tugged gently away from her. "Ayrium," he confessed, "I'm afraid."

"Don't be," she smiled at him. "D'Ander won't let anything happen to you."

"I'm afraid for you, and Perry, and the Purple Alliance."

She smoothed his feathery black hair from his forehead. "We'll be fine."

"Promise me," he said, desperation written plainly on his lovely face, "promise that you won't risk yourself on my behalf. Because you're better than I am, Ayrium."

Ayrium's expression clouded. "Don't say things like that."

"Promise me," he insisted, in dead earnest.

She laughed. "What could happen to me? Oh, I know, I'm supposed to fight a duel with Di Mon, but I've no illusions of Dad actually letting me do it myself, if that's what you are worried about."

He pressed her hand. "Just promise to do nothing for me that could harm you, even if I ask! The Purple Alliance is worth more than everything I am!"

"Amel," she tried to soothe him, "nothing's going to happen to me because of you. Now let me go stop Mom and Dad from taking chunks out of each other, and you stop working yourself up into a panic. Got it?"

He nodded. "You won't forget?"

"I won't forget," she teased. "I'm Demish."

"Thank you, Ayrium!" he gushed, overflowing with a rich and complex gratitude.

"You!" Ayrium scoffed, and messed his hair again. "You're impossible."

§ § §

Back in the parlor, Ayrium found her parents taking tea together. D'Ander had taken off his sword and sat with a teacup in one hand.

"We leave for court tomorrow, Ayrium," he told her, and held the teacup out to Perry. "This needs more sugar."

"You shouldn't be drinking caffeinated tea at all," Perry scolded, "let alone tea with sugar."

"I'm not Vrellish!" he protested, amused.

"Caffeine affects the Demish, as well," she insisted, "just not as much."

"I've just been through tearful farewells at home and a long trip out," he said cheerfully. "I need the pick-me-up."

Perry closed her lips over further objections. She kept quiet just long enough for D'Ander to take a sip of tea and set the cup down.

"Do you have to do this?" Perry got to the point at last. "Di Mon is an Old Sword."

"Which does not frighten me as much as it does you," D'Ander said complacently, then beamed at her. "Besides, if I am clever, it may not be Green Hearth's Old Sword who stands against me at all. It might be Ev'rel's young fighting cock, D'Therd, a boy of fifteen who fancies himself a mean sword because he's the top of his class in the outback, on FarHome!" He plucked a savory treat off the tea tray and popped it in his mouth. "I will try not to kill the lad," he said, after he had swallowed, "just teach him to respect his elders."

Perry muttered, "I still don't like it."

"Would you prefer the Silver and Golden fleets fighting it out on top of you? Because that's the alternative," he said, getting worked up. "Maybe you *would*. Maybe that is why you did something as provocative as sleeping with Amel when you know—"

"Don't start again!" Perry protested.

"You did promise Amel to behave like a gentleman, Dad," Ayrium pointed out.

D'Ander bottled up his freshly stirred ire with a frown.

"Now," said Perry, looking at her daughter, "about you."

"Me?" she asked, taken aback.

"D'Ander needs you to go along as the original oath maker, and I've told him that if he wants our cooperation he will damn well see you properly introduced at court."

Ayrium blinked at her mother. "What?"

"Perry insists," said D'Ander. "I think it could wait, myself. After all, I'll have enough to do polishing up Amel." He must have noticed Ayrium's mixed reaction, despite her effort not to show her feelings, because he got up and set his hands on her shoulders to look into her face with a father's love. "You know I'm not ashamed of you," he told her. "It is just that you are not really a Demish woman, not in the ways expected in civilized circles. Still, I've promised Perry I'll introduce you into Demish society this time, once the business over Amel is settled."

"Getting custody of Amel won't make him Ava," said Ayrium. "Are you sure you want to have me along, as a second liability, while you try to drum up votes for Amel on Fountain Court?"

D'Ander spread his big, capable hands. "I've promised your mother," he said again, helplessly. Then he drained off the last of his sweet tea and excused himself, saying he wanted to get a good, long sleep before the trip to Gelion.

"Oh," he added, leaning back into the parlor before he closed the door. "Amel will stay at Black Hearth. Horth Nersal is honoring his father's promise to act as Judge of Honor for the duel."

Ayrium nodded. "Horth used to serve under Liege Bryllit here in Killing Reach. I know him, a little. He's an honest man."

"Yes," D'Ander agreed, "a bit grim, though. I thought it might be useful for you to keep Amel company in Black Hearth."

And spare you the embarrassment of hosting me at Golden Hearth with your wife's people around, thought Ayrium. But she couldn't begrudge her father that.

"Horth Nersal is still unsworn," concluded D'Ander, "so do try to make a good impression on our behalf." With that, he finally left and pulled the door closed.

"Sit down a moment, will you?" Perry asked her daughter.

Ayrium sensed her gravity at once.

"What is it, Mom?" she asked.

"Something we have to think about," Perry said. "If D'Ander loses—"

"But—" said Ayrium.

"I know, I know, he's a *rel* sword!" Perry silenced her, drew a breath, and started over. "Just hear me out. You know I've done my best to let you be your own person, take risks, and live life as you wanted to. But the fact is, Ayrium, you're our excuse for holding onto Barmi II without the Silver Demish barging in to sort us out for breaking all the rules. And then, of course, so long as we had D'Ander as an ally—"

"We still—"

"Anything can happen in a duel!" Perry silenced her, then added grumpily, "We don't even know who he'll be up against, for sure. It might still be Di Mon."

"I'm listening," said Ayrium.

"If something happens to D'Ander," Perry told her daughter, "we'll be vulnerable. You will have to secure us another court ally, preferably a Silver Demish one." She hesitated before adding, "As a husband."

Ayrium blinked at her. Then she laughed. "Gods!" she said. "All right. I can see your point, but... well, good thing Dad's a mean sword!"

"There is one other thing," Perry told her gravely. "Amel."

Ayrium narrowed her blue, blue eyes. "What do you mean?" she asked.

"If Ev'rel gets control of him he may become our enemy," Perry warned.

Ayrium shook her head with a laugh. "Mom, you wouldn't say such a thing if you'd heard what he just begged me to promise, up in his room! He'd never betray us."

Perry got a pained look on her face. She sat down, picked up her tea, and spoke to it, not Ayrium. "Amel is a sweet young man. A very sweet, very battered young man, trained in the arts of a courtesan." She looked up with a sober expression. "That includes learning to love the one you are with, Ayrium, for survival."

An ungenerous thought crossed Ayrium's mind concerning her mother. "Is that why you started sleeping with him," she asked, "to learn more about how he behaves? Or was it, maybe, just a little bit, to strengthen his commitment to us?"

Perry looked away. "Just think about it, Ayrium," she said wearily, "all of it. Think — don't feel."

"Sorry," said Ayrium. "Golden Demish, remember? We're all heart."

She left in anger, knowing she'd make up with Perry before she left for court because she couldn't bear to fly away leaving bad feelings between them.

Arrival on Gelion

"I am sorry I disappointed you," Amel said, as he hung about waiting for D'Ander to finish taking care of post-flight details such as strapping on his jewel-hilted sword. It had been an uneventful trip in from Killing Reach to Gelion — too uneventful, as it turned out, since Amel had gleaned along the way that D'Ander had expected to soul touch him in the way Ron D'An of the Blue Demish fleet had reported months earlier. But it simply hadn't happened.

"It is nothing," D'Ander assured him, straightening his court attire.

"What's nothing?" asked Ayrium, striding up to join them. Unlike D'Ander and Amel, who had changed in orbit before finishing the trip in a shuttle, she had come in an envoy class *rel*-skimmer and was still in her flight leathers.

"Prince D'Ander thought he might experience me as a, uh, Soul of Light, I guess, in soul touch," Amel said, ending in a mumble.

"No go, huh?" Ayrium teased her father.

"I thought you promised your mother you would dress appropriately while you were at court," D'Ander changed the subject.

"Hey!" Ayrium objected, and spread her hands. "This is appropriate for Black Hearth."

D'Ander sighed. "I foresee days of hard work ahead of me, making you respectable," he lamented. "And we will have to get you women's clothes. I can't introduce you anywhere looking like a Vrellish—" He stopped short of whatever he'd planned to say and muttered, "Person."

Ayrium turned her attention to Amel. "You look wonderful!" she told him.

He grinned back a bit sheepishly. He was wearing a soft yellow tunic with matching pants, a Golden belt and a floor-length vest embroidered in sunbursts. "Thanks," he told Ayrium.

"You aren't carrying a gun are you?" D'Ander demanded of Ayrium, spoiling the moment.

"Dad!" she protested. "I'm not stupid. I know we're at court, and about to get scanned by the best engineers in the empire. Lighten up!"

Their Nersallian hosts provided them with a spacious car powered by *rel*-batteries that ran cleanly and quietly. The driver was a woman dressed in black with red insignia signifying her status as a member of the Pettylord grammar class. A highborn woman got in the back with them. D'Ander put himself between the highborn woman and Amel, but she didn't show any interest in either of them. Ayrium sat up front with the driver.

"*Ack rel*," was all the highborn Nersallian said to D'Ander when she parted from them at Black Gate, one of eight exits from the highborn docks into the underground city called UnderGelion.

"*Ack rel*," D'Ander acknowledged her approval. The phrase could mean many things, but in this case Amel was sure it registered respect for the willingness to settle disputes by the sword, whether the person who said it was rooting for you or the opposition.

The three of them passed through Black Gate's wide, heavy doors, that were left open during business hours.

"Tell your insides to smile for the pictures," said Ayrium chattily. "See that *gorarelpul* over there?" she added, nodding in the direction of a liveried commoner behind a workstation. "He can probably tell you what you ate last, by now."

Amel didn't need Ayrium to underscore the technical skills of their hosts for him. He was already thoroughly intimidated by the somber efficiency of the Nersallians.

On the far side of Black Gate they were met by an honor guard dressed in black with red highlights. It was led by a man with a dragon design on his shirt and liege marks on his collar.

D'Ander stepped forward to greet him. "Liege Nersal," he said with a bow. "Thank you for agreeing to host Pureblood Prince Amel in Black Hearth while custody of him is settled by the sword."

Horth Nersal acknowledged the Golden Champion with a nod. He took Ayrium in with a glance that raised Amel's hackles for the sake of its frank, male appraisal of her as a woman. As Horth's attention flicked over Amel, his thin lips turned downward in a frown.

I haven't got a sword on, Amel realized. He doubted if Horth understood Souls of Light were not expected to bear weapons.

"Liege Barmi, here!" Ayrium introduced herself. "We've met once or twice in Killing Reach."

The silent man nodded again, before moving aside to let them pass.

"Horth was never much for talking," Ayrium tried to reassure Amel as he trotted along beside her.

People were lined up along their route to witness their arrival, and more waited inside the Palace Shell, where a path had been cleared through the money-changing stalls on its main floor. People stood in stands behind the lines on either side, and the balconies above were full.

D'Ander greeted the spectators with smiles and waves, enjoying the spectacle. It was much the same all the way to Black Pavilion on the Plaza, where they stopped.

"Look after him," D'Ander urged Ayrium, and paused to bow to Amel before heading off to Golden Pavilion to join the entourage he had sent ahead. It was strange to think of Golden Hearth being full of people.

Shrinking closer to Ayrium, Amel entered Black Pavilion and went down the spiral stairs at its center into Black Hearth below.

As a courtesan, Amel had visited more than one hearth on Fountain Court, but never Black Hearth. Where Silver Hearth had knickknacks, Black Hearth was decorated with mounted swords and nervecloth vistas of shipyards. Where Green Hearth breathed history, Black Hearth was about utility and power. Signs of wear on the floor had not been fixed or covered by a rug the way they would have in a Demish home. The furniture was made of hard, dark wood.

Only the final room of the Throat struck Amel as homey. In this room there was a cabinet of toys, a bookcase, some comfortable chairs and a couch occupied by a child about ten years old.

Two paintings were given pride of place on the wall: one of a wide-shouldered, aristocratic man labeled Hangst Nersal and one of a full-figured, warm-looking woman named Beryl Nesak. Below these were smaller photographic images of three men and a collection of children. Horth was the third of the young men.

The boy on the couch, who was one of the children in the portraits, sprang up as they entered, letting his book fall to the floor. He was skinny with big feet and hands, and large, gray eyes. He had an expressive mouth and an air about him of having only barely survived a near-fatal shock, expressed in latent nervousness. His name was Eler, according to the portrait on the wall. Eler took a long look at Amel, then fixed his stare on Ayrium and developed an acutely smitten look.

One of the Nersallians escorting Amel and Ayrium nudged the boy with a chuckle as she went past, making eyes at him to show she was amused by his reaction to Ayrium's robust good looks. The bit of horseplay humanized the otherwise grim Nersallians in a way that made Amel feel more comfortable.

He was shown into one room, and Ayrium into another.

"I'll be here if you need me," she told him, and wrinkled her comely nose, "but not quite the way Mom was."

As soon as the door was closed securely behind him, Amel pressed his palms to his cheeks in a vain attempt to force the blood down out of them. It was not mere embarrassment, but shame at his own reactions. He wanted very badly to maintain a clean relationship with Ayrium, but every time she said anything at all suggestive he couldn't help having sexual feelings. How was he ever going to fall in love with one woman, completely and utterly, when his three years as a courtesan predisposed him to sexual reactions?

Or do all men have that problem? he wondered.

A knock interrupted his efforts to purify his thoughts.

"Yes!" he cried, alarmed, and schooled himself to act more like a Sevolite. "Come in!" he amended.

Eler Nersal entered.

"Put it there," the boy commanded the burly servant who was dragging in a large trunk decorated with white and gold inlay.

"A gift from Golden Hearth, for Your Immortality," the servant told Amel, executed a deep bow, and withdrew.

Amel blinked at Eler, wondering why the child did not leave. But he liked presents, and was eager to distract himself. Leaving the question of Eler aside, he went to rummage in the trunk, hoping there might be a musical instrument inside, nervecloth toys, or books to help him pass the time. He was disappointed to discover mostly clothes.

"So you are the Pureblood Prince Amel," said Eler, crossing skinny arms ending in oversized hands. He reminded Amel of a puppy he had seen on Barmi that Perry said would "grow into its paws."

"I'm not impressed," said Eler.

Amel cocked an eyebrow at the boy, his mouth twisting sideways in a quizzical expression. Belatedly, he realized Eler's decision to address him in *rel*-peerage was either disrespectful, brazenly familiar, or both. A Highlord like Eler ought to be up-speaking a Pureblood by two birth ranks. But Amel wasn't sure what to do about it.

"Too bad," Amel said, avoiding pronouns.

"You're sixteen," said Eler. "I'm nearly eleven." He paused to make sure that had sunk in. "That doesn't make you so much older than me."

Amel's stomach fluttered at every taunting pronoun Eler pronounced. Sure he was a kid, but he was also a member of the *kinf'stan*. Amel doubted he could beat even Eler with a sword, and he wasn't at all sure about the protocols involved. He'd never been a Sevolite dealing with Sevolites before.

Eler sat down on the bed and got comfortable, tucking his legs under him. "Tell me all about sex," he commanded, then added more defensively, "everything I don't already know, of course."

Amel's bubble of anxiety burst. This, he knew all about. While a courtesan, he had been pestered by children with questions like Eler's all the time. He gave the boy a sympathetic smile. "Some things are better experienced than talked about," he pointed out.

"I don't want to experience everything you have!" he cried, making a face intended to distance himself from the sordid parts. "Not even half! I just want to know about how bad it can get. You know, the worst possible experiences."

Amel's amusement shaded into wary defensiveness. He might even have been angry, except Eler didn't strike him as a *slaka'st* who took pleasure in the pain of others. So why did the boy ask?

Why doesn't matter! Amel scolded himself for putting Eler's feelings before his own. *I'm not entertaining him with ugly stories!* But his resentment was fleeting. He couldn't help sympathizing, and as soon as he did, his anger dissolved in the acid of his own painful memories forever fresh and charged with feelings he lacked ordinary human defenses against because he could never forget, like a laborer unable to develop a useful callus.

He must have betrayed as much, because Eler's glib manner sloughed away revealing the boy's own distress.

"You don't want to think about the bad stuff, do you?" Eler asked, with a questing hope that touched Amel's heart.

"Nobody likes to remember dreadful things," Amel said, quietly, overtaken by the profound sense of being in the presence of another person's sacred pain: the thing in Eler's life that must be addressed if he was ever to be whole again.

"What do you do about it?" Eler wanted to know.

Amel was briefly frightened by Eler's need to know the answer. He felt privileged, but alarmed. Maybe he ought to send the boy away and avoid any possible repercussions of — what? Helping Eler cope with an agony the child could barely even define?

Me, me, Amel thought. *I must worry about me first, not the child!*

But he had been a child like this, himself, traumatized to his core. He could not resist collapsing into a hopelessly empathic state of mind. It felt good: unguarded, alive and warm.

"A lot of people died in Black Hearth on the day your brother Horth became liege," Amel probed gently, in tune with the child's reactions now. "Ayrium told me," he added, guessing her name might hold a special magic for the boy.

"A few." Eler looked away, picking at the coverlet with his fingers. "My father. My mother. My brother Branst. My sister Beryllan and our baby brother. My other brother, Zrenyl, died as well, but not here."

Amel waited.

Eler continued tugging at a wrinkle he'd made in the previously neat bed clothes. Then, all at once, he looked up with
a skeptical frown and fixed Amel with an interrogating stare.

"Are you a real Soul of Light?" Eler demanded, a pout on
his full lips and unshed tears in his eyes.

Amel passed over possible responses: the honest one, the
glib one, the one that exposed the child's hope of comfort
and threw it back in his face. Instead, he asked, very carefully, "Do you need me to be?"

Eler's eyes darted around the room in search of some escape from the emotions building inside of him. Then, with
little warning, he hurled himself at Amel and burst into tears.

Amel received him openly, and closed his arms about the
boy's back.

"We were waiting!" Eler gasped between sobs, "Mother,
Sanal, Beryllan, the baby and m-my uncle, the Nesak... priest!"
He spat out the last word. "We thought... Father told us...
we expected he'd be coming back, and then, when Horth
killed him instead—" A hiccup made him stop.

Amel guided them both over to the bed where they could
sit with Eler cuddled up against him, one hand locked in
Amel's soft yellow tunic and his face pressed against Amel's
chest.

"Mother loved us!" Eler's story kept spilling out erratically,
with breaks in which he paused to sniffle or to nibble his lower
lip between bursts of words. "I know she loved us! She was
trying to s-save us in her own w-way." He hiccupped again,
trying to hold it all in, and then blurted out violently. "She
was Mother... but she dropped the baby! Then Beryllan ran
to her, right into her knife! Branst tried to stop the priest —
and—"

Eler broke down entirely in violent sobs.

It was hours before Amel had pieced together the picture
of a sensitive child who observed and understood a great
deal of the tensions in the air, but had lived in the security

of his family's strength until the day that strength was shattered over ideology. Everything about the story hurt Eler. Even Horth, his rescuer, had simultaneously become the executioner of both their parents. It was all the more poignant for Amel to realize he was listening to a child as Demish at heart as his ominous brother Horth was Vrellish, even though they were full brothers. Sevolite genetics could be quirky in a line with mixed blood, like the Nersallians.

"And it's not over!" Eler exclaimed, wiping his nose on a sleeve. Amel offered him one of the handkerchiefs from the trunk, but Eler was too worked up to notice. "Horth's been challenged twice! Twice!" Eler stuffed a knuckle between his teeth, tears squeezing out of his eyes again. "The brother who saved us is going to be killed, and Sanal and I will be taken by the Nesaks to be murdered so we can get reborn properly!"

Amel looked up as the door opened, thinking it might be Ayrium. Instead, a tiny, well-coordinated girl came bounding in and joined them on the bed, accepting Amel on the evidence of Eler's attitude towards him.

"She's Sanal," Eler said and fell silent, his torrent of words finally spent.

Amel put an arm around the very Vrellish-looking four-year-old as she cuddled up to him, and did the only thing he could think of. He began to sing, rocking both children as he did. He sang Demish songs about tragic loss, songs that would resonate but with strong threads of hope running through them, as well. After the first few, Eler asked if he could sing a Nesak song he knew, which surprised Amel for the sake of its emotional power. He had always thought of Nesaks, before this, as heartless slayers of commoners. They exchanged songs and poetry for half the night with Sanal curled up on the bed between them, sleeping soundly.

It was much later when the door opened again and Horth Nersal came in, looking for his siblings.

Amel stirred where he lay in a heap with both children cuddled up against him. None of them had thought to turn off the lights, so his view of Horth's looming figure was perfectly clear as the tall swordsman walked over.

A horrible thought flashed across Amel's mind. Here he was, a stranger famous for his smutty exploits, known to have violent fits, lying on a bed beside two innocent children and while he realized, with an inward bloom of joy, that no inappropriate feelings had troubled him as he comforted the children, Horth Nersal had no way of knowing as much.

He'll kill me! Amel suffered the hard bite of terror in the face of Horth's implacable confidence.

But as Amel held his breath in fear, Horth Nersal merely lifted the sleeping form of his younger brother and draped him over one shoulder comfortably, before scooping up their little sister also. Sanal woke and clung. Eler just snuffled and shifted a little.

Amel held his breath until Horth had left, carrying his sleeping siblings.

A *gorarelpul* came in afterwards with sedatives. "In case of clear dreams, Immortality," he told Amel.

Amel swallowed hard as he eyed the vial of brown oil in the man's hands.

He said, even managing the grammar right, "I understand."

But he wished Perry had been there.

7

The Custody Duel

Making Deals

Ev'rel stepped into the big, square room containing all those privileged to advise her as Ava, and fixed her stare on one empty chair in particular. Di Mon was not there. As a *pol*-heir, inferior to Di Mon by challenge class, Tessitatt Monitum could not attend or speak on his behalf, therefore the duty fell to Ev'rel, as Di Mon's liege.

Which is fine with me, she told herself smugly, as D'Ander and Ayrium rose to acknowledge her with the rest of those assembled.

In addition to D'Ander and his bastard daughter, Ayrium, Ev'rel noted the presence of Liege Vrel, Prince H'Us, and the new liege of Nersal called Horth, whom Ev'rel had yet to hear speak a single word. Each liege had a second or an heir along as well. Ev'rel has brought her second son, D'Therd, who insisted on claiming Di Mon's place as her personal champion despite his tender years — a situation she had to put up with for the sake of his Knotted Strings connections. Ev'rel was surprised to see that Eler Nersal, who was even younger than D'Therd and stood no higher than waist height on most adults, had accompanied his reticent older brother, Horth. Vretla had no second, since the only Vrellish she led at court were nobleborn, and she had yet to make her trip to Cold

Rock to persuade the rest of her kin that her treatment at *TouchGate Hospital* had left her uncontaminated by Lorel evil. H'Us had a couple of the usual burly male relatives with him and had supplied half the guards of honor who stood against the walls. Horth Nersal had supplied the other half.

It was the duty of an honor guard to observe without comment of any sort, and to intervene, impartially, only if the protocols of Sword Law were violated.

Ev'rel looked around the assembly with pride. It was, after all, her first Council of Privilege as ruling Ava, and she was determined to enjoy it with as much relish as she had the extravagant birthday parties her father had thrown for her as a child.

She sat down with a regal air. D'Therd sat next, beside her. The rest of the table resumed their seats as one, Vretla doing so just a bit faster and out of synch with the other lieges.

It was up to Ev'rel to begin. She savored the moment a bit longer, taking in the historical ambience of the room with its panels decorated in the work of great artists from half a dozen eras, and the heavy wooden chairs they sat in, carved with the devices of the hearths they represented. The great wooden table between them was eight hundred years old, but the Demish referred to it as the 'new' one. The original, of Earth manufacture, had been destroyed by fire during some debacle of the Purity Wars. Di Mon had told her the story in her childhood.

Judging she had left enough silence to prove it was she, and no other, who commanded the gathering, Ev'rel drew a deep breath and prepared to preside over the matter at hand.

"We are here to agree upon the terms of resolving the custody of my son, the Pureblood Prince Amel," she told them all. "I consider the entire question absurd." She looked to Prince H'Us where he sat at the far end of the table. "I am Amel's mother. He is only sixteen and in need of rehabilitation. He should be returned to me without question."

Ayrium rose, which was quite unnecessary, although not forbidden by protocol. Or rather, the Demish had given up on making Vrellish members observe the finer points of Demish protocol centuries ago, so people at a Council of Privilege could act as they liked within the scope of Sword Law. Ev'rel made a mental note that Ayrium was unschooled in Demish rules of conduct. D'Ander's bastard was an impressive-looking woman, despite her ill manners, and strikingly attractive even in her mannish clothes. But Ev'rel doubted the young woman knew how to make use of her looks.

Earnest and naïve, Ev'rel summed Ayrium up before the Killing Reach woman spoke.

"The people around this table have their differences," said Ayrium, "but *Okal Rel* unites us. It is a well established principle of *Okal Rel* that honorable pilots must be able to make deals in space, and trust each other's word. Liege Monitum and I did so in Killing Reach concerning Amel. We agreed to fight a duel to first blood. Events in Killing Reach have made it unsafe, until recently, to travel. But I am here, now, to make good on my side of our bargain." She looked around the table. "The question is how Di Mon will be represented."

Ev'rel felt D'Therd stir beside her and spoke quickly to preempt any rashness from that quarter. "Let me say, first," she interjected, "how grateful I am that the present Liege Nersal has seen fit to honor the promise of his predecessor, Hangst Nersal, to act as Judge of Honor in this matter."

All eyes turned to the new and enigmatic liege of Nersal but it was his second, young Eler, who answered.

"Naturally Horth will honor the word of our father," the boy said, sounding strained but full of family pride in House Nersal's good reputation.

Curious, Ev'rel thought sardonically, *how none of that prevented Horth killing both his parents in one day on the way to power.* She kept her overt response civil. "Of course. House Nersal is renowned for its uncompromising honor."

"Ava Ev'rel," D'Ander spoke up, bluntly, "you know my house is not sworn to you, nor has Golden Hearth been occupied in recent years in protest over Silver Hearth's abuses of court power."

"Abuses!" Prince H'Us roared, his big fist coming down on the table.

"I understand your dissatisfaction with such language," Ev'rel assured Prince H'Us. "But please, for Prince Amel's sake, let the Golden Champion have his say before we answer. I do not ask it of you as your Ava," Ev'rel added, purposefully playing the 'woman' card, which worked so well with Silver Demish men, "but as a mother."

Prince H'Us grumbled, but subsided, dragging his big fist off the table.

"Ayrium D'Ander D'Aur," Ev'rel addressed her rival, careful not to name her as Liege Barmi, "may your sire speak for you concerning Amel?"

One of the H'Usians coughed at Ev'rel's use of the Gelack naming word for 'sire,' which was a respectable Vrellish term never used in Demish circles, except as an insult underscoring the lack of a marriage to define the social role and standing of the offspring. Liege Vrel frowned at the Demish reaction. Horth seemed oblivious. D'Ander looked angry. Ayrium showed symptoms of being uncomfortable.

No doubt she had always known what it meant to be a bastard in Demish circles, thought Ev'rel, *but she hasn't spent much time experiencing the phenomenon firsthand.*

"I have discussed the matter with my father," said Ayrium, stressing the word father, "and we agreed he would act in my stead as a liege of Fountain Court."

"Sounds reasonable," Vretla barked, with a cranky scowl at odds with the intent of the words.

Does she resent Ayrium's rejection of the word 'sire?' Ev'rel wondered. *How delicious! By resisting Demish slights she insults the Vrellish. Or Vretla Vrel, at least,* Ev'rel admitted in frustration. *It is hard to tell what this Horth Nersal creature thinks about anything!*

"D'Ander will act for Ayrium, then," Ev'rel summed up. Maybe it was the room; maybe it was the gamesmanship of the conjectures flying about in her head; but whatever the cause she felt the heady sensation of a thrill seeker about to take a plunge into the unknown.

Beware of your Vrellish blood, Di Mon had always told her. *Keep it under control.*

To have power and not wield it, Ev'rel lectured his memory, in turn, *is like staring at a man I dare not touch!*

"But who will act for Di Mon?" she said, and let her eyes track towards Vretla Vrel.

She was delighted to see D'Ander's jaw lock. Prince H'Us betrayed mixed feelings. Ayrium gave Vretla Vrel a deeper inspection than she had previously. Horth was stone-faced, as usual.

D'Therd sprang up. "I will do it!" the fifteen-year-old insisted. "I am not afraid of Prince D'Ander! He may have a *rel* reputation, but only against Silver Demish champions!"

A stir of surprise and dismay went around the table, punctuated by a curse from Prince H'Us.

My, my, Ev'rel thought, *swords before parlors is it, Son?* D'Therd would have bridges to mend in Silver Hearth for that remark.

D'Ander laughed. "By all means," he cried good-naturedly, "since it is only a duel to first blood, I've no objection to giving your young champion a fencing lesson!"

D'Therd went for his sword. Prince H'Us rose. Guards of honor descended on them both. Prince H'Us shrugged them off and sat down, nursing a frown.

The table between D'Therd and D'Ander kept them separate. D'Therd jerked his arm free of the Nersallian restraining him to glare at D'Ander where the Golden Champion lounged unperturbed in his chair.

"I am well past fencing lessons," D'Therd said in a dangerous voice, "and to prove it, I will gladly fight you to the death instead of first blood."

"I very much doubt your mother will permit those terms," D'Ander answered glibly. He cast a calculating glance at Ev'rel as he said it, followed by a flicker of his eyes towards Vretla.

He does not want to fight her, Ev'rel decided, *but is it only Demish scruples about taking on a woman? No. He does not think of her that way. I can tell by the way he looks at her. It must be Demish insecurity about the Vrellish, then.*

"I might consider letting D'Therd fight," Ev'rel dangled the possibility before D'Ander, hoping to find out what it would take to make him bite, "but you want more than mere custody of Amel as a possible Soul of Light. You want to make him Ava. If I put the throne on the table..." She smiled. "What have you got to match it?"

"Demora!" he said without hesitation, his pale blue eyes as crisp as ice.

Demora itself! Ev'rel thought. *The coveted homeworld of the Golden Emperor! Breadbasket and trading partner to the Purple Alliance!* It was so huge an offer she was utterly unprepared.

H'Us was all attention. D'Ander's bastard daughter looked at her father as if he had lost his mind. Even Horth Nersal looked more attentive.

D'Therd leaned forward, placing his fist on the table. "If I win," he said, "your heir swears to my mother and I marry her."

"My sister?" D'Ander scoffed. His mouth twisted in an unpleasant smile. "You have ambition, boy! I will give you that. A bargain-bred child from the Knotted Strings, taking the heir of Golden Hearth to wife!" he exclaimed. "You are mad."

D'Therd leaned back again, content. "You are afraid I might win."

"Ambitious," D'Ander repeated, "and foolhardy. You do know, I hope, that I have won a half a hundred fights?"

Yes, thought Ev'rel, wondering what she was missing that explained D'Ander's rashness. *Fifty duels. And you made a point, in every one of them, of grandstanding against Silver Demish with designs upon all things Demoran, including Golden princesses. Yet now you are considering whether to use your own sister as a bargaining chip. Why so desperate?* Then it dawned on her: he was already risking everything back home by promoting an ex-courtesan and *slaka* as a Soul of Light. Ambition had led him too far to back down unsatisfied. He had to win all he reached for, or lose what he already possessed.

So, Ev'rel concluded, *D'Ander is a gambler. Am I?*

She weighed her own circumstances. She was Ava now, yes, but not securely, not with Di Mon's allegiance so obviously half-hearted, D'Ander against her, and Black Hearth occupied by the inscrutable Horth. If, on the other hand, she had custody of Amel and D'Ander dead, she would be in a much more defensible position, especially if D'Ander had enemies she could ally herself with on Demora.

It was a very tempting deal D'Ander offered by putting Demora on the table. And as a Demish male, with his father dead, he had the authority to command his sister's marriage, too, if that was what it took to make D'Therd take the bait. But D'Therd, of course, was the liability for Ev'rel, since success would depend on him being able to kill someone twice his age with three times his experience. It was clear to Ev'rel that D'Ander was convinced he could beat D'Therd.

Ev'rel looked longingly at Vretla, who — although she disdained tournaments like most Vrellish — was understood to be very dangerous.

D'Ander read her mind. "Not an option," he told her.

A powerful feeling of gamesmanship possessed Ev'rel. She eyed her enemy thoughtfully, remembering what he'd said about the duel being to first blood. D'Ander was chivalrous, an honorable Demish gallant all around.

Might he be too generous against a boy? she wondered. She knew D'Therd would not let sentiment hold him back.

Heart racing, excitement thrilling through her like a drug, Ev'rel said, "Done. But only if you are prepared to make it a title challenge, to the death, with your Demoran heir obliged to wed my son, D'Therd, if you fall."

Ayrium looked horrified. "Dad!" she exclaimed, alarmed.

D'Ander's expression hardened. He refused to look at Ayrium, keeping his eyes fixed on Ev'rel. "And this," he said for the benefit of the Silver Demish present, "is the mother you would give charge of a Soul of Light? A mother who offers her second son up for slaughter."

D'Therd was too exultant, just then, to do more than sneer at D'Ander's jibe.

The Golden Champion rose, tugged at his braid-encrusted jacket, and looked straight at D'Therd. "I am sorry if you are nothing but your mother's pawn," he said, "but I must kill you now."

"Acquit yourself well, tomorrow, Prince D'Ander," D'Therd answered him with ringing confidence. "I will want to think well of my future brother-in-law."

"Liege Nersal," D'Ander excused himself to the duel's Judge of Honor. He did not address either the Silver Demish or Ev'rel. Ayrium scrambled out after him, avoiding all eye contact around the table.

Horth Nersal left next.

Ev'rel sat down heavily.

"*Ack rel*," Vretla said to D'Therd, with a duelist's sober admiration for sheer bravery.

He nodded an acknowledgement to her.

On his own way out, D'Therd paused to lean over Ev'rel. "Thank you, Mother," he whispered with naïve sincerity.

Ev'rel looked up at his exultant expression. *He thinks he is immortal*, she realized.

He also thinks I care about him, she thought, bemused and just a little frustrated to know she did not, as he lay his big hand over hers. "It will be all right," he promised her.

"That was a little rash, wasn't it?" the Silver Demish leader, Prince H'Us, asked her in a shocked tone once they were alone.

Ev'rel hardly heard him. She had reached the same conclusion on her own.

What have I done?! she thought.

On the Challenge Floor

Ayrium was waiting by the spiral stairs for Amel on the morning of the duel.

He knew something was up, but no one had told him what, and the drugs made him feel leaden. He had needed a shot of the stimulant, *sish-han*, to climb out of the *klinoman*-induced stupor of the night before.

Seeing Ayrium was a welcome pleasure. She had given up her flight leathers for a blue and white pant suit decorated in braid that proclaimed her Blue and Golden Demish heritage. She had even styled her hair, but she still wore the weapon that gave her a voice under Sword Law.

"Black suits you," Ayrium remarked on his own plain attire, making an effort to sound casual, but she could hide nothing from him. She was distraught.

"What is it, Ayrium?" Amel asked, dismay uniting with the *sish-han* in his veins to make him agitated. He started towards her and was blocked by an errant.

"No contact, please," the Nersallian nobleborn warned.

"It's the duel," said Ayrium. "It's right now: this morning."

Amel swallowed around a lump in his throat. "Wh-what?"

"Dad didn't want you to worry," Ayrium explained. "He thought—" She gave up on D'Ander's reasons and put on a bold front. "Dad's up against a very green sword, Ev'rel's second son, D'Therd. He's just fifteen years old." Maybe she could see this wasn't making Amel feel any better, because she ended quickly. "It won't take long."

"D'Therd?" Amel said, with a deep but ill-defined feeling of wrongness. "He's my... brother, isn't he?"

"Yes." Ayrium struggled with how to explain, finally deciding on the simple truth. "And it is to the death, Amel. You deserve to know."

"Death?" Amel breathed out the word, stunned.

"Let's go," said the errants.

It was much too short a distance getting down the spiral stairs and out onto the Octagon below Fountain Court. The challenge floor lay at its center. The two metallic houses, Gold and Silver, had set up stands on their respective wedges of the Octagon. About two dozen Golden Demish princes occupied the Golden ones. Twice that number of H'Usians were seated comfortably on elegant tiers of upholstered chairs on Silver Wedge, including a few stout-hearted women. The people on the Vrellish wedges — Green, Red and Black — were roughly half male and half female. Amel recognized Vretla, but avoided eye contact. White and Brown wedges stood empty except for a token guard in Di Mon's colors. Di Mon himself was not present, so the Green Hearth contingent was led by Tessitatt Monitum.

At first, Amel tried not to look towards Blue Wedge, but he couldn't help himself. *My mother,* he thought, as his eyes were drawn to Ev'rel. *She's my mother.* His first glimpse sent a jolt through him, followed by disgust at the strong impression that her Demish clothes concealed a Vrellish sexuality. The disgust was not for Ev'rel but himself, for noticing. As her head began to turn towards him, he looked away towards the duelists, his heart rate quickening.

§   §   §

Beautiful indeed, Ev'rel judged Amel. But mere beauty could not hold her attention with a question of power about to be resolved.

Nervous, too, was the last thought she spared for Amel, before returning her attention to the Challenge Floor.

§   §   §

How odd, Amel thought, watching D'Therd, *to have a brother I might know for the first and last time like this, as a spectator. A brother so different from me we'd have much to teach each other. He's younger than me, and he's about to fight a duel to the death! Can he really want to do that?*

D'Ander caught Amel's eye and beamed at him with a look of confidence, as if to share his courage.

Doesn't it matter to him that he is about to kill someone? Amel wondered. It all felt surreal, but he tried to look brave because he was afraid for D'Ander, too.

Ayrium was not allowed to stand beside him. It was Black Hearth errants who surrounded him, backed up by the *gorarelpul* with his drug-laden needle gun, permitted on the Octagon expressly to subdue Amel if necessary. But Ayrium remained within speaking distance.

"Are you scared?" Amel asked her in English, his eyes fixed ahead as Horth Nersal stepped out to declare the duel.

"Terrified," Ayrium said jauntily, "of Dad dragging me off to a West Alcove tailor tomorrow.'

§   §   §

I let D'Ander play me for a fool! Ev'rel berated herself, afraid she was too anxious to hold up through the duel. *I was too greedy for Demora. Too eager to tell Di Mon I could dispense with his half-hearted backing!* D'Therd was brilliant for his age and experience, yes, but she had pitted him against a legend! And all because she could not resist the gamesmanship of the deal D'Ander had offered her. She'd been seduced like a novice! Baited like a stupid man instead of a clever woman, and unworthy of Di Mon's lessons in statecraft.

This would never have happened if you'd been here, damn you, she thought bitterly at Di Mon. *Or if you'd meant it when you swore to me, so I could trust you enough to feel secure!*

It suddenly seemed clear to her that all her life's disasters were rooted in her failed relationship with Di Mon.

§ § §

As Judge of Honor, Horth Nersal was supposed to summarize the terms of the duel and declare it begun. Instead, he simply stood where he had stopped, doing nothing at all.

He's got stage fright! Amel realized, with a flash of insight from his courtesan days of working with novices new to appearing before a crowd. *He doesn't know what to say.*

Amel turned his attention towards the people ringing the challenge floor and decided they did not understand. They saw only the enigmatic liege of Nersal who had perturbed the power equation in the empire by coming back to live on Fountain Court, and they were trying to guess what he meant by delaying for so long.

Seconds passed in silent expectation. Then Horth drew his sword and held it high. Amel felt anxious on the grim Liege Nersal's behalf. But both contestants seemed to understand, at once. D'Ander nodded. D'Therd gave a confirming look. Both watched the raised sword.

Liege Nersal took a step back, then another. When he was clear of the fighters, but not yet off the challenge floor, Horth looked at the combatants to be sure they saw him. Then he swung down his sword, signaling them to start.

§ § §

Ev'rel caught her breath as D'Therd barely survived D'Ander's opening attack.

The Golden prince smiled as he drew back. "Not bad, for a kid from nowhere," he remarked.

Go ahead! Ev'rel thought at him viciously. *Talk!*

D'Therd attacked, but chatty or not, D'Ander held him off like the champion he was.

Ev'rel's heart was in her throat. She remembered flashes of D'Therd as a child, while he was still her Chad, adoring and malleable, before he began to defy and resist her. The vestigial concern, as a mother, gave way to a nasty premonition of the humiliation she could look forward to when she found herself Avim to D'Ander's puppet Ava, Amel. Court would begin to turn Golden. Her transgressions of the past might come up again, discrediting her, and she could die the way her father did, slain by pompous fools for the sake of her sexual appetites.

As D'Therd continued to survive, with difficulty, Ev'rel looked at Amel in this new light and imagined him shielded by a wall of Golden Demish paladins led by D'Ander. A spiteful shiver of resentment went through her in anticipation of humiliation and a long, stupid struggle for respectability in a Golden-dominated court. Then she saw something else that gave her hope.

Amel was humming like the plucked string of an instrument, alive with tension.

Extending her hand without taking her eyes off her quarry, she caught Kandral's wrist where he stood beside her. "Get Mira out here, now," she hissed in a low whisper to her captain of errants. "Tell her it's in case she's needed."

Now, please! she willed Amel, her eyes boring into him as he looked everywhere except at the duel, to distract himself from the drama playing out on the Challenge Floor. *Look this way before it is too late, and see her!*

What she imagined might happen was a slim hope. But it was all she had.

§ § §

Amel could not bear to watch the duel. Every block and blow felt fatal, and he knew what it felt like to be run through with a sword. It had happened to him, once, on the Flashing Floor, while he'd been dancing at the birthday celebration for the princess liege of H'Us. It was an accident that time. It would be purposeful now. And it wouldn't be him who was struck down. But whenever he looked at D'Therd and D'Ander he couldn't help imagining a sword passing through his own body wherever one of them was trying to hit the other. It was making him so jumpy he dreaded it would start a clear dream, so he tried to fill his head with words from poems as gentle as the duel before him was violent, to stop his nerves singing in sympathy with the two vulnerable bodies on the challenge floor.

Then he saw Mira.

There was absolutely no doubt it was Mira, alive and real, across the Challenge Floor. She looked older than she did in his memories. She was the sister and companion of his childhood — his idol, his first love, and his partner in dealing with the politics of their confined existence for the first ten years of his life. He would have recognized her anywhere! As he watched, she moved silently between the people on Blue Wedge to stand at Ev'rel's side, a medical bag in her hand.

Realities clashed inside Amel. The poem he'd been silently reciting was gone. Mira was there, instead, the Mira he had lost when the life they'd shared had been transformed into a nightmare.

An errant turned towards him, aware of some change in him, but by then Amel was no longer on Black Wedge observing a duel. He was locked in a room with a pedophilic sadist in Nersallian black: his first 'client' in the *sla* den called the Bear Pit, where he had wound up after Mira was gone. He never knew afterwards why his unstable memory picked that detail. Maybe it was the Nersallians surrounding him. Maybe it was because, until Jarl had locked him in that room, with that man, he had still been Miff at heart — the little brother who had done his best for his big sister Mira — making this the hour in his own life that separated him from everything she represented. Maybe it was random. But all the second-guessing came afterwards.

Right now it was his new reality. He lost both Von, the cocky thirteen-year-old performer, and Amel, the uncertain sixteen-year-old Sevolite. He was Miff, the ten-year-old innocent, prepared to fight a hopeless battle in which he was about to lose his innocence, brutally, and come close to losing his life at the same time.

§   §   §

From the instant Amel gave a cry of terror, Ev'rel's attention shot back and forth between him and duelists.

She saw Ayrium try to reach Amel at the same time D'Ander broke off his attack to put space between himself and his opponent as he turned his head to look.

Ayrium was blocked by a Nersallian as another one went down before Amel's wild assault on a phantom opponent.

D'Therd lunged.

Ayrium got past the Nersallian restraining her as Amel took a shot from the *gorarelpul*'s needle gun.

D'Ander saved himself by a hair and fell back. D'Therd flew at him.

Ev'rel bit her lip as she watched her fifteen-year-old son prove he had the heart and ambition of a champion. D'Therd's name hovered on her lips, her right hand clenched with tension. She wanted to cheer him on, but knew she had to keep completely silent.

The swordplay was close and furious. Amel had fallen silent. Ev'rel forgot about him and Mira, who had gone rigid beside her. She tried to understand the action of the duel, wishing she had paid more attention to Di Mon's instruction. D'Ander appeared to be in control once more.

A desperate exchange of blows nearly slew her with anxiety for fear it would end the duel! She could make out nothing except that both champions were pushing hard to score.

Her heart stopped as D'Therd staggered backwards, bleeding. Then D'Ander dropped onto one knee and fell on his face with his sword still in his hand. Every witness held his breath, uncertain for a moment who had won.

D'Therd was bleeding freely from a sucking chest wound. But D'Ander did not get up.

"Go!" Ev'rel cried, and shoved her medtech forward to take care of her wounded son.

Mira moved as stiffly as a puppet made of wood, her narrow face white with shock or anger. Ev'rel did not care so long as Mira did her job! She had gambled and she had won! It was all she could do not to squeal with relief and triumph!

D'Therd staggered on the challenge floor and dropped his sword, but Mira did not go to him immediately. She checked first on D'Ander, who lay face down in his own blood, but rose again without disturbing the fallen Golden Champion, leaving him to his own people who had flocked onto the floor.

Silently, Mira went to help guide D'Therd off the challenge floor before he passed out.

Poor D'Therd, Ev'rel thought with a giddy feeling of euphoria. *No chance to stand and take a bow.* She did not expect him to die, though. Mira wouldn't be letting him walk off at all if she thought there was any chance of that.

Ayrium was slow in reacting to her father's loss. Ev'rel watched her with interest where she stood, gaping at D'Ander's body being turned over, respectfully, by his vassals, looking as if her world had just turned upside down. No doubt it had.

Amel was a limp rag in the grasp of his handlers, thoroughly sedated with *klinoman*. Ayrium had temporarily forgotten him.

Only when the eyes of every witness began turning to Horth Nersal, standing on the sidelines, did Ev'rel remember he was still the Judge of Honor, and capable of casting a shadow over her joy. No cry of *Okal Rel* had been raised yet to proclaim the duel fairly won and witnessed. Everyone was waiting for him. Horth Nersal looked directly at Ev'rel across the challenge floor and, for an instant, she thought she glimpsed her ruin in his unflinching stare.

She held her breath, and his stare, willing herself not to look frightened.

Prince H'Us came up beside her, grim-faced with grief over his nephew D'Ander, despite the enmity dividing them. Ev'rel could only hope he meant the gesture as a show of solidarity. She could barely think.

Horth's silence was terrible!

Then Liege Nersal gave a curt nod and sheathed the sword he had lowered to begin the duel.

A sigh rose from the watching crowd.

"*Okal Rel*!" boomed Prince H'Us, drawing his own sword to thrust it up above him. He began to grin then. So did all the Silver Demish. The Goldens looked on with shocked faces.

Ev'rel stayed on the Octagon just long enough to see D'Ander's bastard daughter barred from the body of her fallen father by the entourage of mourning Golden Demish surrounding him.

8

Ava Ev'rel

The Prize

Two Nersallian errants brought Amel over, his body suspended between them with his arms about their shoulders,
delivering the stake of the duel.

"Take custody of Amel," Ev'rel ordered Kandral. "Take
him into Blue Hearth immediately."

She hurried ahead, guessing it would be wise to get out
of sight before she indulged in the ear-to-ear grin trying
to crack through her sober expression. She went sedately
up the first turn of the spiral stairs. Then she hitched up
her long, Demish skirt and rushed up the rest of the way,
suppressing giggles.

I am Ava, I am Ava, and liege of Demora! she told herself
with jubilation.

At the top of the stairs her household had assembled to
greet her with an air of subdued excitement. Perhaps they
thought it unseemly to be happy about the death of so dash-
ing a champion as D'Ander, or maybe it was D'Therd's condition that sobered them. She didn't know and didn't care.
She couldn't cope with their company right now.

Kandral came up the stairs behind her with Amel limp
in his arms.

Perfect excuse! thought Ev'rel. Her only other option was
to seek out Mira, whom she did not want to see just now.

Even seeing D'Therd would have required some posturing on her part that she did not feel up to mustering until the giddy feeling of success subsided.

"I must see to my poor son, Amel," Ev'rel decided, invoking her best impression of a serious liege and mother, and hurried off after Kandral, down the Throat towards Family Hall.

Kandral carried Amel into the bedroom she had set aside for him before the duel. Ev'rel came in and closed the door.

She watched as Kandral laid out her new prize on the bed. He pulled off Amel's short leather boots and put them on the floor. Kandral opened Amel's black silk shirt to make it easier to check his heart.

"Is he in any danger, do you think?" Ev'rel asked.

Kandral straightened up with a frown. "It was only *klinoman*," he said roughly.

Ev'rel nodded, letting herself be calmed by the aesthetic feast laid out in front of her.

Amel was moving slightly, like someone in delirium, all his actions muted by the *klinoman*, but he was breathtakingly alive despite the drug. His chest rose and fell, lips slightly apart. His eyes moved restlessly beneath their lids. His eyebrows and eyelashes were so black and fluid against the creamy whiteness of his skin that they invited touch. His half-naked body was flawless. There was an integration about him that intrigued her; a sort of rolling up of all he was, making it impossible to separate his face from his body or his soul from the flesh it inhabited. He was so deliciously physical and as well made as an artificial image she might draw or shape in nervecloth. But he was all the more fascinating for being alive in ways she had no idea how to extract and duplicate, artistically, so she would be free to move on to the next challenge.

"Leave him with me," Ev'rel said in a sultry drawl.

Kandral hesitated a second. He knew more about her weaknesses where helpless men were concerned than anyone else in her service except Mira, which meant he also knew to keep his mouth shut about it.

He gave a guilty start for being tardy in his response and grinned at her. "Of course, Ava."

Ev'rel smiled back, secure in the knowledge that her strongest hold on him was his sexual obsession with her as a dangerously Vrellish woman. She trusted that bond more than most. It had kept her father attentive to her. Kandral liked the idea of her secret depravity, admired her, even, for possessing desires potent enough to transcend all other considerations.

"Wait," she said, as Kandral made to leave. She spread her fingers in Amel's direction. "What do you think of our new member of the family?"

"Pretty," Kandral allowed, looking Amel up and down in the dismissive, almost angry, way men who do not lust for men dismissed an attractive rival, "and barking mad."

"Dangerous, you think?" she inquired, wondering if she could make him jealous.

The errant captain shrugged. "Not while he's slack, and Pureblood or not, they pumped enough *klin* into him to keep him that way for hours."

"Thank you," Ev'rel said, bored by his failure to show any intensity of feeling, "you may go."

Kandral bowed himself out.

As soon as the door was closed, Ev'rel spun around with a flourish and pounded her fists in the air to vent surplus excitement over her triumph. It was all she could do not to squeal. Once she felt steadier, she sat down in a chair beside her long-lost son to properly inspect her new possession.

This is not the Amel I lost, she realized at once, seeing how the beauty that had looked purely aesthetic to her moments earlier was underpinned by something vigorously male, but not aggressive. The apparent contradiction intrigued her.

She brushed locks of dark hair from his pale face and smiled at the suede-soft caress of his skin on hers. He smelled faintly of sweet vanilla, just like Delm had. The association made her frown. As a baby, he had not yet possessed the signature odor of the Family of Light. He had smelled of clean skin and baby powder.

Ev'rel drew her fingers from his face and trailed them down his arm, watching his eyes moving under closed lids. *Is he still reliving some horror from his childhood?* she wondered, and felt a surge of violent anger laced with a possessive jealousy. The idea thrilled her. She wanted in, to see what was going on inside of him.

She touched his face again and the eye movements stopped. His lips parted and he moved his head a little with a soft moan, struggling for consciousness. She slid a hand over his chest to check his heart and was rewarded with a steady thump-thump. Her knowledge of medicine was more limited than Mira's, but she felt confident he was in no danger, physically. Psychologically was another matter.

As an experiment, she scratched the inside of his arm to see if he would respond, but whatever preoccupied him internally continued to dominate his senses. She wondered what she might do to cause a little more pain and slowly, as if the idea originated in her fingers, she extended her hand towards his groin.

And froze.

What am I doing? she thought, astonished. *He's my son!* A sharp spurt of pleasure surprised her as she failed to resist the inevitable follow-up: *And I was Papa's daughter. Wouldn't Di Mon be horrified,* she concluded. The idea forced a giggle from her.

She remembered how devastated Di Mon had been by the news her father had been sleeping with her. He found out in the wake of Papa's assassination by Delm's cronies. Ev'rel had been beside herself. In her grief, she'd defended the love

Delm had ended but Di Mon had refused to call it love. "Vrellish celebrate sex, yes, but not incest!" he had told her. "Not child molestation!" He apologized for failing her. He did not want to see how she grieved for the father who had loved her as she was, without trying to improve her; loved her because she was his spoiled, willful, sexy daughter, full of delight and desires.

I own you, she thought looking down at Amel, feeling mildly intoxicated.

On impulse, she slipped an arm under his back to lift him, controlling his head with her other hand. His weight felt good in her arms, his body supple; even the vanilla scent that had displeased her earlier became his own, leavened with a spicy male smell that tantalized her with its ghostly hint of Vrellish musk.

There was no one to see, no one to know, not even Amel.

Ev'rel embraced him. His mouth was warm on hers, but unresponsive. She kissed him long and carefully, exploring the experience, and felt his breathing start to deepen. It was enough response to panic her.

She laid him down again, fast, and sat rigidly beside him, staring at his lovely form and processing the buzz she had gotten from handling him.

"Perhaps we're both mad!" she said aloud to herself, and laughed. But the laugh was too shrill and too bitter. Her own voice made her shiver. She got up and smoothed her skirt out with her hands, reassured by acting out such an ordinary, womanly gesture.

Today, she thought, *I gained a world and kept an empire. No wonder I am not quite myself. Who would be?*

She heard something behind her, and turned to find Mira standing just inside the door. She must have come in and closed it behind her silently.

Ev'rel's heart gave a guilty pound that must have showed in the pulse at her neck, it was so violent. She raised a hand to cover it, feeling slightly dizzy.

"Done already?" Ev'rel asked the medtech with an unanticipated flutter of worry about D'Therd. "How is he?"

"Resting. I expect him to survive the wound."

Ev'rel swallowed down a soulful of mixed feelings. She looked down at Amel to prevent Mira seeing her face just then. His own face was sweet and weary, interesting despite his drugged stupor.

"You did that on purpose," Mira said tersely. "You knew."

"Knew?" Ev'rel snatched a breath with a jolt of fear as she spun to face Mira. A glance told her Mira was upset. And Mira did not like to be forced to contend with her emotions.

She's just a commoner! Ev'rel told herself, and gave a rough laugh. "Whatever are you talking about?"

"Amel," Mira said coldly. "He's the boy I grew up calling Brother. You learned it from the Reetion data and you did not tell me. Why? Were you planning this all along? Is that why you were so bold about striking a deal with D'Ander? You knew you could distract him just by having me appear on the challenge floor and make Amel react."

"No!" Ev'rel exclaimed indignantly. "It was nothing like that!" she insisted. "It was nothing I planned!" The qualification made it true.

Mira remained tight-lipped and silent. Ev'rel had never felt so shut out before.

"Check him out, would you?" Ev'rel ordered Mira with a careless gesture towards Amel. "I will need your assessment on how to manage him."

"No," said Mira.

"What do you mean, 'no'?" Ev'rel asked in a louder, sharper tone. "You will give me an assessment on his mental stability."

"I do not want anything to do with him," said Mira. "Please," she added, dropping her voice to a whisper. "We were raised together and my mother loved us both."

"What's this?" asked Ev'rel, relieved by a sense of regaining control. "Sentiment?"

"I saw what you did," Mira said in a bleak voice, "just now... to him."

Ev'rel barked a laugh. She was shocked with herself the next instant, as if being observed had changed something trivial into something she was forced to examine in a different light. She had meant to insist it was nothing, but Mira's bluntness left her no room to maneuver. She reacted with resentment instead.

"Really? And do you intend to be tedious and ruin your career over your little brother again?"

Mira had not expected cruelty. She gave Ev'rel a sharp look of reassessment, making her regret the implied threat.

"Oh, don't look like that, Mira," Ev'rel reversed herself quickly, "I am his mother not his executioner! I was just — excited! I got carried away." More gently, Ev'rel added, "I am not asking you to care about him, just to serve as his physician."

"Of course," Mira said, collecting herself. But there was a new distance, a wariness between them. "It will take time to develop a strategy for managing the total recall episodes he suffers from, but my guess is they are induced by stress." She left a meaningful pause. "You may want to minimize his exposure to trying situations."

"I want to hold his formal reception in three weeks," Ev'rel said. "You will keep him sedated, as required, until then. But right now I want you to wake him up."

Mira drew breath to argue, but instead composed herself and said, "Very well."

Ev'rel watched Mira prepare an injection. She didn't use *sish-han* of course. She used something more subtle, from her store of Lorel medicines secured through House Monitum.

Watching Amel revive under the influence of the drug, Ev'rel was freshly entranced. *He must be exhausted,* she thought, with a wash of sympathy that was curiously pleasant. The wide scope of her own reactions to him fascinated her.

After a few minutes, Mira slapped him lightly and his eyes sprang open. He tried to sit up, but barely got his elbows propped under him in his first, jerky movement. His fear and vulnerability drew Ev'rel to help him, supporting him against her body. His trembling slowly subsided as she stroked his hair, its texture caressing her fingers.

"Welcome home, Amel," she said softly.

Amel's eyes filled with tears. "D'Ander," he said in a choked voice.

"Is dead," Ev'rel said, laying him gently back down again. She settled on her knees at his bedside to bring her face level with his. "And if not D'Ander, then it would have been your half-brother, D'Therd, who died today. *Okal Rel* is like that. I will look after you, now."

The gentle pathos in his wet eyes moved her. She gave his hand a squeeze and liked the way he yielded to the pressure, although he felt strong enough to resist. "I think you need some looking after," she told him kindly. "Don't you, Mira?"

Mira spoke in a perfunctory manner. "Of course."

Amel looked at her directly for the first time, his hand still in Ev'rel's. "I was afraid you had died," he said, plainly ashamed and full of regrets he seemed to be struggling to define clearly enough to put into words, without success.

"I deserved to die," Mira said with a snort. "I was younger then, and stupid, like you were when you thought you could make everything right by taking me to *TouchGate Hospital*. We've both learned that the world doesn't play by Em's rules."

"Em?" Ev'rel asked mildly.

Mira took advantage of the opportunity to take her eyes off Amel and fix them on Ev'rel. "My mother," she informed her clinically. "She told us to look out for each other. We've each done that once now, with disastrous results. I, for one, have grown up. You should too, Immortality," she told Amel, using strictly proper pronouns. "We are not who we once were."

Ev'rel watched Amel suffer through Mira's every word, but he refused to spare himself by breaking eye contact. Only when she finished did he lower his eyes and turn his head askance, struggling to accept what she said.

Such an expressive face! Ev'rel thought. *Like a piece of magic art, as complex as it is beautiful.* She was certain he could have spoken volumes about what he was feeling, if Mira had invited it.

"I need to know about the clear dreams, Immortality," Mira addressed her patient. "They manifest under stress. Is that all?"

"And in my sleep," Amel mumbled without looking at her.

Mira nodded. "The Nersallians drugged you with *klin* to prevent you acting them out, which is hardly a satisfactory long-term solution." She paused. "You spent months living on Barmi II. How did they manage you?"

Amel wet his lips. Ev'rel watched his tongue move, saw his teeth flash, and remembered the feel of his soft, pastel lips and the clean taste of his yielding mouth.

"Perry and I," Amel mumbled, a flush slowly rising on his pale cheeks. "I was clear dreaming and... it just happened."

"What happened?" Ev'rel demanded, her interest piqued by his reaction.

He swallowed thickly. "S-she slept with me... at night... to keep me calm."

"Slept?" Ev'rel stood up, her political interests aroused. "Is she with child?" she asked harshly.

"No!" Amel cried, becoming animated. His emotions had astonishing power. Even though he lacked the strength to stand, they animated him with a quivering vibrancy so strong Ev'rel could almost feel it just by standing near him. "It wasn't like that!" he protested. "It was my fault. I was clear dreaming and she knew I didn't like to be tied down.

I begged her to stay, and then — I don't know how it happened!"

"A strange confession," Ev'rel said, letting her sarcasm show, "for a person with your professional training."

Amel went very still where he lay, aware he had made an error. "Perry is not pregnant," he assured Ev'rel. "She knew it would make trouble with you and on Demora. She wouldn't have done that to D'Ander. I — I shouldn't have told you." The longer he talked, the more agitated he grew. "I just can't bear to be tied up or drugged!" He turned his head to Mira, tears seeping from his remarkably crisp gray eyes. "Please don't use more drugs!"

His desperation was alarming enough to pierce Mira's indifference.

This Em, Ev'rel thought, *has forged a bond between them that still has the power to make one flinch when the other suffers.* She was fascinated, and resentful. Mira was her only friend and confidante. Amel was her son. Their connection should be solely through her.

"I suppose," Ev'rel said, dryly, "we could keep him supplied with disposable bed warmers not likely to be missed too badly if the trick doesn't work and he goes wild."

Amel reacted with profound horror. "Oh, no!" he said, shifting on the bed as if he wanted to get up and flee from it all. "It's true! I can hurt people!" But he could not rise. Whatever Mira gave him had not counteracted the slackening effects of *klinoman*.

"I think he could use medicating now," Ev'rel told Mira. "He's had too many shocks for one day. Make it something to help him feel happier."

Mira obeyed by opening her medical bag. Amel tensed where he lay, looking trapped and betrayed, but accepting it like a beaten dog who knows its place in the scheme of things.

"Do you need anything before you rest?" Ev'rel asked, as if he were a much younger child. "Food, or a bathroom?"

He shook his head ever so slightly, breath locked in his chest. His expression was deliciously bewildered, as if he wasn't certain whether to categorize the intervention as help or harm, and was afraid to decide because once he did there would be no going back.

Amel gave a small start as Mira came towards him with another dose of medicine, then closed his eyes as she administered the shot.

"Leave us now," Ev'rel told Mira without taking her eyes off Amel. "I am going to have a chat with my son concerning an important matter."

"Of course," Mira answered her. She didn't look at Amel again but he forced himself up onto an elbow before she reached the door and called to her.

"Mira! When I betrayed you — when I didn't back you up — Mira, I was conscience bonded to H'Reth!"

Mira did not turn, just stood where she'd stopped with her back to him. "Of course," she said in a flat tone, and hurried out.

Amel fell back with a sob, looking devastated.

"Don't worry," Ev'rel soothed, feeling sorry for the poor fool, whose distress was so sincere and comical. "I'll make sure she learns all about what happened from your point of view. I've learned so much about you from the visitor probe record."

He managed to roll himself over to hide his face beneath his arm, his shoulders shaking with half-stifled sobs of adolescent misery.

Ev'rel went to fetch a damp cloth from the room's private bathroom. She put the cloth down on a side table so she could use both hands to roll him over gently. He was too rung out by the drugs to resist her. Whatever Mira had given him was starting to work, too. Even his misery was mellowing.

"You like to believe the best of people," Ev'rel explained him to himself as he lay looking up at her with a confused expression. "I understand why — you are much too good a person. It is frightening for you to realize other people are more selfish than you, in ways that give them all the power."

She reached for the cloth and began to clean his face up. He stared, but made no effort to resist her, as if something in the scenario felt inevitable to him.

"You deserve a good illusion, Amel," she told him, "an oasis of happiness to shelter you, full of luxuries and simple pleasures. You need the safety of marriage to a woman who is bound to love you." Her smile opened out in a generous, honest expression. "Who could help it?"

"Marry?" he asked, in a daze.

"Would you like that?" she asked him.

He considered a long time, his expression growing more abstract under the influence of the new drug.

"I wrote a poem," he said dreamily. "To my *cher'st*... my one true love. But I told her it would never work." He paused. "I'm used up."

"It doesn't show," Ev'rel assured him, softened by the eerie beauty he projected in this altered state of mind, as if the light reflecting from his wet-crystal eyes really did come from inside.

"Tell me the poem," she invited him. "I promise I will never mock you for it, not for the poem itself, at least. I promise." She gathered his hand into hers as if it was as fragile as his simple-minded affections seemed to her.

He remained silent, each blink taking longer and longer.

"'Art is all the soul dares to love,'" she quoted on impulse from a Demish drama.

A faint smile touched his lips. His eye lids fluttered, trying to stay open. Then he let them close, and for a moment she thought he had drifted off to sleep. Then his voice came, full of love, magically delivering its message across time and the burdens of experience to an Ev'rel who might have understood the sentiments. She listened spellbound as he recited.

To My Cher'st

I know you would laugh at my excesses
if we met each other, whole, some life,
and kiss my griefs to butterflies.
I know you are clean where you are.
When I mourn my virgin hopes
you flash silver as a missed star,
neither rushing up nor falling
past my arc of flight.
I know you between nows.
Doing better without me than I can,
you look up from whoever you are
to smile at my living ghost—
Golden memory and Silver promise,
Today bears the shield of my yesterdays
before my eyes. I could not recognize you
if you hailed me, in a corridor, ablaze in joy.
I would want too much anyhow.
We can unite instead in strangers' arms,
each time you laugh, each time I love,
and live in all the cher'stan *who've had better luck.*

He completed the last word like a pilot making dock, and slipped into the arms of sleep the instant it was done.

She was astonished at the discipline involved in making the last phrase as clear as the first, and the instinctive dedication to the art of oratory itself behind so dedicated a performance under such bizarre conditions.

The content of the poem was foolish. But the idealistic twaddle was redeemed from self-indulgence by a patient acceptance of hopelessness she found amusing. The poem was cleverly structured, in Gelack, contrasting the idioms of the Golden era with the forms and stresses of a later, more cynical period.

She sat back and folded her hands in her lap, feeling as quietly satisfied as she could ever remember being since the hour of her father's death.

Then she cloaked her spirit again in the tools of survival, and left to begin negotiations with the Demish for the marriage of her sweet, ridiculous son to some stuffy Demish princess.

9

Drinks and Duels

Social Challenges

Three weeks after the custody duel, Ayrium halted in sight of Green Pavilion on the Plaza, shoved aside her grief for D'Ander, wrestled down her hurt pride, and strode forward to accost the watch captain.

"I want to speak with your liege, Di Mon," she declared, using the full force of her Highlord rank against the Midlord.

The guard gripped her sword and pressed her lips together.

"I know he is back," insisted Ayrium. "It is all over court."

"Is it?" remarked a sharp voice behind her.

The errant captain saluted. Ayrium spun around. Di Mon was there, in person. The braid on his jacket would have identified him unambiguously even if the errant's reaction had not. He looked as hard and gray as a knife, his expression stiff, his eyes cold, and his skin an unnaturally pale color. It was not hard to believe he had been as seriously wounded as rumored, but it was equally hard to believe it made him any less dangerous.

Ayrium swallowed a mouthful of cold saliva and squared her shoulders, acutely aware of the lack of braid upon her own jacket.

"I want to see Amel," she told Di Mon.

"Good," he said, curtly. "Then you are not as unfashionable as I'd thought, since that is the desire of a good half of the leading Demish families at court, which is why Ev'rel is holding a reception for him tomorrow. Get yourself invited."

"You know that's impossible!" she cried, too stirred up to appreciate his wit. "I have no friends on Fountain Court or among the Silver Demish courtiers of the Palace Sector."

"Yes," he said dryly. "I've heard."

She looked away, chagrined by this unlooked-for confirmation of her less than stellar success making friends among those with the power to be useful to the Purple Alliance.

He thawed slightly, then. "You have my condolences over your father's death. We had our differences, but D'Ander was a man of honor."

A spur of anger welled up and would not be repressed. "He was distracted on purpose," she accused. "By Ev'rel!"

"I will not discuss this with you," Di Mon told Ayrium.

"Liege Monitum!" she called, as he began to turn away, vexed with herself for letting her feelings get the better of her common sense again, because there was one more thing she had to say, however upset she might still be about her father's duel.

She thought he was going to ignore her for a moment, but he turned back, looking ill and irritated.

"Thank you," she said, "for your part in frustrating the Nesaks in Killing Reach. A Nesak occupation in my backyard isn't something I want to deal with, this life." She hesitated then, as she debated whether to risk the next thing she wanted to say to him, because she hated the idea he might mistake it for an attempt to manipulate him. "I'm glad you got out of it alive," she blurted, gauging the narrowness of her window of opportunity by his frown. "I know there are no Vrellish Souls of Light, but there are good souls." She gave a quick bow and ducked out, to make it clear she was taking no for an answer on the other matters she had come about.

She couldn't see how he responded to her thanks because his errants moved to block her access to him. The whole clump of green-clad Monatese disappeared swiftly into Green Pavilion.

Ayrium took a couple of steps back, staring after them, and nearly bumped into a small boy behind her.

"Hi, Ayrium!" a voice piped up to warn her.

Turning, she discovered Eler Nersal dressed in a ruffled shirt and stretchy trousers with no scrap of Nersallian braid about him. His mop of brown-black hair was tousled and he wore no sword. He looked flushed, as if he had been darting about on the Plaza evading shopkeepers like a hungry rascal at a fair on Barmi, or perhaps evading Black Hearth errants charged with the thankless task of keeping an eye on him.

The sight of him raised Ayrium's spirits a little. "Hello, Eler," she said. "What are you doing?"

"Looking for you," he told her, passionately. "I've heard about the bad luck you've been having with the Demish and I've got an idea!" He clasped her hand and towed her in the direction of the arch exiting the Plaza through the Palace Shell. "There's an exhibition tournament on right now," he said. "You could enter!"

She allowed herself to be led for the moment, but she laughed at the idea. "That's no way for a woman to get noticed by a Demish suitor, Eler! I doubt they'll even let me enter!"

"They'll let anyone enter," he insisted, tugging harder. "I know, because someone came to invite Horth and he's not even Demish! Horth wouldn't go. The Silvers who invited him were crestfallen. I told them he only fights for real. I think that's right," he added, with a glance back at her over his shoulder. "I don't know Horth as well as I knew Branst. He left home before I was born."

"I'm sure you'll get to know him soon enough," she assured the excitable child. "He seems to care about you and your sister, Sanal."

"All the more reason not to get fond of him," Eler insisted.

Ayrium stopped him, crouched down, and pulled the skinny child around to face her. "Why do you say that, Eler?"

The boy looked back at her defiantly. "Because he's going to get killed any day now!" Eler slipped free of her grip and tore off again, shouting, "This way! Hurry!"

Reluctant to let him go off on his own, Ayrium decided to follow. He set quite a pace for a scamp with short legs, at first, but he gave out on the flight of wide, shallow stairs leading down to the Palace Plain. She came to sit companionably beside him while they caught their breath together.

"Tell me about the Purple Alliance," he asked, and she obliged him by answering questions about the kind of people who wound up there and the challenges of all living together. She also took care not to make Barmi sound too attractive to an imaginative child.

"Only around the capital are we hopeless renegades and rebels," she assured him. "Most of the habitable parts of the planet are still occupied by good, solid Blue Demish families."

He nodded gravely. "But you're short of highborns."

She ruffled his hair, smiling. "The few we have just fly harder."

He got up, declaring there would be a car for them at the bottom of the stairs and dashed off again. Not sure what else to do, and charmed by his evident regard for her after so much court rejection, Ayrium followed.

There was, indeed, a car waiting — a rather fine Nersallian one. Its custodians eyed her suspiciously but deferred to Eler's wishes.

"You drive!" he sang out to Ayrium as he leaped into the passenger's seat beside her. "Better not waste any time, though," he added, leaning forward. "Those attendants will blab to Horth for sure and he'll come looking."

"In the habit of running away, are you?" asked Ayrium.

"I haven't run away yet," Eler said. "I'm just exploring."

They parked in a thick mass of other vehicles on the boundary of what was, indeed, a tournament of some kind, although not the Pan Demish Games themselves. Even Ayrium knew the dates for those.

"Are you sure about this?" Ayrium asked her diminutive escort as they marched along a wide boulevard filled with Demish families out to enjoy a day's excitement.

"You're having trouble meeting the right people because you're unconventional, right?" Eler lectured. "So flaunt it! But do it in front of an audience big enough to flush out the people who'll like you because of it. Pure logic," he concluded.

Ayrium wasn't so sure, but on the other hand leaving her name with two dozen heralds over the last three weeks hadn't done her any good, either, nor had loitering in cafés or any of her other strategies. The only people of rank who had not avoided her, thus far, were the handful of men to whom she had been obliged to demonstrate she was not desperate for a quickie in a rented room. The worst part about the latter kind of false start was that she had wasted valuable time being nice to the idiots in case they proved to be meaningful contacts.

Eler picked out one of the raised combat rings on their left, three-quarters surrounded with bleachers, and cried, "Perfect!"

Ayrium could see why. The champion holding this particular ring must have scared off all his competition. He was marching around in a half-bored manner, waiting for someone to get up the courage to challenge him.

"Fine," she said, with a sigh, convinced this would also be futile, and strode forward.

"Ayrium D'Ander D'Aur," she told the ringmaster as she uncoupled her sword belt and drew her sword out of it.

The middle-aged commoner blinked at her from under owlish eyebrows. "My Lady," he spluttered, at a loss. "You are—?"

"A duelist of some skill," she told him, handing him her sword belt. As she jogged up the steps to the stage, she heard him drop her belt to the floor, which was disrespectful. He was supposed to hang it up and take care of it for her.

Big surprise, she thought as she ducked through the ropes surrounding the stage area.

The Demish man in possession of the ring watched her with an incredulous expression.

"I've heard of you," he laughed derisively. "You left a calling card for my cousin's aunt and were bold enough to spend half a day in the company of the family rake finding out why the rest of us won't have you mixing with our wives and sisters!"

"Well, I'm not asking myself to dinner this time," said Ayrium, stung to hear so brutal a summary of her social ineptitude, "just to duel."

The Demish man lowered his sword. "I do not bloody women," he told her.

"It remains to be seen who—" Ayrium began, but the man had already collected his fencing mask from the pole it was resting on and passed his sword to a valet. Ayrium realized two things immediately: first, she didn't have a fencing jacket or mask; and second, no one else was going to step up and oblige her, since losing to her would shame any male Demish challenger, and beating her would hardly be the act of a gentleman.

Even the audience was embarrassed for her. She heard people in the stands clear their throats and saw some contrive to look elsewhere. A couple of young men in the front row put their heads together and snickered.

Then something happened. People looked away from her towards a black-clad man headed straight for Eler, where the boy stood staring worshipfully up at Ayrium.

A whisper went around the stands. "Liege Nersal — Horth Nersal — the new liege of Black Hearth — alone!"

Eler noticed people making way as his elder brother approached, and turned to greet him. Eler pointed towards Ayrium and rattled away in an animated manner. Ayrium found herself feeling all the more embarrassed for the sake of the new Liege Nersal's calm stare in her direction. There she was, alone at the center of the exhibition arena, surrounded by a Demish audience and looking ridiculous. No one was going to challenge her.

She was about to cut her humiliation short by simply leaving the raised stage, when she noticed someone studying Liege Nersal in a curiously intense manner. The stranger was a tall man with brown hair, which was unusual in someone who was otherwise quite Vrellish looking. He wore Monatese colors with a sextant on the breast of his jacket, but no house braid to clarify his rank or family affiliations.

A stir in the crowd alerted her that something exciting was happening. She turned just in time to see Liege Nersal halt in front of the attendant minding the stage, draw his sword, and hand over his sheath before climbing up the three short steps to join her.

Ayrium looked for Eler in the people on the street beside the stands and saw him grinning away happily, as if he'd done something truly splendid for her.

Right. Thanks a megaton, kid, she thought as she turned to face her challenger, politely, and was met by a wall of eerie silence.

"Liege Nersal," Ayrium acknowledged her infamous challenger a bit unsteadily, not so much afraid as discomfited by his composure.

Is he doing me a favor? she wondered, recalling Eler jabbering away to his brother moments earlier. *Or is there some reason why he wants to kill me?*

She didn't have much time to ponder. Liege Nersal nodded to her, once. Then he engaged her.

His movement was Vrellish swift. She never saw his sword, but hers found its place even so, between piercing tip and heart; the swords met, tested each other briefly, and then he slipped back, out of range of her riposte. *He is testing me*, she realized, testing her heart as the Vrellish did not her blade, as a Demish swordsman would. Maybe he did not know how to fight a duel to first blood.

Maybe, but Vrenn had prepared her to face even this. Every practice day for the past twenty-one years he had grimly trained her in the style he himself had learned, growing up *kinf'stan*. Had he survived a certain duel, long ago, with his spirit and honor intact, he might have been a sword to match Horth Nersal; she could see his style echoed in Horth's. She would not shame Vrenn, who could no longer contend in this arena.

And she would not shame her father, her other swordmaster, before the man who had allowed Ev'rel and her son to declare him defeated. The Demish did not matter now; she was done with them. Vrenn, her father, and — most of all — her opponent did. She was not aware of movement, or even intention, only of having moved, and its achievement. A parry upheld; his yielding step backwards. She found, though, that after the first glance, she dared not look into his eyes. They frightened her. She focused on his left arm, her target for a wound.

Afterwards, she heard they'd come together seven times before she finally pressed her attack a fraction too deep, recovered a fraction of a second too late, and received his blade not through her heart, but along her right forearm.

The moment she registered the sudden, piercing pain, Liege Nersal stepped back, sword held in guard, quiescent.

I've lost, she thought, followed by, *I'm still alive*.

The smart of losing in front of the Demish hurt more than the nick on her forearm, but she knew what her opponent was waiting for and acknowledged his hit by lowering her own sword. Blood dripped slowly from the cut on her arm to the floor.

Liege Nersal smiled, once. Then he turned his back and walked off the raised arena floor. Stunned silence prevailed. There was no hooting, no shouts, no pounding the arms of seats or chanting slogans.

Only one man, seated in the nearly empty booth reserved for House Monitum, rose to his feet and began to slap the top of the barrier in front of him with an open palm.

It was the same man Ayrium had noticed watching Liege Nersal, earlier. Despite his brown hair — unusual in a Vrellish Sevolite — he had gray eyes and sharp features with a long, thin nose and an air of intense energy packaged in a tall, lean body. Naturally, he wore a sword, but it looked more like a fashion accessory than a statement of his readiness to live or die by Sword Law. All the same, his decision to be the first to applaud the duel was bold.

For long seconds, the stranger's palm slapping down on the top of wooden barrier was the only sound. Then others joined in one by one. In moments, the whole audience was reacting to the spectacle of the duel they had just watched, breaking out in smatterings of slapping or foot stomping in some quarters, and talk in others. There were still no hoots and no songs.

Ayrium took a deep breath and dared to feel pleased. She hadn't won, but she had held her own with a duelist who impressed the hell out of the bashful champions who had declined to face her.

She sheathed her sword, squared her shoulders, and clamped a hand over her cut to slow the bleeding before she marched off the stage. No one greeted her with congratulations, but her arrival at the base of the raised arena floor interrupted a couple of blonde Demish swordsmen in the midst of making sense of what had happened.

"Course he wouldn't go too hard on a Demish woman!" one was saying to the other.

Before Ayrium could decide how, and if, she wanted to react, the Monatese stranger who'd begun the applause was there, taking charge.

"'A Demish woman with a sword... is a woman with a sword,'" declared the Monatese man. "It's a Vrellish maxim. Naturally, one has to appreciate the underlying assumption of a woman with a sword being as threatening as any man wielding one. I have noticed Demish seem to require centuries to digest the notion."

"Who are you?" one of the Demish princes asked with a sneer, declining to be addressed in peerage. He spoke down two birth ranks, instead, suggesting that Ayrium's admirer must be a Seniorlord.

"I am Amra," the stranger introduced himself, "from Monitum. I'm staying in Green Hearth." He refused to up-speak the prince and stuck to *rel*-peerage.

"You aren't a Royalblood!" his opponent insisted, dropping his own estimate of Amra's status by another birth rank. "Not if you're from Monitum!"

Muscles clenched and relaxed in Amra's jaw. "No," he said, "not Royalblood, but I am a highborn — a Highlord from Sanctuary — not much of a sword by your high standards here at court, I grant you, but Vrellish enough to ask the lady I applauded to redress the slight if you won't offer peerage as a courtesy to a naïve, Vrellish visitor." He punctuated the suggestion with a smile.

The Demish prince shot Ayrium a resentful look, glared at Amra, and decided to avoid all pronouns. He punched his friend on the shoulder and jerked his head, instead. Both Demish men cleared off.

Amra turned his full his attention to Ayrium. "May I have the pleasure of buying you a meal to celebrate?" he asked Ayrium.

"Celebrate?" was all she could think to say. "I lost!"

"Far from it," he disagreed, urbanely, "you achieved something no one else has managed. You induced the new liege of Nersal to exhibit his talents." He paused for a heartbeat. "Are you a friend of Horth Nersal's?"

"Friend? No," She glanced down at her arm, which was starting to smart badly. "More of an acquaintance. He used to fly for Bryllit Nersal, in Killing Reach, so we've encountered each other a few times, and he could hardly avoid knowing something about me by reputation. I'm Ayrium D'Ander D'Aur." It was hard to say her father's name. So many unfinished symphonies of emotion were wrapped up in it and doomed to stay that way forever.

Amra nodded. "You are D'Ander's daughter, gifted to your Blue Demish mother in the Vrellish fashion — in Demish terms, a bastard. You are twenty-five, the self-styled Protector of the Purple Alliance, and court-acknowledged liege of Barmi, although your mother runs things back home and a Nersallian exile named Vrenn commands the home guard for practical purposes. But you are a necessary figurehead and a critical asset in the cockpit and on the challenge floor, should the need arise, although you have not yet fought a public duel on the Octagon. D'Ander stood between your alliance and the houses of the Ava Oath since his decision to sire you. I expect you find yourself in need of new connections, given the outcome of the custody duel over Amel."

Ayrium's golden eyebrows had drifted up as Amra talked, lodging in twin arches at their apex. She kept inhaling in surprise as he continued. When he was finished, she searched herself for a reaction and was forced to settle on astonishment.

"You are a bold man!" she accused him. "And a well-informed one."

"Politics," he said, flicking his long fingers with a strangely precise gesture in which each finger snapped out one by one, in a fan which stayed frozen in place just long enough to notice before the whole hand dropped limply back to his side. "It's something of a specialty with me. I am a scholar."

"And a Highlord, apparently," she said. "That's surprising. The Monatese worry about Liege Monitum being their last living highborn, too valuable to risk his life, while all this time there's been another?"

"I was not discovered until recently," said Amra, stroking his tapered chin. "Having chosen a life of scholarship in the libraries on Sanctuary, a genotyping did not seem necessary to me. But with the acute shortage, people were looking. I was tested, and... well, there you have it. So I have come to court to do my duty by House Monitum."

"To marry?" Ayrium asked.

"Too Vrellish for marriage!" he said. "But come, let us find a place more conducive to civilized conversation! And get that arm seen to."

"All right," she said, looking down at her fingers clamped over her bloody forearm. She could use some friendly company and Amra might turn out to be a useful contact. "If you pay," she added. "I have means, but not enough negotiable court currency to squander on luxuries."

"Done!" he said happily.

Amra took her to a clinic on the ground level of the Market Round to get her arm seen to. Most of the clinic's clientele seemed to be lesser Sevolites of the petty Sevolite challenge class, but Amra claimed the place had a good reputation, which he knew about by virtue of his house connections. Monitum supplied the clinic with its Luverthanian medicines. No one mentioned she had earned the nick in a duel with the enigmatic Liege Nersal, so they escaped without incident. Even the bandage they provided was discreetly flesh-colored.

Satisfied with Ayrium's treatment, Amra hired a car and asked her if she had a preference for where to dine. He suggested a place in the Apron District, and another in West Alcove. Then Ayrium remembered the name of the establishment D'Ander had promised to take her to after the duel and she knew she had to go there. It felt almost as if she were keeping an appointment with her father.

"Ameron's Wake," she said.

Amra scowled. "Never heard of it."

"It's a place on the Ava's Way," she told him.

"I know it," their petty Sevolite driver assured them.

"This place," Amra asked the driver with a decidedly snooty air, "is it honorable?"

"It's safe enough, Your Grace," the driver said, "for anyone faithful to Sword Law."

"It's the only place I want to eat dinner," Ayrium insisted. "My father meant to take me there."

"Very well, then," Amra agreed, but with a definite touch of annoyance.

The Ameron's Wake Emporium

They climbed into the back of the car from either side, each of them briefly preoccupied with managing their dueling swords during this operation. But Amra continued to look sulky.

As they got underway, she heard him mutter, "Silly name, *Ameron's Wake*."

Ayrium swatted him.

He reacted with surprise, then relaxed again. "No lack of respect to your late father intended," he mended his manners. "I understand D'Ander was an Ameronite and that he believed Di Mon to be one."

"Di Mon is," said Ayrium harshly. "He just won't say it."

"If you mean that the current Liege Monitum has too great an opinion of Ameron, then I must agree," Amra told her. "But what exactly is an *Ameronite*, if it pleases you to tell me?"

Ayrium wrinkled her nose at his odd diction. "Sometimes you sound like an actor in an old Demish play," she said.

"Sanctuary is a little behind the times," said Amra, frowning. "But I am picking up new patterns of speech quickly." He changed the subject abruptly. "How is your arm?"

"It will do," she said, flexing her hand as she inspected the dressing cuffed to her forearm. The medic had said it would heal cleanly, but it still hurt and was itching like crazy. "But a few stiff drinks won't go amiss."

Amra smiled. They rode in silence for a moment as he studied her and she returned the favor. He was restless in a typically Vrellish way — full of energy. She had a hard time imagining him studying in a faraway library. His scrutiny of her was equally frank and pointedly masculine.

"If you are not at court to marry," she said after a moment, "is it to child-gift?" She was a bit embarrassed to ask a thing like that flat out.

"Yes," he said, as comfortable discussing sex as most Vrellish people were. "I am child-gifting to Tessitatt Monitum for the good of all Monatese." He smiled again. "That is much how Tess thinks of it, also. She is young, and I understand she was in love with one of Horth Nersal's older brothers, now deceased. It can happen, even to Vrellish couples."

"You approve of love?" asked Ayrium, surprised and involuntarily curious.

"Heartily, although Sevolites are best off conceiving it for a *lyka*." He laughed. "Which is ironic, since love is a clever trick of biochemistry meant to benefit an offspring, and a *lyka* is the least important person for a Sevolite to breed with. The trouble with love is that it's indiscriminate. Take Tessitatt's case. Her first child was sired by Branst Nersal, which makes the boy more of a liability to the Monatese than an asset, for fear of encroachment by the Nersallian *kinf'stan*."

"But Horth waived challenge rights!" said Ayrium, goaded by an instinctive urge to defend the tragic romance. "I heard he gifted the child to Monitum with no strings attached."

"Indeed," Amra acknowledged. "But, in the end, his promise will be no better than the strength of his sword arm. Who knows what might happen if young Nersal goes down before a challenger? Although I rate his chances better now than I did before seeing his performance with you."

"You mean beating me?" said Ayrium, with a touch of a resentment for the pointed reminder.

Amra leaned over to lay a long-fingered hand on her knee. "I mean seeing him spar with an excellent sword." He leaned back again. "I think we're there."

Ameron's Wake was a two-storey building one street back from the brothels, theaters and gambling houses that lined the Ava's Way. The district was well-lighted, despite its address on the strip known as Dim Street. All the buildings looked like grand old residences abandoned by circumstance and taken over by commerce. The storefronts Ayrium glimpsed along the way were interesting. She noticed a sign advertising glow-plastic fixtures, and another place that rented out staff to Petty Sevolites to act as temporary pseudo-errants for special occasions. There was also a store advertising braid and house devices worked in lace, weave, or embroidery, which was further evidence that the district catered to those wishing to keep up appearances, but lacked the means to maintain enough servants and retainers to do it all in-house.

Ameron's Wake was an emporium. Its lighted, glow-plastic sign said, "Welcome all who mourn for Ava Ameron!" A placard posted on a board beside the door listed the stores inside, the current menu for the ground-floor restaurant, and the evening's entertainment.

Amra balked, staring. Ayrium tugged.

"Come on!" she cried, as eager to go inside as if her father waited just inside the doors.

A smiling doorman dressed in period clothes of 200 years earlier, during the reign of Ava Ameron, ushered them in and onto the floor of the big square building. A grand portrait of Ameron occupied pride of place at the far end of the hall, hung from the second-storey banister on a heavy chain, like some kind of gigantic locket. The Lost Ava was grand in this portrait, which had been done by a Golden Demish artist famous enough to be significant, but not enough for Ayrium to know much about. The artist's name, Prince Gilanderon was so large that it obscured the details of books stacked on a table by the Ava's side.

Ayrium heard a groan and looked at Amra in time to see him lock his jaw and roll his eyes. The resemblance between the painting on the wall and the man from Monitum beside her was so striking, for an instant, that she had to catch her breath. The next moment the similarity seemed ridiculous. The Ava in the painting was powerful, aloof and arrogant. The man beside her looked peevish and fundamentally languid beneath a habitual air of confidence, more like a broken man.

Family resemblance would, of course, be strong in any group as inbred as the Lor'Vrellish, thought Ayrium. But just the idea that Amra might be more Lor'Vrellish than Monatese was intriguing to her. She had never met a Lor'Vrel or a Lorel. Both White Hearth and Brown Hearth, on Fountain Court, were managed by the Monatese, in trust.

"Must we stay here?" Amra said grumpily, making her break eye contact with the portrait overhead to see what he was looking at.

The pictures mounted on the walls of the emporium, between shops, made her laugh, which alarmed her because the subject matter was grave. They made the portrait by Prince Gilanderon look sober and drab by comparison. 'Grand heroic' was the phrase that sprang to mind.

"It's the story of how Ameron was betrayed by the Demish and saved by his First Sworn, Liege Monitum," said Ayrium, tracing her finger in the air to follow the narrative around the room. She had to admit she was charmed despite — or even because — of the larger-than-life style of the work, and the artist was much better than Prince Gilanderon. More modern, too, she suspected. She gave respectful attention, frame by frame, to vignettes from the drama of how Ameron was wounded by traitorous vassals and fled with Liege Monitum towards *TouchGate Hospital*. The last image was a stylistic depiction of how they were Lost in the first jump along the route, between Killing Reach and Golden Reach.

"It is all nonsense," Amra said, peevishly, "the stuff of legend that thrives in a climate of incomplete information. People think Ameron was lost in the Killing Jump, for example, based on rumors of spiritual encounters with Ameron's Lost Soul reported by Monatese pilots who continued to make the jump to keep it in living memory, despite the ban on re-establishing relations with the Reetions. But Ameron was going to *TouchGate Hospital*! Why not assume he was Lost making the Luverthanian Jump?"

Ayrium hardly heard Amra's curmudgeonly complaints. She had lost interest in the story art ringing the emporium's walls because she had noticed something much more immediate and heartbreaking.

In the middle of the floor, right in front of them, temporarily masked by a mob of shoppers wandering about the emporium, was a prominent exhibit mourning Prince D'Ander.

A life-sized painting of D'Ander rested on a black-draped easel. A replica sword hung off the top, as if the figure in the portrait had only just hung it there while he went in for dinner and would return to pick it up. The most expensive plaque the proprietor of such a place could afford, Ayrium was sure, sat at the base of the easel. It declared D'Ander both a valued client and a brave believer in Ameron as a *zer-rel*, the type of great soul who was sent to guide the living through acts of strength in troubled times. Patrons of the Ameron's Wake emporium had left offerings, in D'Ander's name, in a bowl set before the memorial that was watched by a guard of honor, no doubt hired from the agency next door. Whatever their origins, however, the guards made a good show of standing solemnly at attention, dressed in a uniform plausible enough to not quite trespass on the actual trappings of any house, while managing to suggest something of Lor'Vrellish origins.

Almost as though they had been sent by Ameron, thought Ayrium. D'Ander would have liked that.

Offerings in the bowl included personal belongings such as rings and necklaces, as well as low-denomination honor chips from a half a dozen different houses. Throne chips were most numerous, followed by Silver Demish currency and a couple of green chips of Monatese issue. There were even some commoner coins, used among those too poor to trade in even the lowest official currencies of Fountain Court. Commoners got such coins from money changers whose exchange rates varied with the tides of commerce in UnderGelion, making them a volatile but unavoidable necessity. Such evidence of respect for her dead father from so diverse a spectrum of society fixed a knot of pain in Ayrium's chest that made her wish she could relieve it with tears.

Amra took Ayrium's elbow gently from behind. "Are you all right, Liege Barmi?" he asked.

She turned to him, feeling raw with emotion. "I was half expecting to find him here, you know. Isn't that odd?"

"If it is too uncomfortable—" Amra began.

Ayrium forced a smile, blinking dry eyes that stung. "I wouldn't want to be anywhere else."

She produced a couple of throne-issue chips and tossed them in the bowl. Then she undid a small lacework choker from around her neck, hidden beneath her clothes, and knelt to put that in, too.

"I was angry with him," said Ayrium, still kneeling before the shrine to her father, with her eyes on the donation bowl. "Angry about how he kept hiding me from his Golden relatives, and how he took over and ran things for Amel without really giving Amel much choice in the matter. Or me, either, for that matter. I meant to have it out with him once and for all after the duel. Now..."

"Do you believe the dead watch the living while they wait to be reborn?" Amra asked her, in a carefully neutral tone.

Ayrium looked back at him over one shoulder. "Sometimes."

"Well then," said Amra, tossing in two green-colored chips of his own, "tell him now."

Ayrium looked back at the impromptu shrine and tried, but her anger had gone flat. She said simply, "I wish you were here with me now, Dad." Then, for Perry, she added, "Damn your Golden hide!"

She felt the tears come then, at last.

Amra raised her up and turned her in his arms to wipe the tears away with his thumbs. There was something so matter-of-fact about it that she let him hold her as grief took hold and her shoulders shook.

"Company," Amra murmured, moments later, and shifted them apart.

The new arrival was the emporium's proprietor. He was a dapper little man with a round belly in a period costume, his big eyes fixed on Amra. He had to force himself to revert his attention to Ayrium when she turned around.

"Thank you for this shrine to Prince D'Ander," said Ayrium, swiping at her tears with the back of one hand. It was polite for her to speak first, to spare him the risk of offending her. She pegged him as a commoner, five ranks her inferior. He confirmed it in his answer.

"You are Ayrium, aren't you?" asked the round-faced man. "D'Ander's daughter."

"I am."

The little man bowed. "You are welcome here. Your meal is on the house."

"That's very generous, but—"

"I insist, Your Grace!" cried their excitable host. "Your father did us much honor with his visits and we miss him very sorely now that he's gone." No sooner had he finished than his gaze tracked back towards Amra like a compass needle to a magnet.

"Amra, of House Monitum, visiting from Sanctuary," Ayrium's date introduced himself. "And you are?"

"Penwick," said their host, whose graying hair stood out from either side of his face in tufts, although the top of his head was bald. "Ryan Penwick, descended from—"

"Ameron's valet!" exclaimed Amra, with an unexpected sharpening of tone. Then he laughed, looking around him. "Gods! Is that what all this nonsense is about?"

"It isn't nonsense!" Ayrium came to life again, in no mood for Monatese airs of superiority. Penwick's display might be gaudy, but his love for her father was genuine. "Ameron matters to these people! He mattered to my father. And if this is how they choose to honor him, it's their right."

"You are Monatese," Penwick said to Amra, nodding sagely. "The Monatese sometimes feel a sort of trespass about anyone else admiring Ameron. I completely understand! It is an honor to have you here at all. Why, you might even be a relative of Ameron's on the Lor'Vrellish side, Your Grace. You have the look."

Amra glanced at the life-size portrait hung from the second story balcony above and scowled. "There is Lor'Vrel in most Monatese, of course," he acknowledged in a surly tone, "but you mistake the nature of my objection. I do not resent the way you honor Ameron, but that you honor him at all! I am a historian, good Penwick. It irks me that you cannot see, through the lens of history, how the man you venerate is nothing but a failed Ava!"

They had attracted attention by now, and both staff and customers snatched in a breath at this vehement denouncement of their favorite icon.

Ayrium took Amra by the arm with a forceful jerk, wishing they were on Barmi. She could have solved things with a shove into a manure trough, there.

"Just show us to a table, Mister Penwick," she said, "and I'll put him right about Ameron."

"Yes, of course!" The proprietor said, blinking back astonished tears. But he led them off briskly to his best table.

"Let me guess," said Ayrium, walking with her arm through Amra's. "You also insult Souls of Light at *Okal Lumens* ceremonies and debate rulings of the *zer'stan* with Nesaks."

"Cynicism is a Lor'Vrellish failing," Amra snapped, and then added, "which rubs off on Monatese who read too much. Come, have a drink. You need one."

The proprietor returned with a decanter of Nersallian brandy, apologizing that they had no Monatese Turquoise in stock.

"Fool," Amra muttered as Penwick scurried off.

"My father liked him," said Ayrium.

Amra filled up her tumbler. "Aye," he muttered darkly, "because he fawns over Ameron."

"While you claim Ameron failed as an Ava." Ayrium leaned forward on her elbows. Between D'Ander's shrine on the floor and Ameron's portrait, the notion of being watched was all too tangible. She couldn't let Amra's slurs pass.

"Of course he failed!" Amra said testily, casting the 'he' for Ameron in *rel*-peerage.

"He," Ayrium corrected, up-speaking the long lost Ava by the correct two birth ranks.

Amra gave her a look that would have translated in Killing Reach, as: "I'll up-speak the bastard when the last sun burns out!"

Ayrium rebelled. She set her fist down slowly and carefully between them. "I'm enjoying your company and gods ignore me, but I want to get drunk! So you, Amra of Monitum, will up-speak Ava Ameron as he's entitled, as a Pureblood, or I'll break your nose and spoil the evening for us both!"

Amra looked from her face to her fist. "Peace," he said, and leaned back. "Have a drink, and we'll discuss it like civilized human beings." He raised a palm to signal his surrender. "I will up-speak Ameron out of respect for your father, if it pleases you."

Slowly, Ayrium sat down and relaxed, not sure if she was satisfied, and aware she was about to face a debate with a Lor'Vrel — or a Monatese scholar, which was just as bad. She took a swig of the Nersallian brandy. It was mildly sweet, with a bite to the aftertaste. Comforting warmth exploded through her chest.

Amra gestured with his long, energetic fingers whenever he wasn't drinking from his own tumbler. "Now," he said, "for the facts. Ameron set out to end the Killing War, and succeeded. But he should never have tried to reopen talks with the Reetions. He risked everything else he'd achieved in the previous eleven years by trying to do one more thing than he should have, and failed."

"He was betrayed!" Ayrium insisted, waving her half-empty tumbler in Amra's direction. A highborn had to drink a lot, fast, to benefit from the exercise.

Amra topped her glass up again, and then his own. "He misread the Demish," he agreed with her, although casting it as Ameron's fault once more. "They weren't ready. He was too impatient, and after only eleven years in power. As a result, the important work he had got started fell apart again as soon as he was gone!"

"Not all of it!" Ayrium said stubbornly.

"Such as?"

"He stabilized the throne currency and placed limits on money-changing windfalls."

Amra shrugged. "Any strong Ava could have done that."

"He established freeholds on Gelion," said Ayrium, "allowing commoners to lease property from the Throne on terms with enough stability to make places like this one possible!"

Amra laughed. "Next, you'll tell me he deserves to be revered for introducing the Ava's dole!" He scowled. "All that does is prolong the misery of houseless commoners."

Ayrium inhaled to defend the utility of the Throne-run soup kitchens on the Palace Plain for those without the means to feed themselves, but Amra preempted her.

"The point is," he said, throwing an arm over the back of his chair, "neither the dole nor the freeholds were part of Ameron's agenda to begin with. They were unimportant trivia."

"Not to the commoners of UnderGelion!" exclaimed Ayrium.

"Yes, yes," Amra said impatiently, leaning forward to refill both their glasses. "But what about drawing the Vrellish out of Red Reach and into the empire to neutralize the Nesak threat? What about reopening Avatlan Lor'Vrel's clinic in the UnderDocks to reduce our dependence on *TouchGate Hospital* in the medical sciences? Putting an end to conscience bonding. Establishing emergency relief tax. Bridging the Vrellish-Demish divide at court. Initiating deep-space exploration. Cultivating a middle class. Colonizing the surface of Gelion. And most of all, redefining Pureblood to include anyone more than 80% Sevolite to prevent exactly the sort of convulsions of violence and corruption that erupted around the throne after Ameron's loss! None of it happened!"

Ayrium wagged a finger at him. "All conjecture! I've never heard those particular notions concerning Ameron's goals. And even if you do have access to some secret document preserved on Sanctuary to prove it — so what? No one ever achieved everything they set out to do!"

Amra filled her tumbler again.

"How old are you?" she demanded, on impulse. It was almost impossible to tell with any highborn unless you asked.

He gave a start, spilling the drink he was pouring for himself, and paused to shake drops of brandy off his hand with a distasteful air.

"Penwick!" Amra called in a commanding voice.

Proprietor Penwick had been hovering within hailing distance. He hurried over with a damp cloth to clean up, and another for Amra to wash his hand. The washcloth steamed gently. Amra waited for him to finish in silence, then dismissed him with a curt order to fetch another jug.

Ayrium was starting to feel the first jug's effects but she knew her capacity as a Highlord. Besides, she'd seen Amra drink the other half just as thirstily. He wouldn't get an edge on her that way!

"I am older than I look," he said, and laughed, "older than I am, too, if one could make sense of that!" He sobered up. "Why?" he asked her warily.

"I don't know," she said, feeling foolish now that she'd asked. "It just crossed my mind how it would be the sort of thing the Monatese would do to hide a son or daughter of Ameron's — your mother maybe? — who didn't want to be involved in court politics." She leaned forward on both elbows, feeling the table damp beneath her skin where Penwick had wiped up. "You talk about Ameron as if you knew him," said Ayrium.

Amra gave a snort.

Ayrium poured for them both from the fresh decanter. They drank in silence for long minutes.

"D'Ander should have met you," she said, her eyes filling up at the thought of her father. "He should be explaining to you why Ameron is so important." She looked about her vaguely, as if half expecting D'Ander to offer support from the afterlife. Then she began to cry.

"Oh, no," Amra protested. But he instantly relented, rose swiftly, and raised her out of her chair and into his arms as if he had every right. The mix of grief and brandy made her grateful. She muttered something about being all right, but he said, "Tears are a Demish gift. Welcome them."

She drew back, feeling self-conscious despite the brandy. He grew quiet, watching her gazing back at him, still in the circle of his arms. Then he said softly, "You are a woman of rare beauty for one so vigorous and of rare vigor for one so Golden."

She smiled, feeling flirtatious. "Is that a warning?"

"You are here at court to marry," he said by way of answer. "Does that not still require virginity on the part of a Demish woman?"

Ayrium giggled. "Well, it's too late for me if it does," she said, and kissed him.

"Excellent," he said, pulling her into a prolonged embrace.

She drew back after the first, exciting kiss, feeling breathless. "Discretion, of course, is advised in such matters."

He nodded.

She took his hand firmly in hers. "But I have to show you something first." She grinned. "I haven't conceded the argument."

He followed her meekly enough to one of the stores below the overhanging balcony where Ameron's portrait was hanging.

"These are charms," she said, lifting a pendant off a rack. The face on the stamped metal cameo was a stylized version of Ameron's. "Commoners wear them for good luck, and so do some Sevolites. My father would have, if he hadn't considered it tacky."

"The man had judgment," said Amra dryly.

Ayrium tugged him along to another stall. "Figurines. People collect them for their sideboards and mantles. You can get any Ava, of course, but Ameron's are particularly popular."

"More nonsense, then," said Amra. "A typical display of yearning towards stable times, in unstable ones. It does not mean Ameron achieved his goals."

"How much could he achieve in eleven years?" asked Ayrium.

"My point exactly. He had no business pursuing relations with the Reetions so soon."

Ayrium brightened. "So you really think that's what Ameron was up to in Killing Reach, then? Dad thought so, too. I wish—" She shook her head, feeling more tears threaten. "No, I've already said that. I have to move on. I have to put aside my feelings about Ev'rel, too! I've more important things to do now, and little enough idea of how to manage it."

Amra turned her around to face him. "Do you hate Ev'rel for luring D'Ander into a life-and-death duel?"

Ayrium could hold it in no longer. "I hate her for cheating!" she said hotly, and wiped her nose on a napkin. Her eyes were filling up again, but she wasn't ashamed of the tears this time.

"Explain," Amra demanded. He had a knack for making requests sound like commands, but she didn't mind. She was ready to tell someone. She just wished he looked as tipsy as she felt.

"I think," she said, "Ev'rel used Amel to distract D'Ander. Just for an instant, I grant you. D'Therd is good — better than anyone imagined — but he should have lost!"

Amra looked grave. "You believe D'Therd and Ev'rel, between them—"

Ayrium shook her head. "I don't think D'Therd was waiting for it, no. But he exploited the chance his mother gave him when the sight of Ev'rel's medic triggered a clear dream in Amel. At first I didn't understand why Amel reacted so strongly, but now I realize this medic is the Mira featured in Amel's captured memories. Ev'rel must have known she was, and hoped Amel's reaction would throw Dad off!"

Amra pressed his lips together in silence for long seconds before he ruled on the matter. "Impossible to prove," he said.

Ayrium nodded glumly, feeling hopelessly sad and more than a little drunk.

They had strolled as they talked and arrived, under his guidance, at the stairs leading up to the second floor. Ayrium hesitated only briefly.

What the hell, she thought defiantly, took his arm in hers, and waited for him to take the lead since he seemed to know where they were going.

It wasn't until they reached the top of the stairs that Amra spoke again. "Does Amel want to be Ava?" he asked her.

"No," she told him firmly, "but D'Ander considered himself Amel's paladin. He truly did!" she insisted, adding sourly, "It wasn't all about regaining power at court for Demora!"

Penwick appeared magically, as Amra must have anticipated. He gave them a two-room suite to themselves. Amra waved aside Ayrium's offer to pay half. "Bill it to House Monitum," he told the proprietor. "And send us some food and more brandy, but no entertainment. Leave us to ourselves."

"Certainly!" Penwick enthused.

Ayrium went into the suite and looked around. "Nice," she remarked. There was a table just a little above floor level on the left, with sunken seating all around it strewn with pillows. Tables and couches suitable for a small reception lined the walls. The second room was a private bedroom with hygiene facilities attached. She explored until the food and drink arrived.

Amra had everything set up and waiting for her on the table when she got back. He had loosened his vest, as well, and shed his sword. It was sitting in a rack near the bedroom door.

Ayrium made up her mind and put her own sword into the rack beside Amra's. "There is something... *impossible...* about you," she said.

"Strangely enough," he said, pouring brandy, "I've heard that before."

"How Vrellish are you?" asked Ayrium as she settled beside him on the cushions.

He smiled. "Enough to warn you we are doomed, romantically."

She smiled, loosening her vest. "I thought this was just about good company, and sex."

He helped her undress. His fingers were long, swift and sure. He kissed her face, his fingers brushing the bare skin of her shoulders. She kissed back, in no hurry. It was nice being with him. "I should bathe, first," she said. "It's sweaty work fighting Horth Nersal."

"Later," he suggested.

Typically for a man, he was less interested in shedding all of his clothes than he was in helping her out of hers. But she insisted.

"I am nothing special to look at," he warned her, as she teased him out of the long, loose tunic he wore under his vest and jacket.

"Not from your perspective, maybe," she said, tossing her hair back. She felt pleasantly relaxed with him — safe, in some odd way having nothing to do with prowess in fighting. She did not expect any great martial skills in a scholar.

The ugly scar on his thigh surprised her. It was fresh, the surrounding flesh still discolored in mottled greens, browns and purples, and looked serious enough to have been life threatening. It had been expertly repaired, but there was evidence of hasty first aid, which was now in the process of smoothing out and correcting itself as highborn injuries did.

"What happened?" she exclaimed, looking into his face.

"History," he replied mildly, and kissed her.

He took her to the bedroom, along with the fresh decanter of brandy, and made love to her. They washed each other afterwards and kept on drinking, sitting on the bed draped in dressing gowns supplied by their host. He ordered more food, billing it all to Green Hearth again. For Ayrium, who was accustomed to living on a budget while at court, it felt extravagant.

She was grateful for the food in particular. She couldn't remember being this drunk since her sixteenth birthday, when she'd set out to prove she could drink a less-Sevolite friend under the table. Amra matched her glass for glass and never lost his wits, although he laughed more readily.

Near the end of the meal, on the bed, she spilled a sweet sauce on her creamy white dressing gown and wet it with water to try scrubbing at it.

"Take it off," he ordered instead.

Ayrium looked up, giddily, and blinked at him. "Huh?" She couldn't see how removing the robe would help get the stain out.

He came towards her on his knees across the wide, firm bed, and demonstrated what he wanted by easing the lapels of her dressing gown off her shoulders.

"You are glorious in nothing," he assured her.

"Oh yeah?" she said, glowing pleasantly with a sated feeling. "Fine." She waggled a hand at him. "But if you get to stare at me, I get to stare at you."

"Ack!" he scoffed at her. "That is too Vrellish an attitude for someone with eyes so blue. I am a man, like all men. It is women who are beautiful."

"Depends on your perspective," Ayrium disagreed, grinning back at him. It was true that his face had neither the bold good looks of her father, nor the sweetly expressive glory of Amel's face. But it was so alive! Especially since he'd stopped brooding behind his wall of aloof superiority. And there was something exotically tantalizing about the possibility of him being Lor'Vrellish. His strong features tended toward Vrellish sharpness and his eyes were a Vrellish gray, for certain, but she had decided his black hair had dark brown roots, on close inspection.

In the tussle to divest each other of their dressing gowns they fell off the bed and onto the carpeted floor. He rolled on top of her, bracing his elbows on either side of her face as he stroked her golden blonde hair, smiling to himself as he admired her.

"You are beautiful," he told her with authority, and kissed her. Then he gave his attention to her breasts, using only his hands and his eyes. He seemed quite content to explore her that way indefinitely, for his own pleasure, fascinated by the firmness of her strong body beneath her womanly contours. It was Ayrium who lost patience and rolled him over with a mock growl to get down to business again.

He fended her off playfully. "Art thou sure thy mother did not bequeath thee more Vrellish genes than she owns up to, My Lady!" he laughed at her, lapsing into archaic usage again, like something from a 200-year-old play. She decided it had to be an affectation. Maybe he thought it was cute to sound literary.

They made a game of her needing to get him interested in seconds, until it succeeded too well to sustain the joke. She also discovered he was ticklish along the ribs, which proved an excellent secret weapon.

They fell asleep tangled in each other's limbs, wrapped in an alcoholic haze of forgetfulness.

Ayrium woke with a hangover worse than a bad post-fight migraine.

Amra was sitting up in bed beside her, talking to himself. "Damn thou mad Gods!" he said, and smacked the heel of his left hand squarely into his forehead. "There must have been brain damage!" He followed up with muttered curses less distinct and very definitely out of fashion.

Ayrium bounced onto her knees despite her pounding head. "What is it?" she exclaimed. A quick inspection of the room revealed no danger, but his attitude alarmed her.

"*Ferni!*" he exclaimed with a great sigh and threw himself back on the bed with an arm thrown across his face. "I forgot I am not using *ferni*."

"Oh," said Ayrium. The good news was that they were not about to be hacked apart by assassins. The bad news was that he clearly seemed distressed about the matter on his own behalf, not hers, which was hardly flattering.

Ferni was the Luverthanian drug that repressed fertility. It came in male and female varieties tailored to a Sevolite's race and rank. But more importantly, although widely used on the quiet, it had sordid connotations. Among the Demish, to use *ferni* was to admit sex was merely recreational, which wasn't respectable. For the Vrellish, it was an insult to the Waiting Dead because it denied them access to rebirth. More specifically, in Vrellish terms, a desirable male who used *ferni* insulted his partner by implying she was fine for rolling around with in bed but unsuitable for sharing genes with. It was the males, among the Vrellish, who were scolded for bestowing their favors too freely in the wrong quarters.

Ayrium felt silly about being offended, since she felt more than a little stupid on her own behalf about the risk of getting pregnant — of all things! — at this point in her quest for Demish allies. She should have guessed he wouldn't be on *ferni*, since he was here for the express purpose of child-gifting to Di Mon's niece, Tessitatt. Despite all that, she couldn't set aside the irksome presumption in his tone of voice, as if he was the one who felt exploited by the situation!

He turned to her abruptly. "Are you on *ferni*?"

"I'm sure it won't be a — no," she admitted, and felt her face burn with mixed embarrassment and anger at his reaction because he had the gall to look suspicious!

He waved a hand as if to erase the suggestion she'd seduced him for his genes. "We are a pair of fools, then," he concluded.

He got up briskly and began to dress without washing.

She watched him a moment, feeling awkward. She hadn't expected anything more than one good night together. Yet the idea he might walk out of her life now, as casually as he had entered it, did not sit well, either.

When he was dressed he came and sat beside her. "Breakfast?" he asked, smiled, and kissed her. He did not look as hung over as she felt, which was not fair, either. All she could manage was a limp nod.

"I'll arrange it," he said, and took himself off to place an order.

Ayrium flopped back on the bed and must have dosed off; her nose brought her around again. She dragged herself up, pulled on his dressing gown — hers had a stain, after all — and followed the good smells into the outer room where she found Amra seated at the table, drinking a spicy-smelling herbal tea and running his eyes swiftly over a nervecloth disk mounted in front of him.

As soon as she appeared he snapped the disk closed and flicked his fingers at the servant waiting to serve them.

Breakfast worked wonders for her hangover.

"Ev'rel is hosting a reception for Prince Amel," he told her unexpectedly, making her spill her tea. He waited for her to recover before adding, "It might be the best way to satisfy yourself about Amel's health and discharge your duty to your father to look after him. Not a bad place to meet eligible Demish bachelors, either." He began tapping a finger quickly on the table.

"Amra," she said, a little harshly, "I told you I tried to get Ev'rel's permission to see Amel and it didn't work. I have no chance of getting into his reception!"

"I'll get you into the reception," he said with a certain, self-aggrandizing confidence.

"You?" she sputtered. "Why would Ev'rel let you do that?"

"We'll be with Di Mon's party," he said, as if this was the easiest and most natural thing in the world.

"Di Mon?" she said. "*The* Di Mon — the 103rd liege of Monitum — the same one you keep billing things to?"

"Yes." He smiled at her rakishly. "Remember, I am child-gifting to his niece, to provide the Monatese with a highborn heir."

"Isn't it rather unlikely," Ayrium was driven by his arrogance not to put too fine a point on it, "that the child of a Seniorlord like Tessitatt and a Highlord like yourself will turn out highborn? I mean, isn't the child much, much more likely to be no better than Seniorlord itself? Which, forgive my bluntness, is hardly valuable. The Monatese already have plenty of excellent nobleborns."

He shrugged. "I feel lucky." Then he smiled. "And if not, we'll try again. She's a capable woman, Tessitatt. I like her."

Ayrium gave herself a quick, stern lecture about her re-action. Amra was not hers to claim in any way. She couldn't afford to get stupidly Demish about this 'relationship.'

"I suppose," she said, to clarify it for both of them, "what happened between us last night makes us *sha'stan* — lovers with no greater connection between them than, oh, I don't know, people who got drunk together?"

"Nonsense," he said. "You aren't Vrellish."

Now she was really perplexed. "What are you proposing then?"

He folded his arms across his chest and considered her with his head cocked to the left. "Mistress," he decided. "Yes, I think I much prefer the Demish word."

"I'm not sure I do!" Ayrium said, stung. If he was teasing, it was certainly in poor taste. "The Demish don't think much of mistresses."

"On the contrary," he said, "Demish men think a great deal of them! But peace!" He raised a palm. "I mean no disrespect. Let us dispense, instead, with names for what we are to one another and simply take my word for it that I am in your debt. You move me, Ayrium D'Ander D'Aur of the Purple Alliance. You, who possess so much beauty, strength, and disinterested honesty, but are *rel* enough to face the liege of Nersal on a sparring floor! No blushing innocent concerning sex and yet, I think, you have a woman's heart. I will not obstruct your mission. I'll help you achieve it. But I would, in the meantime, like to see you again." He paused. "So, would it please you to attend Amel's reception with me?"

"Yes," she said, "to see Amel, if nothing else. I am worried about him."

"It's done then," he said, "on one condition. You go looking and acting like a Demish lady."

Ayrium opened her mouth to protest, but he was out of his chair and at her side in an instant, taking her in his arms. "Yes, yes, I know," he said, "you are more *rel* than the lot of them, and not a lady, but I will not take you if you mean to make trouble over your father: not with D'Therd nor with Ev'rel, either. And as to your main purpose, you'll gain more in a dress on that front — believe me!"

Looking into his face, Ayrium glimpsed an immovable will behind his easy manners. Besides, it would have seemed ungrateful to object to such good common sense.

She sighed. "Agreed. But I have nothing to wear."

"Ah!" he cried, delighted. "Then we shall spend the day deciding such important matters jointly!"

10

Amel's Reception

Waiting

It took an hour and three attendants to dress Amel. He liked the servants, particularly the rosy-cheeked, middle-aged woman who went about her work in a serious, bustling manner, frowning or smiling approval as she fussed with the hang of a sleeve or the lacing of Amel's cuffs. His clothing was all pale blue and soft gold, with hints of his lineage echoed in every bit of decoration, but it didn't bristle with stiff braid — it flowed.

Preparing his hair was the hardest part for him to endure. It was twisted up in a scarf that contrived to look casual but was really set firmly in place, flaring out in a big, loose tail to merge with the design of his soft shirt and trousers. Tiny white flowers that had taken hours to arrange cascaded over his shoulders in delicate strands.

A band across his chest carried the weight of his heritage, assisted by the lacing patterns of his pure white boots. He was fitted out with a jeweled sword designed as a fashion accessory. Even his supposedly perfect face had been touched up to disguise the evidence of sleepless nights.

The rosy-cheeked woman finished lacing his boots and sat back, looking pleased, but she staggered as she struggled to get up, as if her heart couldn't get the blood to her head fast enough. Instinctively, Amel reached down to steady her.

"Oh, no, Immortality!" she said, with a sudden blanching of her ruddy complexion. "You mustn't."

"Isn't he beautiful!" declared the man in charge of the whole process, setting Amel's teeth on edge. He felt every bit as much on display in this outfit as he had in a dancer's sheath while working as a courtesan. The only difference he could see was what was being advertised: his pedigree now or his sex appeal then. But whenever he got vexed about it, he just ended up feeling sad. He couldn't get out of this on his own, and he had no defenders now. D'Ander was dead and Ayrium had wisely forgotten him. Mira hated him, which hurt more than he knew what to do with, and Ev'rel disconcerted him. He couldn't think about the Ava as a mother no matter how often she told him she wanted to protect him, and while he sometimes felt a faint urge to prove himself in her eyes, he wasn't sure what that would look like if it happened. More than anything else he felt certain he was powerless to change the outcome of whatever was slated to happen to him next, so he had decided to minimize his suffering by just letting it happen.

Ev'rel herself swept in, dressed in a stunning gown that was just slightly daring by Demish standards. The servants reacted with a round of bows.

"Splendid!" she pronounced upon Amel's attire. "Dignified, but unmistakably desirable." She brushed a cluster of symbols on the sash across Amel's chest. "Best not to deny the past so much as transform it into legend, don't you think?"

The servant in charge bowed. "Just as you say, Immortality."

Ev'rel dismissed the servants with a gesture. Amel kept a concerned eye on the red-faced woman as they filed out. He hoped she didn't have heart trouble. His concern drew his attention after her, as if he could leave with the servants and retire to a tiny backroom parlor where he could make her comfortable, ask after her health, and share the day's gossip with her like a friend. He was startled back to the present by Ev'rel's touch.

"Sit with me," she instructed him, taking his hands.

He let himself be led over to a divan before a three-panel mirror.

"You will make your entrance in a half an hour," Ev'rel told him, holding both his hands lightly in her own. "You may walk up and down Family Hall, if you like, or go pick a book from the library, but do not mess up your costume or there will be consequences. Now, are you ready for good news?"

Amel nodded ever so slightly, feeling perplexed and out of his element.

"I've found a bride for you," Ev'rel told him, "and today is the first time you will meet her."

He went completely still, not even breathing. He had not expected anything like this! The whole idea was too enormous.

"She is the daughter of Prince H'Us's eldest surviving son," Ev'rel rattled on excitedly, "the Princess Elaya Dassa H'Us. She has been widowed for some years now, is fond of literature, and will make a very proper, dutiful wife. She already has a few children, so we know she'll be fertile. But don't worry, the youngest son is twenty-three and enlisted in fleet training, and all the girls are married. Elaya will be the perfect teacher to help you adjust to court — there will be no tolerance for gossip about your past in her household. And you'll be living right here, in the Palace Sector, with fifty servants waiting on you." Ev'rel laughed with delight.

Amel was speechless. *A wife? A princess? Just like that?* All the places inside him that ought to react to such news felt numb.

Ev'rel patted his hand. "Close your mouth, dear, and don't fret. You can thank me later. Now I must go back to my guests. Can I trust you to behave until you are sent for?"

He nodded. It seemed the only way to get rid of her.

Ev'rel rose in a rustle of silk and adjusted her own costume, which was gloriously fresh and floral, with enough veins of rich blue about it to avoid a clash with her slightly olive complexion. She wore a full skirt and a short jacket with a snug bodice and large, puffy shoulders. She looked very much the attractive Demish matron, with a light-colored scarf woven through her mass of black hair to inject pale yellow highlights. There was nothing she could do about her gray eyes, which were so dark they were almost black, but the blues in the dress warmed them. As long as she stood before him, exerting her personal charisma, Amel was unable to think. He just stared up at her.

Ev'rel leaned down to kiss his cheek before she swept back out of the dressing room.

As soon as she was gone Amel began to fear he would suffer a clear dream if he didn't distract himself somehow.

The next moment, Eler Nersal stuck his head in and said, "Perfect!"

Amel had heard Eler would be attending in lieu of his more sought-after, but reclusive, brother. He smiled when he recognized the boy, then looked surprised as a troupe of five actors, dressed up to enact a Demish drama, followed Eler into his dressing room.

The lead actor froze at the sight of Amel in his regalia. The other four stared.

"Wow," said one of the two women, whose own gown displayed a variation on Golden Demish braid considered acceptable for theatrical usage. Her comrade nudged her and all five actors bowed in unison.

"Are you courtesans?" Amel asked the actors excitedly, his heart skipping lightly at the thought of friendly company. All five of them look disconcerted and the women wary. "Oh, no," he added quickly, "I didn't mean... it's just—"

"Because *you* were one!" cried Eler, plainly delighted by the odd tableau before him. "He doesn't mean anything by it that you have to worry about," he assured the actors.

Amel felt the blood rise in his face beneath what he hoped was the dampening effect of the makeup applied earlier. "I'm sorry if I... well, just sorry," he told the actors in *pol*-peerage, which was wrong too. He could all too easily identify with the dread they must be feeling over being addressed much too casually by a Pureblood! He was wildly relieved when he saw them relax, with a couple quick glances towards Eler.

"You were Von, right?" asked the woman dressed up as a Golden princess, daring a shy smile in Amel's direction. "As a courtesan."

"You know me... uh... knew me?" Amel asked, startled by his pleasure at the prospect.

The lead actor swept him a bow. "Of course!" he said gallantly. "Your Immortality was already immortal as a talent on the dance floor, before the truth of your exalted birth was known!"

"Th-thank you," Amel stammered, correcting his pronouns to match the status conferred on him, firmly, by the actor.

"Come on!" said Eler to the actors, hurrying them along. "You'll be wanted any minute now."

"Right!" said the lead actor, and directed the business at hand, which was sewing up a split seam in one of the men's pants.

"It's a good thing I found a place to do this privately, with all those Demish ladies about," remarked Eler, as the man concerned shucked himself out of his pants.

The three men were garbed, respectively, as a Silver Demish prince, a Blue Demish prince and a Golden Demish errant in the mock livery of the lady who had spoken to Amel. The details came together for him in a flash.

"*The Wooing of Demlara's Daughter*!" Amel guessed. "That's the play you're putting on."

"Correct, Immortality," the lead actor took on the job of communicating with their strange roommate. "Have you played it yourself?"

"Not played it, no," Amel said, deciding to ignore Horth Nersal's little brother as Eler giggled at the contrast between such a question and the grammar in which it was expressed. "But I memorized it at a client's place to take it back to Eva's for the novices. I was good at memorizing." Even as he said it, Amel realized that was blindingly obvious, in retrospect, not something to be proud of the way it had been when he thought he was a commoner. Highborn Demish had prodigious memories. Ev'rel came in as the actor with the split pants was getting himself put back together. She was looking for the actors and was clearly nonplussed to discover them in Amel's dressing room.

"I brought the actors in here, Ava Ev'rel," Eler Nersal stepped forward to claim responsibility.

Ev'rel blinked at the short, skinny child who upspoke her saucily, without benefit of the required two-step suffix on his pronouns to quantify the distance between a Highlord and a Pureblood. Amel saw her begin to frown. Then she looked directly at the Nersallian dragon on the front of Eler's dress suit and recalculated.

"You must be Eler Nersal," she said instead, accepting his bold offer to converse in *rel*-peerage. The purr in her voice tried to make the condescension sound natural, but Amel could not help noticing the false note of thwarted pride. "Can I expect the pleasure of seeing your liege-brother, Horth Nersal, also? I understand he is not fond of ceremony. Perhaps he means to come when most of it is done?"

"I don't think he'll come at all," said Eler, and moved a step closer to his hostess with an air that, on stage, would have signaled conspiracy. He addressed her in a stage whisper. "I think Horth is brooding a bit on the custody duel because word is that your medic was Amel's old foster sister, and therefore you had cause to know fielding her might set off those demons of science the Reetions put into Amel."

Ev'rel endured this bit of theater with a clenched jaw. But she had managed to reclaim an air of tolerance by the time the child was done.

"A child's fancy," she dismissed his story with a smile. "You are an imaginative boy, Eler, for a Vrellish scion."

The accusation stung the culprit. Eler's shoulders quivered as he drew himself up with a show of pride that might have been intimidating in a large man instead of a skinny boy. His lower lip protruded. "I'm as Vrellish as you are!" he told the female Ava decked out in a Demish gown.

"Taken literally," Ev'rel told him, genuinely amused now, which gave her voice a deep, rich tone, "I've no doubt." She caressed Eler's mop of black hair with a motherly gesture. "I am grateful to your liege-brother for his excellent service as presiding Judge of Honor at the duel. Please convey my respects to him and the hope we might meet privately some day soon."

"Sure." Eler grinned back at her. "I'm getting good at collecting invitations for Horth. He's keeping to himself between duels."

Ev'rel smiled, inclined her head slightly in Eler's direction by way of farewell, and herded the actors out of the room.

Amel caught Eler's arm as the child made to follow. "What you said about Mira!" he exclaimed, in an anxious voice. "Did it really distract D'Ander? Do you think that's what killed him? Was it my fault?"

Eler pulled free with a sneer. "Is anything ever the fault of a puppet on strings?" he asked.

Amel caught his breath.

"And when the Silver Demish use you to take Barmi II from the woman I love," Eler continued in high dudgeon, "it won't be your fault, either. But I'm going to be there to fight for Ayrium, and maybe I'll even bring half the

Nersallian fleet with me!" Eler's gray eyes grew bright with excitement. "Wouldn't that be something?"

"You love... Ayrium?" Amel asked, astonished.

Eler closed his eyes, drew a deep breath, and sighed like the hero of a Demish play. "Isn't she glorious?"

It was Amel's turn to frown. "She's twenty-five! And you're ten!"

Eler shot him a hot glare. "Horth was only eleven when he attained his full growth. What's two years?"

"For you?" Amel told him off, smarting. "Or your very Vrellish brother? Because I've got news for you, Eler Nersal, the way you talk and make up stories you are way more Demish than Vrellish beneath all your bravado!"

"The actors told me you're a poet," Eler lashed out at Amel with tears in his eyes. "But poets speak truth from their hearts! You are nothing but a frightened puppet who says what he's told!" Then he bolted out the door as if pursued by every errant in Blue Hearth, leaving Amel feeling numb.

Inside Blue Heart

Ayrium was conducted from her room at the Ameron's Wake Emporium to the Plaza of the Citadel by a pair of Monatese errants. Amra and Di Mon met her outside Green Pavilion.

"Lovely!" Amra pronounced judgment on her pale pink and yellow gown. Ayrium was less pleased with it herself. Her bare arms felt vulnerable, the white shawl was a pointless encumbrance, and the shoes were completely impractical. But Amra's appreciation helped to reconcile her.

"You will upstage Amel!" he said, beaming at her. Di Mon's eyes flickered upward at this remark in silent appeal to the Watching Dead to grant him patience.

Both men wore Monatese suits, identical except for the liege marks on Di Mon's collar and the braid patterns on the breasts of their forest-green jackets. Di Mon's braid was concise but explicit. Amra's made fuzzy suggestions of ancient Lor'Vrellish connections.

Amra gave Ayrium his arm to escort her down the spiral stairs into Green Hearth. From there, they proceeded through the Throat and out onto Fountain Court, flanked by errants and preceded by servants stationed to open doors.

Amra paused in front of the fountain at the center of the enclosed, marble-lined courtyard between hearths. Standing beside him, linked arm in arm, Ayrium studied his face in profile, still bothered by his resemblance to Ameron in the portrait at the emporium. She was busy trying to calculate how closely he might be related to Ameron when he suddenly looked right at her.

"You do realize, I hope, what you should care about where Amel is concerned?" he asked, managing to irritate Ayrium with his aloof condescension, despite speaking casually in *rel*-peerage.

"I care about Amel's well-being," she told Amra stubbornly.

Di Mon came up beside them saying, "We've no time for this. We have already missed most of the preliminary entertainment."

"Ah, yes, the play," said Amra, in a thoughtful way that stirred up butterflies in Ayrium's stomach. "The choice of play speaks volumes at a Demish event. Ev'rel chose *The Wooing of Demlara's Daughter*." Amra cocked an eyebrow her way. "Do you know it?"

Ayrium nodded. "The story is about Blue and Silver rivals wooing power in the guise of a Golden prize bride." She paused. "The Silver prince gets the girl."

"Exactly," said Amra, and went from grave to mischievous in a heartbeat. "Do you think the Silver Demish will get it, or is it too subtle?"

Ayrium erupted with a guffaw, taken by surprise by the mental image of Amel as the contested bride. She covered her mouth with a flush of embarrassment over her rebel manners. But Amra only smiled at her, then added, patting her hand on his arm, "Remember, you must keep your temper."

The herald greeting guests outside Ev'rel's door deferred to Di Mon with a bow, but Ayrium noticed Captain Kandral stiffen at the sight of her, creating a matching ripple of alertness in Di Mon's errants.

"How may I introduce your guests, Liege Monitum?" asked Ev'rel's herald, eyeing Ayrium and Amra.

Di Mon's clipped reply was, "Not at all."

The herald bobbed a bow and went ahead. Ayrium saw Kandral go after him at an unseemly jog. Di Mon set their own, more sedate pace.

As they walked through the rooms of Blue Hearth's Throat, towards its central reception hall, Amra leaned in towards Ayrium. "Take a look," he prompted.

She blinked at his expectant expression and looked at the surrounding walls before it dawned on her that this was not just Ev'rel's home base on Fountain Court, but Blue Hearth, the hereditary seat of the lieges of Blue Dem. Ayrium looked about her eagerly for evidence, and suddenly saw heirlooms everywhere. There were story cloaks preserved behind glass, dolls dressed in period costumes, a famous sword hanging above a portrait depicting its exploits, beautifully illustrated books, and displays of handcrafted miniatures.

At the last door before the reception room, a palm-sized portrait of the Blue Demish Ava Xime smiled back at Ayrium from eye level with a woman's air of patient wisdom and a leader's gritty confidence. Knowing how much Perry would appreciate the portrait, it was all Ayrium could do to stifle the impulse to snatch it off the wall and pocket it. It wasn't stealing, after all, to steal from thieves.

"Ev'rel is making a show of possession," Amra murmured by her side.

Ayrium's skin prickled as he said it. Her next reaction was to be angry with herself for worrying so much about Amel instead of the threat he posed to Barmi. Vrenn would have told her she was being stupid, but she couldn't help it.

Captain Kandral stood off to one side, smirking at her, as she and Amra followed Di Mon into the packed reception room. Ayrium's suspicion that Ev'rel's captain of errants had briefed the herald was confirmed when they were announced as: "Di Mon, liege of Monitum, his kinsman Amra, a scholar of Sanctuary, and the bastard daughter of the late D'Ander Dem'dem of Demora and the Barmian mutineer, Perry D'Aur, pretender to the title of Liege Barmi."

Ayrium weathered the 'bastard' part unperturbed, despite the Demish eyes turned on her, but a jolt went through her body at the word 'pretender.'

Amra clamped a very strong hand on her sword arm. "Don't give them an excuse to kill you," he said tersely.

He's right, she realized, struggling to contain her outrage at everything Ev'rel was doing to her and to Amel. *If I attack Ev'rel outside the protection of an acknowledged challenge, her supporters can cut me down like a criminal assassin.* She made herself relax and endure the insult.

The play about the wooing of Demlara's daughter had only just concluded, leaving the tableau of Golden heroine and Silver hero clasped in each other's arms. The Blue Demish rival for the princess's affections lay slain on the floor below them.

Ayrium was soaking in the symbolism when an impeccably dressed prince with washed-out blue eyes and very straight, very pale hair detached himself from an elaborately attired circle surrounding Prince H'Us, the Silver Demish Admiral, walked over and bowed to her.

"Lady Ayrium," he introduced himself, "I am Prince Rail of H'Us, from the Lion Reach branch of the family. Should your father have prevailed, it would have been my honor to woo you."

Rail's wistfully polite manner startled her more than any insult. She was doubly distracted by the glimpse she caught of D'Therd, who stepped in to congratulate the lead actress on her performance. As he bowed over the woman's hand in mock deference, she could not help but imagine her father there and D'Therd dead. Her eyes burned.

"But now, of course," Amra muscled into the exchange with Prince Rail, "you will have to make other plans." He was still holding Ayrium's arm. She decided it wasn't the message she needed to send, and detached herself just firmly enough that Amra could not resist unless he chose to wrestle with her.

"Well, yes," said Rail awkwardly, casting a shy look at Ayrium, "for now, I suppose... for the time being. But I hope it isn't inappropriate to tell you how ravishing you look in that gown, Lady Ayrium."

Why, he's harmless! thought Ayrium. *And almost sweet.*

Amra moved between Ayrium and her admirer with a sudden, sharp elbowing movement. "Look!" he exclaimed, pointing. "There's Amel."

Everyone in the room looked up at this ringing announcement to discover it was premature. There was nothing to see from the entrance at the far end of the reception hall except a few girls in white dresses gathered around a lady who was giving them directions. Commoner musicians in Blue Demish livery stood by, awaiting a signal.

Frowning, Ayrium turned back to take up her acquaintance with Prince Rail, only to find the pale scion of H'Us had slipped away to rejoin his own party.

"You did that on purpose!" Ayrium accused Amra.

"Did what?" he demanded with an air of hurt dignity.

Just then, the musicians raised their flutes to play a fanfare and Ev'rel emerged to command the space vacated by the actors. Instantly, all attention was fixed on her and the food-laden tables lining the walls of the reception hall were forgotten.

Ev'rel waited for the audience to settle.

She's the next act, thought Ayrium sourly. *And just as genuine.*

"I give you," Ev'rel declared, "my son, Amel Dem'Vrel, great-grandson of the Golden Emperor and twice grandson of my father, Ava Relm, the last Blue Demish Pureblood."

A hush fell on the whole assembly as Amel appeared, looking like a carefully staged vision of beauty and innocence. Seeing him like this, surrounded by little girls in white dresses throwing flower petals, it was nearly impossible to associate him with the sordid stories of his courtesan years. He looked radiantly virginal. Even his slightly vacant air contributed. Ayrium decided he was drugged and quietly locked her teeth.

"It is my further joy," said Ev'rel, with an elegant turn in the direction of Prince Rail's party, "to announce Amel's engagement to Princess Elaya Dassa H'Us of Lion Reach, granddaughter of the Silver Demish Admiral S'Reese H'Us and princess-liege, in her own right, of Rose Well on the planet Orchard."

Amel spotted Ayrium in the crowd at that moment, and something strange and moving passed between them. Accepting this marriage would be Ayrium's downfall, and he knew it. But rejecting it would be his. Ayrium stared at Amel, watching as fear — as vivid as a child's dread of fire — displaced the empathic look of understanding on Amel. Her generous heart broke with grief for her people, and melted with forgiveness for her helpless friend who had already suffered so much. And then, as Ev'rel began the next sentence, the distress vanished from Amel's face. A beatific expression replaced it — pure, transcendent, breath-stopping.

Ayrium was not the only one to notice. The audience shifted in a subtle, profound way that raised the small hairs on the back of her neck.

Standing with her back to Amel, Ev'rel carried on, either unaware or assuming that her guests were reacting with respectful awe to her declaration.

"Amel and his princess will wed at the palace," Ev'rel continued triumphantly, "within the month, and—"

"No." It was a small word, but Amel used a performer's skill in its delivery. It reached the whole room. He stepped forward, and around Ev'rel, still inspired by the eerie, inner clarity that made his beauty painful.

"I cannot do it, Your Immortality," he told Ev'rel.

Ev'rel was speechless. She was so completely unprepared to grasp what she had just heard that she froze, blinking at him, as if to erase the spectacle of his inexplicable resistance.

Amel addressed the bride's party simply, in *rel*-peerage, although he and Ev'rel outranked all of them by one birth rank.

"Forgive me, Princess Elaya, for any harm this does you. I am honored you have seen fit to accept me. But I cannot marry anyone like... this." He looked about him with a pained expression.

Ev'rel pulled herself together at last and gestured. "Kandral!" she called. "Amel is suffering one of his attacks. Help him out of the room immediately."

The threat became a self-fulfilling prophecy. Amel caught his breath and went wide-eyed. The spell of his clarity was broken.

Kandral scattered flower girls as he sprang forward. Amel gave a cry of pain and panic, fighting phantoms. One flailing arm caught Kandral across the face, knocking him down. Two more errants piled on, and were slewed about in Amel's ugly dance with his past, the errants shouting for help and Amel screaming like the beaten child he had become, inside.

Ayrium was on her way to help before she spotted D'Therd doing likewise. The sight of him ignited a fierce desire to beat her father's killer to death with her fists if necessary! Amra tackled her. She fell face down. Flower petals stung her nose with an overdone vanilla odor. Ladies and princesses were screaming, while some men in the crowd were shouting directions to others. She heard foot-steps pounding up the spiral stairs, furniture being shoved, and the crash of falling trays, but Amel's cries still pierced her heart and steeled her resolve.

She kneed Amra where it would hurt the most, elbowed him hard in the ribs for good measure, and was up again — only to run right into a blow from Di Mon.

Ayrium staggered back. From the ground, Amra snagged her heel and tripped her.

She fell flat on her back and looked up to find Di Mon's sword drawn and leveled at her throat, close enough it would be hard to fit a finger between it and her jugular.

Amra was up on his knees, looking disheveled in a way that seemed oddly unnatural to him. He was in too much pain to stand, but he put out an arm and shouted, "No!" in a voice like a sword thrust.

Di Mon glared at Ayrium. She glared back, wanting to kill D'Therd as badly as Di Mon seemed to want to shove the tip of his sword through her neck.

Amra struggled to his feet muttering archaic curses Ayrium had only heard used in literature.

"I see," he growled at Ayrium in a rough voice, "that with you, one pays for his pleasures with equal pains."

"She is a liability!" Di Mon hissed through tight lips.

"No," Amra denied, and paused to make himself straighten up. "An asset."

Ayrium's attention was divided between the sword at her throat and the diminishing mayhem around her. She, Amra and Di Mon were ringed by a circle of Ev'rel's errants, but Kandral was not among them. He had disappeared with Amel. D'Therd had also left the reception hall. Ev'rel was doing her best to preside over the disorderly flight of her guests up the spiral stairs to the Plaza or down Blue Hearth's Throat toward Fountain Court. Ayrium could hear her voice in the background explaining away Amel's behavior as a fit caused by the Reetions' mistreatment of him.

"His Golden blood makes my poor son delicate," Ev'rel was saying, "but it is the very finest blood there is, and his lineage is unmarred by the suffering misfortune has inflicted on him. We have to make allowances."

Amra clasped his hand over Di Mon's, moving the sword clear of Ayrium's throat by force. She held her breath, half expecting Di Mon to discipline his presumptuous kinsman. But Di Mon gave way and stepped back.

"D'Therd is gone," Amra said to Ayrium, standing over her. "Amel was taken down the Throat. Pursing either one will only get you killed. There are too many errants."

He was right, although Ayrium resented it with a passion that felt larger than her whole being.

Seeing the message sink in, Amra stepped clear.

Ayrium shot to her feet with a roar of adrenaline. The next instant, she felt helpless and confined because nothing she could do or say would gain her anything she wanted, or defend anything just and right. Being without her sword made her feel naked. And the dress was ridiculous.

A cry breached her lips, half rage and half despair, as a burst of frustrated energy hurled her towards the stairs. She barged past departing guests and knocked aside a servant, making the remaining men turn inward towards their women folk to protect them.

Wrong! It is all wrong! she thought bitterly. She was a great pilot, a good leader, a true friend, and a superior fighter; none of it helped her against Ev'rel's stratagems.

"Ayrium!" she heard Amra's voice behind her, but she didn't slow down.

11

Abandoned Fronts

Forbidden Pleasures

Ev'rel burst into the medical room on fire with humiliation.

Amel was strapped down on the examination bed, awake and begging Mira not to give him the sedative held ready in her hand. His elaborate head scarf still clung where it was glued to his hair, but was badly askew elsewhere. There was blood on his white clothes and the sleeves of his shift were torn. Someone had taken off his jewelry and cloak.

Ev'rel brushed Mira aside. "Out!" she ordered. "All of you!"

Kandral hesitated only briefly. The rest of the errants bowed and fled her anger.

Mira put the sedative on a tray and met Ev'rel's eyes. "There's enough here to make him manageable and still able to talk, if that's what you want."

Ev'rel heard the slate grayness in Mira's voice, but cared nothing about interpreting any coded meanings in her manner or words. Hot fury dominated everything she was, all of it centered on the figure strapped to the bed.

She waited until she heard the door close, then she drew back her hand and lashed it, half fisted, across Amel's mouth.

His head snapped aside with a gasp. She was cagey enough, still, to think about how much visible damage she could write off to his fit at the reception and scanned Mira's trays for something suitable. Then she thought of *sish-han*. It would make him more sensitive to pain, amplifying the impact of small harms.

She looked towards Mira's medicine cabinet with a thrill of transgression rising to displace her bitter fury.

Sish-han was the wrong thing to use on an overexcited teenager suffering from a nervous complaint, of course, but she had told everyone he was fragile. It served her, then, to make it true.

Ev'rel wet her lips, imagining Amel tossing deliriously in his bonds, suffering clear dream after clear dream, exhausted but still driven to remember... what? Would she be able to guess, she wondered, from his body's helpless reenactment of past traumas, even tied down?

Amel lay in the straps, red marks showing where he'd been straining against them, and began to shiver.

Ev'rel looked at the sedative Mira had prepared for her. Then she went to the cabinet to get the case of needles.

"Wh-what's that?" Amel asked, like a prisoner facing execution. He knew she was furious. His fear of pain was palpable in his body's fine-grained tremors.

Remembering the Reetion data chronicling his abuse, she considered it a pity, on purely aesthetic grounds, that all of it was portrayed from Amel's point of view, which robbed the viewer of the yielding vibrancy about him and unwilling responsiveness. She suffered a sharp, inner pang at the thought of recreating some of it herself as art, and reached out with a feeling of intoxication to stroke her fingers up his inner thigh.

His eyes widened with a quick, jerky gasp.

Oh, Amel, she thought, reacting to his spasm with a molten pleasure that wiped out the pain of her failure.

Stress pitched him into a clear dream again. With an oddly detached interest, she watched him struggle, thinking about that fleeting moment of hot passion and whether there was some way to forget it and remove the risks bound up in the impossible attraction it held for her.

While she was pondering, his lips opened in a shallow gasp. On impulse, she bent down and kissed him, one hand locked in his hair and another exploring the smooth-muscled flesh of his flank. He struggled, choking, but she drew back before he could recover from the dream enough to bite her — if he even would! His efforts to gain self-control were scattered afresh by every shock. She tore the scarf from his head when she straightened up, making him cry out for the sake of the hair still attached.

"There are worse things than getting married," she told him. "I suppose I will have to teach you that."

No More Lies

"Wait!" Amra caught up when Ayrium stumbled, blinded by her own tears. He gripped her upper arm, slewing her around. "Talk to me!" he ordered. They were on the far side of the Plaza from where the disastrous reception had been held.

"Leave me alone!" said Ayrium. "I am useless here. I'm going home. We rebels have more honor than you court-iers do!"

Amra glanced in the direction of the naked slab jutting out over the Palace Plain far below. "You are heading in the wrong direction for the docks," he pointed out, "unless you mean to jump down and walk up."

"I know that!" yelled Ayrium. She had, indeed, realized her error the moment she had stopped, but she was not about to admit to Amra how blindly she had been running until then. An idea struck her as she spotted Black Hearth nearby. "I thought I ought to say goodbye to Eler!"

Amra returned the stare of a Demish passerby who took note of Ayrium's torn dress and bare feet. She had chucked the shoes in order to run, her shawl was lost, and her dress was torn. "Maybe," he suggested, "we could sit down."

Ayrium let him steer her off in the direction of a bistro serving both Demish and Vrellish clientele, not sure why she was compliant. She was angry at Amra. On the other hand, except for young Eler, Amra was pretty much her only friend at court. They took a table well out from the center.

"Hot tea, protein crackers, and a traveling cloak for the lady," Amra told an unflappable waiter who acted as if he served disheveled Demish women in torn dresses chaperoned by mysterious Monatese highborns every other day of his life.

"Now, then," said Amra in a businesslike tone. He leaned across their table to take both her hands in his. "You want to rescue Amel, correct?"

She gritted her teeth without lifting her eyes, but she accepted his touch and turned her hands to hold his in return. "And kill D'Therd," she ground out.

"One thing at a time," was Amra's cool reply. "You would like to see Ev'rel deposed and your claim to Barmi II secure. Yes?"

Ayrium's wide blue eyes met his with a leap. "Sure!" she said. Her expression turned sick. "I should go back for Amel. I should have done something."

"And been killed?" He gathered up her hands in his. "Ev'rel would gladly kill you. She will not kill Amel."

"She is making him crazy!" Ayrium lashed out, pulling her hands away. "He was nearly better back on Barmi! She is making him crazy by trying to use him against us!"

"And it backfired." Amra sat back in his chair with a calculating air. "Proving that Amel has a mind of his own. So does Horth Nersal. And we already have Di Mon."

"*We* do?" asked Ayrium, wondering if she had missed something really important.

Amra nodded. "Di Mon counts for three votes, since he stands for Brown Hearth and White Hearth, although with the Lor'Vrellish line being nearly extinct—"

"Nearly?" Ayrium interrupted him. She scowled. "Do you know of any Lor'Vrellish Sevolites I don't?"

"One," he said, and leaned forward on his elbows. "But the point is, a contender backed by White, Green, Brown and Black could stand against Ev'rel four votes to four, which is enough to require the Avaship be settled by a duel. I'd be willing to lay odds on our side with Horth Nersal as champion. And if we claimed Blue Hearth, as well, we might even avoid the duel."

"You're talking about making Amel Ava, right?" said Ayrium. "Just like Dad." She shook her head. "Not again."

Amra stretched out one long arm to comfort her. "Trust me?" he urged her. "For just a bit longer. The challenge is how to get Horth Nersal to — what is it?"

Ayrium had interrupted him by fixing her attention on a table in another café across the thoroughfare from them. Three dour-looking men were sitting there around a table. All wore swords, which wasn't surprising for Sevolites on Gelion, but their livery was very unusual. It looked vaguely Nersallian but wasn't. The men were arguing, and their voices carried well enough for a strong foreign accent to register.

Amra checked over his shoulder to see what had caught her interest. "Those are the late Princess Beryl's retainers," he told her.

"Nesaks!" Ayrium's usually clear brow furrowed.

"Yes," Amra agreed, with academic interest. "One of them has already gone home to SanHome, but those three are still here. Biding their time for vengeance, maybe. Horth did kill their princess."

"From what Eler says it was the only way to save him and his sister Sanal!" Ayrium defended Horth, although part of her still smarted from his refusal to declare D'Therd's win spoiled by Ev'rel's dirty trick on the challenge floor.

"Ah," Amra said, waving one long-fingered hand. "But killing her children was a sacred act for Beryl Nesak, because it set their souls free instead of dooming them to grow up in separation from their people." He smiled with sudden mischief. "Princess Beryl had similar views to yourself about the lack of honor on Fountain Court."

Ayrium was not amused. "I would never kill children!"

He seemed to realize he had taken a misstep and said, simply, "No, of course not." Then he clasped her hands once more. "Please stay a bit longer? I promise you I will do something, very soon, to unseat Ev'rel."

A trio of Monatese errants were loitering about the café behind Amra's back, looking as intent and nervous as Di Mon did when Amra was around. Ayrium narrowed her eyes at her strange lover. "Who are you, anyway?" she asked.

"I will tell you," he promised. "Soon. But first, tell me about young Eler because I think he may be the key to becoming better acquainted with Horth Nersal."

Consequences

Ev'rel caught a glimpse of herself in the dressing table mirror as she paced across her room and stopped. Eyes full of wild panic looked back at her.

She could not sleep. She could not settle. Alarms kept sounding in her head and gut, attacking her attempts to make what happened in Mira's lab seem like an unimportant detail.

I must kill him, she realized. *I cannot let anyone find out. Ever.*

Her sketchbook lay on the top of her dressing table, silently accusing her. It was open and the picture she had drawn there pulled her closer. Helpless to resist, she drifted over, looked down, and felt herself go molten with emotion again, drinking in his beauty, responsiveness, the very fact he was her flesh and blood, as she had been her father's. Even the questing compassion that groped through his hurt to reach out to her, and his stubborn grip on fantasies like love. All of it intoxicated her. His understated gasps stoked her will to dominate him. His hard male body, straining and shifting beneath her, invoked something deep and primitive enough to frighten her. Mira called it an illness. But bloodless, dispassionate Mira — who made love to nothing but science — had no idea of its rewards! Stable, steady Mira, who never lay staring at the ceiling half the night, nursing cold knowledge in a hot bosom, wondering how to be one thing and seem like another, wondering if life's rewards were enough to make up for its disappointments.

I must kill Amel now, she thought again. *But can I?*

Could anyone give up the source of such dark, forbidden, complex pleasure? She searched herself and found no true regret for her transgression, only fear of its possible consequences. She told herself she could not be blamed for her deep, Vrellish impulses. Admittedly, even among Vrellish women what she had done was criminal, but so was the common form of rape that men committed against women. Rape was the right of the powerful. She had learned that in her marriage to Amel's father, Delm. It was only when it got dragged into the light of public scrutiny that it was damaging.

Briefly, she was angry with the cringing crowd who refused to accept life as it really was, but she gave it up as futile.

"Focus," she muttered as she turned to pace the room again. *Focus.*

Amel would not cooperate with her plans to claim Blue Dem. Fine, all she needed was a child by him with a better claim to Barmi II than Ayrium — a child, yes, but not hers. Mother-son incest would be too hard to make the Demish swallow, even if she claimed Amel attacked her in one of his fits.

"Think," she muttered under her breath, stopped, rubbed her palms together, and pressed them to her face with fingers half curled.

She considered Vretla. Might the liege of Vrel be willing to breed with Amel if she pitched it to her right, and kept him incoherent enough not to risk him contradicting her cover story? If not, maybe there were clan leaders in her Sevolite-hungry Knotted Strings who might help her salvage good genes from the mess the Reetions made of her poor, dear son while they had had him. She might even be able to use him herself, in between, until she'd had her fill of him. A bitter kernel of self-hatred mocked and applauded that idea, telling her it would work splendidly. She could child gift to vassals and strengthen the Knotted Strings fleet for the future, while completely discrediting Amel as a possible Demish rival. But could she pull it off? Could she get it past all those upstanding princes, of the sort who had murdered her father for bedding her, and their parlor-bound ladies and princesses gossiping over who danced with whom at a crown ball? Their kind would sooner forgive her for smothering Amel in his bed than making use of all his otherwise wasted genetic vitality. She had to remember to think Demishly if she was going to dominate a court top-heavy with them.

"Gods!" she exclaimed in frustration, and felt her eyes fill up with tears.

She didn't want to kill Amel... not yet. But he couldn't live to tell her secret, either. No matter how she thought about it she could not escape the realization she had made a fatal mistake in the medical lab and had no one to turn to except—

"Mira!" Ev'rel exclaimed in a flash of hope. Mira always argued her problem was a mental illness, a fundamental in-stability of her particular way of handling her half Demish, half Vrellish nature: her disgust for ordinary sex versus the eruptions of wild Vrellish passion which played out through power games; her extremes of cold, detached reason and intemperate passion; the obsessive intensity of her attachment to those few people she truly needed, although she could sentence a hundred to certain death without a twinge. She would take Mira's damned drugs and humble herself to accept her advice if Mira could just get her out of this stupid mistake!

Ev'rel ran to the door, pulled it open, looked for the page always waiting for her orders, and exclaimed, "Fetch me Mira!"

Family

"Wake up!" A child's voice hissed in Amel's ear.

It was hard to obey. He knew he had been drugged, repeatedly. Nothing else was terribly clear.

"Wake up!" A small hand slapped his face. It hurt. He raised an arm, surprised to find he could.

Something very bad had happened, something he didn't want to remember. A clear dream? Yes. And something else... something he was ashamed to think he had imagined! If he had. He felt leaden.

The child started tugging on his arm. "Ayrium wants to see you," he said.

"Ayrium?" The name touched a place in Amel free of sick shame and dread.

He tried to pull himself up on an elbow and slumped back. A residual smell of sex and his vanilla-scented sweat lingered despite a sterile, soapy odor. He was dressed in a loose white jumper that felt soft and cool against his bruised and tender flesh.

Ev'rel, he remembered. And shrank from accepting what he thought he remembered about her. *She was very angry,* he thought — a safe starting premise.

The child's face appeared beside his head.

"I hid," Eler Nersal said conspiratorially. "Ayrium's upset about you, so I figured if I could get you out of here she'd take me back to Barmi with her, too."

Amel squinted at him, struggling to keep his eyes open.
The room seemed so bright, and he felt so tired.

"A woman came and sent the errant at the door away for
me," said Eler. "But we have to hurry! Who knows when the
errant will be back again to check on you!"

"In twenty minutes," came Mira's voice, harsh and clear.

Amel's heart skipped. He heaved himself up and swayed,
his head loose on his neck. "Mira," he croaked.

She came over and began to prepare another shot of something for him. "This will bring you around," she said factually.
"I wouldn't do it even to most Sevolites, not after the cocktail
you've had today, but I think it's in your best interest in the
end."

"Are you a _gorarelpul_?" Eler asked her. "Was it a trap, when
you sent away the errant for me? Are you going to kill me
now that I'm caught red-handed?"

"Nonsense," she said, and paused to give Amel the dose
of whatever she'd prepared. "You would never have got in
without my help."

The drug hit Amel's system fast. His heart rate picked up
and his muscles began to respond again. "Mira," he said,
grasping her arm as she drew away, his tired eyes overflowing
with tears once more. "You told me we mean nothing to each
other anymore. You said it was all a fantasy. You were right!
Don't help me. Look after yourself this time — please — I
promised Em!"

"So did I," she said, tight-lipped. "Now let go. You're hurting me."

He did. She helped him out of the bed. He moved his body
carefully, respectful of its aches. One side of his face throbbed.
His thighs and abdomen had cramped, and his groin was
disturbingly sensitive. He kept trying to believe it was from
clear dreams.

"I'm doing this for Ev'rel, as well," she told him when she
had his feet in the slippers she had brought with her, and

had pulled a cloak about his shoulders. "You can't be here, near her. Go to Rire. Get treatment for the clear dreams there."

A shudder went through him at the idea. "I c-can't," he whimpered. "They d-did this to me."

"That's why they might be able to fix it," Mira insisted.

If I go to Rire, I might see the Reetion woman named Ann again, he thought, trying to believe in the plan Mira offered him. But terror of the visitor probe curdled his hopes of happiness.

"Can you get a ship?" Mira asked Eler.

"Of course!" the boy said with offended pride. "I'm a Nersal of Black Hearth. I can get a ship and fly one, too. But I don't know the way to Barmi II, so I need him. You *do* know how to get there, right?" he asked Amel.

"I'll go ahead and clear the way," Mira said, moving Amel closer to Eler as if handing off custody. "You get him up the stairs."

"No, Mira, no," Amel resisted giddily, "not again. I don't want to ruin you again!"

"You will ruin me if you stay," she snapped at him, then added in a more generous manner. "I can handle Ev'rel, you can't. Trust me."

"She had Kandral rough him up, I bet," Eler jumped in with conjectures. "Look at the bruise on his face! I didn't see that happen while they were dragging him out of the reception! Kandral must have done it afterwards."

Mira caught Amel's wrists and made him look at her. "Tell no one what she did. That's my price. Tell no one, ever. But get out of here!"

Amel gulped and nodded. He couldn't think or speak, just promise with his stare.

Mira seemed satisfied. She went into Family Hall ahead of them.

Amel could barely walk by himself. He felt strong enough but not stable. His heart was hammering. Eler helped him balance.

Room by room, they followed Mira through the Throat.

"There will be guards in the entrance hall," she warned them. "You are two guests going home." She pulled the hood of Amel's cloak up over his head. "All the staff have been told to be deferential to anyone from Black Hearth until Horth gives his oath," she instructed Eler. "Tell them Amel is an acquaintance who's had too much to drink. Say he is some Demish Highlord or other. No one knows them all. Now go."

"Be well!" Amel told her in a whisper. "For Em!"

Mira flicked her fingers at him irritably.

Eler played his part well with the errants. One of them even offered to take Amel to Silver Hearth for him.

"I'm taking him back to Black Hearth," Eler improvised a bit wildly. "He promised to look at my collection of old Demish poetry books and tell me what they're worth, if anything!"

"Odd collection for a scion of Nersal," the errant said, laughing.

"Oh, well," Eler proclaimed unconvincingly, "I only collect them to sell them again."

It wasn't until they got out onto Fountain Court that Amel felt how Eler was shaking with stress.

"We will have to go up through Black Hearth," Eler muttered, "but it's all right. Horth won't be home. He's out looking for me."

12

Changing Partners

Wooing Liege Nersal

"You know Horth from Killing Reach, then?" Amra probed.

"Horth and I crossed paths a few times during his fleet service under Liege Bryllit," said Ayrium with a frown, holding a spicy bread stick in the air between them. She sat with her feet apart like the space-farer she was, making the grandeur of her court attire all the more ludicrous. Her torn dress, disheveled hair and the absence of discarded accessories already made it abundantly clear she was no lady. "I can't say I know Horth really well at a personal level. But I'm telling you, he won't swear to Amel. He's Nersallian. I can't imagine any Nersallian swearing to Amel the way he is right now."

Amra waved away this objection, as usual. "I will explain that part later."

Ayrium set both elbows on the table and narrowed her bright blue eyes at him. "Try right now!"

As Amra inhaled to reply, movement at the Nesak table across the street caught Ayrium's eye.

"Give me your sword," she ordered Amra as she began to rise.

He looked appalled by the idea and inclined to argue, but what he saw next made him swallow his objections and hand the weapon over, hilt first.

Horth Nersal had appeared on the thoroughfare unaccompanied by other members of his household.

He's looking for Eler, thought Ayrium, watching the new liege of Nersal as he scanned the crowd in the half-worried, half-annoyed manner of an adult searching for a troublesome child.

Horth's notoriety had inspired people to collect in his wake, some tapping their companions or pointing in Horth's direction.

"Not good," muttered Ayrium as she watched the Nesaks swarm up from their table. Their leader strode forth to meet Horth.

Had it not been for the witnessing circle gathered around them, including herself and Amra, Ayrium suspected the three Nesaks would have mobbed Horth to bring him down.

It was legal on Gelion for duelists to accost each other anywhere in public, within challenge class, but only if they did so one on one. It was everyone's duty to keep the fights fair.

The lead Nesak came forward stiff-legged with hatred. "Die!" he challenged Horth. "For Princess Beryl!"

Horth cleared his own sword with a practiced motion, while releasing and shedding his sword belt with his right hand. The sword in his left hand held its place in the air, as steady as if it had been set in concrete. His whole attention focused on his opponent with impressive clarity.

The circle of witnesses fell silent, breathing like a single animal.

The first challenger attacked with a yell. Horth gave a few steps and dodged. They flew at each other again in a slamming barrage of blows.

The duel transformed Amra. He was keenly alert, taking in the action with a hungry and purposeful intensity that made the hairs on Ayrium's neck prickle.

An exhalation from the crowd snapped her attention back to the duel in time to see cold skill prevail. Horth threaded his opponent's defense in the midst of a lethal attack, escaping injury himself by a finely calculated margin. He stepped back untouched as his impaled opponent staggered and fell, struggling to breathe with blood-filled lungs.

The second attacker came on with a roar. The third made to join him, and then hesitated, eyeing Ayrium and the sword-carrying men in the watching crowd.

Horth met his second opponent as calmly as he had the first one, but this Nesak was less hot-headed and very good. Ayrium found herself holding her breath as she watched Horth deflect a protracted series of clever attacks. He was on the defensive for too long and the pace never let up! It was an agonizing fifty seconds before the Nesak backed off to study his opponent like a locksmith intent on a particularly complicated mechanism.

Damn, damn, and damn! Ayrium thought, her own heart rate picking up. It half surprised her to realize how strongly she was rooting for Horth, despite her unanswered questions about his decision concerning D'Therd's win against her father. *It would serve him right if Eler distracted him right now!* she thought despite her nobler impulses.

The second Nesak picked his strategy and plunged in. Ayrium's eyes widened as each man's blade suggested first one thing, then another, all within the mere scrap of time before they came together!

Horth is going to die! she thought. But the next instant it was the Nesak who was sliding backwards off Horth's sword, a vengeful grin of victory still fixed on his face for a strange moment. Run through the torso, he lost the strength to hold his sword and buckled to his knees on the floor.

But Horth's victory had come at a steep price.

Horth put his sword into his right hand, flexed the blood-streaked fingers of his left, and wiped it on his thigh, then he put his sword back in his left hand and raised it again with no overt sign of weakness, at first, except the blood dripping from his soaked, black sleeve to splash, drop by drop, on the floor. Within seconds, however, his damaged muscles could not sustain the steadiness that had been there before. Face grim, he lowered the sword to rest the damaged arm, keeping his eyes on the third Nesak, kneeling beside his fallen comrade. Horth's right hand was uninjured, but he did not change hands.

He's too strongly left dominant! Ayrium realized with a gulp. *He's dead if the third Nesak's any good!*

Then it dawned on her: there were rules about serial challenges. Only a named heir could challenge immediately. *Or is that only in a title challenge, not a grudge match?* she wondered, rueing her lack of a court education.

Doesn't matter, she decided. *This is wrong!*

Ayrium stepped into the open center of the witnessing circle, barefoot, in a Demish gown, and with a borrowed sword.

Horth grinned at her with a nod and stepped back, willing to be championed. He was shaking slightly in reaction to trauma and blood loss, and his sword hand was losing power.

Ayrium nodded back, conscious of the compliment he was paying her, in sharp contrast to the startled looks among the Demish men surrounding them. At the same time, she was less than thrilled by the prospect of fighting for her life in a torn reception gown. *Trust the disapproving Demish gallants to do nothing but watch!* she thought bitterly. She had expected to be the first of many, not the only one.

"Fine!" the third Nesak spat out. He rose from the side of his fallen comrade, his eyes flinty hard as he reached for his sword.

Suddenly a voice was raised behind and all around them, in ringing tones. "*Okal Rel* has been served here! If there is more blood to pay, let it be done on the Octagon with the houses of Fountain Court to bear witness, after a three-day respite!"

Is that Amra! Ayrium was almost sure, but dared not take her eyes off the third Nesak.

"Or will you have it said that this woman you call a bastard and a rebel has more honor than any man among you with a sword?" the commanding voice cried.

The crowd reacted to the criticism with a restless stirring and general stiffening of posture among the Demish men. In her peripheral vision, Ayrium glimpsed a man reaching for the hilt of his weapon, only to have his hand captured by the woman at his side, her face white with alarm.

They're afraid, Ayrium realized. Her next thought was, *Which is reasonable.*

"Who will lend me a sword, then?" came Amra's bold challenge.

Even the Nesak looked at him now, freeing Ayrium to do likewise. She was confident Horth would warn her if she was going to be jumped.

Amra was holding out his palm in an imperious gesture, his figure straight and his face set in the scowl of a disappointed parent. A couple of Monatese errants hovered anxiously at his back, unable — as nobleborns — to draw in his support, but projecting a clear sense of solidarity despite that. Their presence startled Ayrium. They had been hovering on the periphery the whole time she had sat talking with Amra. Now this! It seemed clear enough that looking after Amra was their job.

A half dozen spots around the circle showed signs of disturbance, like loci of decision in the body of the crowd.

Horth was as calm as living stone. He never took his eyes off the Nesaks, neither the angry one still confronting them nor the one curled up around his wound on the floor. He made no move at all except to twitch the fingers of his wounded arm and let them relax again, blood dripping — pit, pat — from the longest finger.

A Demish Highlord stepped into the circle to join Amra, sword in hand. "I say, schedule the duel for the Octagon."

A friend was close behind him, and another. In seconds the circle was clogged with defenders of orderly conduct, speaking with many voices.

"Give Liege Nersal time to find kin to act as champion," someone suggested.

"Three days respite is usual," another Demish defender piped up.

"Take your dead and wounded and leave," said the first Highlord.

"We'll help, if you agree to go," concluded a Silver Demish prince fresh from space and still in flight leathers.

The Nesak was hopelessly outnumbered. He glared at Horth. "Matricide! Patricide! You'll pay with your very soul!" Then he snapped his sword into its sheath and went to accept the help offered for his comrades. One was dead. The first still moaned.

Ayrium looked for Amra and found him fending off the two Green Hearth errants.

"I will come when I'm ready!" Amra's voice lashed out, down-speaking his would-be nannies with an exaggerated weighting on his suffixes that she could only presume were meant as an insult. Certainly the man and woman in Monatese livery looked appropriately unnerved.

What is it with him and the Monatese? she wondered, and remembered he was child-gifting to Tessitatt Monitum. *Guess it hasn't taken yet,* she thought, and discovered she disliked the idea. She had relegated the arrangement between Tessitatt and Amra to the past. *Not that I should care,* she reminded herself for good measure.

Horth was surrounded by his own errants, at last, who had shown up with three friendly members of the *kinf'stan*. One of the errants was inspecting Horth's wounded arm in a manner far from painless to judge by Horth's set expression. He became more animated when he caught sight of Ayrium through the loosening clumps of crowd milling around. The respect and thanks Horth conveyed in a look rankled on her lingering resentment.

Right, thought Ayrium, tired of harboring mixed feelings about him, *let's have this out!*

Squaring her shoulders to help compensate for the silly dress, she marched straight to where Horth stood in the midst of his retainers. He acknowledged her arrival by drawing his arm away from the errant applying first aid, holding it cradled in his sound arm, instead, as he waited for Ayrium to speak first.

Given the situation, Ayrium got straight to business.

"You sparred with me when I was hard up for a partner," she said. "I acted for you, here. I'd say we're even."

He nodded, eyes narrowed, but whether in suspicion or just pain she couldn't be sure.

"Now I have to know why you ruled as you did, for D'Therd," she told him, shaking with an excess of emotion, "even though Ev'rel distracted my father."

Horth was silent so long she began to feel ridiculous standing there, getting glared at by the errant waiting to treat his bleeding arm. She counted five drips of blood fall to the floor as the seconds passed. Then Horth said, very clearly, in his deep voice, "Ev'rel, not D'Therd."

Ayrium was forced to do the thinking to decipher the remark. "Do you mean the distraction, if intended, was not D'Therd's fault?" she said, unable to keep the anger out of her voice on her father's behalf. "That he only took advantage of D'Ander's concern about Amel?"

Horth shrugged. She was outraged until she grasped it was not a dismissive gesture so much as an admission of his own inadequacy to explain himself further.

She had given up hope of further clarity, and was wondering how to disengage, when Horth spoke for the second time.

"In a duel," he said, "do not be distracted."

Ayrium's face burned at this answer. It sounded like a tacit criticism of her father for letting Amel's distress draw his attention. Except criticism was the wrong word. Horth dealt in facts. To be distracted was an error, nothing less nor more. Errors could be fatal in a duel. She got the feeling he would have ruled the same way, from the afterlife, on his own behalf, if Eler had distracted him today as she had imagined he might.

"*Ack rel,*" Horth Nersal concluded in a curiously heartening tone which let her feel his respect for both D'Therd and D'Ander for settling their quarrel within the scope of *Okal Rel*, without threatening those they wished to govern with a destructive war.

Ayrium managed to raise a smile. "*Ack rel,*" she answered him and turned away to look for Amra as the Nersallians closed around Horth again.

Amra caught her unexpectedly by an arm. "Introduce me to Horth Nersal," he demanded.

Ayrium pulled free. "He's wounded! His people are seeing to him."

"Now!" insisted Amra. His altercation with Di Mon's errants had left him over-stimulated, each breath flaring his thin nostrils.

"No!" Ayrium rebelled.

Amra let loose with one of his curiously quaint curses and bolted off in the direction Horth's retainers were headed with Horth.

"You forgot your sword," Ayrium called after him, but he didn't hear.

Her knees began to feel weak. She walked back over to the table — noting how people were keeping clear of her — and sat down.

I'm not dead, she thought. *Again*.

She tipped her head back to stare at the lights overhead. She supposed this kind of excitement could become addictive for people who liked to poke the world with a finger, or a sword, and watch it wobble onto a new axis. Not for her. Although two things could be said for the day's experience: first, that anyone maneuvering to challenge her for Barmi would be thinking twice now, given the respect Horth Nersal had shown for her swordsmanship; and second, when she found a way to challenge D'Therd, she'd heed Horth's advice. *In a duel, do not be distracted.*

"Easy to say, hard to do, Dad," she muttered, by way of apology to the Watching Dead.

Di Mon emerged through the increasingly chatty crowd beyond the clear space surrounding her. He had a whole hand of errants with him, all looking as agitated as their leader.

"Where is Amra?" Di Mon demanded.

"Gone off after Horth Nersal," said Ayrium, suddenly not caring much anymore. She was thinking about D'Ander and her heart felt bruised.

Di Mon cursed in more current usage than Amra had, and tore off in the direction Ayrium had indicated before she remembered to give him Amra's sword.

She was watching him sprint away, wondering if she ought to chase after him with the sword, when Eler popped up beside her. "You are awesome!" he told her worshipfully. "You saved my brother!"

Ayrium looked down at Amra's un-bloodied sword in her right hand and chuckled. "That's a little generous," she said.

"But you might have!" Eler insisted, drinking her in with blatant hero worship, spiked with a dollop of infatuation.

Ayrium ruffled the boy's hair, suddenly too happy they had all survived to stay sad. She could even forgive Eler for his obvious appreciation of her torn dress as she tugged a drooping strap back up onto her shoulder.

"I've got something to show you," Eler told her suddenly, and tugged at her arm.

She had seen he was excited from the start. Now she saw that he was also as nervous as a bad swordsman on a challenge floor, which convinced her not to brush this off as childish folly. She owed it to Horth to keep an eye on his flighty little brother.

Eler led her past tables to the core of a nearby café where the proprietors lived and stored their valuables. To gain entrance, he showed a pass card to a sword-carrying guard whose attire claimed no allegiance to any particular family, although his braid hinted, vaguely, at a Silver Demish background. A scar on his face suggested he was no better than nobleborn. All in all, a typical sell-sword — houseless and reduced to hiring himself out to commoners.

They entered a dimly lit room filled with boxes. "Where are you taking me?" asked Ayrium, annoyed by the sneaking suspicion he might have precocious ideas about romance.

"To their crash room," said Eler. "Most places like this have at least one. They rent them to people who are desperate to hole up for some reason — pilots who have fallen out with family, duelists needing a place to bleed in peace, Vrellish customers who can't wait for sex, or Demish ones who don't want anyone to know they're getting some."

"I know what a crash room is," said Ayrium when he left her space to get a word in.

"This way, then!" Eler led her down a short, dark corridor to where a second sell-sword rose from a seat set outside a closed door. The guard accepted a Nersallian honor chip from Eler with a grudging bow.

Sell-swords are lost people, thought Ayrium. This one also looked like a Demish nobleborn of some description, down on his luck. He acknowledged her with a polite nod, trying to keep his eyes off her bust, and slunk off.

"He doesn't know who I've got in here," Eler told her as soon as the sell-sword was out of earshot. Then he opened the door with a memorized combination of punches on a side panel and ushered her into very cramped quarters containing a bed and a tiny hygiene closet.

There were two people inside. Sanal sat cross-legged on the floor snatching at jacks as she bounced a small red ball.

She looked up only after she had completed the round she was on.

The form stretched out on the bed was Amel. He struggled up onto an elbow, looking woozy, and lighted up at the sight of her.

Ayrium sank down beside him to gather him into a warm hug, and was alarmed by the hurt sounds she elicited.

"What's Ev'rel done to you?" she exclaimed, trying to separate them so she could get a better look.

He didn't answer, just clung to her with his face against her neck.

She tugged free to place her hands on either side of his face. It broke her heart to see his bruised and luminous beauty looking back at her.

"You stood up for us," she said, "against all common sense and self-interest. I am done being wise myself, too. I'm taking you home with me. Right now. Before something else can go wrong."

His expression stirred with awe at her approval, and then terror. His pushed back. "No! They'll come after you, Ayrium." His eyes glistened. "You can't do this. You promised!"

She gripped his arm with one hand as she stroked his sleek hair with her other one. "I have always known, ever since I was old enough to understand, that the Silver Demish might invade us at any time, and even D'Ander's status, the Golden Princess Dar'cynth's support, and the blessing of the Fountain Court Vrellish would not keep us safe forever. You are an excuse, Amel — a politically sanctioned excuse to inspire the average family who will have to risk their sons in *rel*-fighters. But it isn't about you at all."

"Oh, Ayrium," he said in a hushed tone, his expression so open it almost felt like soul touch. A delicate whiff of hope mingled with his mild vanilla perfume, as tangible as light in a dark room. "Who was the man with you at the reception?" he asked suddenly, with an inexplicably keen interest.

Her surprise broke the spell of his fey beauty. "Amra," she said, with a blink, "a Highlord from Sanctuary — a scholar. The Monatese brought him here to child-gift to them," she said a bit huffily. "He's no good for much else, although he does have his moments. He inspired the Demish to act on their convictions just now, with nothing but a few choice words!"

Amel's eyes grew wider.

"Does he have a plan?" Amel asked. "What is he doing?'

Ayrium frowned. She presumed he meant Amra, but it was always hard decoding Amel's pronouns. Sometimes he spoke as a Pureblood, sometimes as a commoner. More often he stalled halfway in some foggy compromise. But what he could possibly mean by up-speaking Amra, commoner to Pureblood, she had no idea whatsoever!

"Amra is a bit scrambled up here," she said, tapping her temple, and using *rel*-peerage for Amra. "He's obsessed with Horth Nersal. But I doubt he can get himself in trouble at Black Hearth with Di Mon tagging after him like an anxious mother."

Amel's elation just kept growing. He wriggled with barely contained excitement.

Eler was getting impatient. Ayrium raised a palm to forestall what she feared would be a barrage of words from that direction. She wanted to clear this up with Amel.

"Who do you think Amra is?" she asked her disturbed young friend as delicately as she could, thinking she might have an idea. It would only be natural to jump to conclusions given the family resemblance, especially for someone as impressionable as Amel.

Hope burst out of Amel openly now, in a wide grin. "He's Ameron! Ameron Lor'Vrel!"

I was afraid of this, Ayrium thought sympathetically.

"Oh, Amel," she said, unable to keep a note of pity out of her voice.

"It's true!" Amel cried, with infectious excitement. "He must have time slipped! It's possible! I can't believe he would have stayed away so long otherwise!" He inched closer to her on the bed. "I think he loves you, Ayrium. I saw how he reacted to Prince Rail at the reception."

Ayrium smiled at him indulgently. *Only Amel,* she thought, *would put love on a par with the idea that the man concerned was Ameron Lor'Vrel, time slipped by two hundred years!*

"It's so unfair!" Amel plummeted from rapture to dejection. "D'Ander should have met him! He should have seen—" Emotion choked off the rest of the sentence.

The lump in Ayrium's throat for the sake of Amel's ruined sanity kept her silent.

Eler snatched the opportunity to drop to one knee, snatching Ayrium's hand as he did. Looking up at her, in a posture of passionate drama, he declared, "I swear allegiance to you, Liege Barmi, the greatest sword in Killing Reach and most beautiful woman in the whole of Sevildom!"

Unfortunately for his noble intent, the strap of her dress had slipped again, and his eyes slid slowly downwards towards what this might reveal, which rather spoiled the effect of his glorious declaration.

Ayrium swallowed a chuckle and put out a large hand to ruffle the boy's hair. "I suspect, Scion Nersal," she said, "that what you need is a girlfriend your own age with a good right cross to keep you in line — not a liege."

He had the grace, and the most un-Vrellish instinct, to looked chagrined as she pulled her dress together again.

Sanal spared her any further protestations of devotion from Eler by losing patience with whatever scheme her brother had in mind for her. She scooped up her jacks and began to leave.

"No!" Eler shrieked, and sprang to intercept the wiry child. Ayrium watched just long enough to hear him refreshing promises of a long trip in a *rel*-ship to a place the child had

never been. It made her wonder how much of his plan to run
away to the Purple Alliance he had shared with his little sister.

Amel lost his balance struggling to get out of bed. Ayrium
caught him and sat down on the bed with him, letting him
lean on her.

"We should find Ameron," Amel said. "We should help
him."

Ayrium compressed her lips, unsure whether to indulge
him or set him straight. "Amel, dear," she said. "What makes
you so sure Amra is Ameron?"

"It just... came to me," he admitted, closing his eyes as
he leaned against her chest. "I think it's been in the back of
my mind since I saw him at the reception. Seeing you again
made me remember. I can picture it all perfectly. How he
looks. The way he studied the room like he could read stories
in people's faces. The way he looked at you. And how Di
Mon was so fixated on him."

Ayrium smiled. "You do have a marvelous memory," she
murmured, thinking to herself, *which can be both a curse and
a blessing.*

"Listen, Amel," she said, hoping to penetrate his drugged
fog and touch reason, "Amra looks like Ameron because he's
from old Monatese stock with Lor'Vrellish ancestors. I fancy
he might even be a descendant from some youthful affair
the Monatese chose to keep secret. I wouldn't put it past them!
But Amra's just a Highlord, like me."

She patted Amel's hand, sorry to be forced to rob him of
a hope so comforting as one of leadership large enough to
bridge house rivalries. "There is no Ameron to save us, Amel,"
she said gently, as she stroked his hair. "There is just us —
ordinary people. We have to be the ones to say *enough*, no
more lies and maneuvering, this is right and that is wrong.
Then act accordingly, like Horth did when he challenged his
own father. That is why—" She rose, pulling him up with
her. "—you're coming home with me."

"But—" he began, the hope of a miracle still animating his expressive features.

She put a finger to his lips. "No buts. I owe you for what you did today. Good people have to stand together if we are to have any hope of saying 'no' to the greedy ones who don't care about anything but their own ambitions."

"Let's go already!" wailed Eler.

Amel and Ayrium both looked at him.

"I left Horth a note," explained Eler. "It said I was running away to Red Reach, so there's no need to worry he'll suspect I've joined the PA. But we have to go soon, or something will go wrong!"

Gods! thought Ayrium. *What am I going to do about Eler? The last thing I need is complications!*

"Eler," she said with strained patience, careful not to promise him anything. "I can't fly in this dress! I have to fetch my flight leathers from Green Hearth. Will you and Sanal come with me?"

Eler shook his head. "The Green Hearth errants might report me to Horth. I'll wait here with Amel."

Ayrium pressed her lips together. She'd hoped the issue of Horth's young siblings would sort itself out if she could lure them back to Green Hearth with her. It would even give Amra the excuse he wanted to get a foot in the door with Horth Nersal. But she was no good at deception. Honesty was going to have to be her policy here, as well.

"I can't take you to Killing Reach with me," she told Eler. "It is true that you and your sister would be a great asset as pilots — in about ten years — but you'd be the cause of too much trouble until then."

"You are going to take risks for Amel!" he cried, bristling with hurt feelings. "You just won't risk offending Horth for *me*!" He lapsed into a sulk. "*Ack rel,*" he muttered, drawing his skinny shoulders up towards his ears. "Go get your flight suit. I'll mind Amel for you and help you smuggle him down to the docks, even if I can't come with you."

Ayrium leaned down to kiss him on the forehead. "Thanks," she said. "You'll make a great PA irregular one day, when you're old enough. Okay?"

Sanal climbed onto the bed and scrambled into Amel's lap, making him grunt when a sharp knee came down in a sore place.

"Sanal!" Ayrium exclaimed, reaching to snatch her off.

"It's all right," Amel deflected Ayrium, his face gray. He displaced the child from his lap. She knelt beside him on the bed, instead, playing with his silky black hair.

Ayrium hesitated on the brink of needing to ask Amel about his injuries. *It's nothing*, she told herself irritably. *A man doesn't need any special reason to be sensitive there!*

She was loath to leave the three of them alone, all the same. She looked down at her torn dress, then back at the three children: Amel sixteen, Eler ten, Sanal three. They would be as safe here as they could be anywhere on Gelion for the twenty minutes it would take her to change, say goodbye to Amra, and reclaim her sword from Green Heath. And she didn't dare take Amel with her. Di Mon would turn him back over to Ev'rel.

"Wait here for me!" she told them all sternly, and dashed away.

Confession

Mira sat impassively through Ev'rel's recitation of what had taken place in the medical lab with Amel, giving Ev'rel the space she needed to vent her stormy feelings over the events of the day. She wept more than once. She locked her hands in her wild mass of loose hair and raged at Amel's betrayal. She struck her fist to her forehead as she paced, berating herself for not listening to Mira's warnings, or to Vretla's. She wrapped her arms around herself and talked incoherently about her father, and how she had never felt as close to anyone since he had died until the moment when

Amel was at her mercy, on the laboratory bed, looking up at her with his beautiful face full of emotions she could paint in, with pain or ecstasy.

"Perhaps I am mad," Ev'rel concluded, "sick in my mind, as you say. But it can be fixed! You've always said so. I'll even take your damned drugs that leave me less than all I am, or do as Vretla says and find a secret way to be a Vrellish woman in a Demish court. Only please, tell me how to wipe out Amel's memory without killing him! We can blame any side effects on the Reetions! I could start over with him. Socialize him properly for his role. Can you do that, Mira? Can you erase his memory for me?"

Ev'rel hung on the answer, atremble with hope, her eyes red with crying and her hair disheveled. "Please?" she begged her unorthodox friend.

Mira drew a slow, deep breath. "I have already taken care of the problem with Amel," she said.

Ev'rel blinked. Her mouth toyed with the start of a relieved, joyous smile, and then faltered as her eyes grew wary. "Explain yourself," she said, reverting to Gelack and its status-laden pronouns from the free-wheeling English of her long, satisfying rant.

She could tell Mira was afraid now, which made her more confident even though the medic spoke with the stubborn, clinical aloofness that was Mira's weapon against Ev'rel's social superiority.

"Amel's brain is designed to defend against memory loss during reality skimming," Mira said. "Rehearsing threatened memories is the physiological priority of the Demish brain. The amount of cellular damage you would have to do to be sure of making him a blank slate would be life-threatening... not to mention torture."

Ev'rel sank onto the divan beside Mira, her hand spread to brace herself. "Then you think I should kill him?" To her own dismay, she found herself choking up at the idea. "I don't want to — it would be like destroying a work of art."

Only someone who knew Mira as well as Ev'rel did would notice it, Ev'rel congratulated herself, but she saw the austere medic flinch. Her cool, self-interested scientist may not be willing to let her foolish little brother mess up her life again, but she didn't like knowing too much about Ev'rel's feeling towards him, either. Instinctively, Ev'rel grasped the fact as a fulcrum upon which the balance of power between them could be shifted again. The insight stirred the molten passions Amel invoked in her, making it easy to improvise.

"You don't care about such things, I know," Ev'rel told Mira, "but he was rewarding to love even as a baby. He laughed when I laughed. He put up his little hands to touch my face, and explored it ever so seriously, not like the average brat who only pokes and smiles for his own reasons. Amel responds. He blends with you, willing or unwilling. And since he has grown up, ah, Mira," she indulged the whim to stroke her friend's hair, teasing a bit out of its confinement between playful fingers as she watched for the tightening about Mira's eyes and the way her throat worked while Mira's eyes kept staring stubbornly ahead. "Your little brother's body is sleek power packaged in satin sheets. Hurt him, and the music of it plays across him like a symphony. I took him in too great a hurry this time. I should have made it last longer, to explore lesser joys, but it was too delicious to drink the breath from his lips and feel the way it shuddered when I—"

"Stop!" Mira shot up and turned around, stiff and agitated. "I know what you are doing and I won't have it — hurting him, taunting me. It's not good for you, Ev'rel! If you want to get your obsessive tendencies under control, you cannot start by indulging them! So yes, I don't like to hear you talking that way, but I dislike it for your own sake as much as mine or Amel's! The more you indulge such feelings, the more power you give them. I am no threat to you. You have complete control of my fate. I depend on you for the means to do the work I love and to protect me from those who would condemn it out of superstitious terror. But I am no use to you if I let you upset me. So stop it."

Ev'rel was taken aback by this outburst. *Mira might be right,* she realized. The seething, restless feelings of desire her own recitation had stirred up again in her were proof of it. She sobered and pulled her robes together.

"What do you advise, then, if we cannot safely wipe his memories?"

"Separation," said Mira. "The farther the better."

"But he knows!" Ev'rel wailed at her.

13

New Plans

Runaways

Sanal was trying to braid Amel's hair, but it wasn't co-operating. She gave the strand in her hand a resentful tug when it tried to slip through her fingers.

"Ouch," Amel said softly, wishing she'd be gentler. The innocent physical contact was a comfort, however, and he looped an arm lightly about her as he tried not to dwell on the delirium-drenched memories troubling him.

At first, he had tried to believe they were clear dreams. Clear dreams could feel real enough to make him react psychosomatically, which would account for any physical evidence of abuse. But he knew all the incidents from his clear dreams right down to the last detail. These drug-sodden memories were different. They were set in Mira's lab and Ev'rel was in them. He may have been conscious only half the time, but he had breathed in the heat of her passion. And he remembered, quite clearly, what Mira had told him. She would not have said that if Ev'rel had nothing to hide. She would not have freed him, either.

And if I do tell, he thought, *Mira will be punished.* The trust that implied made him feel whole again.

She trusts me to be stupidly loyal to her, he thought, *even with brain damage.* He was proud of it, and terrified of the responsibility.

Eler came back from seeing Ayrium off and closed the door behind him.

"Right," he said. "Let's get going."

"What?" Amel asked. "Where?"

"To Barmi!" cried Eler. He grabbed Amel by the loose tunic he was dressed in, making him catch his breath. "Ayrium won't take me, so you've got to!" the excited child insisted. "Horth can't keep saving us forever! Besides, one day he's going to look at me the way he looked at Branst and expect me to fight and I can't. I froze! Do you understand? I froze like a coward! Even little Sanal fought back, but I didn't. I just stood there and screamed like a Demish girl. And if I hadn't — if I'd been Vrellish enough to fight, too — Branst might still be alive!"

Eler's aggression broke down in a sob when he reached this confession and he threw himself into Amel's arms. His tears disturbed Sanal. She rocked back on her haunches, Amel's hair forgotten, and stared at them.

Eler's hug squeezed pain from Amel's abused body but he didn't care.

"Don't, Eler," he said, clutching the boy back as if Eler's agony anchored him. "Don't blame yourself. Sometimes we're splendid and sometimes we're not. Anyone can get overwhelmed."

"Not Horth!" Eler cried, face buried against Amel's shoulder.

Sanal curled up at Amel's other side, making a low moaning sound. She was too Vrellish for tears, but Amel thought she understood what Eler was upset about and shared his distress in her own fashion. He freed an arm to include her and she snuggled closer.

"Horth can't cope with too many people talking at once," Amel pointed out to Eler.

"That's different!" Eler cried, rearing back. Impulsively, he caught Amel's hands. "Take us to Barmi, Prince Amel! That way you will save us and spare Ayrium, because if

Ayrium is caught smuggling you off planet, she'll be strung up on Ava's Square and lashed to death by anyone who wants a turn!"

Amel caught his breath in horror. "You really think Ev'rel would do that to her?"

"Sure!" said Eler. "I know how Fountain Court works, you know." He shuffled closer. "But if you leave with me, it won't be her fault. I'll tell them on the docks that we're going to Red Reach, like I told Horth. Your disappearance will have nothing to do with Ayrium."

Sanal raised her head to look up at them. "Fly?" she asked, with uncomplicated expectation. All she wanted was an outing in space, Amel felt pretty sure.

"Black Hearth consumes its highborns," Eler said darkly. "Branst died to save my life. I will not waste it on mere carnage over who gets power. There's so much more to discover! Please save us, Prince Amel!"

Maybe it was the desperation, or maybe it was the poetic cadences of the appeal, but Eler managed to deliver his payload straight to Amel's heart. A quivering sense of huge potential fluttered about Eler and his little sister like an aura. They deserved to grow up safely. But was Eler right about the dangers at court, or was Ayrium right to think that Horth Nersal could protect them? And was it safe for the PA to shelter them? He needed someone he trusted to consider all of these things to decide for him.

"Perry," he muttered. Once he'd made up his mind he felt stronger. "Are you sure you can get a ship?" he asked Eler. "Isn't your brother always worried about you running off?"

"You think Horth would ground me?" Eler was mortified by the idea. He scowled with such gravity Amel believed he must, indeed, have access to pride derived from many former lofty and successful lives. "A Nersallian would sooner break his brother's legs to ground him than deny him dock rights! It's unthinkable!"

"Let's hope so," Amel told him with a tight frown. He heaved himself up, braced this time for the pain and dizziness. Sanal clasped his hand. Eler scrambled to his feet.

Cold sweat stood out on Amel's forehead, but his body was equal to the demands he made of it. "We must go fast," he said, "before Ayrium discovers we're missing."

Be Careful What You Wish For

Di Mon watched the man wearing out his library rug with awe.

He really does pace, he thought.

Di Mon had insisted on genetic tests, naturally, and even then it had been weeks before he dared to let himself believe that the man he and Ranar had knocked out of a jump was truly Ameron Lor'Vrel, two hundred years time-slipped. His joy, once he knew it was true, had been dampened only by his inability to hand Ameron back his throne. He had plans for that, though, to which Ameron had not objected, even though they were cautious ones. The idea of exposing Ameron himself to any risk, at all, was out of the question.

What Di Mon had not understood was that he had been dealing with a depressed and convalescent Ameron. Until now.

D'Ander's rebel daughter is behind all this impatience! Di Mon thought darkly as he watched his incalculably valuable charge pace the length of the library once more, his hands clasped behind him.

Ranar was the first to address the proposition placed before them. "Your plan seems a little... incomplete," he ventured, in English.

Ameron stopped pacing to whirl on Ranar like a *rel*-sha facing down a hand of enemies, pushing Di Mon close to panic at the thought of trouble breaking out between the two of them. He was still bewildered about why Ranar was part of this discussion at all, except that he'd been in the middle of it from the start, on *TouchGate Hospital*. The Reetion had got along remarkably well with the staff there while he and Ameron were incapacitated by their injuries.

"I declare who I am and force a Swearing," Ameron snapped back at Ranar. "What's incomplete about that?"

"What if you don't have enough houses to tip the balance?" Ranar asked. "Then you'd be Avim, not Ava."

"I am listening," Ameron encouraged him in a cold tone.

"I am thinking of Di Mon's position," Ranar went on boldly. "If Ev'rel remains Ava, he must maintain influence with Silver Hearth to hold his right to speak for both Brown Hearth and Green Hearth, and to back up your right to speak for White Hearth. You may be, well, Ameron... but you are only one person and the House of Lor'Vrel has no tangible assets in this era. Ayrium is the other problem."

Ameron's cold stare became a hot glare.

"She appears to be... part of your plan," Ranar came close to floundering. "And that's certain to antagonize Ev'rel. In essence," the Reetion summed up as tidily as any *gorarelpul*, "you don't have a shot without Horth Nersal. And from what I understand, even if he swears to you he's likely to be taken out any day. It could be weeks or even years before the *kinf'stan* stop testing his ability to hold on to his title — if he lives that long."

"Huh," said Ameron, pouting slightly. "All the more reason for young Horth to swear to me immediately. An Ava can help him solidify his standing faster."

"Ranar's point," Di Mon overcame his awe of this transformed version of his idol to help make him see reason, "is that even if you get Horth's oath, it's bound to be a risky business because he might be replaced by someone else any day!"

Ameron scowled at him.

"Mine is not the Monitum of your day," Di Mon was driven to impress upon him. "I have nothing but nobleborns to put at your disposal."

"And no matter how tradition-bound the Silver Demish may be," Ranar picked up the thread, "they can count the number of highborn *rel*-sha in flight leathers! You will not be taken seriously without at least one highborn fleet in your oath to counter Ev'rel's Golden Demish, Silver Demish, Red Vrellish, and Knotted Strings vassals."

"The Knotted Strings are insignificant," Di Mon disagreed with a flick of his fingers. "They're nothing but nobleborns, except for Ev'rel's sons, and not even a court power."

"But they are a fleet power as significant as yours or Ayrium's," Ranar reminded him.

Di Mon had never thought of it like that. He found he did not much like the idea.

"Your pet Reetion is correct," Ameron told Di Mon, oblivious to Ranar's shocked reaction at his choice of words. "But all it proves is that I must win Horth Nersal to my oath if I'm to succeed. I would have held out hope for Vretla Vrel, as well, if you hadn't offended her so thoroughly by sending her to *TouchGate Hospital*."

"She would have died it I hadn't!" Di Mon insisted.

"Yes," said Ameron, "but her successor would have remained favorably disposed towards you, which might have been the better outcome in the end."

"I am not his pet!" Ranar spluttered unexpectedly.

The next instant, Di Mon felt a stab of anxiety for fear Ranar intended to reveal the true nature of their relationship. He knew it was irrational to fear such a thing. Ranar was not stupid! But his dread was so intense he contained it only by promising himself he would draw his own sword and end his life rather than live with the shame of it, if he'd misjudged the Reetion's common sense.

Ameron did not seem to know what to make of Ranar's outburst. He switched from English into Gelack to speak to Di Mon about it, using *rel*-to-*pol* address for Ranar and his own, infamous, peerage-of-convenience for Di Mon.

"What is he to you, this Reetion?" Ameron asked the very question Di Mon could not answer.

Di Mon swallowed, feeling sick to his stomach. "Ranar wants to learn about us for the sake of informing his own people how best we might be dealt with, diplomatically. He is... interesting."

Ameron turned his attention back to Ranar, still speaking Gelack. "And do you inform Di Mon of your own people's nature and customs, in exchange?"

"Yes," Ranar assured him.

"Sensible arrangement," Ameron concluded, and clapped a hand on Di Mon's arm. "You've had your time to think. Make up your mind — come with me now, or stay here. Either way, I go to tell Ayrium what I intend. I have to do something and she wants to know how Amel will figure in it. I will invite Amel to swear to me as liege of Blue Dem. That gives us another house."

The one Ev'rel has claimed! Di Mon thought, alarmed. He expressed it in other terms. "Amel? But he's deranged!"

Ameron herded Di Mon out of the library into the hall. Ranar made to follow, but Ameron closed the door on him, precluding it. He smiled conspiratorially at Di Mon. "Amel is not as deranged as Ev'rel would have him be, methinks... I think," he corrected his archaic Gelack. He tipped his head towards the closed door. "A wise policy keeping this Ranar by you. I fear we are not yet done with Reetions and they are much changed from my own time. There is much to learn. But see you keep him close until we know what use he makes of what he learns, in turn, from you. Commoner or not, he is too intelligent to underestimate as a potential enemy."

"Yes, Majesty," Di Mon agreed, pleased Ranar had made so significant an impression.

Ameron surprised him with a short laugh. "Do not call me Majesty yet! Be careful, too, of where you up-speak me. I wish to declare myself, yes. But I am Amra until I say otherwise. Now," he said, smiling with a boundless enthusiasm, "to Ayrium! To tell her!"

Leaving Court

An errant followed Ayrium to her quarters within Green Hearth and lingered outside her door as she changed into her flight leathers and snatched up the few possessions she cared about enough to bother with. Her sword was the first item in that category. She also stuffed a token from D'Ander's shrine into a pocket of her flight jacket and, after a second's hesitation, the necklace Amra had bought for her.

"I want to see Amra," she told the hovering errant as she emerged from her room, "to say good-bye."

"This way," the woman said, and led her to the family sitting room, called Azure Lounge, near the mouth of Green Hearth's throat.

"Wait here," the woman said, and left her.

"I'm in a hurry!" Ayrium called, starting to follow. But the errant closed the door on her.

Annoyed, she went to the door at the other end, opened it, and saw two errants standing guard. They nodded to her politely but she wasn't fooled. She was a prisoner.

Unless I fight my way out, she thought, and paused to think through the technicalities under Sword Law. As a highborn, she had the right to barge past any nobleborn she liked, and they couldn't touch her. Not, at least, on general principle. She was less certain of the rules if a visiting highborn was a guest in the errants' own hearth because she knew it was common, at court, for errants to act on their liege's behalf in special circumstances. *Is this one of those cases,* she wondered? *And what happens if I kill an errant or two getting away? Would it be legal or illegal — not to mention moral?*

"Damn!" she exclaimed softly, realizing she just wasn't sure.

Amra entered from the inward side of the room, nearest to Family Hall.

"Ayrium!" he cried with booming relief. "I was afraid you might have lost patience."

He swooped down upon her with a passionate kiss that made her forget everything else temporarily. She drew away breathless.

"We've no time for this!" she pleaded with him. "I came to say good-bye. I have to leave immediately." She repressed the urge to tell him about Amel. It was better to withhold that detail for as long as she was able. She had no cause to trust him too thoroughly.

Amra was shaking his head at her. "Ayrium, no. Truly, I will act now."

She scowled at his pretentious use of *rel*-to-*pol* address. They were both Highlords, which made them birth peers! What sort of insult was he playing at by down-speaking her?

He must have realized his mistake. He took her by both shoulders and stared into her face with a hypnotic force of character. "Believe me," he told her, speaking in *rel*-peerage now, "I can help."

Ayrium was moved enough to raise a hand to his face. "I believe you want to," she said kindly. The way he looked at her made it hard to break away. "But I have failed here," she explained, instead, painfully. "I must go home and let my mother know."

"Ayrium—" he tried to interject.

She put her fingers to his lips, smiling at him. "There is one way we may be able to help each other. Eler Nersal and his sister, Sanal, asked to run away with me to the PA. I can't take them, naturally. But if you come with me and collect the two of them, it might be a good way to earn Liege Nersal's gratitude. Will you do it?"

"Of course!" he said, beaming at her.

"Alone?" she pressed him.

"Whatever you require!" He took her hands in his.

Di Mon came in just then. He frowned at the two of them, looking thunderously anxious about something.

"I am going out on the Plaza with Ayrium," Amra said, speaking in *rel*-peerage. "You will wait here."

He is giving Di Mon orders! Ayrium marveled, and held her breath, waiting for Di Mon to admonish him. It was Di Mon, after all, who was liege here! She was half afraid she might be forced to draw her sword in Amra's defense!

Mom would be so pleased at my progress wooing Fountain Court! she thought in a fit of black humor.

Di Mon's jaw locked and his eyes smoldered. His thin nostrils flared with each breath. Then, to Ayrium's further amazement, a third man entered Azure Lounge and went to stand quietly beside him.

He must be Ranar, the Reetion, thought Ayrium, after one glimpse of his dark skin. She had heard about him.

Ranar spoke in English, which eliminated the complexities of Gelack pronouns.

"On the other hand, of course," the Reetion said quietly, as if continuing a debate Ayrium had not been party to previously, "the time comes when a leader kept too safe to lead is just a prisoner."

Ayrium made nothing of the remark, except that it was meant for Di Mon, who shot a fierce look in Ranar's direction. Then, between one instant and the next, the infamous Liege Monitum went from murderous to vulnerable.

"Gods," Di Mon muttered, like a broken man, and raised a hand to press long fingers to his forehead.

Amra snatched Ayrium's hand. "Let's go collect Black Hearth's strayed children," he told her gleefully.

They paused no longer than it took to snatch up traveling cloaks in Green Pavilion, Ayrium helping herself to a spare one for Amel, which Amra noted but said nothing about.

Ayrium set a steady pace across the Plaza. Running flat out might draw attention, but like a mother separated from her infant for too long, she was beginning to get anxious about Amel. "This is the place," she told Amra when they halted minutes later. A few people stared, but most looked away after identifying the source of the disturbance. It was common enough for cloaked figures with swords showing beneath their hems to be scurrying about furtively on Gelion.

Ayrium put both palms on Amra's chest as he began to head inside with her. "No! You wait here!"

She left him at a table while she went to fetch Eler and Sanal. But the crash room was empty.

"Where are they?" she yelled at the first staff member she discovered, shaking him. "Where are the people from the crash room? Who's taken them?"

"No one, uh, My Lady?" the man floundered, flustered by the contrast between her Demish coloring and Vrellish-looking attire. He had probably never in his life seen a Demish highborn woman in flight leathers.

Amra appeared at her side. "They left on their own?" he asked the man, who nodded with a gulp. "How long ago?"

"Fifteen minutes?" the man guessed. "Maybe more."

"The Nersallian docks," said Ayrium. "It's the only place Eler could command a ship."

Amra looked over his shoulder instead of answering and cursed in an obsolete, Lor'Vrellish dialect. *"Impa'har'l!"* The elided phrase he used was short for "ignorance empowered will triumph over helpless wisdom." It was delivered in a way that felt roughly equivalent in meaning to a Barmian explicative of disgust over stepping in a cow patty.

Etymology is hardly important right now! Ayrium told herself, but she couldn't shake the feeling it was a clue to the larger picture that was still eluding her.

Di Mon's arrival interrupted her decision to confront Amra, again, over his peculiar behavior.

The liege of Monitum came running towards them, flanked by a dozen of his errants, all in livery and armed with swords. Ayrium looked about her swiftly, half expecting to see twenty of Ev'rel's palace errants bearing down on them, but nothing else had changed yet on the Plaza.

The next moment she was swept aside by the mob of Monatese surrounding Amra. From the outside of the tight circle she heard Amra's voice raised in anger, but he seemed to be in no danger. To the contrary, it was Di Mon who appeared to be under attack, at least verbally.

However intriguing that was, Ayrium knew this might be her only chance to get out, alone, since all the Monatese seemed to care about was Amra and none of them knew Amel was even part of the equation, except her.

Ayrium backed away under the baleful stare of one of Di Mon's tense-looking errants. She ran all the way across the Plaza to the Palace Shell and through it to the promenade leading to the highborn docks, glad she could be confident of Horth Nersal's offer to let her come and go through Black Gate, since Ev'rel now controlled both of the gates her blood should have entitled her to use.

Doctor's Orders

At first, Ev'rel could not take in what Mira had told her. She stared at her medic for long seconds.

"Escaped?" Ev'rel asked, stunned. "And you helped him?"

"I had to," said Mira. "I guessed what had happened, and knew you would face the choice you face now. Everything that you've told me convinces me that you can't keep him near you safely. Ev'rel, it was kill him or free him. This is better for all concerned."

"Better?" Ev'rel choked on a strangled laugh, her body gone cold at its core. "You've destroyed me!"

"No," Mira assured her. She reached out and closed her hand firmly on Ev'rel's lower arm looking steadily into her eyes. "He will not tell anyone. I told him it would mean my life. He'll die before he tells, now."

"Are you mad!"

Mira shook her head. "I know him. I knew him before. I thought he had changed when he betrayed me three years ago, but after your trick on the challenge floor I located the Reetion data and I understand now. He has not changed because he cannot forget. And his gentleness masks a potent will. The very force of will you aroused by trying to use him against his friends on Barmi II is on your side now, Ev'rel. So long," she concluded with emphasis, "as you do me no harm."

Ev'rel stared at her blankly. She knew when she'd been outmaneuvered. She did not like it. Her respect for Mira increased. Her bond with the medic diminished.

"You are sure?" Ev'rel asked, once, far from certain herself. Trust based on love felt too flimsy a thing to rely on to her.

"I will go over the data from the Reetion object with you," Mira promised. "I'll show you why, if anything, their intervention only strengthened his potential for altruism." She paused. "His freedom is my insurance, while I am yours."

Ev'rel let the new political possibilities slide soothingly over her raw emotions. Provided that Mira's analysis convinced her Amel was fool enough to keep his mouth shut, she could put her mistake behind her, at least for the moment. She would have to make sure she kept hold of Mira, but that shouldn't be too difficult. There might even be an opportunity to woo Horth Nersal in connection with the role played by Eler in Amel's escape from Blue Hearth. She'd have to work on that angle. In the long run she might still get Amel back, one way or another, and see him married to her advantage. Or if he proved recalcitrant on that front, offer him up to the Knotted Strings for child-gifting in the Vrellish fashion. It would all depend on who she needed to please most, and in which quarter he was still acceptable. There were all sorts of ways this might work out, if Mira really was the key to controlling Amel.

"Let's see your data, then," Ev'rel told Mira, coolly.

Mira said, "It's in the lab."

Ev'rel followed, feeling the thickening in her blood that came with thinking about Amel, and guessing she might find some pleasure in making Mira explain the Reetion data to her. The victory was Mira's, here, but it would be a small revenge, at least, to see if she could make her squirm. As Ev'rel anticipated the pleasure, her wiser nature warned her against doing further damage to their relationship, but wisdom was the weaker voice.

A sla *secret can be a fatal weakness,* Ev'rel thought, watching Mira's stiff, narrow back, as she followed her. *If only Di Mon had one I could discover,* she added, wistfully, to herself.

She and Mira never reached the lab. They were interrupted by Kandral, who came tearing down Family Hall at a run, crying, "Immortality Ev'rel!"

"What is it?" she snapped, expecting him to give her the stale news that Amel was on the loose, and at a loss to know how she should cope with it in an official capacity. She fidgeted as she drew her dressing gown about her shoulders.

"Something is amiss on the Plaza," Kandral told her, instead. "Di Mon and his household errants are out there searching frantically."

"No doubt," Ev'rel said in a coldly neutral tone, anticipating with pleasure the shock she was about to deal her captain of errants, "they are looking for Amel. He would most likely be somewhere on the Plaza if he escaped through Blue Pavilion, past your guards."

"Impossible!" Kandral cried, then cast a hard look in Mira's direction. "Unless—"

Ev'rel dismissed the inquiry with a wave of her hand. "Never mind. The important thing is to recapture him before he does himself or someone else an injury in his demented state of mind. Who knows what he might do or say, or how he might confuse past and present, damaged as he is. Wait—" Ev'rel added as Kandral seemed about to dash away. "—I will come with you myself!"

14

Taking Flight

Leaving Court

Eler treated the ground crew imperiously on the highborn docks. They acted as if he were not a mere child, but an old soul in a young body, owed the respect unnamed past incarnations had earned. They took Eler's word about Amel when he walked past, cloaked in his borrowed traveling cloak and holding Sanal by the hand. Eler claimed he was Horth's cousin, Rowl, who had volunteered to teach them a new jump.

"Horth said it will be good for us," Eler elaborated. "Clear our heads after the excitement with swords on the Plaza."

That prompted the dockworkers to launch into an admiring round of discussion over Horth Nersal holding off three Nesaks, single-handed. Eler couldn't let that go. He corrected details like a born raconteur, being sure to entrench Ayrium's role as savior in the story. It took no more than three minutes, but to Amel, waiting in the ship with Sanal, ready to launch, it seemed like forever.

Then, suddenly, Eler was in the passenger seat beside Amel.

"Right!" the child cried excitedly. "Let's go!" He spun around immediately to check on Sanal, who was riding in a Vrellish-style child sling in the cargo compartment at the back. "Remember now," Eler lectured Amel, "when the tower asks, say you are my Cousin Rowl."

"If I was your cousin Rowl I'd be wearing a sword!" Amel said, feeling cross. He was hurting all over in minor ways, and the waiting had got on his nerves.

"You don't know Cousin Rowl," Eler said with a cocky grin as he climbed into his own seat beside Amel, in front, and strapped himself in. "You're a bit short for Rowl, but it's not as if the docksmen notice him much. Not every Nersallian is Horth, you know."

"Eler?" Sanal spoke up from the back. "Why is Amel Rowl?"

Eler twisted around to look back at her. "You want to go flying, or not?"

"Fly!" she decided.

Eler gave her a Nersallian salute, putting his fist to his heart with a thump and then snapping the arm out with an open hand. Sanal answered with a little squeal of pleasure.

Amel got the ship going and out onto the floor.

Departure procedures, including remembering he was supposed to be Eler's cousin, occupied him until they had made it out of the chutes and been cleared by the tower, with Eler prompting him with details of Nersallian protocol as required.

Eler started babbling. He talked about everything and nothing at all, describing the real cousin Rowl, who was apparently supremely mediocre on all fronts; and pointing out everything Amel should know about the ship's interior and controls.

Amel let the child talk, soothed by the stream of words, and aware they soothed Eler's nerves, too.

A hail came over the radio while they were still taxiing away from Gelion, just shy of the planet's challenge sphere.

"Ignore it!" cried Eler. He fidgeted a second. "Go to skim!" he blurted when the signal came again.

"I can't yet!" Amel answered.

They passed a tense two minutes ignoring the radio until Amel was certain they were far enough away to engage the ship's phase-slicer. Eler's silence gave away his fear.

"Now!" Amel cried as soon as possible, and heard Eler sigh in relief at the prospect of escaping light-speed signals.

Reality skimming hit Amel's battered body with a sickening dropping feeling, but he stabilized quickly, his Pureblood physiology designed to endure this, even though it grated on his lush nervous system. Sanal whooped happily. Eler swore a blue streak of barracks language.

"You know any Demish poetry?" Eler demanded as soon as they were smoothly underway.

§   §   §

Damn those kids! Ayrium fumed as the ship she was following into space flashed on her nervecloth and disappeared. She felt certain it was them. The studious silence that answered her hails as they climbed out of the atmosphere only reinforced her hunch. *Damn Eler*, she amended, deciding this fiasco was all the young Nersallian's idea.

She couldn't splice into the medium while she was still in the top layers of Gelion's atmosphere. She'd wind up plastered all over the lining of her hull as air molecules ripped through her body. She hoped Amel would take a straightforward route to Barmi. Options for communication were limited under skim, but she could provide an escort to ward him clear of any bad weather.

At least, she reminded herself, *we know he has got grip to spare.* But talent aside, it worried her to know Amel had logged fewer hours in the cockpit than the greenest member of her PA irregulars.

A Higher Power

In the midst of a clump of Green Hearth errants screening them from curious on-lookers, Ameron stalked up to Di Mon and struck him, backhanded, across the face.

The errants gasped. Even Di Mon had to check his impulse to retaliate.

"I told you not to follow me!" Ameron raged. "All this," he gestured at the mob of errants, "will attract attention!"

It already has, Di Mon realized with chagrin. Errants from Blue Hearth were headed towards them, led by Kandral.

Ameron seized Di Mon's vest in both hands, crumpling his Monatese braid and lifting him off his feet, slightly, to growl into his face. "I am going to Black Hearth to tell Nersal where he can find his little siblings and to travel with him to Barmi, where I hope to find Ayrium, as well. I want you there as soon as you can follow. But I will not have you come with me to Black Hearth or interfere in any way with what I do there."

Released, Di Mon found it hard to draw breath into his chest. He nodded dumbly, mutely astonished by the impact this man's anger had on him.

Ameron was off with a single, parting glare.

I have lost his respect, Di Mon thought, devastated, watching him weave through the loose clumps of people surrounding them. The next instant he nearly tore off after his idol again, despite the dressing down he'd received, fearing doom from every sword-bearing body Ameron sprinted past. But he remained rooted to the spot, smarting from Ameron's anger.

"Is there some problem here, Your Grace?" Captain Kandral asked, shouldering his way past Di Mon's errants, who all looked as strung out about Ameron as Di Mon felt. "My liege Ev'rel heard there might be a problem," Kandral said. "She has dispatched me to offer help."

"No problem," Di Mon snapped.

"We thought it might concern Pureblood Prince Amel's unfortunate escape," Kandral volunteered.

"Amel?" Di Mon blinked, and then narrowed his eyes suspiciously. "You have cause to suspect he was near here?"

"We're searching everywhere," Kandral assured him. "The Ava is requesting access even to hearths on Fountain Court."

Ranar! Di Mon thought, heart in his throat.

"With the permission of presiding lieges, of course," Kandral added. "Do we have yours?"

"No," Di Mon said without thinking. "I will speak with Ev'rel about it myself."

"As you wish," Kandral replied with a sly smile, and departed with a bow.

One of Di Mon's errants jogged up, followed by two more who were managing a prisoner between them.

One look at the prisoner made Di Mon's heart lurch in his chest.

"My liege!" the excited young errant reported. "We caught the Reetion trying to escape."

Ranar stumbled as his captors thrust him forward. He was dressed in hearth clothes and slippers not intended for wearing in public. His jacket was rumpled from handling and his dark hair was tumbled about in disarray. He looked angry and perhaps embarrassed, but unafraid.

Di Mon's temper flared, shattering his brittle self-restraint.

"Give him to me!" he ordered.

"What are you—" Ranar protested, in English, as he was shoved forward.

"Shut up," Di Mon told him harshly in Gelack, taking hold of him by the wrist.

Ranar stumbled. Di Mon just moved faster, towing the soft-bodied Reetion man after him like a helpless child. Either wisdom or shock kept Ranar quiet and cooperative.

Di Mon didn't care. He didn't care about anything, suddenly. He was all action, caution shoved to the margins of his normally calculating mind.

The empty crash room Ameron had discovered, with Ayrium, was the closest bit of privacy Di Mon could buy. He shoved Ranar through the door so hard the Reetion fell forward onto the floor, and gave a yelp of pain where his outstretched hand landed on a stray jack left by Sanal.

Di Mon turned, locked the door, and pushed Ranar back down as the Reetion began to get up. He pinned Ranar beneath him, the hilt of his sword pressing into the Reetion's hip, and spoke into his upturned face.

"Ameron has gone to tell Horth Nersal his siblings are on route to Barmi II with Amel."

"What?" Ranar asked, bewildered. There was fear in his voice at last, but not for the sake of Di Mon's words. It was Di Mon's behavior that frightened him.

Di Mon didn't care. He was beyond believing he could control anything, least of all himself. He pressed down the body beneath him, his hands in Ranar's hair, not knowing whether he needed sex or help to see clearly again — he only knew he needed something immediately, and he needed it from Ranar.

Ranar's dark face was hard to read in the room's dim light, but Di Mon could sense the Reetion's turmoil from his disturbed breathing.

He had Ranar off balance. Finally!

"Stop! Wait!" Ranar lodged an elbow against Di Mon's chest. "Are you sure this is safe? Now? Here?"

Di Mon snapped, "I don't care!"

"You do care!" Ranar insisted. He shuffled back far enough to prop himself up on his elbows. Di Mon pulled him down and kissed him. Ranar broke them up again.

"Talk to me," Ranar demanded as Di Mon caught his breath. His hands were firm against Di Mon's chest. His eyes shone in the soft light. "Please!"

Di Mon rarely regretted being too Vrellish to shed tears. He did now. He gasped a dry sob, instead, his whole body screaming for relief. "Ameron," he got out past a strangled knot of hard emotion. "He ordered me not to follow! Not to protect him! Not to interfere!"

"He was angry?" Ranar guessed.

"I'm afraid!" Di Mon admitted, burning inside. "Ameron is progressive, Nersallians are conservative, and Horth is deadly. I know! I've known him since he was a child!"

"Listen," Ranar demanded, putting a hand on his face, "you can't control everything! No one can."

"It's that damn Demish swordswoman!" Di Mon wailed. "She's made him reckless!" He ground his teeth, loath to admit his disappointment even to himself. Ameron was supposed to be all about wisdom and strategy, not the slave of an infatuation with a beautiful woman!

Ranar made sounds that alarmed Di Mon for fear he was crushing him with his strength, until he realized the Reetion was chuckling. "I'm sorry," Ranar said, wiping a tear from one eye with a hand trapped so tightly between them it was hard for him to use it. "But Di Mon, look at what you're doing right now and tell me you can't understand Vrellish passions! They don't negate the rest of what you are — nor him. Surely the Ameron you have so long admired has some talent for survival!"

Di Mon's heart swelled with giant, broken feelings about duty and reason, mistakes and desires. He wanted to destroy Ranar for mocking him, and he wanted to ravage him to clear his own head. He wanted to talk to him for hours, in his library, with books piled up between them. He wanted to possess the cool rationality that never failed the Reetion, even when he could not quite manage it himself.

He kissed Ranar's forehead, then his face, and the worst of his unbearable need to do something to help Ameron began to dissipate. He could think again. Ranar answered him in kind with less physical confidence, but enough receptivity, to make it clear that he was done resisting. They grinned at each other between touches, and Di Mon felt he was not alone in his private hells.

"Ev'rel is searching hearths for Amel," he tossed out the worry that had seemed so insurmountable seconds before. "I don't want her in Green Hearth. She might find evidence of you. Even if she didn't, it's a trespass — a bullying tactic, the sort of thing despotic Avas did when the Avim wasn't strong enough to balance power. It violates court culture and threatens the stability of the empire."

"It isn't *traditional*, then?" Ranar said in a pointed way.

"No, it's—" Di Mon caught his drift. "The Demish. You don't think they will let her get away with too much?"

Ranar smiled back up at him. "They are good for something, you know, your tradition-bound Demish peers."

There was a pause in which Di Mon digested Ranar's remark.

"This floor is really hard," Ranar said. "Do you think we could..." He tipped his head in the direction of the bed.

Di Mon braced himself to haul them both up when a sound alarmed him. He sprang to his feet, putting Ranar behind him.

One of Ev'rel's errants stood in the open door, a control rod in his hand, no doubt on the mission to reclaim Amel. Di Mon realized in an instant that the proprietor's right to grant his customers privacy had not held out against the weight of a Throne search order. The proprietor had given the errant the access code.

The errant had a funny look on his face. He lowered the control rod with an embarrassed gesture, his hand shaking violently.

He has seen us, Di Mon knew with cold certainty.

"Your pardon, Liege Monitum," the man began to babble. "The proprietor said — but I didn't—" He ran out of words, his eyes fixed on Ranar, sitting up on the floor, his clothes disheveled.

Di Mon sprang. His hand closed on the man's wrist. The control rod dropped, clattering. Di Mon kicked the door closed, thankful he glimpsed no one else outside in the narrow corridor.

"No!" Ranar cried.

The pleas reached Di Mon's ears in tandem with the sound of the errant's cervical vertebrae snapping. The man had barely recovered from the shock of what he'd seen inside the room enough to raise an arm to defend himself. He died staring wide-eyed at his murderer.

15

Journeys

Soul Touch

"Recite something juicy and complex with lovers and court intrigue in it," said Eler.

"I thought I just did!" Amel protested. The ship was equipped for two people, not three, and their water supply was getting too low for recitations, hour after hour. Not that Eler had shirked his share of storytelling. He had also interrupted Amel with suggestions for improvements to plays that had been part of the Demish canon since the Golden Age, and asked interminable questions about poetic structure.

"Are you sure we shouldn't acknowledge Ayrium?" Amel asked again, glancing at the ship on his nervecloth display that had been shadowing them the whole time. He was sure it was Ayrium. "We're getting close to Barmi II."

"How do you know it's her?" demanded Eler.

"I've felt her," Amel confessed awkwardly.

"What? Soul touch?" Eler muttered. "Doesn't happen to me. Sounds like a fairy tale. Like getting messages from the Watching Dead while you're reality skimming. People imagine it."

"No, it's real," Amel insisted.

"Mm," said Eler, with a tip of his head, "to you, maybe. Everyone knows your brains are scrambled." He leaned forward to peer into the nervecloth lining of their envoy-class shuttle's blunt nose as if he might read answers there, instead.

There were three ships now, in addition to Ayrium's. This had happened before. Each time, Eler had urged Amel to exceed nobleborn tolerance for reality skimming and soon it was just Ayrium tailing them again. She had tried, on and off, to shimmer dance commands at them, but had finally given up. Amel believed she was resigned to the inevitable and only wanted to escort them safely through potentially hazardous territory. He didn't mind. He felt safer knowing she was there. And he needed to keep calm for the children.

Eler's denial aside, Amel had been sharing emotions with both him and Sanal ever since he'd first brushed feelings with Ayrium. He knew, once he'd touched her, that someone else believed in people, in love, and in doing the right thing regardless of whether it served their own ends. After that, he didn't dwell on what he'd have to face after he delivered Eler, although it could be exile or execution, either on Barmi or on Gelion. He lived for the moment, instead, and the miraculous sense of connection with both children.

Sanal was quick to trust where she sensed no threat, and attracted by Amel's easy mastery of the navigation data flowing through his unconscious awareness. Amel had the odd sensation she was learning from him. He had never experienced anything quite like it, but although odd and intimate in a sensory way, he felt more privileged than trespassed against.

Eler was another matter. Horth's little brother was a churn of passions, soothed and fired by Amel's recitations of Demish poetry. Words acted like drugs on him, molding themselves over Eler's deep fears surrounding the upheaval in his young life. Amel answered with silent resonances though their shared reactions to the poetry. But Eler never

gave up digging. He basked in conclusions, then went rooting about for contradictions to disprove them in a way Amel
found tiring.

None of this, however, could be put into words. Eler
would deny it. Sanal wouldn't care. And Amel didn't want
to spoil the strange rapport among the three of them.

Then, between one breath and the next, there were problems!

Maybe it was Sanal's intensifying interest in Amel's navigational talent, or maybe it was Eler's rapacious plunge into
whatever it was he and Amel had begun to share through
literature, but all at once the low-level soul touch between
them got out of balance, and what had been beautiful became
a demanding invasion.

The ship stuttered for a few rough stitches, gap slapping
all three of them silly. Amel could sense Eler responding
exactly like himself, with an instinctive scramble to rehearse
and record the experience. Sanal was an intense well of desires.

Amel gasped as he came to himself and took a second
to ensure he was still master of the ship.

"What was that?" Eler demanded in a loud, astonished
voice.

Sanal said buoyantly, "Do again!"

Amel blew air and blinked a couple times before turning
his head to look at Eler, instinctively trusting Sanal to keep
her eyes on the nervecloth for the unexpected. But all he
could do when he met Eler's wide gray eyes was shake his
head.

"Soul touch, I think," Amel said momentarily, and
watched the child scowl at him.

But Eler kept quiet for the rest of the trip.

Ayrium cued them to reduce speed as they entered
Barmi's solar system. She took care of everything. All he
had to do was follow her lead, cutting back to cat-clawing
when she did.

They cut out of skim at the edge of Barmi's atmosphere and began their descent, gliding on the stubby wings of the envoy ship.

Ayrium hailed him on the radio. "Are you all right?" This time he answered. "Yes."

"I'm going back up to watch out for other arrivals," Ayrium told Amel. "I've already called down. Mom's expecting you. Do you know the way?"

"Yes," he said again, feeling sheepish about being here at all now, where he probably wasn't welcome, but whatever happened, it would be good to see Perry D'Aur again. The Reetion named Ann sprang to mind next, with a sense of profound loss over what might have been if he wasn't Pureblood Prince Amel. He knew he wasn't Perry's first priority, but when he felt lonely he liked to imagine Ann might have been his *cher'st*. In more sober moods, he strongly suspected she would not have liked him so much if he hadn't been a bit of an exotic novelty to her, which wasn't the stuff of which legendary love affairs were made. Nevertheless, he felt entitled to daydream about Ann to distract himself from thinking too hard about his fate. The future was a blank wall in his mind. He would let Perry decide what would become of him.

Amel set the envoy craft down like a veteran, figuring he'd done pretty well for someone who could count the number of times he had made planet-fall on one hand. It was a small achievement really, since piloting was almost instinctive for highborns, but it pleased him anyway.

Just like the last time, two people were waiting to greet him: a man and a woman. Unlike the last time, it was not the Golden Prince D'Ander who stood beside Perry D'Aur now, it was Perry's ex-Nersallian *mekan'st*, Vrenn.

Sanal seemed to grasp, instinctively, that Vrenn was a relative, and showed no fear. She might have run right up to him if Eler had not bolted after her.

Vrenn let Perry greet the children. He came straight for Amel, meeting him halfway. From a distance, Amel supposed the gesture could be taken as a friendly one. But everything about Vrenn projected menace, from the set of his shoulders to his grim, straight-mouthed frown. Amel froze.

"I don't care who you are," said the fallen Nersallian, offering no more than *rel*-peerage, grammatically, which Amel figured it was a safe bet to assume was an insult rather than an offer of intimacy. "You are expendable."

"P-Perry doesn't l-love me," Amel struggled to mitigate the cold contempt streaming off the man he considered a rival for Perry's affection. "She loves you."

Vrenn almost laughed. "This isn't about you warming Perry's bed," he assured Amel in a disinterested tone. "Good on her if she's found herself a Pureblood whore."

Amel concentrated on breathing evenly, his heart running riot.

"Think twice," Vrenn told him in a voice full of murderous promise, "before you imagine you can take shelter here from whatever the Ava's court wants of you. Because I'd take it as a personal challenge to see if I could outdo the little catalog of pain and suffering the Reetions put together on your charming childhood, if you bring either Perry or Ayrium to grief protecting you. Understood?"

Amel nodded. He groped for an elusive dignity, resentful of the threats that stripped him bare.

"You'll say nothing to either of them about this little welcome," Vrenn concluded, taking Amel by the arm to march him over to where Perry knelt, speaking with Eler and Sanal.

"Here he is," Vrenn delivered Amel, smiling. "I am going to support Ayrium upstairs. Who knows what might come out from court looking for him."

Perry stood up as Vrenn left. Whatever she had been saying to Eler had managed to subdue the excitable child for the time being.

"Amel," Perry said sadly, and took him in her arms. "Why did you come back here?" she asked him forlornly, as she held him. She had to stand on her toes to hug him properly. He stooped a bit to accommodate her, hurting inside and out.

"Ev'rel tried to marry me into Silver Hearth," he said simply. "I couldn't let her."

She measured him with grave eyes as they drew back. "I see." She paused. "But is this any better? They will come after us for harboring you, and call it kidnapping."

"I won't stay," he promised her. "Eler wanted to come here. He had the ship. I will go away again."

"Where?" Perry asked mildly.

This was the very question he did not want to face. "Ayrium thinks I can lose myself in Killing Reach," he babbled. "Mira thinks I should go to Rire." He thought of Ann, and wondered if he could trust them not to mess with his mind again with her help, but she didn't seem to be 'in' with the Reetion equivalent of highborns. *Was Mira thinking about the visitor probe when she recommended Rire to me,* he wondered? *Did she think about how they could force me to betray her, again? They could make me tell what I know about Ev'rel.* It was easier admitting he knew what Ev'rel had done to him when he thought of it as a secret locked inside his heart, where nothing short of the visitor probe had the power to force it into the light of day. He knew how to ignore such secrets and enjoy life hour-by-hour.

"It doesn't matter where I go," he said out loud, "so long as I am seen far away from here before—" *I die?* he finished silently. Certainly he had little confidence in his ability to survive, alone, in Killing Reach. It didn't matter. He had come here to ask Perry's advice, but there was nothing she could do to fix his problems. Vrenn was right. He was nothing but a danger to the PA.

"I have to go now," he said stupidly.

Perry caught his arm. "Amel—"

He pulled free and took a few steps away from her in the direction of the ship they'd arrived in. He'd just have to take it. The loss would hardly be crippling to House Nersal. But his heart was pounding too hard and his vision blurred with unshed tears. On the third step, something gave and he buckled forward. He barely got his hands out to break his fall. He felt boneless.

Perry helped him to his feet. He pushed her away, chagrined.

"It's nothing," he said, and paused to sweep loose hair off his face, one palm smarting. "Clear dreams." It was a lie. The failure was physical. And frightening.

Am I dying? he wondered. *Am I bleeding to death internally?* He knew of people who had died that way after *rel*-skimming.

Perry said, "You look pale, Amel."

He felt dizzy, but he told her, stubbornly, "I said it's nothing. I'm a Pureblood!"

He took a step and pitched forward onto his face again. He must have grayed out then, because the next thing he remembered, people were gathered around looking down at him. He recognized Maverick, biting her lip in concern.

Perry gave orders; he was scooped up and carried into the palace. They took him to his old room. He was relieved to see the bed had been replaced by one without straps punched through it to bind a mental patient. They kept him horizontal the whole time, which helped him feel better.

A medic came in to examine him. "We'll have to get him out of those clothes," the man said matter-of-factly, "if I'm going to examine him."

"No!" Amel pushed Maverick's hand away. "Leave me!"

"Don't be hysterical!" Perry admonished firmly.

Her tone told him he was panicking. But he didn't want them to see marks on his body he couldn't explain and was trying hard not to believe in himself. At the same time, he wanted help. *I can't die here!* he rationalized it to himself. *It has to be somewhere else, or it will only make things worse, not better!* Where was Vrenn when he needed him?

Paralyzed with indecision, Amel let Perry take over stripping him, starting with his flight jacket and borrowed Nersallian shirt.

She stopped there. "How did you get disrupter bruises having clear dreams?" she asked him, a brittle edge to her voice.

"Ev'rel's errants," he mumbled. "They had trouble subduing me."

Perry's eyes lingered on the hint of discoloration showing above the top of his belt that was darkest where it disappeared under the flight pants. "Right," she said, paused, and added in a measured tone with a hesitance that told him she did not want to know, really, "So, when the marriage plans didn't work out, was Ev'rel... angry?"

"I don't know," he said, as guilelessly as possible. "I had one of my fits. And when I woke up I ran away with Eler." He closed his eyes, feeling sick and foolish. "I'm so tired, Perry."

"Rest then," she said, looking sad again, and turned to the hovering medic. "Let him keep the rest of his clothes on if you can, but I would like to know he's not in danger."

"Exhaustion is my guess," said the medic, "aggravated by drugs and the physical trauma of manhandling while he was clear dreaming. I'd need blood tests to know what to prescribe, if anything, and an examination to assess the injuries."

He shrugged to convey his acceptance that he wasn't likely to get either. "His vital signs are stable. I can monitor them. But I can tell you now, even though he's sound internally, he'll need a respite before he can fly again. Even Pureblood stamina isn't bottomless."

Exhaustion! Amel thought miserably. *How pathetic!*

He willed himself to get up and get out of there, like a real hero in a Demish drama bleeding from a fatal hurt, but undeterred. He could do it, he was sure, if he could just close his eyes first, and rest a minute.

Culture Shock

"You killed him," Ranar sounded stunned.

The crisis averted, the body at his feet in the crash room, and the door securely closed behind him, Di Mon allowed himself the luxury of turning around.

Ranar was speaking English, not Gelack. He sat on the floor with his arms braced behind him and his legs extended, staring.

"You murdered a man outright just because he might have seen us together," Ranar said, clearly upset about it. He shook his head. "I can't live like this!"

The cold fear of discovery had not yet released its hold on Di Mon. "I cannot live any other way," he told his Reetion lover. "It is not just about me, or you. Discovery would ruin Monitum." He paused, then added with a touch of irritation, "I thought you understood."

Ranar looked at the motionless body on the floor between them. He said nothing, only drew his knees up and slowly wrapped his arms around them.

"I have no time for this!" Di Mon told him impatiently. "I should be back at Green Hearth! Surely Ameron will send word, at the very least, if I am needed! Who knows what he may require? And I must find some way to explain the death of this errant to Ev'rel."

"You killed a man," Ranar said hoarsely, "with your bare hands, for nothing more than doing what he was told — and it means nothing to you."

"Nothing!" Di Mon challenged sharply, his whole body tingling with pent-up energy, "I have told you, time and again, how impossible this thing is between us. You kept telling me there's nothing wrong with it!" He stabbed a finger at the body. "I ask you in return, is a dead man nothing?"

"I think... I should go home," Ranar said quietly. "To Rire." He made himself look up at Di Mon, his expression sober. "Or will you ever dare to let me?"

A surge of confusion went through Di Mon. He shook it off with a curt gesture. "For now, you must come back to Green Hearth," he said gruffly. "Perhaps we will discuss it later."

A strange look came over Ranar's face as he took Di Mon's hand to let himself be pulled to his feet.

"Do you realize," Ranar asked, in English, as Di Mon released him, "that you just switched into Gelack, and down-spoke me, Highlord to commoner?"

Di Mon had not realized. He didn't know what it meant, either. He shook his head.

"Do not forget what I tell you, now," Ranar said, speaking Gelack himself in *rel*-peerage. "I am not your *lyka*... now or ever. To be *slaka'stan* might even be better."

There was a new hardness in the Reetion's voice. It hurt Di Mon and made him want to strike out — not at Ranar, but at something too intangible to kill as he had the hapless witness.

He forced breath from his lungs to make them work properly, looked down at the body by his feet, and said gruffly, "I kill people. You've always known it."

"Not because of me," Ranar said stubbornly.

"Yes," Di Mon snapped back at him, "there was Sarilous."

Ranar was startled. "That was different!"

"Was it?" Di Mon demanded angrily, remembering how his mentor and first *gorarelpul* had insisted he kill Ranar, and then died trying to do it herself because he could not.

Suddenly, he had nothing more to say to the Reetion.

Homecoming

Ayrium touched down ahead of Horth Nersal's envoy ship.

She knew it was Horth. She had sensed the clean, hard essence of his personality while they were *rel*-skimming. She'd also sensed Amra as a presence — large, energetic, and complex. The other vibe she had picked up from both of them didn't bear dwelling on too much and could be summed up by the fact they were male and she was female. A bit too much involuntary truth could be a downside to soul touching, though it could be an excellent way to convince yourself — if it even worked at all — that an approaching *rel*-ship could be trusted. And it had worked with a vengeance this time! The sharing already established between the two men when Ayrium matched wakes with them had been so wide open that she couldn't help falling into it, especially given how well disposed both of them were to her — to put it politely. Horth's interest had been general, frank, and physical. Amra's was personal and riotous. She suspected he had also picked up on the gist of her own responding passion for him, which was doubly embarrassing.

She'd stayed clear afterwards, until they dropped out of skim.

It was Amra who had hailed her on the radio, but she didn't do more than give him the essential directions after confirming that she did, indeed, have good cause to believe Amel had brought Eler and Sanal with him to Barmi. Amra had already convinced Horth this was the more likely scenario than the Red Reach destination in Eler's note to him.

Amra signed off saying he looked forward to meeting her mother.

Which means what, exactly? Ayrium fretted as she parked her ship on the runway and climbed out of it. Amra had sounded positively jocular. He had also been inflating his pronouns again, shamelessly. If it weren't for the sheer impossibility of someone time slipping two hundred years, she'd half dare to imagine Amel might be right about him being Ameron.

Or thinking he is! she thought, alarmed. *If Amra has convinced Horth he's genuine through soul touch, Amra must be as crazy as Amel!*

Poor Amel! She thought next, involuntarily. She'd heard about his condition from Perry, by radio. Maybe it was just as well, since it would give them a little time to decide what to do with him. Unless the Silver Demish fleet showed up first.

Nah, she thought, *if there's one good think about the shiny metal houses — they don't do anything without a basketful of councils and hearings. If they're going to mobilize, it will take them at least a week.*

Nersallians were another matter, so she dearly hoped Amra was behaving himself with Liege Nersal.

Once down, Ayrium hopped out of her ship, pulled off her flight hood, and shook her hair out. Then she strapped on her sword. They were, after all, expecting respectable company.

"Ayrium!" Perry called to her from the edge of the machine yard. "Come and talk some sense into Eler. He doesn't want to see his brother, and we can't have that!"

Nodding, Ayrium trotted over to where Eler sat sulking while Sanal played on derelict equipment nearby, getting greasy.

"I've given up trying to keep her still," Perry commented on Sanal. Ayrium decided the child was Vrellish enough to be safe on a jungle gym suspended over a chasm, and reverted her attention back to Eler.

The skinny, imaginative child looked up at her with big eyes, and declared with a seriousness much larger than his frame, "I am going to marry you when I grow up."

She tapped him with the gloves she held in her hand. "Nersallians don't marry. You're Vrellish."

"I'm half Nesak!" Eler protested, and frowned. "I mean, not that I'm proud of it, I guess, except—" he gave up on the complexities with a scowl.

"I'm flattered either way," Ayrium assured him, and gave him a sideways hug. "But you are still a bit young."

Eler kicked at a clump of grass stubborn enough to survive the constant tromping of boots over the much-abused back lawn of the rundown palace.

"I know," he muttered.

"So what's wrong with growing up back at Black Hearth, with Horth?" Ayrium asked. "You can come back out here when you're old enough to join the fleet and woo the blonde." She flashed him a big grin to let him know she meant herself.

Eler looked troubled. "Horth is... scary," he said, adding even more truculently, "and I've told you, I don't think he's permanent."

"You think I am?" Ayrium asked, and ruffled his mop of dark hair with one hand. "The Demish have always thought Barmi II should be taken back. Without a patron like my dad to hold them off, I could be fighting a space war one day soon, or standing challenge if I'm lucky enough to keep it to an honest duel. There are dangers here, too... maybe *more* of them."

"So nowhere is safe?" Eler asked with a shiver.

"Some places are safer than others," she assured him, "and I wouldn't count your brother out too soon." She leaned towards him. "He's made quite an impression on the rest of Sevildom, even if he isn't impressing you."

Eler frowned. "Oh, he impresses me," he said. "It's just he doesn't talk much. He's hard to get to know."

"It was Branst you got along with, right?" asked Ayrium. "What did Branst think about Horth?"

Eler rolled his eyes. "Branst worshipped Horth! I mean, he thought Horth was this paragon of *rel* virtues, like honor and swordsmanship and piloting." He paused, then added with a pedantic air, "You do know what paragon means? Because some people don't. I could explain it if you need me to."

"Nope," Ayrium assured him, "Demish, you know." She tapped his nose. "I bet I've got a larger vocabulary than you."

Eler made a rude noise. "Nobody does!"

"You just don't hang out with the right — oh," she interrupted herself. "Here comes Horth now... with Amra."

"Mm hmm," Maverick remarked to Perry as she watched the new arrivals approach. "All the sexiest men in the universe are coming for tea at the palace on Barmi II."

The impossible juxtaposition of Demish tea parties and Vrellish sexual appetite was classic Maverick. It made Ayrium smile. Then she noticed the way her own dear mother was taking in the young liege of Nersal. She gave Perry a quick kick with a sideways movement of her foot.

"Mother, do not even thing about it," Ayrium hissed under her breath, keeping eyes front.

"Who, me?" said Perry. "Think what?"

Ayrium frowned.

Horth Nersal was, indeed, a sexy looking man. Even his sharp Vrellish features were better proportioned than Amra's long face, pronounced nose, and thin nostrils. It was Amra, all the same, who made Ayrium's nerves crackle, not Horth. She was no blushing virgin herself, even if she lacked her mother's knack for collecting interesting men as lovers, but she couldn't remember anyone who had excited her the way Amra did.

She loved him. It was that bad.

Facing it was almost unbearable because she knew they would never again spend an evening together like the one at Ameron's Wake. Whatever half-baked plan he had to put Amel on the throne was nothing she could support, given all Amel had already been through. Besides, she was probably going to die within the next year defending the PA from Ev'rel, one way or another.

He loves me, too, Ayrium realized, watching Amra's high
spirits melt into affectionate obsession as he gazed at her.
She smiled despite herself. *Maybe*, she thought, *we can get
in a couple of nights together.*

Sanal broke the ice. She leaped off the bulldozer she had
been scaling and charged, hitting her liege-brother like a
small missile. Horth received her with a well-timed grab
that absorbed her momentum without interfering with his
balance. Ayrium noticed he did it with his right arm. He
hugged Sanal with natural affection before setting her down
to hop and skip along beside him the rest of the way.

When he reached Eler, Horth went down on one knee
in the dirt to put himself at Eler's eye level and set his right
hand on the boy's shoulder.

Eler stared at him slack-jawed. "You shouldn't have come
all the way out here, alone!" he told his liege-brother.

"Not alone," said Horth, his deep voice always sounding
to Ayrium like something freshly uncovered for use, like
stored furniture. "Come back to court?" he asked Eler.

"No!" Eler said fiercely. "I want to stay!"

Amra touched Horth's shoulder, which the black-clad
liege of Nersal tolerated, much to Ayrium's astonishment.
Amra must make quite an impression in soul touch! she thought.

"Eler Nersal," said Amra, "we are all friends here, and
bound to become more so, therefore I will use peerage of
convenience to underscore the informality of this setting.
Does this suit you?"

Eler pulled a face. "It isn't peerage of convenience, stupid,
when we're both Highlords." He made a dismissive noise
as he shook his head. "And for somebody trying to be casual, you sure talk like an old Demish play."

"Ah, good point," Amra said, with good humor. "I shall
endeavor to sound less formal and more modern. Here's
the thing I wish to say: you are not alone — not you, and
not your brother. Not Di Mon." Next, he looked straight

at Ayrium. "And not the woman I want to claim, at the very least, as my *mekan'st*. If she'll have me."

O-kay, that's embarrassing, Ayrium thought, stung by the sudden sensation of two dozen penetrating stares.

Perry let loose first. "You hooked up with a Monatese — whatever he is — scholar? Gods, Ayrium! What sort of use is that supposed to be?"

"It just happened!" Ayrium flared, willing her cheeks to stop glowing to no avail. She looked daggers at Amra and mouthed words she hoped might inhibit him.

"The Monatese back Ev'rel!" cried Perry.

"Officially, yes," said Amra, amused by Perry's hopping-mad excitement. "But things are about to change."

Perry could barely contain herself. "I'm sure you are used to being fawned upon as rare and superior among your own kind on Monitum," she told off her pretentious guest. "But this is the PA. We don't put Green blood above any other color here, and we're in a damned serious predicament."

"Of which," he assured her, "I am well aware."

"Ah, Amra," Ayrium cautioned, but he raised a palm to silence her with such aplomb she backed down and left him to Perry's tender mercies.

Perry folded her arms. "Oh, really?" she said. "Look, Ayrium's a striking woman. I don't blame you for falling for her. But we've got serious business to—"

"Liege Nersal!" Amra cut through Perry's harangue. "Tell these people who I am!"

Silence fell like a brick from the heavens as Horth Nersal turned from Amra to Perry. The inevitable delay ensued, in which Ayrium blinked twice, at a loss for what to expect.

"He is Pureblood Ameron Lor'Vrel," Horth said eventually, paused, and then concluded with slow, deliberate emphasis, "My liege."

A dumbfounded silence followed. Eler was the first to giggle. Half the PAers surrounding them joined Eler. Perry's jaw dropped open, just before she started to look angry again.

Thinking back on all the little hints and slip-ups, Ayrium was deeply afraid this was no short-term case of post-flight *rel*-fatigue.

"Is it just me," Maverick asked rhetorically, "or is this getting really weird?"

"Of all the—" Perry began, in exasperation.

"Wait, Mom!" Ayrium jumped. "I think he really thinks he is! I mean, he must, if he's convinced Horth of it through soul touch on the way here. And considering the fact he has Horth Nersal sworn to him is very real, whoever he really is, we don't want things to get out of hand for no good reason, do we?"

Horth's steady stare convinced Perry to simmer down. Turning to Eler, she asked curtly, "Who is he really?"

Eler shrugged. "Like Ayrium told you, he's Amra, a Highlord from Sanctuary who is staying in Green Hearth." He reconsidered. "Although Amel says he's Ameron, as well."

"I time-slipped," Ameron explained, with an air of condescending patience rapidly wearing thin.

Perry cocked a disbelieving eyebrow at him. "Nobody time slips two hundred years!?"

"I do not recommend it," Ameron agreed dryly.

"You will be pleased to know," he interrupted himself to tell Ayrium, "that Horth considered the duel with your father fair, as far as D'Therd was concerned, but his doubts about Ev'rel were profound enough to prevent his swearing to her. I regret I never met D'Ander, for if I had, from what you've told me, I'd have Golden Hearth, as well, but I am in his debt for thus exposing Ev'rel to Liege Nersal, and I will pay the debt to his daughter and her people as best I may."

"You're talking funny again," Eler said, with a peculiar look on his face.

Ameron continued talking to Ayrium. "I need Amel," he said, "to leverage the throne from Ev'rel and block her claim to Blue Hearth... which will serve both you and me."

"I don't think we can allow him to upset Amel with this nonsense," Perry said firmly.

"Nonsense?!" Ameron shouted, caught himself, and laughed instead. "I know who I am. What will it take to convince you?" He glanced at Horth. "If you do not believe Liege Nersal."

Perry folded her arms. "Horth Nersal is a swordsman, a fighter, and an engineer — a very promising young man," she added, "but not necessarily a match for a devious courtier."

Ameron put out a hand towards Ayrium. "Walk with me," he ordered.

She hesitated.

"Please?" he added, looking more like a man in love and less like an irritated Ameron-impersonator.

"Just a few minutes, Mom, okay?" Ayrium said with an apologetic look, before she went to join him. Crazy or not, she couldn't help loving him.

"We may as well have out the business of how things stand between us, personally," he told her in a curiously practical fashion, once they had put enough distance between themselves and the others, "while we have the opportunity."

16

Loose Ends

Cover Up

"I am here about my dead errant," Ev'rel told Tessitatt Monitum as imperiously as she could manage in her current state of stress.

Tessitatt was not happy to see her. Ev'rel drew comfort from it as evidence she was on the right track. The young woman's face showed signs of the Monatese affliction of feeling overwhelmed by great responsibility coupled to inadequate power.

It is always about power in the end, Ev'rel reminded herself. She'd come well prepared. She had Vretla Vrel on her left and Prince Rail of the Silver Demish on her right, each with four of their own armed retainers. These were the people whose support she needed to outwit Di Mon and, therefore, the only ones she ought to care about right now. So why was she haunted by an unstable hunger that gnawed on a rawness she could never salve? Why must she be thinking about Amel, and Di Mon, himself?

Tessitatt eyed Vretla Vrel and Prince Rail. "Di Mon is not home," she told Ev'rel.

"I did not say I needed to talk to him!" Ev'rel exclaimed.

Prince Rail put a hand on her arm in a solicitous, male-Demish manner. "Would Your Immortality like me to handle the investigation?" he asked kindly.

Ev'rel pictured the stupid fop incinerated to a cinder for such addlebrained condescension based on gender. *Or even better*, she thought, *watching me with Amel, where he couldn't avert his eyes and keep pretending I am something he understands because I am female. That would rearrange his world view!*

"No, thank you, Your Highness," is all she actually put into words, underpinned by a brave smile. "A liege may not flinch from her duty to those who serve her, even if she is a woman."

Vretla gave an impatience grunt and barged in without waiting for Ev'rel's leave.

"Tell me where Di Mon has gone and what he's up to!" the liege of Red Vrel demanded, down-speaking Tessitatt with a courtly precision rarely accomplished by a Red Reach highborn. *Di Mon taught her how to be a courtier,* Ev'rel realized with a delicious thrill of irony.

Tessitatt drew her head up. "Do you imply, Your Highness," she asked Vretla, with equal precision, "that a liege of Fountain Court should be obliged to register his comings and goings with the Throne?"

Vretla reacted as if stung. "Of course not! And I would challenge any Ava who said otherwise!"

"So would Silver Hearth!" Prince Rail insisted. "If it was at issue. But it isn't. Di Mon is alleged to have killed one of the Ava's errants and he has to answer for it with an explanation."

"Word on the docks is that Nersal left with Di Mon's houseguest, Amra," Vretla contributed with a scowl, "the one with the Lorel smell about him who has been making friends with Ayrium D'Ander D'Aur. Tell us what he is up to or we'll come in and search this hearth!" she threatened Tessitatt. "You have no highborn at home to bar us, under Sword Law, if the Ava asks."

Tessitatt showed signs of being game to bait Vretla to accept her as a challenger, which might not have been hard to do. Vretla preferred action to talk. Ev'rel was rather disappointed when Di Mon's *pol*-heir overcame her Vrellish impulses and yielded, backing deeper into Green Hearth's entrance hall.

"As you will then, Ava," said Tessitatt. "Come in and look."

Vretla, Prince Rail, and their errants poured in after the retreating Tessitatt. Ev'rel hovered near their hostess, waiting for her to finish barking orders to the Green Hearth errants not to interfere.

"We will be careful not to break the heirlooms," Ev'rel assured her in a civilized tone. "I've great respect for objects of art."

"But not, apparently, for your First Sworn," Tessitatt spat out with no signs of civility beyond the accurate differencing of her pronouns.

"On the contrary, dear," Ev'rel assured her. "I have far too much respect for Di Mon as a kingmaker to risk turning my back on him for too long. Has he found Amel?" she added quickly, hoping to catch Tessitatt off guard.

Tess blinked in apparently genuine surprise. "No."

Ev'rel's mouth settled into an involuntary scowl, not sure if she was relieved or not. She was terrified of Amel telling Di Mon about her mistake in the med lab. Di Mon could ruin her if he were armed with proof of what she'd done, unless she could discredit Amel — which was possible. On the other hand, if Di Mon didn't have Amel up his sleeve then what — by all the mad, vindictive gods of Earth — was he playing at?

"Well, then," she said as calmly as she could manage. "Does your liege-uncle imagine Fountain Court is ready to consider any highborn for the Throne? Is that what this Amra is about? Dispensing with the requirement that an Ava be Pureblood would, admittedly, give Di Mon a much wider pool of candidates to draw upon. Except, as I recall Di Mon's own lesson on the subject, having thousands of potential pretenders would rip the empire apart." She paused to reconsider. "Or has he so much faith in young Nersal, as champion, that he thinks between the two of them they might win the day on the challenge floor? In which case he should really be taking Vretla Vrel and my own son D'Therd into account, as well as every Demish champion in existence!" She realized she was getting shrill, and made a conscious effort to contain her rising temper.

"My liege-uncle," replied Tessitatt, looking positively cool by now, "is not given to schemes that depend on things as chancy as duels, as Your Majesty well knows."

"Perhaps not," Ev'rel allowed, prowling her opponent's defenses with caressing tones. "But he settles a fair number of his problems with a sword despite what he professes in his lessons."

Tessitatt responded with an indifferent shrug intended, Ev'rel felt sure, to seem aloof, but Di Mon's niece was too Vrellish to disguise her pleasure at the backhanded compliment Ev'rel had just paid her uncle's reputation on the challenge floor.

Ev'rel clacked her back teeth, once, with annoyance. "Green Hearth is hiding something from me," she warned Tessitatt, "something worth the life of an innocent man. Di Mon would not kill a bystander lightly — I know him. So it must be something bad. But tell me what is going on, and I promise you, whatever it is, Di Mon will remain my honored mentor and First Sworn." She let that sink in before bringing the stick out. "On the other hand, if he should fail in some desperate ploy to displace me he will end up both defeated and forsworn. How well do you imagine you could cope, as his *pol*-heir, the day after he dies a traitor's death on Ava's Square?"

Tessitatt reacted to the final image with visible shock. Her stare cried, *You wouldn't!*

Ev'rel's answered, *I would.* Then something oddly upsetting happened that Ev'rel had never anticipated would feel so like the severing of a cable anchored to her heart. One moment she and Tessitatt were siblings, squabbling for power under the umbrella of a shared connection to Green Hearth; the next moment they were strangers on two sides of a fatal struggle for the throne.

Ev'rel was spared the need to process the lump in her throat and the pain in her heart by the arrival of Rail and Vretla, herding a brown-faced Reetion before them at the end of Vretla's sword.

"My, my," Ev'rel said, wondering where this piece of the puzzle belonged. The Reetion hardly looked like a prisoner. He was dressed in an expensive, quilted jacket worked in abstract patterns of Lorel origin on an emerald background and worn over black slacks. He also possessed the calm of a truly balanced being, the same inside as out, that she herself would never have.

He knows things Di Mon doesn't want me to, Ev'rel guessed intuitively, and smiled.

"This is the Reetion who was sent out to *QuickSilver* with the Monatese embassy and who later left there with Di Mon to accompany him to *TouchGate Hospital!*" Prince Rail volunteered. "The one called Ranar."

"Really?" said Ev'rel, resenting Ranar's implacable stare. "Ranar — the leader of the Reetion expedition to Killing Reach who violated the Americ Contract, as I recall. How curious!" she said, turning to Tessitatt. "We were just talking about executions on Ava's Square."

"Excuse me, but is that appropriate?" Ranar asked in an academic manner — and in flawless Gelack — so incongruous with his situation it drew everyone's attention. He fixed on Prince Rail as the correct authority to address. "I mean, since I'm a Reetion not a Sevolite, can I be executed in a way reserved for dishonored Sevolites?"

"Not actually, no," Prince Rail acknowledged, too startled by Ranar's grammatical assumption of peerage to admonish him for it.

"He is under Green Hearth's protection!" said Tessitatt, but Ranar himself stayed her with a firm look and a touch.

"Better not," he said quietly, in English. "Wait for Di Mon."

"Bring him to Blue Hearth!" Ev'rel ordered Vretla curtly, peevishly disappointed to have no excuse for killing the nobleborn niece Di Mon loved.

The Romantic Agenda

"Over there is a communal field worked by the village co-operative, which is made up of anyone the guild admits, regardless of birth rank or bloodlines. The agricultural holdings on the far side of the palace, on the other hand, are held by an old Blue Demish family who backed Perry during the revolt against the last liege of Barmi II."

Ameron looked thoughtful. "And the rival systems do not compete?"

"Well..." Ayrium rubbed an itch in one eyebrow where a trickle of sweat had collected and dried in the breeze. It was a perfect day. The sun stood in the sky directly overhead. In the field before them a small tractor powered by *rel*-batteries labored side by side with a yoked farm horse, while a pair of young dogs squabbled over the ball a young boy was throwing for them. "We have our problems," Ayrium confessed, thinking about the lack of manufactured goods, the growing population, the friction between irregulars and traditionalists, and a host of other technical and cultural challenges that plagued her mother every day.

"I am glad to hear it," said Ameron, putting an arm around her, "or I would not believe in this experiment. I expect there are also displaced Blue Demish families who have not forgotten what was once theirs?"

Ayrium sighed, always troubled by this aspect of post-rebellion politics on Barmi II. "Oh yes! Some days I'd like to believe we could relax all the rules and things would just work out, then someone poisons a neighbor's well, introduces a polluting factory that gets them lynched, shoots up a commercial rival with power weapons like a mob of thugs, and you wonder how mankind survived before *Okal Rel*."

Ameron turned her around to face him and kissed her, long and passionately, his hands cupping her face. "I think I love you, Ayrium D'Ander D'Aur," he said.

There was a long pause in which she did not know how to deal with the silly, girlish joy his words inspired in her, and wondered if she might be able to keep him with her after all, as a harmless madman, if Di Mon could be persuaded to relinquish his kinsman to her.

Then Ameron frowned and looked away. "It is impossibly inconvenient," he said, sounding as vexed as a traditional Barmian liege whose heir had run off to become an irregular.

"Pardon?" Ayrium sputtered.

"Come," he said, heading back towards the main road to the palace. "It is time we returned and I have put off all I must say to you for too long."

A pompous harmless madman, Ayrium amended, wondering how long it would take for such behavior to wear down the gleeful feelings that kept bouncing around in her chest like happy dogs in an open field whenever he looked at her.

"I have enjoyed more women than I've loved," he explained in a curiously clinical fashion as they walked hand-in-hand, "but I've never been in love with one, until now. Infatuated, yes. When I was young. And there are women I have loved as *mekan'stan*, but..." He trailed off, pulled himself together, and stopped to pull Ayrium around to face him. "I had assumed I was too Vrellish for this sort of idiocy," he told her, bluntly, in a faintly angry tone of voice, "but I had no tolerance for Prince Rail's attentions to you at Amel's reception. I denied it to myself later. But it's no use. I was jealous." He paused, adding with a gravity that seemed ludicrously out of proportion to the whole situation. "This is an unmapped reach for me, Ayrium, and I fear what we may run into exploring it."

Ayrium kept a straight face with difficulty. "I love you, too," she said, feeling it was only fair to let him know. She forgot his disturbing delusions momentarily as she touched his face, soaking in his sober earnestness. "More than I have ever loved before, either."

He laughed, letting it drive him away from her. "But you think I am deluded about being Ameron — a mad eccentric? Maybe you imagine that's why Di Mon has been so attentive, lest the world discover Tessitatt is pregnant by a flawed sire."

Ayrium opened her mouth, and then closed it again, struggling with mixed emotions.

"I realize it must seem fantastic," he admitted, taking hold of her again by either arm as if he could squeeze belief into her. He felt strong enough to do it for a moment, until he relaxed his grip.

"Di Mon would not admit it either until he had me genotyped. He wanted me to be Ameron too badly to dare hope I might be until he was sure. And I was hardly myself. I was depressed for weeks, almost catatonically so when I learned what had happened in the wake of my disappearance. It was history to Di Mon, but it was my life to me. It is true what I told you in that silly emporium, Ayrium. I failed them. It is you who made me realize that I cannot keep failing them, and Di Mon, and everyone else who believes in me. Like your father, D'Ander. Like you." He stepped closer again, unable to keep his hands off her. With tantalizing tenderness he kissed her hairline. "Once Di Mon was convinced," he breathed, intoxicated by her nearness but still sober enough to be rational in what he said, if not the throaty way he said it, "he started acting like a she-cat with one kitten. Child-gifting to Tessitatt was the most he would allow me to do for him. I had to insist I come to court. He'd have kept me safe on Monitum. It was you who made me realize I cannot be Ameron in secret! That way, I can only be Amra. My legend is a great advantage. I must wield it, which I can't do from hiding."

Tears welled up in her eyes as she stared at him.

"You still don't believe me?" Ameron asked, crestfallen.

She made a wry face. "I want to believe you, Amra, really! But Ameron? I mean, if you said you were someone else, anyone else!"

"Ameron is not a man, to you," he said insightfully. "Ameron is larger than life, a legend, a lost Ava idolized by a father you loved and respected, whatever his shortcomings in not knowing how to value undemish strengths in a daughter." He kissed her again, pulling her so close the power of his desire ignited her own. They stuck like magnets. "And you know very well I am a man, Ayrium D'Ander D'Aur, a man like any other. Therein, methinks, lies the problem. You do not believe a mere man could be Ameron."

"There's a barn not too far from here," she found herself whispering urgently. "It's usually deserted."

"Straw?" His passion wavered. Then he clasped her hand, muttering a mild, astonished expletive to himself that marveled at his own behavior. His body language told her he would follow.

A voice drove them apart — Di Mon's — calling out to them breathlessly from down the road. "Amra! Amra!"

The man in Ayrium's arms gave a shudder, frowned, and sobered. He stood clear of her, retaining one of her hands in his as they squared off to greet the new arrival.

The normally dignified liege of Monitum sprinted toward them down the dirt road in his flight leathers, minus the jacket which might have encumbered him. He had also neglected to put on his sword and was all alone.

Ayrium squinted against the glare of the sun as she watched him come, Ameron's hand in hers the only thing about the whole scene that felt real to her.

Di Mon charged up and lurched to a stop in front of them, clearly ecstatic to have discovered his kinsman in one piece. His agitation boggled Ayrium.

"You do not need to call me Amra," Ayrium's lover greeted the famous Highlord coolly, down-speaking him Pureblood to Highlord. "I've told her. But I believe she needs to hear the truth from you."

Di Mon caught his breath with a gulp, scowled his distrust and resentment at Ayrium for the threat he clearly thought she posed to Ameron, and then spoke with reciprocal, fully-differenced pronouns. "He is Ameron Lor'Vrel," he told Ayrium. "I knocked him out of time slip in the jump to *TouchGate Hospital*."

The next moment, Di Mon forgot Ayrium. He dropped on one knee before the man he clearly venerated. "I will obey you henceforth as your sworn vassal ought to," he pledged, "even to the extent of accepting any risks you choose to take for your own reasons, if you will hear me out and grant your understanding. In all the years of my reign, whenever I gave my oath to others, I did it because I believed it was what you would expect of a disciple. You have always been the touchstone of my purpose and my honor. But it has been trying work. And now that you are here, alive, I find I lack the courage to face such work again without you. Promise me, therefore, you will permit me to shield you with my life, should it ever be required, and I will learn to trust your judgment and obey you better."

Ayrium couldn't get breath into her lungs as she bore witness to this impossible scene. There was no doubt that it was Di Mon, liege of Green Hearth, who knelt before Amra; she could think of no inducement to make him do so unless he, too, believed he was speaking to Ameron Lor'Vrel!

"Convinced now?" the man she had known as Amra asked, with a slight tug of her hand in his, unconcerned about leaving the 103rd liege of Monitum kneeling in front of him, unanswered.

Ayrium's eyes kept getting wider as she stared at him. She could tell, by his smile, he was enjoying the spectacle of her dawning awe at the enormity of what this meant, but she didn't care. Tingling thrills washed up and down her body gleefully.

"I can't believe I slept with you!" Ayrium erupted aloud. And flushed crimson, because that was not what she had meant to say first.

Ameron's smile faded ruefully. "I cannot believe I forgot I was not taking *ferni*," he replied.

"What?" Di Mon yelped, still on his knees, and quickly shook his head, as if to erase the involuntary protest from the air.

Ameron clasped Di Mon's left arm in his to pull him up, and set his right hand on Di Mon's shoulder with confidence. "Devotion to a living man can be harder to stomach than devotion to a legend, Liege Monitum," he lectured him. "Be warned, and think twice before pledging your obedience to me. It's true I learned my values in the archives of Monitum on Sanctuary, but equality among humans of all stations is a matter of philosophy with me — a truth to school my arrogance." He glanced at Ayrium. "Like past failures." He looked hard into Di Mon eyes. "Do you still wish to make this pact with me?"

Ayrium had never imagined Di Mon like this — a sounded gong, quivering with the will to devote himself entirely to his heart's liege — as he said, "Yes!"

"*Ack rel*, then," said Ameron, and heartily embraced his newly confirmed vassal. "I accept all you offer me with gratitude, Di Mon, liege of Monitum." Ameron made up for his earlier neglect of Di Mon as he stepped back to Ayrium's side again, speaking in English, the language of Monatese scholarship. "I am moved by all you give me of yourself. But where I rule, make no mistake, I will be king."

"I would not have it any other way," Di Mon insisted, staring at Ameron so serenely and seriously that Ayrium might not have been on the same planet for all it mattered to him.

"Good!" Ameron declared, and reverted to stiffly differenced pronouns in Gelack. "Then you will accept what I say next," he told Di Mon, and turned to Ayrium.

"If you are pregnant," Ameron told her, "keep the child as my love child and my gift. If you are not pregnant," he smiled, "it can be arranged."

Ayrium did the math and arrived at a Royalblood child, one birth rank superior to her, with a father who might just be the empire's ruling Ava if Ameron managed to displace Ev'rel. If not, its sire would be liege of White Hearth and master of the Avim's Oath, at the very least, with Green and Black Hearths sworn to him.

"The gift," Ameron continued, a bit pompously, "is well deserved. Ayrium brought the leader in me back to life by reminding me past failures did not excuse me from taking up my work again. It is people like the two of you, and D'Ander, who deserve to be legends. Will you, therefore, accept the gift I offer you, Ayrium, if not as husband, then as *cher'st*?"

"*Cher'st*?" Ayrium blinked, going weak in the knees.

"Yes," Ameron elaborated, his misty-eyed romantic air overtaken by a more pedantic manner. "I think it might do the trick to plead a *cher'stan* relationship, acknowledged by Vrellish and Demish alike as an obstacle to child-gifting and marriage, respectively. Children grow up and become unstable factors in equations of power on Gelion. On the whole, my life has not encouraged me to view mine positively. I owed House Monitum an heir, but there will be no end to the demands if I do not stop there. Being your *cher'st* will take me off the breeding market; while for your part, a child, and a relationship rumored to be dangerously intense, is the best protection I can afford to extend to your fascinating social experiment here, since I can neither marry you nor accept your oath, I fear. Silver Hearth would never swear to me if I did." He looked at her as appreciatively as a horse owner thoroughly pleased with his latest acquisition. "But no male in the empire will find it hard to understand an ill-advised passion where you are concerned. A half-secret love affair with you might even mitigate the Lorel stigma of being too calculating politically!" he concluded with glee.

He was obviously pleased with his solution. Ayrium was less sure how she felt, except that for someone trying not to appear calculating, he was bombing in a big way with her.

"Are you asking me if I want to have your baby, Immortality?" she asked him, differencing her pronouns carefully.

"Am I not being clear?" he asked, surprised.

"Let's see," she said, raising her hands to tick off points on her fingers. "You are offering me a baby to act as a surrogate for some kind of official recognition by the empire, and proposing I become your mistress — in Demish terms — because an official connection with the PA would be disastrous for you, politically."

He considered for a moment, but on the whole seemed pleased by her intelligent analysis. "Yes," he said.

Ayrium scowled at him. "That has got to be the most cold-blooded proposition a Demish girl has ever received, in a thousand years, from a scheming Lorel jerk!"

Belatedly, Ameron realized his mistake and had the decency to look dismayed. "Is it unacceptable?"

"Hell, no." She grinned, her feelings much relieved by his reaction. "Let's get ourselves off to that barn and get to work."

Ameron's concern about straw reasserted itself. "Willingly," he said, "but is there not a nearby inn or sympathetic householder who might provide a proper bed?"

"I will find you somewhere safe and decent," Di Mon said, looking thoroughly irritated about the whole thing.

Ayrium could hold out no longer. Her sunny nature overtook her desire to make Ameron suffer a bit longer for his backhanded compliments, and she flung herself on him with a joyful whoop, tears flowing freely. "Dad, I know you're loving this!" she cried loud enough she hoped D'Ander could hear. "Mission accomplished, Mom, and how!"

Ameron received her with reassuring affection. "I hath," he lapsed into archaic dialect, "concerns about your mother's reception of the arrangement." More ominously, he added, "I must speak with Amel, as well, as soon as possible."

17

History Lessons

The Drainage Room

"Why is it called Ava's Square?" Ranar asked Ev'rel in his maddeningly unruffled fashion, as if her intent in showing the place to him was strictly educational.

"A good question," remarked Ev'rel. "But unfortunately I was remiss in paying attention on the day Di Mon attempted to enlighten me about its history."

"You were his pupil?" Ranar asked.

"Yes, for many years."

They were speaking English, which kept them on even footing, grammatically, and their conversation private from the errants with Ev'rel. The square itself looked ordinary enough when no executions were in process — just a court-yard between buildings in the Palace Sector, with pedestrians emerging from irregularly spaced lanes and a few people on the balconies overhead. The floor was tiled in stones radi-ating out from the center in fractal patterns littered with black and white triangles. Both the stone and the swirling shapes painted on them grew larger towards the edges of the square. The buildings were white with gold and silver trim. Ava's Square was a commercial district, with shops at ground level and families of poor relations from lesser Demish families occupying the residences above. Ev'rel's arrival with Ranar and a hand of her palace errants had cleared most people off the square itself. Those who continued to cross it, for reasons of their own, made a point of avoiding them. Some cast furtive glances at Ranar's light brown skin. Others looked away as if he frightened them.

"Come with me," she told Ranar, and walked to the center of the empty square to show him two metal-rimmed holes straddling a drain in the floor. "This is where the whipping frame stands," she said. "The drain collects spilled blood, funneling it into a collector underneath. Tradition encourages people in search of miracles to rub the blood of Sevolites on their withered limbs or cancers to be cured. Weak pilots drink the blood of better ones for prowess in space. Foolish women think they might conceive by smearing themselves with the blood of a man more Sevolite than they are. The list of absurdities is endless, and all have been committed in the room beneath this drain, in eras when the people were indulged in such superstitious whims. Lines of supplicants filed through for days. People could take a long time to die in the whipping frame if they were tended. Supplicants came in one end of the drainage room and went out the other, when they'd had their ration. In some eras they had to pass through showers on the way out, for fear they might use the blood to forge honor chips, signets of passage, or to open blood ciphers sealed for the use of the condemned traitor. There are all manner of stories, and some of them must be true, I suppose, or the showers would never have been built."

"Would it be possible for me to see the drainage room?" Ranar asked with an academic eagerness that baffled Ev'rel.

She cocked her head towards him. "I could have you killed."

"All the more reason to enjoy life as fully as possible while I may," he said.

"Enjoy?" she asked, curious. "By inspecting a room where our citizens performed a silly, morbid ritual?"

"I am an anthropologist," he said. "I study cultures."

"And you find ours fascinating," she surmised.

"I do," he assured her.

"Very well," she said coolly. "Kandral! I am taking Ranar to the drainage room. Wait here and see we are not disturbed."

§ § §

One of the buildings on the square was a barracks housing palace errants upstairs, with a station below where duty officers could be called upon by residents — a sort of local police station. The men inside were mostly petty Sevolites, which meant they belonged to the challenge class below nobleborn and were less than 18% Sevolite. They made way for Ev'rel with fawning gestures. Their nobleborn captain merely muttered, "Immortality" as he bowed to her.

An officer led the way into a tunnel below the barracks that crossed beneath Ava's Square. The tunnel was lighted with blobs of fading glow-plastic. Ranar stopped all the way along, looking at everything.

"When was this place established?" he asked, peering at the unevenly lighted mosaics that lined the tunnel walls. Pieces had fallen out, here and there, and never been replaced.

"No idea," Ev'rel said. "Hundreds of years ago, certainly. It was used in the reign of the Nesak *K'isks*. There were a lot of state executions then. Blood magic predates them, however, and not all of their priests approved of it. Such things have their roots in the era of the Purity Wars, I believe. You'd have to ask Di Mon for details. He's the historian."

"I will," Ranar assured her, touching a wall with careful, inquisitive fingers.

"If you ever see him again," she said. She had expected a reaction at her remark, but she could not tell whether he had even registered the implied threat.

The officer went ahead to open the door to the drainage room itself, at the end of the corridor.

"This is the only way in or out, these days, Your Majesty," he informed Ev'rel, demoting himself to a commoner through his pronouns to flatter her. "The old exit, through the showers, has been sealed up ever since it was used in a poisoning incident. At least that's what they say. The pipes are plugged and the showers themselves are packed with sand bags. No one can get through that way."

"Yes, I know," Ev'rel purred. "It is very private down here."

Ranar turned. She caught his expression as their guide turned up the lights.

He knows he is in trouble, she thought, smiling false reassurance at him.

Ev'rel went inside and drew down the handle of an apparatus below the collection pan. "For dispensing," she told Ranar.

"Mm," Ranar said thoughtfully. He turned in place, taking in the mosaics on the walls depicting miracle cures. "This looks more like a holy place than a charnel house, as if the sacrifices were voluntary... even part of a ritual."

"We have a long history," Ev'rel told him irritably. "Anything is possible."

She moved between Ranar and the door. "Leave us," she ordered their guide.

"Majesty!" the man obliged, bowing his way out.

Ev'rel followed him to the door to make sure it was closed and the bar on the inside lowered. She knew the bar was there. She was not the first powerful Sevolite to use the drainage room for secret purposes. Di Mon himself had told her about the mad prince who had ravaged servant girls down here, emulsified their bodies in a recycling unit, and decanted them down the drains of the showers.

"I have seen enough," Ranar said, coming towards her as she locked the bar in place on the inside.

She seized him, and was gratified by his surprise. Knocking the air of out him, she shoved him back against the wall.

"Yes," she said, her face close to his. "I am a Pureblood, and much stronger than you, even though I am a woman."

"I assure you," he said, when he had regained his breath, "I have no delusions concerning our relative physical prowess based on gender."

Her old trouble kneaded her in the gut with an instinct brewed in the endless clans wars of Red Reach, and stirred in the caldron of millions of life-and-death dramas. To have a willful enemy within her power was to desire him. Di Mon had explained it to her once, in his clinical manner, telling her man-rape strengthened genetic lines among the inbred, warring clans of Red Reach. Conquered Vrellish women did not breed well, but men were needed for only a few hours. It was all so academic the way Di Mon had explained the phenomenon. He, of course, had no idea what it felt to be in the grip of a lust so powerful it squeezed out reason! The urge to possess and kill throbbed in Ev'rel like a second heart.

Ranar had gone very still.

"What happened in the crash room where my errant died?" Ev'rel demanded, getting herself back on track with an effort. "You were there. Witnesses saw you enter and leave with Di Mon. What did my man overhear that made Di Mon kill him?"

"Nothing!" Ranar cried, eyes wide now and his composure shaken. "It was an — accident. Di Mon was startled."

"Startled?" Ev'rel pressed him against the wall harder, leaning her weight into his chest. "That does not sound like Di Mon to me."

"I — hadn't thought so either," Ranar gasped, his face betraying an echo of his own dismay over the murder.

Ev'rel let him up, to gain respite from the impulse fueling her aggression. "He will kill you, too, one day," she impressed upon Ranar, "when you threaten whatever he's hiding from me."

"P-possibly," Ranar admitted, looking miserable.

She brushed down his quilted jacket and straightened out his collar, speaking in honeyed tones. "I can protect you better than Di Mon can. I could send you home safely. Will he?"

"No," said Ranar, his dejected tone making her hopes soar. She had punched past his defenses into a real vulnerability!

"Tell me what he's been hiding from me," she urged. "Tell me, and I will not only send you home, I will send you with a library full of history books! Di Mon's own, if you want them!"

Ranar said nothing.

"Tell me." Ev'rel's almond eyes narrowed. "Or defy me at your peril."

Un-sworn Allegiances

"Ameron!" Amel cried. The word trembled in his mouth, too exciting to hold in any longer. "He really is! And you believe him?"

"Unfortunately," Perry D'Aur said stoically. She stood over Amel's reclining chair with her arms folded. Spring bloomed all around them in an indoor garden, now yielding useful vegetable crops instead of the exotics that had once thrived here, but it was still fragrant and airy. Amel was dressed for the first time since his collapse and feeling rested after twenty hours of doing little except sleeping and eating.

"Of course I'll talk to him!" Amel blurted, nearly levitating off his recliner.

Perry crouched beside him and attempted to ground his enthusiasm with a hand set firmly on his forearm. "Listen to me, Amel. He's Ameron, yes, but no fairy tale. He's a Lor'Vrellish Pureblood who wants to be Ava. You are a potential ally — or rival."

"But this is good, isn't it, Perry?" Amel asked her eagerly. It felt as if the excitement bounding about his body was spilling out through his eyes as he stared at her. He knew it, but he couldn't help it. "I mean, he's Ameron! And he's in love with Ayrium."

Perry grunted noncommittally.

"Ameron will fix things at court!" Amel's euphoria continued to bubble out. "There will be no wars and no duels! And the PA will be safe under his protection."

Perry's face contracted painfully. "Stop it!" she accused him angrily.

He blanched, and fell quiet.

She rubbed her forehead irritably. "He will want to use you," she impressed upon him.

Amel nodded eagerly. "I want to help him!"

"No, Amel!" She sprang on him unexpectedly, seizing his shoulders and making him catch his breath and gulp at her. "Think about yourself, too! You hear me?"

He nodded, chastened by her harshness. "I will," he promised.

She let go. "Let's hope so," she muttered. "But I'm staying here just in case. You tell him to let me. Understand?"

Again, he nodded. "Thank you," he mumbled uncertainly.

Perry gave a soft grunt and went to fetch in Amel's amazing visitor.

Amel rose to greet the long-lost Ava.

"No," Ameron said, coming forward quickly to guide Amel back into his reclining chair and take the seat beside him. "Rest," he ordered.

Amel had never felt so safe in male hands, and let himself be mastered without the least resistance. Ameron was as large as the sky and irreproachable. Amel felt simple and fuzzy-headed in his presence, all the more so because his guest was dressed more like an Ava than previously. He wore Lor'Vrellish white decorated with a beige-colored fern that someone must have embroidered for him here on Barmi, unless Di Mon had brought it with him. The fern was the emblem of Lor'Vrel.

"We must return to court soon," Ameron confided in a serious manner that flattered Amel with its frank inclusion of him as an equal. "Di Mon has gone ahead with Liege Nersal. He asked me to wait here a bit longer, and I find I

am not loath to spend the extra days with Ayrium," he concluded with an awkward smile.

Perry frowned, skeptically. Amel glowed with pleasure.
*He doesn't even want to admit it, but he can't help it. They've got
to be* cher'stan, he thought, delighted, wishing he could make
Perry see it the way he did.

"Many scenarios could play out with your mother, Ev'rel,"
Ameron went straight back to business. "But only one will
end without bloodshed."

Amel nodded, holding his breath in expectation of the kind
of miracle only Ameron could possibly make happen.

"You must convince her to concede the throne to me,"
Ameron told him.

Amel's elation evaporated. "Me?" he croaked, a great
weight of dread settling on his chest again.

Perry stepped forward. "He's a child!" she said stubbornly.
"Oh, I know who you are and I'm grateful for what you are
trying to do for us, despite the way you're doing it...."

"But offended I do not offer oaths and marriage?" Ameron
interrupted her with a smug air that said he knew his place
in the world and pegged it several ranks higher than Perry's.
Amel squirmed uncomfortably watching them.

"I'm hardly one to criticize on that score," said Perry, her
chin high.

"But you resent me." Ameron shrugged. "Fair enough.
I've no love of liege killers either, whatever the provocation,
which—" He raised a palm to forestall Amel's objection
"—was considerable in the case of the late Liege Barmi, and
I am certainly grateful to D'Ander for the solution he provided." Ameron's eyes laughed in a way Amel trusted
whenever he made reference to Ayrium. But Perry only glow-
ered.

"Now leave us, Midlord," Ameron told Perry curtly.

"I'm a Blue Demish Midlord," Perry answered him, taking
up a post beside Amel. "I'll stay unless it is Pureblood Amel
who asks me to leave."

She put one hand on Amel's shoulder. He laid his over hers, stroking her fingers with slow, tiny movements to calm his own mounting anxieties.

Ameron cast the weight of his frown upon Perry before turning pointedly to address only Amel.

"Do you have influence with your mother, Ev'rel?" he asked bluntly.

Amel froze in the act of denying it. He had worked for three years as a courtesan. During that time he had encountered other part-Vrellish women like Ev'rel, and he knew about handling difficult customers. He also knew he shouldn't be thinking along those lines, but it was the only skill he knew how to apply.

"Maybe," he admitted, and dropped his eyes to hide the shame his thoughts inspired.

"Help me strike a deal," Ameron appealed. "Find out what might induce her to signal her acceptance of me as Ava, by swearing to me, and I will let her hold onto what she already has. My return will force a Swearing, especially now that I command Liege Nersal's oath, and if she chooses to stand against me she may lose more than the throne. Make it clear to her you will not marry to please her in a direction harmful to the Purple Alliance nor support her claims against Ayrium for Barmi. Warn her that if she presses those claims, despite you, we will take the Golden Demish from her, because you could, Amel, with my help."

Perry's hand tightened on Amel's shoulder. "Why don't you help him do it, then?" she demanded. "Get back the allies we lost with D'Ander's death, and set up Amel, here on Barmi II, as liege of Blue Dem?"

Amel saw the muscles in Ameron's jaw clench. Anger and impatience stormed over his face before he could summon the will to discipline them. "You severed your ties with the empire when you overturned your liege," he answered Perry. "This is your reality. Embrace it. I will even help you to the extent that I am able without compromising myself at court. But you cannot win a space war without highborns, and you cannot gain the years to breed them without court acceptance. If you think I am exploiting the 'child' you hover over so protectively, let me assure you, woman, it is you who will bring destruction down on him if you try to set him up as liege of Blue Dem while Silver Hearth is hostile to the idea."

Amel watched Perry struggle to hold back her rebuttal. She must have known it was ill-advised to voice it, but in the end she couldn't stop herself.

"You don't say?" she snapped at Ameron, her compact body shaking with anger. "That's how it is, then. Nothing to do with your plans, your throne, or the fact Amel could damn well claim more Demish clout than either Ev'rel or you if he married Ayrium and the two of them laid claim to both Barmi II and Demora in the names of their respective ancestors!"

Ameron was on his feet the second Perry mentioned Ayrium, coldly furious. "Leave now," he told her.

"I won't!" she cried, her whole body rigid with anger.

Ameron started around Amel's chair as if to physically remove her, but Amel sprang up between them, tipping his recliner and causing both of them to grab for him simultaneously. Ameron was faster.

"Thank you," Amel said sheepishly as the legendary Ava set him on his feet again at his side.

Perry watched, crestfallen. "I'll go," she said. "But tell me one thing first, Ameron Lor'Vrel. Tell me what Amel gets out of brokering this deal for you, if he can do it. Or is his role to be shut up in Ev'rel's hearth with her forever, refusing to marry or child-gift for her as she desires, but vulnerable to both of you and neutralized as a potential rival?"

Ameron snorted like a stallion bothered by a pesky insect, but the scowl he leveled at her proved her sting had penetrated.

"It is true I want the throne," Ameron admitted, "but only because I'll make the best Ava, and while the Nesaks remain a threat, the rest of Sevildom must remain united to oppose them." He turned to Amel, asking gently, "Is there something you want, for yourself, Amel?"

"Let Perry stay here, now," said Amel, "to..." he groped for the right world, "advise me!"

Ameron looked as if he would rather have been asked for a few planets, but he sighed, twitched a lip in an involuntary symptom of vexation, and gave in with a flip of his fingers. "Fine," he conceded ungraciously.

"What about Demora itself?" Perry ventured. "D'Ander would expect you to save the Golden Demish from his folly. Can you make Amel heir to Demora?"

Ameron was shaking his head before she finished. "I have made a study of Ev'rel and her methods," he said. "She achieved worthwhile things in the Knotted Strings, but the emerging nation of Dem'Vrel needs trade connections with a green world. Her stewardship of Demora may be a good thing for both territories, particularly if Di Mon is able to gain Silver Hearth for me, which will force her to pay more attention to what Demora needs. I promise you both, and D'Ander—" Ameron made the quick glance skyward that was idiom for including the Watching Dead. "—I will do my utmost to ensure the Goldens do not wind up in the same oath as their Silver rivals while the rancor he stirred up between them is still fresh. Now, what do you want for yourself, Amel?"

Amel looked at Perry, wet his lips, looked back at Ameron, and decided how to put his longing into words. "I want to belong somewhere."

"That must be under your mother's roof," Ameron said quickly. "You've insulted Silver Hearth by refusing their princess. I cannot accept your oath, now, if I mean to win them."

Amel nodded, trying to deny the scrabbling thing in his stomach.

"Ev'rel will not agree to placing you anywhere else," Ameron insisted. "She will want to keep you close to ensure you do not become a focus for discontent seeking to undermine her."

"Then I... want," Amel said haltingly, worrying the fingers of one hand with those of the other, "to be able to come and go... to have duties that make it necessary to fly away from her regularly, even if I always have to return."

Ameron tapped one fist in the palm of his other hand, thinking. Then he turned away to walk about the garden room.

Pacing! thought Amel excitedly. *He's pacing, just like it says he does in the* Ameron Biography *by Sela Lor'Vrel!*

Perry put an arm around Amel's shoulders. He looked up to smile at her nervously.

"You're afraid to go back," she guessed. "Why?"

He thought of Mira. He thought of Ayrium and Ameron, of Perry, and of Ev'rel herself. He thought about explaining what had happened to him in Mira's laboratory, and realized he didn't want to tell anyone, ever. What could Perry do about it if he told her? Nothing but feel helpless and know he was pathetic. He didn't want her thinking of him as Ev'rel's *slaka*. If Ameron knew, and insisted Amel put up with it for the cause, his new hero would cease to be the Ameron he needed to believe in. But it would be even worse if Ameron put himself in peril to protect Amel from Ev'rel... or, worst of all, failed to believe him. Ayrium would believe him, he felt sure, but at what cost? She was already too eager to fight D'Therd, and he would not be responsible for her death the way he had been for D'Ander's. Besides, this way he could do something more than be a pawn who was moved about and fought over. He was afraid, yes. But it was the kind of danger he had plenty of experience with, and at least Ev'rel was female, unlike H'Reth, who had victimized him for years. It was creepy that Ev'rel was his mother, but he suspected incest was integral to her fascination with him for reasons connected to her father, and she really felt nothing like a mother to him. That was Mira's mother, Em, and always would be. He might even be able to help Ev'rel. He remembered her listening to him recite a poem in the midst of all that had happened, and knew he could connect with her through art. Mira thought Ev'rel was worth protecting, and Ameron believed Ev'rel had been good for the Knotted Strings.

Would it be too much to hope we might come to mean something to each other? Amel asked himself. *Maybe a* slaka'st's *love is the only kind I have the right to expect, but it is still love. Or could be.*

"An envoy!" Ameron cried, spinning back suddenly to where Perry continued to wait for the answer Amel would never give. "Amel can be the first royal envoy in three hundred years!" Ameron explained himself. "It used to be common for Avas to send other Purebloods out to act as their surrogates in far away situations, or just deliver messages requiring a special emphasis." Ameron was pleased by the inspiration. "Prince Amel will look splendid in Lor'Vrellish flight leathers," he concluded with a wide smile in Perry's direction, "don't you think?"

Perry's pursed lips relaxed just a little. "It would give him the opportunity to visit us here," she said.

And the Reetions, thought Amel, with hopes of seeing Ann of Rire again, quickly confused — though not entirely dashed — by his earlier decisions about Ev'rel.

"I'll do it," Amel said. "I'll live with Ev'rel, on Fountain Court, as her son, and be Ameron's royal envoy."

18

The New Order

Pureblood Amel

"Liege Monitum is—" Ev'rel's herald was silenced by a shove.

Di Mon barged into Ev'rel's visiting lounge swarmed about by errants, both his and hers. One of hers was half-fainting from a body wound. Di Mon's sword was out and ever so slightly shiny in the way that told her it had been used. Six errants poured in after him and squared off against each other again, hers taking up protective positions between her couch and Di Mon.

"Killing off more of my staff, are you, Di Mon?" Ev'rel asked her visitor pleasantly, once everyone had decided where he or she meant to stand. Two of Di Mon's errants were female. Everyone else was male.

"Where is the Reetion you took out of Green Hearth?" demanded Di Mon.

Ev'rel set down the sketch she had been doodling and got to her feet. She moved one of her own errants out of the way with both hands as if he were furniture.

"I'll tell you," she said, "if you'll talk with me alone." She smiled. "You might prefer privacy when you find out what I have to say."

Di Mon had been breathing hard but by the time she had finished her sentence, he had stopped breathing altogether as his face went slowly gray.

Got you, thought Ev'rel, mentally flicking the sword out of his hand.

"Go," he told his errants, barely able to find the breath.

She dismissed her own with an impatient gesture, eager to have her victim to herself and confident he would not attack her. He would expect her to have taken precautions, to ensure the secret she'd extracted from Ranar would not die with her.

It undermined her confidence a little when he didn't put his sword away. But he didn't point it at her, either. He shifted it in a curious manner with the hilt facing outward and the blade angled towards himself. His pounding heart made his shirt flutter.

"What do you know?" he asked her in a voice like death.

She held her breath. Even now, seeing him taut with suspense as he waited, she could hardly believe the mad thing she had learned from Ranar in the room below the Ava's Square. It seemed impossible! But nothing else could account for the transformation she was witnessing in Di Mon, from the maddeningly self-possessed man she had schemed to conquer for as long as she could remember into the trembling figure before her now.

She sipped a breath. "It's true, isn't it," she said.

The silence stretched between them. It was Ev'rel who could not stand it in the end.

She cried, "You've found Ameron Lor'Vrel!"

Di Mon gave a cough and staggered. His grip on his sword changed as he lowered its tip towards the floor.

Her eyes narrowed. *Was that relief?* she thought, bewildered.

"How do you know?" Di Mon asked gruffly.

"I fed your Reetion enough drugs to make Horth Nersal talkative," she told him, forcing an aloof exterior to hide her inner devastation. This was not going the way she'd imagined! She had expected the secret to give her power.

"Ranar reminisced about your trip to *TouchGate Hospital*," said Ev'rel, pushing hard to try to disconcert him again. "You were talking about Ameron when my errant burst in on you. That's why you killed him. You didn't want to tell me until you were ready, but it's too late now! I know. You'll be forsworn, and he'll be no more than Avim, if he can achieve that! I don't care who he is! I'm secure!"

Di Mon shifted his grip on his sword again. *He won't kill me in cold blood*, she told herself. *He would never get out of my hearth alive. He'd be ruined on Fountain Court even if he managed it! He'd be executed on Ava's Square!*

But he killed Delm, she couldn't help remembering, and took a step back.

Di Mon was murderously angry with her. She had never seen him look so wildly irrational. Was it over Ameron? Or had Amel told him something? Surely it couldn't be something as trivial as outrage over her interrogating his brown-skinned commoner!

Di Mon charged. She shrieked as he swept back his sword arm. Her arm flew up to shield her of its own accord. Smooth metal in a hard fist slammed her down.

The floor had never felt so hard! Ev'rel rolled over. Di Mon glared down at her in a fury, his thin nostrils shivering with every breath.

Defend yourself! Di Mon had tried to teach her, long ago on a very special day she remembered so clearly that suddenly time stood still for her. *You are half Vrellish, girl! Defend yourself!*

But she couldn't. He had hurt her trying to teach her fencing and she had cried. She begged her father's errants to take her home to Blue Hearth. Di Mon gave up in disgust. She ran home. She looked everywhere for her father, Ava Relm, certain he would pet and comfort her. She looked for him eagerly, afraid of running into her hated older brother while she felt so vulnerable. She found Papa in his great empty bed. He was crying, too. He took her in his arms, under the covers. She told him how she wanted to be Demish and not Vrellish at all. He told her how her Vrellishness made him mad with sick desires. That was the day she discovered there were two ways to be Vrellish, and what happened in the bed, with her father, for the first time, was easier than Di Mon's hard tutelage. From that day, she had feared Di Mon for what he might do to Papa if he found out he was bedding her; feared him, and longed to test her new skills on the man she feared — to win him, to master him, and to make him her protector. But she had never been able to — not then, not now.

I love you! she thought at him, staring into his paralyzing hatred, as she marveled at herself for what she felt.

She never found out if Di Mon meant to kill her. A lithe shape stepped between them, clad in sweet-smelling, cream-colored flight leathers. He clamped Di Mon's wrist in one hand, standing over the fallen Ev'rel.

"Ameron sent me," he said, in a voice full of quiet strength, "to see Ev'rel."

Ev'rel found her voice, at last. She gasped in relief and astonishment, "Amel!" For the stranger was, indeed, her own Amel, dressed in white flight leathers with Ameron's device over his left breast.

Amel drew her up. Di Mon took a step back. Shaken, Ev'rel clung to her oldest son. His leather-clad arms felt good around her.

Alive! she thought, rejoicing. *I'm alive!*

Di Mon was distracted by the emblem on Amel's breast: the Lor'Vrellish beige fern. "Why are you wearing that?" he demanded with a streak of pique and bitterness, granting Amel no more than peerage.

"I am Ameron's envoy," Amel answered, claiming Pureblood status through his pronouns. "And as Royal Envoy, I am here to speak with my mother, Ava Ev'rel, on Ameron's behalf."

Di Mon stabbed an accusatory arm in Ev'rel's direction, trembling in the aftermath of his anger. "She took a guest out of my hearth — the Reetion named Ranar. I want him returned immediately."

Amel set Ev'rel down on her own couch. She stretched her arm out along its back, clinging to it like a shipwrecked woman. She had been so certain she was about to die. The couch beneath her hands felt like a miracle.

"I know where Ranar is," she heard Amel tell Di Mon. "He's in the drainage room beneath Ava's Square."

Di Mon made a growling sound in his throat, spun, and left.

Amel sank onto the couch beside Ev'rel.

"Are you all right?" he asked her, looking genuinely concerned.

Ev'rel groped for him, attracted to the calm strength he exuded, and was repelled by a painful suspicion. "M-Mira," she guessed. "Mira told you where to find the Reetion!"

"She didn't need to." Amel picked up the picture Ev'rel had been drawing when she was interrupted by Di Mon. It showed the drainage room, complete with details of a background mosaic and Ranar lying asleep on a pallet on the floor, with his face turned in profile.

Ev'rel clung to her resentment. "Maybe she didn't need to tell you," she said spitefully, "but she did, didn't she? She always thinks she knows best."

Amel tucked a lock of her hair back behind her ear. "Mira told me you had drugged Ranar to make him talk, and let Kandral push him around a bit. She said you were starting to find him attractive, so she made you stop. She thinks," he touched her face, "you have a problem that way. People with problems sometimes need help."

She struggled to reclaim her dignity and sense of power. It evaded her. But she had no fear of Amel. His concern felt much too genuine.

"Oh gods," she muttered. She ran a quivering hand across her brow.

"I'll take you to your room to lie down," he said, and picked her up as if he had the right to do it.

She knew she had lost the upper hand. He had seen her diminished to a frightened child staring up, stunned, at her executioner. She suspected he knew what she'd done to him in the medical lab, and the persistence of his old bond with Mira also felt threatening. Mira must have told him about Ranar! But she couldn't feel distrustful of him, somehow. She let herself relax in his arms, surprised they were so strong!

But why shouldn't he be strong, after all? she thought. *He is a Pureblood.*

Amel had lived in Blue Hearth prior to his reception and knew the way to her room.

"Ava Ev'rel has just heard that Ameron Lor'Vrel is back at court, returned from time-slip," he told an errant who might have stopped him. "It's a shock. I'm taking her to her room to rest."

Ev'rel turned her head to make eye contact with the errant, but did not contradict Amel.

They entered her bedroom and Amel laid her on the bed. He closed and locked the door. Then he shed his short boots and stretched out beside her, his head propped up on one hand.

"Ameron wants you to concede the throne to him," he said without preamble. "He's willing to discuss the price. He has Horth Nersal's oath and Di Mon's. Di Mon controls the Lorel vote by proxy, of course, and Ameron himself is liege of White Hearth. But he knows Brown and White Hearths are vestigial. With Blue Hearth, Red Hearth, Silver Hearth and Golden Hearth, plus the Knotted Strings, even if they are not a court power, you hold the stronger oath. Except..." Amel lowered his eyes to the non-repeating patterns on her chocolate-brown coverlet, touching it with sensitive fingertips. "I think Ameron should be Ava."

"You do?" she asked, blinking at him.

"I do," he told her. "And this place can't be Blue Hearth, either. Name it something new, for your own house of Dem'Vrel, the house you founded in the Knotted Strings."

"Purple Hearth?" she suggested, mocking his presumptions.

He made a face and shook his head. "Too much like the Purple Alliance."

"Would Lilac Hearth do, then?" she asked tartly. "I always loved the lilac trees on FarHome."

He brushed hair from her face tenderly. "You were a great leader on FarHome. Everyone says so, even Ameron."

"Ameron!" Ev'rel sat up, halfway to a robust and healthy anger at the sheer magnitude of how the universe had undermined her. "Di Mon must be too thrilled to piss straight!"

Taken by surprise, Amel laughed. He caught himself fast, but it was too late. His laughter was contagious. Ev'rel began to laugh as well and couldn't stop. They leaned towards each other, clasping arms to steady themselves.

"Ameron!" she gasped. "I mean, of all people dead or alive!" She freed a hand to wipe her eyes. "It just isn't fair!"

"No!" Amel agreed, swallowed a chuckle, and sobered up. "Things have been going wrong for you since you came to court, haven't they?"

"Not at all." She pushed herself up with a grunt, pulled a skewed clasp out of her hair and shook her midnight tresses out about her shoulders, pleased to see Amel take notice. He appreciated women. "Things were going fine until you got bride-shy on me!" said told him.

"I won't marry against the interests of my friends," he said, looking painfully earnest. "And I won't child-gift to please you. But I won't threaten you, either, and I won't let anybody use me to try to gain the throne again. You can trust me to be stupidly unambitious. And you can trust me to keep what happened in Mira's lab between us."

"Really?" Now he was bothering her. He was too self-assured and well-balanced. She leaned into a kiss to disconcert him and became unexpectedly engaged in it. Her breathing deepened. He put his arms around her and they sank down together on the bed.

"You're good at that," she remarked blandly as they separated again. She was more than surprised. She had never felt so stimulated by mutual participation since she had lost her father.

"Perhaps you need someone who's good at what you need," he told her.

A shiver of *sla* desire stirred in her, giving her power. "You don't want to give me what I need," she told him, squeezing the tip of his earlobe between her thumb and forefinger. She saw the discomfort of her pinch reflected in his beautifully expressive face and body tension.

"You wouldn't like it if I did," he said, with no hint of naïvety. He was a little sad, a little frightened. She longed to touch him intimately, to wring emotion from him like an elixir. But she had to be careful. She couldn't go too far or she'd risk shattering the trust he offered. Then she'd have to kill him. She didn't want to... not yet anyway.

Maybe never, she admitted, staring at him.

She kissed him again, slowly, noting with satisfaction that he was far from immune to her. She felt him respond. She saw his pupils darken.

"There would be rules," he said, and swallowed thickly. "No drugs — not ever, and no tying me up without my consent, either."

"Rules?" she teased, amused and oddly comforted. She folded her arms on his chest and propped her chin on them, enjoying the aesthetics of his face and thinking about the many, many ways she'd like to draw him. "Will we keep score as well?" she asked, mockingly.

"If you like," he said.

"Maybe Mira will do it for us," Ev'rel suggested. "I can tell her you are my new medicine."

He grimaced. "I would rather you left Mira out of it."

"I'll tell you what I like," she told him, and kissed him again, taking his lip in her teeth afterwards just long enough to make him wonder if she would bite him — but she didn't. She felt no desire, just now, to mar his beauty.

"I like to win," she said, and smiled at him, pleased to feel him tense. But she was not really feeling competitive. She simply wanted sex, now, with this puzzling and lovely creature lying next to her; and, for the first time since her father's brutal death, she hoped she would not feel lonely afterwards.

He made love with a dancer's self-possession. She never thought of Delm, despite the light vanilla body odor Amel shared with his father.

"You are good at this," she told him when they had finished, speaking for the first time in an hour.

"If that's true," he said, and rolled onto his side to see her better, "it's the only thing I am good at."

She plucked at his dark hair, remembering he was her son again with a curious, forbidden pride in his luscious physicality. "I don't know," she said, feeling surprisingly mellow. "You are proving a very effective negotiator."

"Then you'll do it?" He sat up excitedly. "You'll be Avim?"

"Haven't you heard?" she asked him. "Purebloods are immortal. There will be time, yet, to be Ava." She pulled him down again, marveling at how hard it was to satiate the craving he inspired in her. But she felt at peace despite the craving, as if a great weight had been lifted from her.

Maybe there is something to this Soul of Light business, she thought, and decided to have Mira analyze Amel's sweat for evidence of exotic pheromones. *Best to know what I'm up against*, she told herself.

"Of course," she added to Amel as she caressed him, "there are a few more details left to settle."

The Naming Word

It wasn't until Di Mon was in the drainage room, with the door barred behind him from the inside and his errants on guard against intrusion — that he realized how scared he was. First dread, and then anger had masked his great horror of losing Ranar. Now he had no choice but to deal with the sight of the man-shaped mound lying beneath a blanket on the floor of this obscene little room he'd always despised for being a superstitious vestige of the Purity Wars. Perhaps there was understandable cause for anti-Lorel superstition about the medical sciences, due to past abuses, but nothing could possibly justify the sheer stupidity of thinking a highborn's blood could cure disease without the mediation of those very same forbidden sciences.

Ranar did not belong in this room, on the floor, maybe dead, maybe broken — Di Mon did not know which he feared more. Facts impacted him like blows. He could not tell if the body was breathing. He could see it was Ranar. He could see Ranar's eyes were closed, not wide and staring.

Ev'rel did this! It was a bitter thought. Ev'rel, who had shown so much promise of being a great statesman. Anger collapsed on itself and grief transcended. He remembered the day she had stopped trying to please him and fled home to her father, in tears — the day he had lost the power to influence her. His lessons had warped in transmission from then on. When he tried to teach her wisdom, she learned contempt for honor and all moral constraints. He attempted to show her how to channel her Vrellish passion through the discipline of swordsmanship, but lost her to secret perversions because he did not dare to become her lover. Looking at Ranar, now, he had never felt so inadequate: as a man, as a leader, or as an heir to Monatese scholarship. It was his own pupil and ward who had done this! And to this man of all men!

Ranar was everything Di Mon respected but could never be, from his unshakable faith in the power of knowledge to improve the world, to his complete acceptance of his own homosexuality. Di Mon felt no Sevolite superiority as he stood over the still figure. He hated himself, instead, for being unable to trust this precious, unique friend, or to love him as unguardedly as he deserved.

Di Mon might have stood there for an hour without moving if Ranar had not moaned and stirred. Catching his breath, Di Mon dropped like a stone to his knees to examine his injured friend.

Ranar caught his arm as he forced himself up on a elbow, his usual cool rationality displaced by a disordered anguish.

"Di Mon!" he gasped. "Forgive me! I've been so naïve!"

The emotional pain in these few, wrenching words broke Di Mon's restraint. He pulled Ranar into his embrace, desperate to protect him.

"No, you don't understand!" Ranar struggled for enough space to look up at Di Mon in the circle of his arms. "I knew nothing — nothing! — about the kind of threats you live with every day! I told her about Ameron! I was trying so hard not to think of other things. Then, once I'd started, it was easier to tell her about Ameron in order to hide the rest. Di Mon, the drugs! I couldn't help myself! It was all I could do to edit out what I couldn't say about... about..." The inhibition was still there, too powerful to let him put words to their relationship in this locked and guarded room, with Di Mon's arm around him. "It was like she was a student I had to help keep focused on the relevant work," Ranar said instead, "that's how I thought of it. How absurd!" He broke down in sobs, his eyes still puffy and red-rimmed from his ordeal.

Di Mon's heart broke to see Ranar's face so distorted by failure and humiliation.

Ranar's hand groped its way up the arm of Di Mon's jacket, clutching him. "If something happened to Ameron — if you have to kill me — just do it!"

"No," Di Mon said hoarsely. He tried to make himself smile and failed. He touched Ranar's face with tenderness instead, speaking in a voice thick with tortured pride in his brave friend. "Ameron is beyond Ev'rel's reach. He sent Amel back to deal with her. I've just come from there."

Ranar looked confused. "Amel?"

"Amel is a Pureblood," Di Mon snapped with flat finality. "Let the three of them solve it together." He lifted Ranar in his arms, and felt reassured by the living weight of him.

"What you have done for me," he said, switching from English to *rel*-peerage, "by keeping from Ev'rel what Monitum could not survive her knowing, is more than my thanks can ever express. I will not doubt you again." He paused, thinking of Hangst, and how they had relied on one another before politics had parted them. "*Brerelo*," Di Mon named Ranar.

The Reetion's anguish softened. A hint of his linguistic curiosity returned. "*Brerelo*," he repeated. "I like it." He paused. "A bit evasive maybe, but we'll work on it."

Then he closed his eyes and let Di Mon take care of him.

The Rival

Ayrium ran out to the meadow where Ameron was sparring with a couple of Nersallian retainers, too excited to change out of her summer shift. Her long legs flashed through the wild grass that fringed the field. The airy dome of Barmi's sometimes-treacherous atmosphere loomed benign and sunny overhead. She couldn't help grinning all over her face.

"Ameron!" she cried as she got close, and watched the Nersallians peel away, the one who had been politely exchanging blows and parries with the new liege of their liege lowering her sword respectfully.

Ameron pulled off his fencing mask, sweat in his hairline, and handed his gear off to someone who was simply and suddenly there to take charge of it. No one seemed to mind performing even the most menial services for Ameron, except for Perry and her closest minions. Ayrium figured her mother would come around, because she couldn't see how anyone could be anything but delighted by the miracle man who stood smiling back at her as she ran towards him.

The Nersallians had deployed a type of flat, rubberized roll of flooring that, once unrolled, stiffened into an instant practice floor. Ayrium reached the edge of it and kept on running flat out. Two of the four Nersallians went on alert, misunderstanding her intent at an instinctive level, and forced Ayrium to break her stride in case she needed to defend herself from them. She was not going to risk anything stupid! Not now! The Nersallians relaxed again just in time, but her timing was off. She tumbled into Ameron's arms off-balance.

The two of them went down, laughing, on the portable practice floor.

Nersallians came to help them up, but Ameron waved them off. "No, thank you. Leave us please! Tell your liege I will meet with him as soon as Amel lands and I've debriefed him."

Ayrium watched the Nersallian honor guard for signs of knowing smirks or doubting glowers, but they took her in stride, saluted Ameron where he sat beside her, and left with military precision.

Four disciplined highborns trained in space combat, thought Ayrium as the Nersallians walked away. *Sure be nice to have them flying with the irregulars.*

"I don't suppose you could lend us a hand or three of those to help Vrenn clean up Vrellish pirates on a wild hunt, could you?" she asked Ameron wistfully.

"You would have to negotiate that with Liege Nersal," he said, his tone disappointingly serious. Then he rolled her under him and kissed her.

"I love you in these peasant clothes," he told her. "And I love you with a sword in hand, in flight leathers."

"How's your own swordsmanship coming?" she inquired mischievously.

"Much as always. It needs work." He abandoned bruised pride with a shrug. "Liege Nersal believes it is wise to stay in practice, nonetheless, so I oblige him. It will not do much good," he added ruefully. "I long ago realized I'd never be more than decent on a challenge floor. But that is not what you came to discuss with me?" he guessed.

Ayrium gave up trying to contain her excitement. A bubble of joy was building up inside of her. It popped the second he fell silent. "I'm pregnant!" she cried.

He smiled at her with tolerance and pleasure. "I am glad," he said soberly. It was not quite the response she had anticipated. Then his expression lightened as he arched an eyebrow in a teasing manner. "Mine, is it?"

Ayrium slapped him playfully. "No!" she said, but she couldn't help grinning. "It's Amra's. He's the man I fell in love with."

"Then I hope that Ameron can keep you interested," he said, getting up and helping her join him. His arm went about her waist, but his attention strayed over the lands surrounding them, his eyes narrowed against the sun and the breeze. "It is an interesting experiment you have here."

Ayrium's heart sank a little. "Then... you haven't reconsidered finding a way to reunite us with the empire?"

He turned, placing his hands on her shoulders. He was taller, although about the same weight as her, given his lean, Vrellish build. "Ayrium," he said gravely, "to do that you would need to resurrect Blue Hearth. And Amel cannot do it — not now — perhaps not ever. He would need the goodwill of all the better stocked and landed Demish houses, from the Goldens to the Dem'Vrel. Silver Hearth would have to be prepared to stand by and let him do it. I can think of no scenario in which they might do so, except the marriage that Ev'rel set up and Amel rejected." He stroked her hair. "Besides," he asked her, "is that what you and yours really desire?"

"Mom does," said Ayrium, mesmerized by his touch but loyal to her roots despite everything. "She's a Blue Demish patriot. It isn't right that she, of all people, should be remembered as the rebel who broke Blue Dem."

Ameron said nothing. She could feel him waiting. At last she shrugged, unwilling to let politics come between them. She was trying to be mature about her disappointment over his reaction at the same time. *He's had kids before, of course,* she realized. *They worry him. And as the higher Sevolite, it is him doing me a favor. Why should he be as giddy about it as me?*

"Will your new vassals mind you gifting to me but not them?" she asked him.

"I have already gifted to Monitum," he reminded her. "And I fully expect the mixed feelings about my Lorel side to keep Horth, himself, the sire of preference among the Nersallians for the time being, unless my swordsmanship and prowess in the cockpit get much better." He smiled. "As for the Demish, even if Di Mon succeeds in wooing Silver Hearth to me, I have no plans to marry." He gave her waist a light squeeze. "I have my *cher'st* to protect me from such peril."

He paused then, noticing she seemed subdued.

"What is it?" he asked her solicitously.

She shook her head, feeling more childish than she had in ten years. "Nothing." She lay her head on his chest and closed her eyes, enjoying the nearness of him.

I guess I can't complain when I'm the one who woke up Ameron to displace Amra, she reminded herself, and indulged for just a moment in an imagined scene between her and Amra at proprietor Penwick's emporium, in which Amra had shown all the right feelings.

Ameron was looking off over her head. "There's Amel," he said, his body no longer relaxed in her arms, but intently alert, like a hunting dog with the scent of the chase in its nostrils.

They separated by mutual consent and stood, watching as Amel walked steadily towards them: a lone figure in white flight leathers, lovely as a dream against the blue sky, with his feathery black hair fingered by an attentive breeze.

What Amel has to say about Ev'rel will decide everything, Ayrium refocused her own thoughts and feelings. *Things like whether there will be a duel... or even a civil war!* A sharp twinge of shock jabbed her in the stomach at the thought of war, which had never loomed quite so large and plausible before. *Would Ameron let it go that far?* Ayrium wondered. Even moments before she would have said, *Never!* But standing beside him as they watched Amel approaching, she was no longer so sure. He wanted to be Ava. She could feel it. He was a Lor'Vrel through and through and Lorel blood was never content to let the world move in its own, well-worn channels. Ayrium tried to force the old maxims about the Lorel urge to control others out of her head. *That's what Avas do, isn't it?* she thought. *All of them!*

Amel halted in front of them.

"I'm pregnant," Ayrium greeted him, on impulse.

Amel's face lit up. He laughed, put out his arms, and the next moment they were hugging each other.

"That's wonderful, Ayrium!" he cried when they drew apart, his eyes shining with a rich reflection of her own joy. His entire attention was on her, as if she had given him a rare gift.

"Ev'rel," Ameron interrupted them. "What was her answer?"

Amel sobered up to face the imposing Lor'Vrel who demanded it. "She will swear to you as Ava," he said, and swallowed, with a guilty glance at Ayrium, "but there's a price."

"What is it?" asked Ameron, painfully intense.

Amel squirmed with discomfort, struggling to put it into plain words. "Ev'rel wants... a child... a throne price," he told Ameron, his face growing paler by the second. "Yours."

Ayrium caught her breath, taken off guard. Her mind refused to picture her Ameron and her enemy, in bed.

Ameron was less perturbed. "A rival Pureblood?" he conjectured with a knowing nod. "She'll expect to have the raising of it, which is no more than a woman's prerogative, of course, by Vrellish standards." He frowned. "I suppose she has measured the harm it will do her with her Demish vassals?"

"She thinks the Silver Demish will swear where Liege Nersal does, and there's nothing she can do about it," said Amel. "There's some—" He looked sick and miserable all at once. "—discomfort at court concerning the way she won Demora from D'Ander. Nothing that can be argued openly — it's just whispers — but it is enough to tip the balance, given how popular Liege Nersal is right now, and the debacle over the arranged marriage for me, of course," he tacked on in a mumble, quite unlike his usually clear diction, before he rallied to resume the businesslike tone of his report. "Di Mon has been working on Prince H'Us, on your behalf — even to the extent of playing on the Silver Admiral's preference for a male Ava over a female one. That particular ploy has only made Vretla more determined to stick with Ev'rel, which Di Mon says can't be helped. And Ev'rel's consolidated her hold on the Dem'Vrel by promising them Blue Hearth will be their new foothold at court." He looked apologetically at Ayrium. "She is going to rename it Lilac Hearth."

Ameron was nodding. "And the Golden Demish will stay with her because they want to be within whichever oath the Silver Demish leave," he extrapolated with the air of a dueling enthusiast commenting on game strategy.

Ameron paused to think for five long seconds, as Ayrium and Amel maintained a mutually sympathetic eye lock, each sensible of the losses, as well as the gains, in the new deal. Ayrium could feel his respect for her feelings about Ameron child-gifting to anyone, let alone Ev'rel.

And he's thinking about Perry, thought Ayrium. *He knows how she'll feel about Blue Hearth being given to the Dem'Vrel, even under a new name.*

"Yes!" Ameron exclaimed aloud, surprising both of them. "Tell her yes! And well done!" he congratulated Amel with a hearty slap on the shoulder. "Was there anything else?" he added the next moment, setting aside excitement to make room for new, dangerous details.

Amel hesitated. "Only that I live in her hearth, as her... son," he said, awkwardly. "But she's accepted my status as a royal envoy," he added, looking towards Ayrium with a solar flare of optimistic energy. "I'll be able to come visit all of you, here, frequently."

Ayrium could do no more than acknowledge Amel's hopes with a slight nod. Her chest hurt. Her head told her she must accept this: it was the way of things within the empire; it wasn't the same as a deceitful infidelity; it didn't matter. But she couldn't help taking it personally, and her feelings toward Ev'rel thickened by another dark and vengeful layer, so contrary to her sunny nature the emotions felt like alien intruders in her own breast.

Belatedly, Ameron noticed her discomfort and guessed the reason. He pulled her close, overcoming her uncertain resistance with his own fierce certainty. "It is nothing," he said. "It's only politics!"

Easy for him to say, she thought numbly. But she could not resist.

She found the strength to smile at him, her love for this extraordinary man rising like a sun to conquer the darkness choking her. "I know," she promised him.

Ameron smiled. "That's my rebel princess," he said, with real pride and affection.

Ayrium was glad he didn't know how much it still hurt. She sought Amel's eyes, instead, and knew *he* did.

"Just politics," said Ayrium, understanding at last that she was naming the rival who would always come first:

politics, not Ev'rel or any other woman. She forced a smile as she remembered it would have to be true for herself, as well, and shared a glance with Amel, revealing more than any words could tell.

It is good to know Amel will be around, she thought, *to share the heartaches and the joys.*

Her heart went as hard as hullsteel as the next thought occurred to her. She tugged free of Ameron's embrace to confront both Purebloods.

"Make sure Ev'rel keeps her hands off my baby — Heir Barmi!" she said. "Make sure she knows that if she doesn't there'll be nowhere in the universe she can hide!"

Ameron blinked, surprised and impressed by this first glimpse of Ayrium as a protective mother.

Amel answered with unbounded love in his voice and a hint of things left unsaid. "Ev'rel won't harm the PA while I'm living," he promised her.